Bridesmaids

Zara Stoneley is the USA Today bestselling author of *The Wedding Date*.

She lives in a Cheshire village with her family, a lively cockapoo called Harry, and a very bossy (and slightly evil) cat called Saffron.

Born in a small village in the UK, Zara wanted to be a female James Herriot, a spy, or an author when she grew up. After many (many) years, and many different jobs, her dream of writing a bestseller came true. She now writes about friendship, dreams, love, and happy ever afters, and hopes that her tales make you laugh a lot, cry a little, and occasionally say 'ahhh'.

Zara's bestselling novels include *No One Cancels Christmas*, *The Holiday Swap*, *Summer with the Country Village Vet*, *Blackberry Picking at Jasmine Cottage* and the popular Tippermere series - *Stable Mates*, *Country Affairs* and *Country Rivals*.

🐦 @ZaraStoneley
f http://www.facebook.com/ZaraStoneley
📷 www.instagram.com/ZaraStoneley
www.zarastoneley.com

Also by Zara Stoneley

Bridesmaids

Zara Stoneley

A division of HarperCollins*Publishers*
www.harpercollins.co.uk

Harper*Impulse* an imprint of
HarperCollins*Publishers*
The News Building
1 London Bridge Street
London SE1 9GF

www.harpercollins.co.uk

This paperback edition 2019

First published in Great Britain in ebook format by
HarperCollins*Publishers* 2019

A catalogue record for this book
is available from the British Library

ISBN: 9780008320652

Set in Birka by Palimpsest Book Production Ltd, Falkirk
Stirlingshire

Printed and bound in Great Britain by
CPI Group (UK) Ltd, Croydon CR0 4YY

In memory of my Dad.
The best friend a girl could have had.

ACT ONE

With Friends Like These

Chapter 1

'Oh my God! You're kidding? Wow, that's fantastic!!' And just like that I've looked my best friend in the eye and told a whopper. I pause for breath and lean forward to hug Rachel. 'That is absolutely amazing. I am so pleased for you!' My words are muffled by her shoulder.

I'm not in the habit of telling lies. I have been known to exaggerate slightly (and maybe tell the occasional little white lie), mainly to make myself feel better about my (currently) shitty life, or to make somebody else feel better about theirs.

I mean, when cuddly Liz who runs the 'Olde Fashioned Sweet Shoppe' in town told me she'd lost weight, I felt duty bound to tell her she was looking amazing, even if the missing poundage was probably down to her severe haircut (think scalped-elf) or the fact she'd gone for leggings rather than jeans (think scalped skinny elf).

Eating less and exercising more is torture, isn't it? Specially when you spend your days staring at chocolate and boiled sugar. So, when I saw her a week later and she said she'd won the slimmer of the week award, the last thing she needed was

3

me asking, 'Are you sure the scales were working?' or 'Are you the only slimmer there, ha-ha-ha?', wasn't it?

Whereas, hearing my little white lie, 'Wow! You look fab!' followed by, 'I read somewhere that liquorice can really help' was just the right incentive.

Us girls need to stick together, don't we? We need to present a united front and kick ass. So, if that involves smudging the truth at the edges now and then, that's fine.

I smudge rather a lot. But I don't lie. Especially not to my best friend.

Until now.

This isn't a smudge, this is total truth wipe out.

I should be ashamed of myself. I am.

I also feel slightly queasy, and I'm not sure if it's because the whole idea of this is bringing me out in a cold sweat because of what happened to me, or because of what might happen to her. My bestie.

If I hadn't lied maybe things would have turned out differently.

Maybe all this wouldn't have happened.

It started with the phone call.

Well, let's be honest, it started a long, long time ago. When we were teenagers with fragile hearts, dodgy self-confidence and far too many hormones. When we were sure that the first guy who tried to get into our knickers could be 'The One'. When love and lust were the same thing.

But anyhow, the lie and the big stuff started when she called me. All breathless and excited.

Bridesmaids

I was distracted with work, knee deep in fluffy kittens, or I might have been concentrating harder, and might have had some inkling of what was to come and where it might lead us.

Chapter 2

'Thank God I caught you before you jetted off! Is it okay that I rang you at work? You are at work, aren't you?'

'I am, well, I'm not actually at work, but I am working. Will you stop that?'

'What?'

'Sorry, not you, Rach. I'm at home, but I'm trying to ... sit still, please, pretty please? Oh, for fuck's sake.' I growl, and Rachel giggles. 'I am working, well, trying to. Shit, why are kittens so bloody bouncy?'

'Kittens? You've got kittens?'

'Three. I think. They keep moving, it's hard to keep track, but they're colour coded. If they'd all been black I'd be totally up shit creek without a paddle. Stop it!'

'Kittens! Like, real ones?'

'Definitely real.' I untangle one from my hair. 'Would Sellotaping a paw to the table be considered cruelty? I mean, it's not like I'm using glue, is it?'

'Oh my God that's so brilliant! Oh, I wish you lived closer, I'd be round there!' She's gone a bit shouty. I am confused. I never knew she was a cat lover.

'Sticky tape?' Nobody normally considers my ideas brilliant, and it's not like I've just invented the stuff.

'Not the tape bit, the having kittens bit!'

'Well, er, fine. I've not given birth to them or anything clever.' I'm not really concentrating on just how weird she's being, I'm too busy trying to get one to remain upright. It just keeps keeling over onto its back and doing that 'paws up' thing. Cute, but unhelpful.

'No, but it's brilliant, you're moving on, that's so ace.' She sighs. The sigh of relief. 'I've been so bloody worried about you.'

I let go of the bundle of fluff that I've been holding in a 'sit' position and it flops over, then paddles the air with its little front paws.

'Worried?'

'Yeah, oh come on Jane, I've course I have. You've been so …' she pauses, 'not you since …' She lets that dangle in the air, much like the kitten I've just spotted hanging from the back of a chair.

'Andy?' Andy is my ex. As in ex-fiancé. As in the man who decided he didn't love me somewhere between going down on one knee with a ring and accompanying me up the aisle. Being dumped can leave you feeling kind of worthless, useless and totally unable to distinguish between 'the one' who actually loves you, and the fuckwit who didn't at all.

He has been 'he who must not be named' for quite a while now. Mainly because hearing his name led either to an irrational outburst (from me), featuring lots of swear words, and descriptions about what I'd like to do to various parts of his anatomy, or, and this was so much worse, horrible, snot-inducing tears. Don't you hate it when that happens, when you end up inside out and can't stop?

'Er, yes, him.' She says it hesitantly, and there is a pause. I know she's holding her breath hoping nothing horrible is about to happen.

'Oh, Rach, please stop worrying. I told you, I'm fine. Totally fine. It was ages ago, I am *so* over him.' The git. For a long time, I wasn't sure I was, but I've taken this one day at a time. I've stopped dating, because to be honest now I know my judgement is so far off it's too scary. I've buried myself in work (not hard with my job) and talked a lot to the two people who mean most to me in the world: Freddie my flat-mate, and Rachel.

There are many things I love about my best mate, Rachel: 1. She's patient; 2. She's caring; and 3. She's honest, top the list.

She's always been there for me, no questions asked. Good friends just know, don't they? When to skirt round an issue because they know the wrong word could lead to a major incident, and when only a hug will do.

She's obviously decided that kittens are significant in some weird and wonderful way though, which is slightly disturbing.

I just wish she didn't worry quite so much. I'd always been the one looking out for both of us – as she's so damned nice and easy to take advantage of. But lately we'd had a role reversal.

This time I'd been the one taken advantage of, and I guess

I'd crumbled before her eyes (not a pretty sight). I've always liked to be in control. And I'd been in total control of planning my bloody wedding. Until Andy had pulled the plug, and suddenly I felt like I hadn't got a clue what I should be doing. Everything I thought I stood for had been tossed into the air. I'd floundered. Well, more like come to a complete halt. Scared of doing right for doing wrong.

Then I'd woken up to the realisation that although I might not have had control over him and my love life, I did have control over the rest my life. So, with a few snivels along the way I'd pulled my socks up and prepared to kick ass. Of the work kind.

'I can't stop worrying, Jane! I love you, you know that. But this is brill, you're committing. I'm proud!'

'Proud? Committing? Stop right there Rachel.' I hold my hands up in a stop position, even though she can't see. Committing is not a word I want to hear. Commitment is a pathway that leads to disappointment and humiliation.

The kitten tilts its head on one side then makes a leap for me, misses and drops to the floor. 'It's just a kitten, oh, shit, it's fallen off the table! Hell, hang on, hang on while I ...' I'm down on my hands and knees. 'Do they break easily? I'm going to be drowning in the brown stuff if I send any back damaged. Lora will kill me.' A second one follows it, lemming style and just misses my head.

'Damaged? Send it back? Who is Lora?'

'The girl up the road, you know at Number 20, the one with bright red hair and a nose ring? She fosters animals for that rescue place. She lent the kittens to me and I need some bloody good pics of them, or Coral will sack me. Christ, I can't even catch the bloody thing now, it must be okay.'

At this point, I need to establish something, I am not an animal batterer. I love them. I especially love cats with all their haughty indifference, independence, and demands to be fed and petted when they feel like it. On their terms. They are ace. I'd quite like to be reincarnated as one.

You may pet me now, you may feed me tuna (well, not tuna; chocolate brownies, maybe), you may tickle me just here. Here! You may go away and leave me, or I will turn nasty.

See, cats have got life sussed.

Cats are totally within their rights to show their displeasure by yelling or swiping. There are times when swiping would work for me.

I realise I am about to growl, as an unbidden image of Dickhead Andy sneaks into my brain. Maybe I'm not completely fine. Anyway, I definitely haven't forgiven him. I would so like to swipe him, claws at full stretch until he is shredded into something resembling pulled pork.

I know I need to rise above his fuckwittery and take the moral high ground. Karma will come and bite him on the arse one day, not a cat.

Okay, so you're wondering what Andy did? Did he take me out for a romantic meal, then break the news that it was over? Did he walk out, and leave a 'Dear John' on a sticky note stuck to the fridge? Did he get cold feet when we booked a wedding date, a venue?

Oh, no. Andy did this properly.

I mean, what kind of fiancé tells you IT IS OVER in the

middle of your flaming hen party? There I was with my leg wound round a Chippendale look-alike (as in semi-naked man, not item of furniture) when I felt a funny sensation in my lower regions. It wasn't the over exuberant entertainment, it was my phone buzzing in my new super-tight leopard-skin trousers (yes, it had seemed a good idea at the time, they were on-trend and freebies from a photoshoot I was doing for my fashion-diva boss Coral).

I know I shouldn't have looked. But I did. I thought he'd be sending me a funny text message. Not the cryptic 'this isn't working'.

'It is for me! Ha-ha.' texted back jovially, as the Chippendale gyrated, and cast off another layer of clothing.

'We need to talk.'

This is not something Andy ever said in real life. It's on the scale of him declaring he'd given up beer or football.

'What's up?' I'd typed with the thumb that was holding my phone, because my other hand was otherwise engaged catching cast off clothing. I was expecting him to tell me his stag night had been cancelled or he was missing me.

I wasn't expecting a 'Dear John'.

A very long one. It definitely wouldn't have fit on a sticky note. Not even a whole pad of them.

That should have set alarm bells off. I mean, who sends a text that is so long it doesn't fit on the screen? This was saga length in shorthand. But I was on a high, having fun, excited that soon I would be walking down the aisle with *my One*.

Or not.

Apparently, my darling fiancé had realised we were totally incompatible. That I didn't need him because I was far too busy with my job. That he knew I was building my career and wouldn't want to be a stay at home mum, which, according to Andy, was the only way to bring up kids (I didn't even know kids were on the table, let alone a clause in the mental pre-nup – or had he been planning an actual pre-nup?). That I had to be grown up and realise it wasn't going to work (that bit made me want to be totally un-grown-up and yell like a toddler). That he also thought I needed to spend more time cooking (like his mum did) and ironing (like his mum did) and entertaining his bloody boss (you got it). I am paraphrasing a bit here, but all this came completely out of the blue. Domestic goddess I am not, but I didn't think I needed to be. I am the 'licking fingers and inviting people round' side of Nigella, not the 'slaving over a hot stove' side.

I slithered down my Chippendale onto the floor, all melting and pathetic, and had to be scooped up by Rachel and helped to a chair. My bones had become all bendy and non-supporting, my brain scrambled, and my chest felt like it was fit to burst with pain.

When I got home I tore up all the scraps of paper I'd been practicing my new signature on, in a fury, then collapsed in a soggy mess on my bed and left lots of pleading messages on his voicemail.

Next morning, I was ashamed of my pathetic-ness and sent a few abusive ones.

Then I cut his head off all my photos. And a triangle out

of the crotch area. And looked if Amazon Prime supplied Voodoo Dolls. They do, just in case you need to know for future reference.

Two weeks, lots of cancelled wedding arrangements, and a few crates of wine later I'd moved my (very) few odds and ends out of his flat and shoehorned them into my bedroom at Mum's, rejigged all Andy's carefully constructed playlists, sent his boss an invite to dinner at his mum's (FORMAL DRESS! PLEASE BRING CHAMPAGNE! CABS WILL BE ARRANGED FOR MIDNIGHT!) and left iron shaped holes (to match the ones in the photos) in his best shirts. I know, it was childish, but it made me feel better for a short time.

'Jane, Jane, are you still there? What's happened?'

I shake my head, and blink, trying to regain my inner haughty cat composure and remember what Rachel was talking about.

'Sure, sure. Just trying to catch the damned thing.' I adore cats. I just love them less when I am trying to photograph them. Never work with animals or children? Yeah, yeah, yeah, whoever said that had a point. But some of us like a challenge. Or are slightly deranged.

Or desperate to impress the boss and rescue their job.

I wriggle on my stomach under the chair, my head on one side, cheek plastered to the floor so that I'm all squishy faced, making 'Here, kitty-kitty' noises. The wide-eyed kitten backs off in a kind of weird tarantula dance on its tip toes, until it has emerged on the other side. Its little back is arched and its tail all puffed up like a loo brush and it is jigging sideways, which makes me laugh. Mistake. The noise makes it spin round in alarm and it's off.

'Are you okay, Jane?'

'I think,' my cheek is still squashed so it comes out as 'sink', 'I'm stuck. Not quite sure how I got under here.' The trouble with this apartment is, it literally isn't big enough to swing a cat in (not that I'd do such a thing, obviously).

'How bijou!' Mum had exclaimed – poking round into every nook and cranny the day I moved it.

'You mean small. Bijou suggests small but tasteful.' I'm not kidding myself.

'Yes, dear. I mean small.' She'd poked into one corner too many and was pulling her 'dirty' face. 'But you can make it bijou darling.' Then she'd spotted the gooey shaving foam without a top, and the toothbrush that looked like it had been used to scrub a skirting board, and doubt set in. 'A small flat and a man doesn't really work, believe me, darling. I do know. They take up too much space. Just look at your father, if he hadn't had a shed we'd have been divorced before you'd left primary school.'

I'd bundled her out of the place, muttering the phrases the estate agent had about prices and bargain and aspect and foot on the ladder.

Small it is though. And we've crammed it with two people's furniture. My flatmate and I both arrived with baggage – of the emotional and physical variety. Both can get in the way of life.

At the moment, though, I have more pressing problems that are getting in the way of life. I am currently jammed head first under a chair with my feet under a table and I'm going to have to perform a snake-like manoeuvre to get out.

'Ouch.' Snakes don't have ankles, I do. A sore one. 'Bugger.'

'You okay?'

'Think so, I'm out! It could be worse, I could have still been stuck under there when Freddie got back.'

Rachel giggles. 'He might have taken advantage!'

'Ha-ha. Bugger, it's heading up the blinds now.' The little ginger ninja is moving like Spider-man on a mission, mewling and rocking from side to side, and two more intrepid explorers have decided to join in. 'There are three kittens scaling the blinds!'

I snap a quick shot with my mobile phone – I can't not – and WhatsApp it to Rachel. Kitten number 1 is traversing chimpanzee-style (which is no mean feat when you haven't got thumbs), while the other two are leaping about intent on grabbing its spiky, Christmas-tree tail.

'Oh, God, you are so funny.' She's laughing, and I think from the sniffles, crying a bit. She also seems to be having difficulty breathing. 'Oh, this so needs to be on YouTube.'

'What? Oh, bugger! Don't you dare!' I suddenly realise I've accidentally gone into vid mode, and this is something I don't even want to share with my bestest of best friends.

'Hang on, I'm going to put you down, I need both hands.' I throw my mobile onto the couch, then spin round suddenly scared I've squashed one of the fluffballs as there's an alarmed squeak. I haven't. Kitten number two has now made a leap from the blinds and is mid-air and dropping like a stone, with four rigid legs stuck out in all directions flying-squirrel-style.

I stick my hands out, and its more luck than judgement that the soft furry lump lands splat in the middle of my palms. 'Phew.'

'What's going on? What's happening?' Rachel is squawking from the couch.

'I caught it!' It stares up at me, all wide-eyed innocence. And those baby-blues catch at something in my throat as I pull it closer to my body and stroke it reassuringly. Though, I suspect the cuddling bit is more for my own benefit than the kitten's. It doesn't seem bothered, but it does start up a raspy uneven purr that rumbles straight to the centre of my heart. And finds a squishy bit I'd almost forgotten I have.

I swallow hard to dislodge the lump as it snuggles its way deeper into my hands, then sigh. I can feel the beat of its heart through my T-shirt, feel the warmth of its tiny body. Maybe I do need a cat. Or something. I've been acting like I've been allergic to bodily contact of any kind since Andy did the dirty. And I have in a way. I've been air-hugging as well as air-kissing, and it's probably not good for my mental health. Humans need contact, warmth, touch … not just wine, Krispy Kreme doughnuts and Pringles. Although those do help, don't diss the simple solutions until you try them.

I glance up, and commando kitten number 1, the ginger ratbag, is slowly sliding down the blinds. It makes a leap onto my leg and clambers up me. I'm a human kitten tower.

I slump onto the couch, suddenly exhausted, scooping up the third kitten which is determinedly clambering up me and settle all three in my lap, then pick Rachel up.

'You still there, Rach?'

'I am.'

I take another quick photo and forward it.

'Aww, aren't they the cutest! Which one is yours?'

'None of them!'

'You've got to keep at least one.'

'No, I have not!' But I might. 'They are props. I'm supposed to be taking photos for Queen Coral.'

'Aren't you always!' She laughs, but it's a little bit strained. My job is definitely a vocation. Nothing nine-to-five about it at all. 'She never struck me as a kitten type of person, though.'

'She's not. She wants me to take a picture of her flaming lipstick and an apple, the kittens were my idea, a kind of peace gesture.' I shrug. 'She can take it or leave it.' I flop back further into the cushions. 'Do you ever wish you hadn't started something?' One of the kittens stretches out in its sleep, tiny toes splayed, and I can't help it. I stroke its cute pink pads, and its paw curls round my fingertip in a baby hug. I want to kiss those tiny toes, that little nose. I think this is the closest I've ever felt to maternal. 'I think I need to ditch the felines and concentrate on the apple. Still-life is a bloody sight easier.'

'And since when did you do easy?' I can hear the smile in Rachel's voice.

'True. Look, soz, Rachel, but I suppose I better get on with this and at least take the shot she's after before I lose the light. I'm expecting her to call soon with a new set of demands.'

'Yeah, sure! I just wanted to catch you before you jetted off, check you were okay and tell you,' there's a slight hesitation in her voice, 'I've got some news. Big news.'

'Big?'

'Mega!'

'Tell!'

'I can't! But something exciting has happened, crumbs I hope you're as excited as me! I think you will be, well, I hope ...'

'Rach! You can't do this to me! Of course, I'll be excited. Tell!' Even if the actual thing doesn't excite me, the fact that Rachel loves it so much will mean I will, too – for her.

'I've got to. You'll never guess! But you mustn't, no, no don't even try, I'm not telling you! I can't tell you on the phone, I need to see you in person. Face to face, so I can check what you think.' I smile to myself. I love it when Rachel is excited, she makes the whole world seem a brighter place. It's infectious. 'I just,' she hesitates, 'need to know you're okay with it. You might be ...'

The silence lengthens.

'Be what?'

'Upset?'

'Why would I be upset? Rach, you're worrying me!'

'Soz. I don't mean to, I mean it is good, honest, just a bit, well, I need to see you when I tell you. When are you back, Jane?'

'You're honestly not going to tell me? You're going all weird on me, and not telling me?'

'Nope. I want to tell you in person.'

'FaceTime?'

'In real person! How long are you here for when you get back? You're not going to tell me you're zooming off straight away again?' Rachel runs out of steam and sounds breathless. Giddy with excitement, as my mum would say.

'No, I won't be zooming anywhere!' I laugh a bit self-consciously. I might, or might not, have mentioned to my mate (well, all my mates, and most of my family, and everybody I know on Facebook) that I am about to jet off on an important business trip to New York. I couldn't help myself, it's the most exciting thing that's ever happened to me.

'Promise? We can meet up as soon as you're home?'

'Promise.' I won't be going anywhere, apart from work, for quite some time. My credit card is totally maxed out because I've been on a massive spending spree.

For a moment I forget about my lap full of kittens, and I even forget about Andy.

I've been buying clothes for *the trip*. Talk about excited, I've never been to New York before, I've never set foot in any part of the U. S. of A. This is the trip of a lifetime, well worth a new outfit or six. 'We can meet up the moment I get back.'

'So, you're back on the 25th? Can you make the 26th? Or will you have jet lag?'

'I'll be fine, the 26th is great.'

'Brilliant! I need to see you, Jane! How about we meet me at that new Jax Bar in town at 7 p.m.?'

I've known Rachel for years, since we bonded over a stolen ciggie (yes, I packed them in years ago) behind the bike sheds at high school after we'd both found out we hadn't got tickets to see the Spice Girls.

We were in different school years, but right then it didn't matter.

I was eleven, coming up twelve, and Rach had already hit that milestone. And back then she seemed way, way older than me. She was an August birthday, just into the second year of big school but one of the youngest, and I was a September birthday, one of the oldest in my year but still trying to find my feet. A newbie to the scary, big world of high school. But that day we gelled.

I had a sneaking suspicion that my Dad hadn't actually tried very hard at all to get the damned things. It was probably his idea of hell being surrounded by screaming teenyboppers leaping around as bubbly Emma Bunton and Scary Spice strutted their stuff round a Christmas tree (although thinking back, maybe not). But, anyhow, I'd found out over toast and marmalade that I had lost possibly my last ever chance to see some real Girl Power live and I was in a strop.

So was Rachel.

It was a defining moment, our own small act of Girl Power defiance, as we wagged Wednesday afternoon PE and stomped on the weed-ridden tarmac, punching the air and yelling 'Tell me what you want, what you really, really want' at the top of our voices. I reckon we got a far better work out than we would have done with Ms Stainton and a wooden horse in the freezing gym.

We were mates after that. In school she had her gang, and I had mine, but we'd walk home together, hang out at weekends and as we got older the fact that we were in different school years mattered less and less. By the time I walked out of those school gates for the last time, we were inseparable. Joined at the hip, as Mum laughingly said.

After school we were closer than ever for a while, but then

she started spending more and more time with her boyfriend Michael, and I made the decision to move further south with Andy when he got offered a better job. Then I took on a job that involved loads of travel and unsociable hours, so we saw less and less of each other, even though we'd gas on the phone for hours sometimes. It's not like we're miles from each other, but life can kind of get in the way, can't it? But Rach is always the person I tell first about anything. Well, anything major, my flatmate Freddie often finds out the minor stuff first these days, because he's there. In situ. As in, on our shared couch.

I told Rach I was engaged before I'd even told my mum. She helped me pick my dress, the flowers, the bridesmaids, even my undies. Then she was the person who put me back together again when it all went wrong.

She took a week off work and camped out in the flat. Then she left strict instructions for Freddie and made sure she rang me every single day when she went back home.

'Oh, come on Rach! What's so big you can't tell me over the phone?' I shake my head and can't help but smile.

'I'll tell you when I see you, it's a surprise! I know I shouldn't have mentioned it now, but I couldn't help it. Now, are you all ready for the trip?' This shows how excited she is – Rachel is a very considerate, caring person. Asking about my trip would normally have been her top priority.

'Nearly! I've just got to do this one shot and then I've got two days off before we go.'

'Wow, the mighty Coral has given you time off?' She giggles, and I join in. The hours I put into this job (and the crap I put up with) are ridiculous, but I see it as an investment. This is my apprenticeship. One day, I won't be the un-credited photographer for a glossy Instagrammer, I'll be taking the photos I want, my way. But for now, as my only qualification is a GCSE in Art and I can't afford to take time out and do a course, this is my way in. Along with my role as unofficial pet photographer for the local animal rescue centre. I'm working on that one though. Pet Portrait-er might not have the same ring to it as Photographer to the Stars, but I reckon it's a good second string to my bow. There will always be dogs, right? And it has to be easier than taking pics of babies. Or cats.

'She has, we've got a backlog of photos to post over the next few days, then the next ones will be in New York!'

Rachel squeals. 'Ooh, I'm so excited for you! You're my jet-setting friend, I tell everybody they're your photos and not hers.'

'I was lucky to get this chance.'

'Bollocks to you being the lucky one!'

I was though. Serendipity don't they call it? It was one of those one in a thousand things when I'd bumped into Coral on Millennium Bridge. Literally. Well, I was trying to take a photo and she nudged me with her bony elbows so hard I would have toppled in if Health and Safety precautions hadn't been in place.

We had a bit of a stand-off, mobile phones at the ready. Me wrapping one leg round a rail so she couldn't dislodge me from the prime spot.

Normally I'm an easy-going kind of person, and if she'd

have asked nicely I'd have budged over, but it was her attitude that made me bristle.

She told me who she was, expecting me to recognise her name (I didn't), then showed me her Instagram feed which was full of pretty boring photos. Then I saw her stats. She had tens of thousands of followers. *Tens of thousands*. Most of them under age for at least some kind of legal activity. I don't think I'm her demographic, but I ask you, how had she got so many followers? I had more like ten.

Turns out Coral was a blogger, big time. She had sponsorship, bucket loads of free stuff sent to her every week, and a devoted following.

We compared the shots we'd just taken and before I knew it I had a job taking the pictures for her Instagram feed. Sadly, my role as photographer had also morphed into PA and general dogsbody, as she was a bit of a madam and had nobody else to boss around. And sometimes I find it hard to say no.

Now don't get me wrong, I love my job. I'm doing what I've always wanted to do. And before I met Coral I'd been on the verge of taking a part-time admin job with the company Andy worked for, just to help boost my income until I started to build a reputation. He'd never been that interested in my career to be honest and saw taking photos as my little hobby and had done his best to persuade me to turn it into just that. And he had the killer reasoning that we did, after all, have to save up for our wedding. So why couldn't I do a proper job for a bit?

So it felt like fate meeting Coral that day. It had stopped me putting a hold on my dreams and spending my days filing and photocopying. Andy wasn't keen at all, but, I mean, if I'd taken that role he'd wanted me too, I'd really be in a mess now. No way could I have faced up to him every single day. I'd have been far too tempted to feed him into the shredder or slip something nasty into the water cooler and accidentally kill everybody in the company.

But I need this job more than ever now. I don't want Andy to be proved right, that it's just a hobby. Because it isn't. This is my apprenticeship, and one day the time will be right to strike out on my own. But right now, it's my security blanket.

Without Coral, I wouldn't be able to pay my rent, and I'd lose my flat, and Freddie, and everything.

I love Freddie my flatmate. Not in a lustful way – the shag-a-thon way would completely wreck everything, and I could never in a million years do that to us. He's the best thing that's happened to me in a long time.

A man who I don't need to shave my legs or comb my hair for. Though I do of course. I just don't always have the time or inclination to de-fuzz bits of me that nobody is going to see. And after a burger it is just *so* hard to hold my stomach in and think sexy. It's actually a relief to be living with some-body and not have to think about all that.

So that's me in a nutshell. Wannabe photographer, average weight, slightly above average height, red hair, green eyes, no five-year plan, slightly forgetful, verging on sluttery, one flat-mate called Freddie, half of a very small flat.

'She was lucky to get you!'

'Oh, I do love you, Rach.'

24

'Love you back.' I can hear the smile in her voice. 'I'll see you on the 26th then?'

'You will! Can't wait to hear your news.'

'Hey, Jane? Keep one of those kittens! That ginger one, it is *so* you.'

'I can't, I'm away too much. I'm off to New York!'

'Get it when you get back, ask Lora to keep it.'

'But I'm ...'

'Freddie will feed it when you're not there! You know he will, he'd do anything for you. See you soon,' I can hear her blowing kisses. 'Keep it!'

I put my mobile down, and stare at my lapful of purr-i-ness, they're rumbling so much my legs are vibrating. How on earth can she say that a kitten is so 'me'?

It has its tiny pink tongue stuck out between its lips and its toes are twitching.

I know for a fact I don't do that.

Chapter 3

'Hi, honey, I'm home!' A waft of air from the front door, and the clunk of a heavy bag being dropped sends the kittens scattering in all directions.

Freddie is standing in the doorway, his big trademark grin on his face. He even uses it when cold callers and religious types knock on the door. It makes their day.

I'm not his honey, it's a joke. We're flatmates, but we're like an old married couple without the married bit. Or the old.

He's all lanky and loose-limbed, like a Great Dane puppy. But with the floppy fringe of a cocker spaniel. I don't normally liken people to dogs, honest, but it works with Freddie.

Kitten number 1 has emerged from under the couch and is staring up at him, with a look of wonder on its little face. It's cute, okay, I admit it. Very cute. Big eyed, button-nosed cute.

'Oh my God, cuteness overload.'

See? 'You sound so soppy.' I look at all the ginger and white hairs on my black leggings. I so shouldn't even consider keeping one.

'I don't care.' He's down on his hands and knees making

baby noises, and the kitten is onto him in an instant. Literally. Marching over with a slightly sideways swagger like it thinks it's a real big cat, with its spiky tail stuck in the air. All mixed up attitude and neediness in one small package.

Freddie scoops it up and rolls over on his back and I swear I see the tiny creature fall in love. The other two kittens emerge from their hiding places wondering what they're missing out on, then scramble up onto his chest and join in the purr-a-thon. 'Aren't you the handsomest guy in the world?' Ginger purrs louder, then opens its little pink mouth in a soundless miaow. 'Aww, baby.' Freddie props himself up on his elbow and looks at me, head tilted slightly on one side. 'This mean you're ready for love again?' He winks.

'Oh, God, don't you start! They are kittens, right?'

'Right on,' he holds one up in the air, 'definitely kittens.'

'I need help, Freddie.'

'Don't I know it.' He raises an eyebrow and chuckles. 'Though that is the first step to recovery, admitting—'

'Sod off.' I can't help but grin back and nudge him in the ribs with my foot. 'They're a photoshoot not a therapy session.'

'Shush. Don't call them that.' He covers the kitten's ears with his hands. 'Kitties have feelings too you know.'

I ignore him. 'And they won't stay still. Why won't kittens just sit?'

'You're confusing them with dogs, and men.'

'I need to get a decent shot, and I need to get a photo of that flaming apple on a white plate with lipstick before Coral rings.' He raises an eyebrow. 'Don't ask.'

'Well, how about,' he pulls himself up, so he's got his back

27

resting against the couch, 'it just sits on my knee? I could hold it sneakily to make sure it doesn't move. You know put a finger on its tail, out of sight? Like this?' He demonstrates, and the kitten rolls over in indignation, wraps its whole body round his finger, kicks like crazy and bites him. I hope that this isn't what Rachel means by the 'so you' bit.

'Ooh, you're a little tough nut, aren't you?' He tickles its tummy and it flops back, all languid and blissful. Feet in the air, and I'm a tiny bit jealous. 'Aww, so gorgeous, are we keeping them?'

'No, we're not! I'm taking photo's for Coral's Instagram page, and said I'd do a few for promo for the rescue centre.'

'We should rescue one! A house is not a home ...'

'Well, you can clean the litter tray!'

'Really?'

I groan. 'You're being serious, aren't you? You want a kitten! Gawd, you're as bad as Rach.'

'Maybe.' He tickles the kitten under its chin, and the purring starts up again. 'Look, the perfect picture.'

'Cute, but your finger is in the way, and I'm not sure the ripped jeans make the perfect backdrop.'

Freddie's jeans are not ripped in a designer way, they're ripped in a 'we've been through a lot together and I can't bear to part with them and they're very comfy' way.

It's not Coral's way. Coral doesn't do comfy. Coral would sue me if I posted anything resembling un-touched-up reality on her Insta feed.

And I'm not convinced it will help with re-homing the kittens.

'I could put a blanket on my knee?' He pulls the throw off the sofa.

'It's a bit up and down, they're only tiny. You can't see its legs now.'

'We could put a board underneath?' He improvises with a magazine. 'Mag, blanket, kitten. *Ta-dah!*' He throws his hands out and the kitten slides off his knee, faceplants between his ankles then rolls over and attacks his leg. 'Maybe not.'

I have to laugh. See what I mean about him being the best thing? What boyfriend would go to that kind of trouble? I'd be a total fool to ever think about him in any way other than just a mate, despite him being ever so slightly sexy when he pads through the place in the morning; bare-chested, with bare feet and his hair all tousled.

And makes me coffee.

Then goes away without a word.

No conversation required.

He is priceless.

I bumped into Freddie a few days after my world imploded, and he more or less saved my life.

There I was, at an all time low, my life all but over (I'd got a bit melodramatic, which I think I was entitled to). I'd been dumped mid hen-party, had a horribly demanding boss who just then was doing my head in, and had nowhere to live. Even though I love my mum, living with your happily married parents when you've just hit thirty, and it looks like you're going to be a spinster for ever, and you've just woken up to the fact that there's more chance of your eggs getting hard-boiled then producing babies, is not a recipe for happiness. One more day and one of us would have cracked. Nastily.

So, I'd strolled confidently into an estate agents' office. All naïve and excited about my new life as a single independent woman earning a wage.

Okay, I wasn't excited, I was exhausted from crying, full of self-doubt and needing to find a cave to hole up in. But I was naïve. That bit is true.

'I'm looking for a flat to rent. Something like that.' I'd said to the guy by the desk, pointing at what I thought was an unassuming but nice apartment.

'Nice, isn't it?'

'It is.' He wasn't being very helpful. 'Very. How, er, much are they charging?'

'Haven't got a clue.' He grinned. Quite a nice grin. 'A lot I'd imagine.'

I smiled back, feeling slightly awkward, not quite sure what to say next.

'I'm sorry, I can't find much in your price range.' A tall, slim, blonde, immaculate vision in killer heels and a tight skirt rudely interrupted our smile-a-thon. 'Apart from this.' She passed him the details with a dismissive sniff.

Ahh, so that figured, he didn't actually work here. I felt myself colour up but couldn't resist a glance over his shoulder.

It was the smallest hovel, next to a railway line, overlooking bin-alley and on the drug dealing route. Okay, I might be exaggerating the very tiniest bit. About the drug-dealing. But it was daylight hours, so who knows? The really terrifying part of it all though, was that the monthly rent was roughly the amount I'd had in mind as affordable.

Turned out my type of salary didn't stretch to a roof over my head *and* food. The two would appear to be mutually exclusive.

Bummer.

Anyhow, gloomy was not the word. I mean I'd thought I'd be able to at least afford something that was halfway decent. And I really, as in *really*, liked the flat that I'd spotted when I walked in. It said 'home' to me.

Turns out I was delusional.

'Were you interested in that one?' She'd dismissed him and moved on to me. 'It's in an up-and-coming area. Very on-trend.' She'd looked me up and down and made me not feel on-trend. 'Well-maintained.' She was doing it again. Cow. Bits of me might not be particularly well-maintained, but other bits are fine. I nodded mutely. 'Very reasonable.' She named a figure and I reckon I blanched. Reasonable it was not. Well, not for a normal person.

I think I may have squeaked.

Anyway, the smiley guy realised I'd been stuck dumbstruck. 'I think she needs to think about it, we'll come back later?' His hands were on my shoulders and he'd spun me round and whisked me out of the office and before I knew it we were walking down the street together.

'That's shocking.' I'd finally found my voice again.

'Totally. Shit isn't it trying to find a place round here?'

'It is indeed shit.'

'You don't fancy a restorative coffee, do you? Just to get

over the shock of that place?' He pointed up, and I realised we'd slowed to a halt outside a café.

'Yes, er, well, I don't normally have coffee with strange men, I don't want you to think ...'

'I'm not strange. Trust me!' He winked, and I wanted to. Trust him. I felt a kind of glimmer of recognition, like I'd known him for years. Comfortable is the word I suppose. Safe.

'Well, I suppose you do look harmless.'

'Now,' he held a finger up, 'I didn't say that!'

Anyway, just as I was wondering whether this was how you met 'the One', and if this was the moment to state clearly that I was never, ever going to get my knickers off for a man again in my whole life. That I was all about getting my career established and some money saved up for a house deposit. Though, ha, fat chance of me being able to ever do that solo. Unless I slept in a bin. Or trawled the streets for somebody who wanted to share a flat with me. Just as all that was whizzing through my brain, he interrupted me.

'You don't recognise me, do you Janey?'

Turns out I was right. He was familiar.

He wasn't a random stranger, and my feelings weren't those of kindred spirits destined to be together, but meeting at the wrong moment in their lives. It was much more down to earth than that.

'It's me, Freddie! I hung around with Matt at school?'

'Oh, shit, you're kidding? Freddie! Wow, sorry, I just didn't recognise you, it's the hair, the top, the ...' Body, I wanted to say, but stopped myself.

Now he'd told me, I definitely did remember him. But he'd

changed. Back then he'd been a bit of a geek; lanky, quiet. Sweet. Whereas his mate Matt was all front. A cocky bugger who was a bit of a dish and knew it.

Freddie was the cheeky one, who played the fool some of the time (like when he nicked my yoghurt) but most of the time blended into the background. Into Matt's shadow.

I grin. 'You said you weren't strange!'

'I'm not. Now.' He grins back. 'I was a teenager back then, we're all strange.'

'You can say that again!'

'All we think about is getting off, footie, having it off, computer games, what a normal sex drive is, food and, well, sex.'

'Most of those seem to be the same thing.' I arch an eyebrow in what I hope is a sophisticated not a pervy way.

'Exactly, being a 'yoof' is bloody hard work.'

I laugh at the way he says yoof, it's so completely not-Freddie.

So, anyway, I did know him. Otherwise I wouldn't have done what I did.

Well, who knows, I might have done. I was bloody desperate. And he was laid back and friendly, not pervy at all.

We got chatting over coffee, then ended up being practically swept out at closing time, and we moved onto the pub on the corner and realised we were in the same boat. Roughly.

Well, he hadn't been dumped, and he wasn't currently living with his mum. But he was being chucked out of the flat he was currently sharing, because the other two flatmates had become a far too cosy couple. And he wasn't really ready to settle for living in a dump but couldn't afford somewhere up-and-coming on his own.

After two drinks, Freddie waggled the card that the estate agent had given him. 'Shall we call her? We could just about afford that flat you'd fancied, between us. Or is that a bit weird? You can ignore me if it's too weird. I'm not usually this forward but it's just I'm solvent, got an okay job, pretty well house-trained, you're, er,' I wait for him to say desperate, but he doesn't, 'keen on the same place as me, and we do kind of know each other, and, er, I think it could work.'

When I'd spotted that flat I'd just felt deep down it was the One. Even though the rent had made me feel queasy, I'd been tempted with youthful optimism, to arrange a viewing anyway. Even if it was far, far more expensive than I could afford.

I'm not quite sure what I thought would happen, even I knew that estate agents didn't tend to come with soft hearts and big discounts.

In my head while the agent had been talking to Freddie, I'd been fantasising, but all the while knowing that I couldn't really afford to take it on, on my own.

Freddie was peering over his pint at me. 'You really liked it, didn't you?'

And with those few words there was some kind of unspoken agreement between us. We'd hit on the idea. We could take the place on together. So, we did.

Without knowing it Freddie had turned into my knight in shining armour.

That was well over a year ago, so we've been together longer than a lot of couples I know.

We also bicker a lot less. Though he does take the mickey a bit sometimes. But he has supported me through the Andy years, and I've supported him through the revolving doors years. Don't get me wrong, it's not like he shags round, he just seems to pick the wrong girls. Which I am beginning to suspect he does on purpose.

'Oh, sugar.' My phone beeps with the alarm I set earlier and stops my musings about Freddie. 'I'm going to have to ditch the kittens for now and do the apple. You couldn't look after them for a bit could you?' I give him a slightly beseeching look. 'Please, I'm begging?' I indicate the kittens, then do a go away flap with my hands, and try to do my own imitation of cute, which I'm not sure I pull off.

'Boy, you're demanding, if only I'd known what I was letting myself in for when I signed that flat share contract!'

But I know he's kidding.

He gets to his feet and expertly scoops up all three little felines in his big capable hands. 'Come on fellas.'

'I think one of them might be a fellee.'

'We'll be in my room if you need us.'

'You're a star, I owe you one!'

'Several I'd say.' He winks and kicks open the lounge door. 'I can take them back to Lora's if you like, on my way to the pub?'

I feel a totally irrational twinge in my stomach. Freddie likes Lora. He keeps saying he doesn't, that they're mates like we are, but he's round there in an instant if he has an excuse. And I've seen the look in his eye.

I want Freddie to be happy, but I'm ashamed to say I'm

selfish enough to not want to lose him. Not yet. And anyway, Lora would be a disaster. She's far too calculating for Freddie, and she's had more men than hot dinners this year.

Okay, I'm being bitchy. I confess. I don't want to lose my best – well, only – male friend. Though Lora is a bit of a 'rum 'un' as my uncle used to say. Freddie deserves better.

I'm also being daft. He's offering to help me out, and I'm not so silly that I don't realise what a good move it would be to say, yes.

'Wow, would you? That would be so helpful. There's a basket thing in the kitchen. I'll pop in and see her later, tell her I'll try again tomorrow if she likes. I'd do it myself, but Coral will be calling any sec to discuss last minute plans.'

Freddie rolls his eyes. 'We're definitely out of here if Queen C is calling. See you later, and don't take any shit from her ladyship.' He blows me a kiss, then holds up a kitten and waves its little paw in the air. 'Bye-bye Mummy! Love you! Don't send me away, purry pleeeease!'

I shake my head at him. 'Shoo!'

Chapter 4

I have an apple, and I have a white plate. Oh, and a very red lipstick. And less than an hour to create an Instagram image that will leave Coral's fans and sponsors wetting their knickers – with excitement not incontinence. She has a very youthful following.

She wants to plug a lipstick she's been sent (*Oh, God, I love these cosmetics, I need them to send more, make it good or I'll fucking kill you*), and she also wants a nod towards her (or should I say our?) trip to New York. She suggested I took a bite out of it and left an artistic lip print. Have you ever tried to do that? This apple looks like it's been ravaged by a vampire two seconds after a blood sucking session.

I doodle a lipstick heart on the plate and reach for a fresh apple just as Darth Vader suddenly explodes into the silence. Well, not actually Darth himself, it's my ringtone. Which means it is her: Coral – you have to find fun where you can, don't you?

'Where are you?'

No 'Hello' or other pleasantry. 'Hi, Coral! I'm just doing this lipstick shot; I think the bite isn't—'

'Oh, forget that.' I can picture her making a dismissive motion with one red-talon-tipped hand (she gets a free weekly manicure as well). 'Take the day off.'

'But I—' I was about to point out that it is already five o'clock and the day is nearly done, and I was also going to say I needed the money so I wasn't about to *forget* anything, but she interrupts me again.

'What difference is one more day? You'll be taking nearly three weeks, anyway.'

'Three weeks? But, New York isn't hol—'

'Oh, didn't I say? I don't need you tagging along with me any more.'

'What? Tagging? But—'

'I've decided you'll cramp my style – this is New York, darling, not some suburban—'

'But, photos, you need photos taking.'

'Crystal will help me.'

'Who's Crystal?' I know I sound suspicious but I can't help it.

'She's American.' She says it like that means she is everything I am not. Stylish, for one. 'She follows my blog and suggested this trip, she's so dynamic, so savvy, so ... with it, you know?' I'm already sick of hearing about Crystal. 'And it's more of a holiday than anything. You can run off and do whatever you do, water plants or find a boyfriend, or something. You're always saying you don't get enough free time. When was the last time you had sex? Use it or lose it love.' She makes a disgusting squelchy noise, which, luckily, I find easy to ignore.

'But ... but, I've got a ticket and everything. I've told everybody I'm jetting off with you in two days. *Two days!*'

'Oh, I cancelled your ticket after ...' there is a long pause, then, 'the incident with the dog.'

The line goes silent. My bitch of a boss is letting her words sink in.

'You cancelled it three days ago and you never told me!' My hand clenches into a fist. If she was here now, I'd be having trouble resisting the urge to strangle her or shove the bloody lipstick-scarred apple down her throat.

She is a complete cow – she knows how much this trip means to me and this is the most evil payback ever. I (apparently) screwed up with her #MondayMotivation picture. Daniel's dog-in-a-bag photo had ten times as many 'likes'. And Daniel is her arch Insta-rival. Which is why I've called in the kittens.

This was not my fault though. Everybody knows a puppy will trump the latest trend any day of the week (apart from #FreebieFriday), and how was I to know he'd spring Lucy the long-haired Chihuahua on the world?

'I told you he was looking at luxury pet stuff!' I'd spotted Daniel had started following a designer of diamanté dog collars – but Coral had poo-pooed my suspicions. So it's her fault she's in the doggy-do not mine.

'Have you finished?' She's sounding bored.

'But I've got kittens!' I haven't had time to talk kittens. I was going to surprise her once I'd got the perfect shot. With her flaming lipstick at the side if necessary.

'I haven't got time for that now. We'll talk about kittens when I get home.'

'They'll have grown by then.'

'Well, get new ones. Very cute ones. Very tiny ones, smaller than Daniel's cock-sized offering.'

'I don't think kittens come that sma—'

'Oh, whatever, I don't care. I pay you to come up with the ideas, not bother me with-'

'You pay me to take—' I am about to say, take the photographs, but I don't get the chance.

'Do what you have to,' she's hissing, 'to make this up to me. Then we'll see.' I can hear the click of her nails tapping on the phone. It's a horrible sound and normally I'd just ring off.

'So, I can come?' My little begging voice sounds pathetic even to my own ears. I hate myself.

'No.'

'It is so not fair to pull the plug on my trip. I work evening and weekends and ...' I spend my whole life trailing round after her. She has killed my social life, and any hope of ever getting laid again, dead.

'You should just count yourself lucky you've still got a job. Now, I must fly, I've got packing to do, and I need a manicure.'

'Fine. I'll have a holiday.' I sound like a stubborn child, I know. 'I'll go to Ibiza.'

'You do that. Don't forget to post those photos, though, will you? Have you done my big apple?'

I feel like telling her where she can stuff her big apple, and let's just say it's in a place where the sun doesn't shine. I reckon there is steam coming out of my ears. I can't speak, just mouth soundlessly. But it doesn't matter, she just takes my silence as agreement and goes off *to pack*.

I throw the bloody apple across the room, where it hits the window with a satisfying squelch, then I sink down onto the floor and put my head in my hands.

How could she do this to me? Devastated is not the word. Not that I wanted to go with *her*, but *New York*, I ask you. I could have begged, I should have begged. I think I might have been whimpering, and if she'd have been here, I might have been tempted to lick her feet (no, I wouldn't, I take that back).

I don't know why I put up with her.

Well, I do, I need the money.

I need the flat. I need Freddie.

My phone pings. Maybe it's a last-minute reprieve? Maybe she actually has got a heart?

It's a text from Rachel: *Have fun in New York, I'm well jel!* xx

Me, too.

Chapter 5

'Trouble with the apple, babes?' Freddie, slumps down on the settee behind me and ruffles my hair, which is slightly annoying, but I can't be bothered to thump him like I normally would. For the ruffling and for the 'babes' – which he only does to get a reaction. He leans in to take a closer look at me, and his brow furrows. 'Wow, you really are upset. What's up? What's Coral the cow done now? Demanded the kitties have a mani, pedi and close shave before she even entertains the thought of them appearing on her feed?'

I can't even raise a glimmer of a smile. I sigh and blink. As well as being an excellent kitten wrangler, he's also good for chatting to, but I can't work out how to speak about *her* without either screaming or crying. So, I change the subject.

'Was Lora okay?'

'She wasn't in. Some long-haired lout in a biker jacket answered the door. I gave him my hard "Hurt these kittens and you are so dead, mate" stare.'

'I bet he was quaking in his biker boots.' Deep inside, I feel a slight lift: I'm pleased Lora wasn't there, it makes me feel very slightly better.

'Crocs. He had pink Crocs on, not boots. That's why I dared glare at him.'

'Ahh ... you're just a big wuss at heart.'

'Sure am. You did explain to Coral what you meant by close-ups of a ginger pussy, didn't you?' He nudges me with his elbow.

'*Eugh*, stop it. That's disgusting.' But I can't help the tiniest of smiles from teasing at my taut face muscles. I actually feel like I've got a very thick face mask on and it's set like concrete.

'Wow mate, this is serious, isn't it?' He's spotted the debris on the table. He eyes up the bottle of Sauvignon Blanc I've opened, the biggest pizza the guy at Domino's would make for me (sometimes even a Mighty Meaty needs extra toppings), the tub of Ben and Jerry's Salted Caramel Brownie, and the box of man-sized tissues with suspicion. 'None of this was here when I went out a couple of hours ago.'

I nod.

'I thought you said you were going carb free until you got to the Big Apple.'

'If I do that,' I swallow away the lump in my throat, 'I will die of malnutrition.'

He waits. He's good at waiting and listening. Like the old Golden Retriever I had when I was a teenager.

'Because I'm not going.' I take another big bite of pizza and try to swallow it down past the lump in my throat. And nearly choke. Freddie bangs me hard on the back, helpfully. 'No Big Apple for me.'

'What? But, you're flying out in two days, you've bought

stuff, you've packed. I thought she was dead set on going, that she had her eye on the U.S. and—'

'She is, she has, it's just me that isn't going.' I take a deep breath. 'She cancelled my ticket.'

'Why the hell would she do that? She needs you!'

'She doesn't need me, she's got Crystal.'

'Crystal?' There's a hint of a smile tugging at the corner of his generous mouth, and I know he's dying to laugh. 'Coral and Crystal, you're kidding me? Are they a new double act?'

'Crystal is her American friend.' I smile, despite myself. It's hard not to.

'So, she dumped you for some American photographer?'

'She dumped me because of bloody Daniel.'

'Daniel? Is that her new shag?'

'No, he's that stupid flaming Instagrammer she's at war with.' I bury my face in my hands.

'Ahh.'

'Sorry,' I glance up at him through my fingers, 'I was shouting, wasn't I? Sorry. He's the one with the puppy.'

'So that's why you'd got kittens?'

'You got it in one.' I top up my wine glass and wave the bottle in his direction.

'It's okay, I've got beer!' He sinks down onto the carpet next to me and helps himself to pizza. 'Bloody hell, what are those brown bits?'

I peer at his slice. 'Anchovy.'

'Are you sure that goes with the sausage?'

'Anchovy goes with everything, and so does sour cream.'

'Wondered what that was. So, this Daniel?'

'He's got more likes this month than she has, way more. This is her way of getting even. She says if she loses any sponsorship she will *die*.' I try my best to say the last word in her melodramatic way.

'What a cow. Shame you didn't tip her into the Thames while you had the chance.' Freddie knows all about how Coral and I met, and most things that have happened since.

He drapes his arm over my shoulders and squeezes. It's nice, even nicer than the image of Coral flapping about in the murky brown water in her designer gear.

I'm tempted to just grab him and blub into his shirt, but I don't think he signed up for that level of interaction when he agreed a flat share.

'And ...' I bite my lip, trying to hold in the sudden rush of anguish. I've not really come to terms with the New York bit yet, it's not sunk in, but this bit has. It is here and now, and it hurts. I wave my mobile his way. 'I was just trying to book a cheap deal to Ibiza.' A tear trickles past my defences, so I scrub my cheek with the back of my hand and hope he hasn't noticed. 'But I can't.' It comes out as a bit of a wail. 'My credit card won't play ball, I can't even book the most economy of economy flights, the crappiest airline in the world refused to take me because I'm maxed out,' I rub my forearm over my face, the back of my hand isn't coping, 'buying all those frigging clothes.'

'Oh, shit. Oh, hell, Jane, but you don't need to go away, do you? You can stay here, have some free time and ...' His voice tails off. Then his eyes twinkle at me. 'We can play with kittens?'

'What is it with you and kittens?' I frown at him, suddenly worried that he has some unhealthy fetish and I've got him all wrong.

He sighs. 'I was thinking about you, not me. But hands up I'm man enough to admit that I need cuddles and cute as much as the next person.'

'Amy was quite cute …' I pause. 'And cuddly.' Amy was the girl he brought back a couple of weeks ago, and boy was she into cuddles. In a man-eating, down the throat, kiss your face off, crawl all over you like a rash kind of way.

I'd hidden in the bedroom in case she'd accidentally got confused and clambered over me as well. And because it was making me feel a bit queasy.

'Cuddly as a polar bear.' He pulls a funny face and does a clawing gesture. Girls flock to Freddie like bees to a honey pot, but he rations the stuff, then tells them to buzz off after a very short time. If he hits three weeks with the same girl I start to get scared she'll be moving in, or he'll be moving out. Three weeks for Freddie is heavy. But the moment they get familiar with the contents of our cupboards, he starts the retreat. There was one girl, Annie, who he seemed to like; he ended up rearranging all our food (I nearly had an incident when I grabbed the coffee and it turned out it was gravy granules) so that he could kid himself that she hadn't got her feet under the table. I've not got to the bottom of it yet, but I will. 'But kittens don't come with strings attached, do they?'

'I hope not.' Although strings might have been handy on the photoshoot front.

'You can just chill with them, they have no expectations, they're not planning the future you've not agreed to.'

'Just their next meal.'

We both contemplate a relationship with a cat. Then I snap out of it. If I'm not careful it will be slippers and cocoa next.

'I can't have a staycation. I told Coral I was going to Ibiza, and she lives on social media so I've got to post photos on Facebook because if she gets the slightest hint that I'm still here, or pissed off or sulking then she'll be onto me in an instant. She'll be gloating, making my life even more of a misery, then she'll probably sack me for being a wuss.' I grimace. 'She hates wusses.' Coral loves to be in control, she's an out and out bully, but she likes to think she's controlling people with backbone, not easy targets. God, the woman is totally power crazy. And deluded.

Freddie munches on some pizza for a few minutes. Then swills it down with his beer. 'Hate to tell you, but this anchovy idea is wrong on so many levels.'

'Name one.'

'Salt. Too much.' He tries another bit, flicking the fishy bit off onto my slice. We're like an old married couple, swapping the bits we don't like. 'I've got it!' He sits upright, abruptly. 'We'll go to Brighton.'

'I've got it' and 'Brighton' aren't two phrases I'd normally put together.

'Come again?'

'My parents place. Come on,' he nudges me, 'you'd be doing me a favour, it's boring going on my own.' I don't know that much personal stuff about Freddie, but I do know that his parents are currently swanning around in their villa in Italy and his good-son duties including regular trips to check up on their house. Tidy up, move post, weed the path and generally make sure it doesn't look neglected.

When we first lived together, his periodic disappearing act had intrigued me. Me and Rach had invented all kinds of elaborate scenarios – like he was a spy on a mission, or had a secret wife and family, or had a cannabis den.

Then I spoiled things by asking him, because I'm nosy.

I mean, Brighton is a bit of a killer on the exciting escapades front, doesn't exactly say 007 or Mission Impossible, does it? Though I'm sure it's a lovely place. And lively. And the home of DJ's and raves and stuff.

'We'll use it as a hideaway, then you won't get spotted and you can pretend you're in Ibiza.'

'I can?'

'You can.'

'Er, there are holes in that solution. Like no sun and a pier.'

He winks. 'Post photos of Spain – I won't tell if you don't. I've got some rave ones from when I was a student.'

'Oh, Freddie.' I can't help myself. It's the wine and the emotion and the relief. I fling myself at him. He freezes for a second.

We do occasional clap on the back type hugs, but not this type. Then he pats my back awkwardly, in a there-there kind of way, then unexpectedly hugs me properly. Then disengages. We both launch ourselves at the pizza, gorging on chunks of stuffed crust, and surreptitiously edge an inch or two away from each other suddenly mega aware that our knees had been touching.

I clear my throat.

'So, er, you got pissed in Ibiza? You went to raves?'

'All-nighters, making the moves, babe.' He makes a few *very* strange moves.

'I think it might be better to stop doing that.' I giggle.

'You've seen nothing until you've seen techno, Freddie.'

'Haven't you got to go to work?'

'I'm owed time off, and besides, it'll be good going together. It's fun. You really do need to tell that cow where to get off though.'

'I know.' I nod. 'I know, and I will, just not yet.' I've only just got used to the idea that Andy could change my life like he did and that I could do nothing about it. Right now, I've got a reliable income and a home I like, I'm not ready to risk losing it all.

'I know. You'll get there.' He winks, then holds his beer bottle up. 'What do you say? Brighton then?'

'Brighton.' We clink.

Desperate times require desperate measures – so, Brighton it is.

Chapter 6

I need to pack for Brighton, and right now I'm thinking a rucksack with spare jeans and a few T-shirts is all I need.

This is partly because, 1. it is probably all I need, and, 2. I don't want to have to unzip my flaming suitcase and face all my lovely US-bound clobber, which I still haven't unpacked.

I'm not quite ready for a reminder that I should soon be heading to the airport for a long flight, and bubbly, and hilarity and jetlag and the promise of NEW YORK (yes, I know I've gone shouty) and cocktails and, well, New York.

'Jane, door for you!'

Freddie's yell stops me giving my innocent suitcase the evil eye. Sugar, I'm not supposed to be here! I'm supposed to have jetted off. Why is anybody at the door for me? Unless Coral actually has realised not even she can be that evil, and has sent a taxi?

I realise I'm flapping round, spinning in a circle. Trying to decide if I should dive in the wardrobe or under the bed, or if Freddie will come in after me and I'll look even more foolish than I already feel.

I stop.

Stop panicking. That's tomorrow. I am supposed to be here today. I am here.

'Surprise!' I spin round and it's Rachel.

'Rach! What the hell are you doing here?' Rachel is never here. Rachel doesn't live anywhere near me.

'Crappy work conference, so I thought I'd see if I could catch you before you went!' She throws herself on the bed, dramatically. 'You've got to save me from my earnest colleagues.' She rolls her eyes, then spots the case. 'Wow, are you sure that case is big enough? I'd be taking one double that size if it was me. You are just so cool about all this.'

'No, I'm not.' I shove the suitcase off the bed and flop down beside her. 'I'm not being cool.'

'God, you are. I am so envious of your jet set lifestyle.'

'Don't be.' I close my eyes, then open them and peep at her. Lying on the bed next to me. 'Can you keep a secret, Rach?'

She props herself up on one elbow.

'Course I can! We can do swapsies. You first.'

'I'm not going to New York.' I avoid her eye as I say it.

'Really?' She sits up a bit higher and I can feel her staring at me. 'But, you've packed, and ...'

'You don't need to tell me.' I groan and put my hands over my eyes. 'I've packed, spent up and told the whole world about it. What will everybody say?'

'Fuck everybody else. It's you I care about!' She drags my hands away and looks into my eyes, which have gone a bit blurry.

Saying it out loud has made me feel sorry for myself.

51

'Aww, hell, Jane, you were so looking forward to it.' She wraps me in a hug and I try not to sniffle. 'What happened?'

'Coral happened.' Freddie's deep voice rumbles unexpectedly into the room. 'Mind if I join you?'

'Bugger off.' We both shout at the same time, then Rachel levers herself up.

'She's not sacked her? She's not sacked you?'

'No, she's not sacked me. She just decided she doesn't need me.'

'Oh, Jane, what a cow.'

'I'm fine.'

'You're not.'

'It was just a shock. I will be fine.'

'She'll be fine once she gets to Brighton!' Freddie is still lounging in the doorway, a safe distance away from the girlie fray.

'Wow, you're going to Brighton?' Rachel's eyes have gone all big and wide, and I can practically see her brain going into overdrive. 'Together? Have I missed something?'

'You've not missed anything.' I sigh and dig her in the ribs to cover my embarrassment. 'Freddie's got to check his parents' place and I'm going with him.' I shrug. 'That's all. No big deal!'

'What do you mean, no big deal?' Freddie acts hurt, but winks to show he doesn't mean it. 'And we're going to pretend we're in Ibiza!'

Rachel chuckles. She's got one of those deep, rolling infectious laughs which makes you smile. 'That'll take a special kind of filter, won't it?'

'I'm going to post old pics. I can't admit to Coral that I've not gone.'

'Ahh.'

'But you mustn't tell.'

'I won't.'

'Nobody, not a single person. If it gets out she will crucify me.'

'Promise. I guess I owe you a secret then?' Her eyes are twinkling, and she's gone a bit pink and bashful looking, which isn't my normal Rachel.

'Tell!'

'Well ...' She takes a deep breath, then glances at Freddie, and back at me. 'That's why I came round. I'm so crap, I just can't keep secrets, I can't wait until you get back, I can't not tell you!'

We're all holding our breath. The suspense is killing me. The silence goes on, and on, and she's glancing from me to Freddie and back again.

'I'm getting married!' It comes out in a whoosh.

'Shit, you're not?' I realise the second the words explode from my big mouth that this is not the right thing to say. I give a 'Help me' glance over her shoulder at Freddie.

'Oh, God, I knew you'd take this badly. I'm so, so sorry, Jane. I mean, I know you've had such a shitty time, that's why I needed to tell you in person.' She glances at Freddie again and I realise now, she hasn't just come here because of a boring conference, she's come here to tell me because she knew Freddie would be here. The guy who helped her pick up the pieces after my wedding-that-wasn't. 'Weddings can work out, Jane. I'm as sure as I can be, I just know he's the One for—'

'Stop it, you two! I know exactly what you're both thinking.' Rachel colours up, but Freddie brazens it out. 'I'm not anti-wedding.' They both avoid my gaze. 'I'm not! I'm so over Andy. This is nothing to do with me, it's you I'm worried about. You hardly know him, Rach!' I feel weak at the knees, good job I'm sat on the bed. 'I know not every man is like Andy. But he could be an axe murderer, or a swindler, or, or, a bigamist!' I know I'm clutching at straws here, and the duvet actually, but I'm in shock.

My bestie can't be allowed to plight her troth to smooth-talking Jed, who's persuaded her he's the One. As far as I know, she's only had a chat on Facebook, two dates and a shag with him. That does not a relationship make.

I don't want to be a damp squib, but there's rushing and there's going at the speed only required after far too many drinks when you need a bucket, or an extremely spicy curry that's turned your tummy to molten lava and is demanding a quick exit.

And this is indecent haste, and the stunning blonde-haired, blue-eyed, bubbly Rachel is not a girl who needs to grab the first guy who offers. Not that anybody should, but Rachel has always had them queuing up.

'What?' She frowns at me, looking puzzled. 'Of course, I know him! I've known him ages. What are you on about?'

I take a deep breath of my own and put my hands calmly on her shoulders. 'Rach, you've only just met Jed.'

'*Oh!*' Relief settles on her face as she puts her hand over her mouth, and giggles. 'It's not Jed, you idiot!'

Phew.

'It's Michael!'

This is the point where I should sigh with relief and say, 'silly me'. But I do not. Instead my stomach bottoms out. 'You are kidding?'

Her face says it all, this is no joke.

So, I do it, I tell that whopping great lie.

'Oh my God! *Wow!*' I pause for breath and lean forward to hug her. 'That is absolutely fantastic. I am so pleased for you!'

She tilts her head back, looking worried.

'Honest?'

'Really. Sorry, it was just a shock, I thought you guys had split for good. That's what I meant by kidding, ha-ha. Wow, that's amazing! Fab! Ace! I'm so pleased for you.' A glance at Freddie confirms that I might be overcompensating here, his eyebrows are raised so high they've gone past his fringe and merged into his hairline.

I mentally reel myself in and zip my mouth.

But my head can't stop thinking this is wrong. A mistake. Someone tell me I'm dreaming.

Michael? How can she be marrying Michael? Bastard two-timing Michael who I caught doing the dirty with luscious Lexie (I only know her name because he happened to be chanting it at the time) and made him swear he'd never do it again or I'd tell Rach everything, just before I tore him limb from limb.

We had never had any secrets and I'd hated not telling her, but I hated more the thought that if I told her the truth it could wreck our friendship. I mean, who would she believe, the smooth-talker she loved and planned to spend the rest of her life with – or her friend? I didn't want to put her in that position.

And he did say it was just one stupid impulsive action that he'd regret forever and had promised it would never happen again. But he'd also called it 'a minor transgression' – yes, he really does talk like that.

And I'd umm-ed and ahh-ed but, I have to be totally honest, it all happened just before my hen party and I was so caught up in all *my* wedding stuff, that I kind of didn't give it the thought I should have.

Daft thing is, drunk on vodka and love on my hen night, I'd decided to come clean with Rachel and was on the verge of spilling. She was my best friend and I'd felt secure in the knowledge (ha-ha) that I'd found true love, and I wanted to make sure she'd be as happy as me. I wanted everybody to be in the same state of bliss as I was!

Can you believe it? Talk about rubbish timing.

I never got to tell her. The Andy bombshell hit and it went right out of my head, it just didn't seem as important as my own broken heart. Nothing was as important as my car-crash of a life. Which obviously makes me a pretty shitty friend.

How could I not have told her?

We spent so many hours together, on the phone, FaceTime-ing, texting, while she was doing the good-friend bit and looking after me. And I just felt sorry for myself and let her do the propping up.

And now I'd left it far too late. Telling her just after it happened would have been one thing, but telling her so long after? How could I find the right time to explain? And I didn't want to lose her. I'd been totally selfish. How pathetic am I? I was scared sick of losing her, the very thought brought me out in a cold sweat.

Without her and Freddie looking after me in the aftermath, who knows what I would have done? I mean, I've never thought of myself as the suicidal type, but without somebody to kick me out of my wallowing in the mornings I would have lost my job, and without somebody to tell me when I was very close to the line between enough and too much drink life would have been seriously blurred.

Instead, it had just been normal pissed blurred and hazy.

And so, I'd decided to believe Michael when he said that he'd ever never hurt her, rather than doing what a good friend should. What she'd do for me.

And then Rach and Michael had split over some girl he'd snogged at an office party. So, it had all been fine. Over. Finished. I could breathe again, no need to sweat about whether I should tell her.

I mean, I did still hate myself for not having the guts to tell her, but I convinced myself that what she didn't know couldn't hurt her now.

Michael was history.

Or not, it would seem.

I stop talking, hug her hard, and bury my head in her

shoulder, which gives me chance to compose myself and plaster a bright smile on my face, rather than burst into noisy tears. Which is what my face wants to do.

Michael is back. Forever.

I hate Michael. There, I've said it. I'm not the jealous type, but I am the protective type. And lovely, generous, and it must be said slightly too trusting Rachel, needs somebody to watch her back. I used to do it at school, and I can't seem to break the habit.

I need to stop her marrying a douchebag.

He's just not good enough for her, and there's just something about him that makes the hairs on the back of my neck stand up. And made me punch the air and inwardly whoop when she'd told me they'd split. Though I did of course make all the right sympathetic noises and say things like 'for the best' and 'there's somebody better out there for you.'.

'Oh, Jane, I'm so pleased you're happy for me.' Rachel hugs me stronger. 'I know it's been hard for you since Andy ...' She lets his name hang in the air between us. We both know that he left a rather sour taste in my mouth, and a slight (mega) distrust of the whole 'love you 'til the day I die' thing.

'This isn't about me and Andy, it's about you!' The pressure is definitely on to make sure that she doesn't think any of this is sour grapes on my side. That my bad experience hasn't poisoned me against the whole marriage idea.

And it hasn't. I'm happy for her if she really has found 'the One' and wants to tie the knot. Just not happy about it being Michael.

Though who knows what affect her hen night is going to

have on me – but I'll tackle that one when I get to it. I'm sure there are enough legal highs, combined with gin, to get me through one evening without tears.

'But what about Jed?' I've disentangled myself, and am now thinking that Jed might have been a good option after all. 'He seemed really nice.'

'Oh.' She giggles again. 'He was just to show Michael what he was missing and make him jealous, and it worked! Jed knew it wasn't serious, we never actually slept together, you know.'

'You didn't?'

'Oh, God, no. Well, we slept, but we had all our clothes on.' Seems like I'm not the only one who tells little white lies. 'He totally knew all about Michael, and how I was still mad about him. Me and Jed were just mates!'

Is it wrong that I am feeling deflated? I'd inwardly cheered when I'd thought she'd engaged on a moving-on night of frantic passion.

'Oh, God, Jane, Michael was so sweet. He said it was a complete wake-up call and he'd realised he never wanted to risk losing me again, and, well ...' She glances at me, her eyes bright and shiny with emotion. She's genuinely about-to-cry happy.

The rush of emotion catches me unawares, and I find myself blinking back the tears then hugging her again.

A manly cough interrupts our love-in. 'Well, there's no bubbly, but I can do a mean mini glass of beer if you want to celebrate?'

I look at Freddie. 'Mini?'

'We're going to have to share a bottle. Last one, I was saving it for ...'

'A special occasion?'

'The footie.'

'I appreciate the sacrifice.'

'So do I.' Rachel is nodding furiously.

He grins and we toast the bride to be with a tot of lager in shot glasses.

'I suppose I better get back to the hotel and,' she does little quote signs with her fingers, 'get networking.'

'I suppose I better get back to my unpacking and packing.'

We hug on the doorstep, Freddie yells a goodbye from his position where he's hunkered down on the sofa.

'Have a great time in Brighton.' She winks. 'You never know!'

'Rachel, don't be disgusting, that would be like shagging your brother!'

She shrugs. 'Well, you never know, and he is kinda cute now he's grown up.'

I do an eye roll. 'So are kittens.'

'Well, get one of those!'

'*No!*'

'Shit is that the time? I'm going to get crucified if I don't make it before the bar shuts. I better run.'

We hug again and she half steps out, then turns and grasps my hands in hers.

'Christ, I nearly forgot! You will be my bridesmaid, won't you? I just kind of assumed, but say, yes, please say, yes!' She's crushing my fingers and jiggling about.

'You betcha.' She finally let's go, so I high-five her. 'I'd have been gutted if you hadn't asked!'

'Girlie night when you get back, so you can meet the others! That's what I was planning at Jax. You are going to get such a shock when you see who they are!'

'Really? So, I'm not your one and only.' I do a pretend pout. 'Who?'

'You'll have to wait and see, but you will be totes gobsmacked!' She shakes her head, then suddenly whoops and claps. 'Oh my God! Wow! I know!' She's got a crazy grin on her face, which is a bit scary. 'Why didn't I think of it earlier? Scrub Jax bar, we'll all come to Brighton! It'll be way more fun.'

'Brighton?' I stare at her blankly.

'Brighton! Next week! Oh my God, it'll be ace, we can all get the late train back or stay over. I'm sure they will be up for it. You are going to be so amazed!'

'But ...'

'Oh, no, I'm ruining your love fest, aren't I?'

'It's not a love fest!'

'You've gone red!'

'I always go red when I'm embarrassed.'

'Because you'd planned a shagathon!'

'No.' I clamp my hand over her mouth. 'Shhh, he'll hear.'

'You do fancy him though.' She's all muffled, but I know exactly what she's saying. She might as well be shouting it through a loud hailer.

'I bloody don't. He's just Freddie.' I am embarrassed, I am as hot as a hot tin roof that a cat can't stand on. 'He's he's

...' Has she been in my head, seen all those rude visions of Freddie licking cream off my nipples and kissing my neck? I mean, all that doesn't mean I fancy him in real life, nobody would ever accuse me of thinking I could have a relationship with Bradley Cooper just because I can totally see him throwing me naked onto the lid of a grand piano, are they? See.

'You've gone really bright red now! I knew it!'

'You don't know anything! I was thinking about Bradley Cooper actually. Freddie is a friend. I don't think of him like that!' Which is partly true, I don't actually think of him being like that in real life, it's just a weird fantasy that keeps me happy. It also saves me spending hours on Tinder trying to find somebody I want to swipe right.

'*Ha!*'

'He's not sexy!' I might have shouted that bit. Partly to cover up the fact that the in-my-head Freddie is sexier than any man I've ever known. But that is because he's the fantasy Freddie. Not the real Freddie.

'Whatever.' She shakes herself free. But she's grinning. 'So, are we on, then? Can we all come to Brighton?'

'You can come to Brighton!'

'That is *so* cool.' She has a broad smile on her face and looks very pleased with herself. 'Brighton rocks!' She gives me the thumbs up and squeals.

'How many is all?'

I don't get an answer. She is off down the steps and slamming the front door behind her before I can object.

I stand, catching flies, then close my mouth.

There are two big issues here: 1. Michael. Michael is a very big issue. If she's actually going to marry him, do I tell her now about his 'transgression', before it's too late? I mean, what if he was lying and he's had 'transgressions' before? What if she thinks I'm trying to fuck up her wedding on purpose? Or just un-asks me to be a bridesmaid, and un-friends me. In real life, not just on Facebook. And issue number 2. The (as yet unnamed) bridesmaids. Pretending I'm partay-ing in Ibiza when I'm pounding the prom in Brighton had at least a remote chance of success when only me and Freddie were in on it, but is the week really going to be leak free if there's a big girls' night out involved?

I turn round and Freddie is there, a strange half-smile on his face.

'Shit, did you hear that?'

'Some of it.'

'Sorry, she's mad. She's just desperate to hook me up with another guy, God she's so embarrassing.' My voice tails off. Which bit did he hear? I was pretty loud when I said he wasn't sexy. And he is. Not that I want him to know I think that, of course, but I'd be gutted if even Ron, the beer-bellied, bum hanging-out, belching builder from number 27 bellowed that down the street about me. And if I heard Freddie say it I'd be mortified.

Devastated.

'You are, er, sexy. Very.' I think I'm digging a hole here. 'Lots of people think so.'

'But not you?' He's smiling, but it's tinged with something I don't quite understand.

'Oh, I do, too. Definitely. I just didn't want Rach to jump to any kind of, you know, she's about to get married and she's all loved and thinks everybody else should be.'

'And you don't want to be?'

'Not, er, right now.' I flap the bottom of my T-shirt, hoping the fresh air will go all the way up to my face. 'You know I don't.'

I look at Freddie. Freddie looks at me. 'And not with me?'

'Well, er, if I was looking, I mean, I wouldn't, er, put you in the "no-way" category.' He's frowning. 'You'd be much higher than "no-way". Definitely. I think maybe I should stop now before I embarrass myself. You. Both of us.'

'I'm cool, not embarrassed at all. In fact, I'm quite intrigued about this no-way category and where I fit. Feel free to carry on.' He grins. A proper Freddie grin.

Right now, I could just jump him, give him a smacker and tell him exactly where he sits on the sexy scale. But he's my bloody friend, and one kiss would ruin everything for ever. On an embarrassment scale if nothing else. And, I mean, let's face it, I'm totally in love with him as a friend, but I already know he's not ready to settle down, don't I? We'd be doomed. I'd be in a worse mess than post-Andy. Because at least then I had Freddie.

'I'll shut up. Safer.' I need to change the conversation here, I glance round, desperate for inspiration. Then spot my case. Ha-ha! 'We need to talk about Brighton, what the hell are we going to do about Brighton? They're all coming!'

He shrugs, takes the one and half strides it takes to reach

the sofa, and switches the TV on. Then he pats the sofa, inviting me to join him. 'We need *Mission Impossible* – Tom would know what to do!'

We're cool.

Chapter 7

I am in shock. The whole 'no New York' thing rattled my cage, and after that wedding announcement I feel like Rach has dropped a bloody big boulder on me and left me feeling totally flattened. I can't get my head round everything.

I feel like my best friend is heading for a car crash and I can't do anything about it. Feeling helpless and out of control is so not my thing.

I should have told her, I know I should have. Ages ago. When it happened.

But if I sow the evil seed of doubt in her mind now, then everything could be off – our friendship, and her wedding. I know what that feels like. I went to pieces and I've always thought of myself as a strong person, so what would it do to Rach?

And I could be wrong. Saint Michael might have cast off his sins and been reborn. Now all I can think about is St Michael's mount, and it's the word mount that is bouncing around in my head. *Eek*, bounce was so the wrong word.

This could all go horribly wrong and I could let her down. Andy is bound to be there, because he knows Michael, and so will lots of other people who were supposed to be coming to *our* wedding. And she's asked me to be her bridesmaid! I think I'm fine, I think I'm totally over it, but what if the whole walking down the aisle in a pretty dress brings me out in hives and makes me puke? Or yell blue murder at an inappropriate point, such as when the vicar asks if anybody sees any reasons why they can't be married. Or bump the bride out of the way and yell 'it should have been me'? Or (and let's face it, this is most likely), just look glum and tearful on what is supposed to be the happiest day of Rachel's life.

Note to self: not only do I not make an appealing enough bride, I also do not make a good best friend.

I need her to get married on a desert island with only a monkey and coconut tree in attendance.

Or I need to develop some kind of lurgy that is non-life-threatening but highly contagious. I could say I've caught ringworm off the kittens (sorry kittens). Nobody likes a fungal infection, do they?

I spend the first couple of days in Brighton licking my wounds, and many slices of pizza, and quite a lot of fish and chips with Freddie and then I realise that I really do need a kick up the arse. This is because, 1. It isn't fair on him that I'm such a miserable git, 2. My jeans will burst if I don't quit eating so much crap, 3. The girls will arrive soon and I have to put on a happy face for Rach and, 4. being here is actually fun. Though I am very sad that I can't post my hilarious photos of us on Insta.

The one I got of him with a seagull hovering six inches above his head is a classic. And our selfie with the top of the Royal Pavilion looking like it's a crown on my head is pretty good, even if I say so myself. And so is the sunset, and the one of Freddie snogging the giant terrapin in Sea Life – honestly, you'd really think they were puckering up for real.

Okay, the sunset wasn't hilarious, or even funny, but it was beautiful. We'd sat side by side in silence, in awe, and I'd really wanted to reach out for a hand to hold.

But that was fantasy Freddie. The version of him that somehow manages to occupy my brain every now and then (and sometimes brings on a hot flush).

Real Freddie is different.

There is no hand-holding involved. He is a friend. Just a friend, who turned to look at me just as I'd turned to look at him. For a second, we'd shared a look, then we'd both glanced away, back out to sea and been disproportionality interested in the waves.

'Thanks for this.'

'The ice cream?' Freddie grins.

'No, you idiot, for everything. Bringing me here, cheering me up.'

'That's what friends are for, isn't it?'

I smile. I've never had a male friend like Freddie before. He's currently nearly on a par with fantasy Freddie, the one who (in my head) is currently walking with me barefoot on the sand, rubbing that spot between my thumb and forefinger that makes me go all tingly.

I mean, we all need dreams, don't we? And dreams are a safe option – no disappointments, no ugly reality, just pure unadulterated pleasure and total control.

'Cockle?' He dips his cocktail stick into the tiny tub and lifts the ugly little mollusc into the air. My tingles stop.

I grin and shake my head, thinking of my gran's old saying about 'warming the cockles of your heart'. Freddie warms mine. At least I think it's my cockles. 'Yeah, but it's kind of going above and beyond ...'

He shrugs. 'I was due some holiday anyway, and I like coming here.' He stares at me, and for a moment his gaze locks with mine. I'd never noticed how beautiful his eyes were before, how intense and dark. I feel a brief shiver of some feeling I can't pin down, then he glances away and points at the seagulls. 'Hurry up and eat that or they'll be dive bombing you.'

I am about to hurry up, when my phone pings. 'It's Rach!' Freddie nods, waits, as I look at the text.

'*How's Brighton?*'

'*Great.*'

'*How's Freddie?*'

'*Rach! Will you stop it?*'

'*Ha-ha just wondering. We're all set for the bridesmaids booze up – see you Friday!*'

'*Aren't you going to tell me who's coming?*'

'*Nope.*'

'*Oh, come on, can't you give me at least a hint? I've spent all my spare time scouring your Facebook and Insta feeds for clues!*'

'*No way, I want to see your face!*'

This is a teensy bit worrying. I have, in between ice cream eating with Freddie, been wondering why my best friend cannot tell me who am I going to be walking down the aisle with.

There are several worrying scenarios: 1. One or more of the girls were supposed to be *my* bridesmaids. This thought makes me a bit queasy; 2. Some of Rachel's gang are girls that really didn't like me at all at school; and 3. A combination of both.

'*See you Friday, can't wait! Love you Rx*'

I know they say that your school days are the best days of your life, but how often is that true? I spent a huge proportion of mine worrying about not being liked, not being kissed and not wearing the right gear.

And, as far as friends go, well, I trusted Rach ... but the rest? Girls can be bitchy, cliquey and spiteful, as well as supportive, lovely and generous. And there's often a fine line ...

I frown at Freddie, well, not at him. Past him. 'At least I know it won't be Andy!'

He raises an eyebrow.

'Sorry, Rach was talking about the bridesmaids.'

'True, he'd look rubbish in a dress, not got the legs.'

We grin at each other, mine a bit strained, his soft at the edges. 'Stop worrying.'

'I can't help it. What if they're people I hate?'

'Is that really what you're worried about?'

'Yes. Well, no. Gawd, it's the whole wedding thing, Freddie.' I bury my head in my hands for a moment, which is better than in the sand I guess. 'Why does all the crap stuff come at once?'

'It's to test your mettle as one of my up-themselves teachers used to say.' He squeezes my hand. 'You are okay, aren't you?'

'Oh, yeah, groovy, babe! I've got a rubbish job, got ditched just as I was about to go to New York, and now I've got to be thrilled for Rach with all this wedding stuff, and I've got to go to her hen party! *Arghh.*' I pretend to tear my hair out and he laughs, then hugs me.

'I mean it Jane. Are you sure you can do this?' The concern in his eyes brings a lump to my throat. 'The wedding I mean.'

'She's my best friend, Freddie. I can't *not* do it.'

'You haven't got to do anything. She'll understand if you say you can't cope.'

'I can cope.'

'It's not going to send you loopy again?' His voice is light and his words funny, but I know that he's bothered. Oh, sweet, sweet Freddie, where would I be without you?

'Look ...' I've got to be honest with him. I'm never anything but, we've always been able to talk, and after I'd poured out my heart (and most of my insides) after Andy had dumped me, there'd been no going back. I'd not wanted to go back. 'Okay, part of me is dreading this.' He nods. 'But I'm excited for her as well. I'm just a bit nervous about what it will be like, doing all the stuff I did.' Our gazes lock. 'It's the hen party that's going to be the weird one, I mean, I never actually walked up the aisle, did I? So that can't be such a biggie.'

'It can.' He smiles, a soft smile that reaches his eyes – and my heart.

'Okay,' I sigh, 'it can, it is. I think I need to know that these other bridesmaids are going to be there to pick me up if I fall.'

'I'll be there, if they're not.'

'You're too nice for me.' I kiss him on the cheek, and the roughness of the slight stubble against my lips sends a shiver down me that I didn't expect.

'Hmm, I'm not sure nice is what my manly side needs to hear!' He chuckles, then gives me a brief tight hug. 'You're not going to fall.' It's odd, but just for a second, with his warm hand on my shoulder, I totally believe him. I can do this.

'Come on, eat up, before—'

Right on cue a seagull swoops down and it's heading right for my nose. 'Shit!' I scramble up and take a couple of steps back, and it swoops back. I run, dodging the benches, dashing round the bus stop and the damned thing is preparing to dive bomb. Jumping in the air, I fling the ice cream Freddie's way (it's all me, me, me it appears when I'm under attack). He swerves, my lovely cornet goes splodge and the bird lands next to it and stares. Giving me the beady eye and a squawk.

I double up, hands on knees, panting from the unexpected exertion, and shock. 'Bugger, I was enjoying that.'

'Told you! Never fling food around in Brighton, they're the food police.' He nods at the bird.

'Mafia more like. That bird looks evil.'

We share a look. The dangerous intense-stare bit has been forgotten, which is good. Lick the icing off the cake and you risk ruining the lot, don't you? Then feeling sick and wishing you hadn't.

I reach for my camera, but the seagull has scarpered, and Freddie is laughing. 'You always did take photos of everything, didn't you? I remember at school.'

'Everything!' It's cute that he remembers, but a bit embarrassing. I don't remember much about him at all. I guess I was one self-obsessed teen who didn't look beyond my groups of girlfriends, and the odd show-off cocky guy who was hot. I don't think Freddie was hot back then, he was the quiet, geeky type.

But as I think about it, something deep in my memory stirs. Freddie helping us set up our photo exhibition for our GCSE exam, Freddie embarrassed when we both reached for the same picture, then more embarrassed when we dropped it, and both bent down to pick it up.

Freddie who painted the unassuming black-and-white still-life pictures that made something catch in my throat, even though I was a brash teenager who couldn't explain why.

'Your pictures were ace.'

'Pretentious, "chocolate box" was how one art teacher described them, I think,' he says without a trace of rancour.

'They were good.'

'They wanted Banksy and anger, not broken hearts and whimsy.'

'They were wrong.' I snap a picture of him, then one of our feet on the sand, so that I don't have to look him in the eye and be embarrassed. 'You've got quite big feet, haven't you?'

'You know what they say?' He jiggles his eyebrows, then glances down, a cheeky grin on his face.

'No, what's that then?' I try to keep a straight face and fail.

He colours up, a slight tinge of pink along his cheekbones, then suddenly laughs and sweeps me off my feet. The whole world is whizzing round, I can feel the warm imprint of every single one of his fingers, especially the one that has somehow slipped under my T-shirt, and it could be awkward.

'Bugger.' He staggers off balance, does a daft pirouette and we collapse to the ground. '*Oof.*'

I think that noise is because a fair bit of my weight landed on his stomach.

'God, you're a weight.'

'Your own fault.' I wave a finger at him, secretly, smugly glad that he did his silly dance so that I'd be the one that landed on top, and he'd be the one that was crushed.

We dust ourselves down, avoiding eye contact. Rolling on the beach isn't exactly standard flatmate stuff, is it? And even if it was, I wouldn't be doing it, because I still haven't figured where I want to fit in the whole relationship arena. Not since Andy did what he did. I think I need casual, except I always seem to duck out of actual dates – because what's the point, if you know from the start that it's never going to work out?

'At least it stopped you taking photos.'

'You've done it now.' He's not looking, he's bent over, so taking his feet from under him is easy. So is planting one foot, warrior style, on his chest and taking a photo. 'When this is all over, that is going viral!' I glance at the picture on my phone, check it's not blurry. It's not. He's laughing, a hint of white teeth between his parted lips, lines fanning out from his eyes which are looking straight into the lens. There's a single strand of honey-brown hair on his brow, curled by the sea air. I want to reach out, brush it away. So instead I stare at my screen. 'I'll have to do some retouching of course, sex it up.'

He laughs, then, with one sweep of his long leg, he's taken mine from under me and I find myself sitting on damp sand.

As I go down, he gets up, and strides away before I can retaliate. He's grinning though as he looks over his shoulder. 'First one back gets to pick the movie.'

'That's cheating!'

'Says she. Come on, you've got to get your latest dose of Ibiza online.'

I struggle to my feet as he jogs on the spot. But the second I'm upright, he's off.

Bugger. He'll pick some really gory, scary, film and I'll have to spend the evening peeping out from behind a cushion or googling the ending.

Chapter 8

'*Surprise!*' Rachel leaps up and waves madly as I walk into the dimly lit bar. It's not so dimly lit that I wouldn't have spotted her though. 'We're here! We're in Brighton!' She makes a whoop noise before launching herself at me for a mega hug. And she looks so happy, I immediately resolve to never even think about not liking Michael ever again. Once I've warned him that castration is still on my agenda. And as long as I don't have to sit next to him. 'Look who's here!'

Rachel is grasping my arm and has moved to one side so I can see who is behind her. I look, and forget all about Michael, and cutting his balls off.

Surprise is the understatement of the year. I've been swept back to my days of spots and teenage angst.

'Remember Maddie?'

'Oh my God! Of course I do! What a brilliant surprise, how long has it been? You've not changed a bit!' She hasn't. Maddie has still got the neat, glossy swinging hair, kitten heels and matching accessories that she's always had. Her perfection could be annoying. But it never has been. She's too sweet, kind and considerate, and for want of a better word, nice. She is the Audrey Hepburn of the modern day.

Maddie waves wildly with both hands and looks genuinely pleased to see me. In fact, she looks relieved, if I'm honest, which is odd. I don't ever remember being her favourite. We got on fine, but when we were at high school I drank, smoked and laughed too much for us ever to be bosom buddies.

'Hey, stranger! You've changed lots ... in a totally good way, though!' Her smile and tone is so warm that I get all choked up inside. I think I've forgotten what is was like to spend proper time with real friends. Apart from Freddie. But time with girlfriends is different, isn't it? 'Look at you, all super star and you're looking amazing. Those photos on Instagram are fab, you always were dead artistic! Rachel told me they were yours really, not that woman you work for. I look at every single one, I'm so pleased for you!'

I blush and feel guilty. Not out of false modesty (I am quite chuffed with my work for Coral), but because while Maddie has been following my career, I haven't got a clue what she's been up to since she picked up her exam results and walked out of high school for the very last time.

Maddie wasn't a high achiever at school, all she'd ever wanted was to get married and be a stay at home mum. She'd been a natural when it came to looking after people. She cared. Out of Rachel's group of friends, she had been the one that had welcomed me in without question, even though we were so different. She was the one that didn't raise an eyebrow because I was in the year below them, the kid that Rach found behind the bicycle shed.

She was also the only girl I knew at school who never dated wildly. While the rest of us were oozing an hormonal smog and snogging in all directions, she only had eyes for one boy: Jack. Jack was her first, her only and I bet you any money they married the moment they left school and have a mini-Maddie and a mini-Jack and live in one of those semis on the new estate by the park, with perfectly manicured lawns and carefully trimmed shrubs. And a hybrid car. And I bet they never accidentally put stuff in the wrong recycling bin.

'Wow, thanks ... and how is—'

'Jane, Jane, look, Sal is here as well!' Rachel spins me forty-five degrees with some force.

I don't get chance to find out what Mads has been up to, or how Jack is, or how many children they've got, because I'm trying not to fall off my heels. But I will do later. Definitely.

I stare in shock at the girl sat on the other side of the table. Sally. Who is not at all like Audrey Hepburn. Sally was the girl at school who either already had it all or was damned well going to get it soon. You know the type? You get that longed for pony, next minute she's got a unicorn. A pink one, that makes dreams come true and farts rainbows. And she was the school swot. You worked three hours on revision for your exams last night? Well, Sally worked all bloody night.

Sally always eyed me suspiciously whenever Rach invited me along on their outings, and she did make a big thing pointing out when *they* were all teenagers, when *they* were all sixteen, when *they* all had bras, when *they* were all off to the school prom ... and I wasn't. Like I say. Competitive.

Sally was *not* my best friend at school, but Rachel loved her. They'd met at primary school and did ballet lessons and pony club camp together, so what can a girl do except suck it up and smile? And I never actually disliked her, it was just all that competitiveness could sometimes totally get on my wick and I would have quite liked to have thumped her. Or trumped her unicorn.

Two 'friends' I haven't seen for years – and never imagined I'd see again.

Rachel though had obviously kept in touch with both of them.

I bet they didn't think they'd see each other either. They are chalk and cheese, the opposite ends of our friendship spectrum and it kind of shows. The vibe isn't one of giggly reminiscing.

Now when I say 'friends' I do mean real, actual friends, as in met at school and drifted apart friends. Not mates from work or people I've met on social media.

Sadly though, like a lot of people, I chat less to the real ones because Facebook is about work connections, and all I ever seem to do these days is work. And, let's face it, these were Rach's friends. I did have friends of my own, in my own class, as well. Rach was just cooler.

'Long time no see!' I bet Sal is running a mega corporation, has an office bigger than my flat, a personal trainer, and survives on quinoa, Japanese poke bowls and kefir (I only know these exist because I have taken photos for Coral – who then proceeded to joke with all her friends about the fact I'd called it quin-o-a not keen-whaaaaa). In fact, I bet Sal grows the stuff herself because she only needs thirty-five seconds sleep a night.

I'm not going to ask. I'm more Krispy Kreme doughnuts than quinoa, if you know what I mean. And most of that healthy stuff just seems to get stuck in my teeth and annoy me for the rest of the day. Whoever thought a rice cake was a good idea? I mean, who dreamt that the words rice and cake should even be in the same sentence?

'You look amazing, you both do!' I glance to Maddie, then back at Sal.

Sally looks like she's put on a few pounds, but she's glowing. Though Maddie looks a bit sad if I'm honest. Peaky is the term my gran might use.

'Aww, thanks, Jane.' Sally slips elegantly off her stool, in the way only tall people can do, and stands up. She towers over me. She always was tall, but now she's got killer heels on, a waft of expensive perfume, and the type of nails and complexion that says she spends more time pampering than working. So maybe I'm wrong about the mega corporation – unless somebody pampers her while she works. I can see that, I can really see it. A shoulder massage from behind, and a foot massage under her desk, as she shouts out orders on speakerphone.

She's probably one of those people that has multiple orgasms every time, without losing the place in her book.

She air-kisses me, grins and sits down.

'Wow, how good is this? The Fab Four reunited!' I'm aware I sound a bit lame, but I'm temporarily at a loss for meaningful words.

'I was aiming for the Fab Five!' Rach looks mischievously at us all.

'What? Not Beth?' I look round wildly. Beth with her vodka habit, and Saturday Night Fever dance steps that could clear a floor in seconds, was my naughty-sides twin. She might have brought out the worst in me, but she was so much fun, with a capital *F*.

The real Fab Four had been Rachel, Beth, Sally and Maddie – until I'd come along and been shoe-horned into the group. But then one day, I'd been tagging along on a night out, and Sal hadn't, so Beth had declared me an honorary member of the group. I reckon she did it to piss Sally off, but I didn't really care. I was in.

'Beth with the boobs?' That bit comes from Sal, but we all know who she means.

While the rest of us were considering whether booster bras, balconies, or foam fillets would do the trick, slim and petite Beth was displaying her super-sized wares with ease. Sometimes life isn't fair.

'Where is she?'

'She couldn't come.'

I groan, but I swear Sal perks up. She doesn't like the competition.

'But wait for it girls ...' Rachel really is taking the stage now. 'She said no because ...' She is drawing this one out, but we're all leaning forward in anticipation. 'She couldn't get a babysitter!'

Whatever I thought she was going to say. It wasn't that.

'Bloody hell.' Sal is wide-eyed. 'Who'd have thought hell

raiser Beth would have got up the duff. She was so not the mothering type, she even had her nipples pierced!'

'She was nice.' Maddie's quiet comment gets lost in the excitement. 'I'm sure she's made a lovely mum.'

All I can think of is a baby with a mouthful of titanium nipple bar. It is not a pleasant thought.

'I'd not actually seen Beth for yonks 'cos she did a bit of a disappearing act, moved away, then my mum bumped into hers and she passed on her phone number! She said she'd love to meet up with old friends, 'cos she's been a bit isolated being stuck at home with a baby. I've not actually seen the baby yet, but it's only tiny, and Beth said she's been all hormonal, and bigger-boobed than ever,' this is mind-boggling, 'and her head isn't in the right place at all, and ...'

'Wow, she's married! She beat us all in the adulting stakes!' I'm a bit gobsmacked. Beth, in my head, will always be the hell-raiser. The one who said boyfriends were for losers (unless they were studded to within an inch of their life, had more nose rings than a herd of bullocks, and more tats than teeth), and pulled a puke-face if she ever saw a baby attached to a nipple – which could be why she got the piercings, I suppose, the biggest barricade to natural feeding ever.

The image of Beth with a baby clasped to her bosom and a husband doing the dishes is just weird.

'Well, not exactly ...' There is another long Rachel pause. 'She's on her own, and she won't say who the father is!'

I'm not really into these reunions, I mean, there's a reason you drift apart, isn't there? And sometimes those reasons are bigger than others. But this one is turning out to be slightly surreal.

Beth has to be the biggest shock. From teenage hell-raiser to worn-out single mum with a secret before I've even made a decision on whether a tat would be cool or trying too hard.

'But she said next time we get together, she'll be there!' I think this is Rach-speak for 'she'll be at the wedding', but it looks like she hasn't broken that nugget of news to the others yet. The wedding bit.

There's a lull, while everybody thinks about Beth. I decide I need to fill it.

'Any other births, deaths or marriages I should know about?' I'm clambering onto a stool as I speak, when Rachel starts to manhandle me and nearly knocks me flying. Looks like I said the wrong thing.

'Hang on, don't sit down yet; help me get the drinks in before we get chatting.' She's got hold of my arm and is sweeping me along with her towards the bar before I can object. We don't stop though. After a brief glimpse over her shoulder to check we're not under observation, she charges onwards, like a mini rhino on a rampage, and I find myself bundled into the bathroom.

Maybe she has been recruited as a spy, as well as getting married.

She slams the door shut, then spins round.

I've never been in such posh loos. Except I'm not getting much opportunity to look round or take photos, as Rachel has me pinned against the dryer, which goes off every time I flinch.

'Sorry I didn't warn you before, but ...'

'Warn me? What, about Beth?'

'No, no. About the situ.'

'Situ?' I try to edge away as I'm getting more hot air down my neck than I can cope with. Rachel is so close though, there's not much room for manoeuvre. It's either bounce off her boobs or get all hot and bothered.

I duck down and pop up the other side of her.

'Fuck's sake, Jane. Will you stand still and listen? We've not got long, we've got to get back to them, we can't leave them together.'

'This was your ... What do you mean we can't leave them together?' I get an uneasy prickle down my spine and it's nothing to do with the dryer.

'It's awkward, well, I need you to be a bit like ...'

'A bit like ...?'

'Like a, well, a barrier?'

'A barrier?' I fold my arms, barrier-like. But she has my interest well and truly piqued. 'What do you mean a barrier? Between what?' I frown.

'Between Sally and Mads,' hisses Rachel.

'You've invited me out to be a barrier?' As evenings go, this is not panning out as my best. 'Is this why you wanted Beth as well, then we'd be a double barrier?'

'No, no, no. Oh, God.' She runs her fingers through her blonde bouncy waves. 'I never thought it would be this compli-cated, but I wanted all three of you to ...' She sniffs. 'Please, please say you'll help me make this work?'

I sigh. 'What's happened, Rach?'

'It's just that, well, you know Sally and Mads?' I nod. It's a strange question seeing as we've all just been reacquainted. 'They've not seen each other for like yonks.'

I nod. 'Same here, bit of a shock actually!'

She ignores me, I think she's had this speech planned. 'I mean I've seen them separately, but we've not all got together.' I nod. 'Well, there's something you need to know.' There's a long pause while she waits for the other occupant in the bathroom to wash her hands and leave. 'Sally got married.'

As bombshells go, that's a bit of an anti-climax. 'Good for her.' So maybe I am totally wrong, maybe she does not run a world dominating company. Maybe she is supreme nappy changer. Flannel ones of course. Expensive monogrammed flannel ones. And a maid to dip them in the bucket. Sal is a shit stirrer, not a washer of shit.

Rachel takes a deep breath, then turns to face me. 'To Jack.'

My image of Sally in marigolds, dunking nappies in a silver bucket is gone in a millisecond. The world does a hiccup. 'Jack?' I can hear the note of suspicion in my voice.

She nods.

'Jack, Jack?' I think my lower jaw is dangling. 'Maddie's Jack? Are you sure?'

'Positive. I went to their wedding.'

'You what?' I think I might be shouting. 'But, but, they, we ...'

'Jack and Mads split up like ages ago, when he went to uni, so it's not like Sal barged in and nicked him or anything, and it was Maddie who did the dumping, but, well, Mads didn't know they were an item until Sally and Jack moved back into the area after, well, you know ... the wedding.'

I cringe. I mean, can you imagine? The love (ex-love) of your life suddenly reappears on the scene. With a wife. Your (soon to be) ex-friend.

Then your old school friend invites you all to a big night out in Brighton.

Whoopee!

I'm not surprised poor Mads looks a bit peaky.

'Rach, how could you! How could you ask them both here, if you knew ...?'

'I didn't.' She gulps. 'Honest. Well, I knew about Sal and Jack, obviously.'

'And you didn't think ...'

'I thought Maddie knew! Sal had told me at the wedding that she was totally cool with it, that it was her who had dumped Jack, and he was the broken-hearted one, and Maddie had moved on!'

'So?' I look at her suspiciously.

'I think Maddie's still got a bit of thing about him.' The words tail off. 'I didn't realise.' It comes out a bit plaintively. 'Honest.' Pleadingly, if that's a word. 'Jack rang me this morning, when he found out from Sal we were all coming here. She went white as a sheet apparently when she saw them in Tesco.'

'So why the fuck did you ask them both here, at the same time?'

'Because it was too late, and I love them both, I love all of you, and I need us all together. I need all three of you.' She's hanging on to my arm. 'Please help me. I did tell Maddie that Sally was coming as well, and she said it was fine with her, if I really wanted her to come then she'd come because I'm her friend.'

'And Sal was fine with it?' Sal would be, I don't need to ask.

'She said it was water under the bridge and we were all adults, and what Jack and Maddie had was just puppy love.'

'I bet she did.'

We both go back to staring at each other in the mirror. Then my shocked brain (good job it's not alcohol sodden yet) snaps out of its strange state.

'Shit. And we've left them together?'

Chapter 9

'I need vodka.' It's more of a plea than anything as we slide past the bar at full pelt (luckily, the place is quiet), and the rather sexy barman grins as he slams it on the bar. 'On the tab!' I don't even know if we've got a tab, but I don't care. We need to get back.

Rachel is panting down my neck, and I'm a bit breathless myself as she grabs my arm and hisses in my ear.

'Slow down, slow down, we need to look casual.'

Casual? *Ha!* I flap my arms away from my body because I'm sure I've got sweaty patches forming, and take a deep breath, because I'm wheezing like I've just run a marathon.

World war has not broken out. They are sitting slightly woodenly when we saunter up to the table, smiles pasted on our faces; Maddie studying her drink, Sal people watching.

'Hi! All back, drink!' I hold it up, to prove the point. 'Just had to nip to the bathroom'. Did we miss anything?' There are no visible scars or crumpled up tissues. 'Everything okay? Ha-ha, why wouldn't it be? I mean, have you got drinks? Great here isn't it? Cool! And such a surprise seeing you guys.' I inwardly cringe. Since when did I call people guys?! 'Great surprise!' I'm gabbling and force myself to slow down. Be normal.

Rachel slides out from behind me and sits down. 'Isn't this fab? I'm so pleased you could all make it! But this isn't the whole surprise.' This is good, what is also good is that Rachel has distracted us all, so it stops me staring open-mouthed at Maddie and Sal.

'Guess what?' She doesn't give anybody time to answer. 'I'm getting married!' Rachel actually squeals and claps her hands. 'Isn't it brill?'

With this reminder about why we're all here, I completely forget about the Sally and Maddie stand-off. They could be scrapping like two cats over a fish head and right now I'd be oblivious. What is important now is that my smile is genuine, that I really do show my best friend that I'm happy for her, and that I really can set aside all my doubts about Michael, and happy ever afters in general.

And stop feeling slightly sick about the prospect of walking up the aisle. Or going to a hen party. Or wearing a pretty dress.

Rachel shoves her hand out, so we can admire the rock. It is my first glimpse. If we hadn't been talking earth-shattering Mads and Sal stuff in the Ladies', I would have noticed.

Whatever she did to change Michael, it definitely worked. This is one serious diamond. This says commitment in capital letters.

Sal shrieks and hugs her. 'I knew it! Didn't I say! I just knew it!'

'Oh, God, girls, you should have seen him! He came to

pick me up in a limo and had posh champagne, and everything.'

I fight to ignore the churning in my stomach. It's just excitement, nerves, something. But I never did trust flamboyant gestures, although that is what people do when they propose, isn't it?

Maddie is fanning herself and making *aww* noises, and Sal is dabbing the corner of her eye theatrically, and I'm welling up all over again.

Maybe Michael has changed, after all it is a while since I've seen him (which suits both of us). And he has come running back with his tail between his legs, begging her to marry him – so maybe he's learned his lesson, and will love and protect my best buddy 'til the end of their days. I have to believe that.

'What are we waiting for, let's order a bottle of bubbly!'

'Yes, yes!' Rachel is grinning, hugging herself and looks so happy that I'm happy for her. 'After you've all said you will ...' She pauses and looks at us in turn.

I look at Maddie and Sally who raise eyebrows and shrug in turn. They obviously haven't heard this bit yet.

'Be my bridesmaids! That's why I asked you all here. Oh, you will, won't you? You have to, it won't be the same if you don't!'

'I'd love to!' Maddie smiles, but it's a little uncertain and I notice her slightly shifty 'Princess Diana' sideways look towards Sally. She blushes when she realises I've noticed and clears her throat. 'It would be an honour, thank you so much for asking.' The pinpricks of pink on her cheekbones, and the slight sheen to her eyes makes me frown. She's also clasping her hands so tightly together in her lap that the knuckles have gone white.

Maddie is sweet, kind and unconfrontational. I'm suddenly sorry about the fact that I've not seen her for years.

Rachel waves a hand and the barman arrives with a bottle of champagne that has obviously been pre-arranged.

'Abso-fucking-lutely!' What else can I say? I can't spoil the perfect moment, can I? 'I wouldn't miss it for the world!'

Sally grabs Rachel. 'I am *so* pleased for you, it's going to be ace. I can honestly say *my* wedding was the best day of my life!'

There is a squeak, it actually sounds like a small rodent in pain. Maddie's hand is over her mouth and she practically vaults over the table (not easy in that skirt) in her rush to the Ladies'.

We all freeze. Then Sally starts to twiddle with her glass, and Rachel throws me a guilty look.

'Sorry.' She mouths the word barrier. 'She said she'd be okay, she did know about …' She throws a guilty look at Sally, who sighs.

'I suppose we should have warned you.'

'Warned me! What difference would being warned have made? It's Maddie who's upset, not me.'

'I thought you'd already know, you know Rachel might have mentioned it, or you'd have seen it on my Instagram.' Sal's voice has a defensive, scratchy edge.

'Seen what on Instagram?' I didn't even know Sally had an Instagram account, like I said before, we were never close.

They both seem to be stuck for words. 'Oh, you mean your wedding pics.' I hope I don't sound as cold as I feel.

'Well, it's not like I've done anything illegal, is it? She finished with Jack, he was heartbroken!'

I could thump her. But I don't.

'So you stepped in to console him?'

She shrugs. 'Something like that. Oh whatever, it was ages ago, she should be over it all. He was available for fuck's sake!' Sal's eyes are narrowed as she looks at me, then delivers her final blow. Sweetly. 'And now he's not.'

Chapter 10

'Maddie? Mads?' I'm back in the bathroom checking to see if Maddie is okay. There are only two cubicles in the posh unisex bathroom (it's that type of trendy bar), and one is empty, so I'm guessing she's in the other. If she isn't, this could be embarrassing. 'Mads?' I bang on the door politely, then a bit harder. 'You know I won't go away until you come out!'

I know this full on approach will work, as Maddie has always hated a scene.

'Hang on.' There are some snuffling noises, then the sounds of the flush and she comes out. Her cheeks are pinker than before, and her eyes red-rimmed. She peers into the mirror, then wipes her finger under her eyelid so that her eyeliner is restored to pristine condition.

'Oh, God, Mads. Are you okay?'

'Of course.' The bright smile is wavering at the edges. 'It's nothing, I'm fine.' There's a definite quiver to her bottom lip. 'I'm just being silly.' It comes out as si-i-i-lly.

'You are not fine, or silly.' I hike myself up to sit on the side of the washbasins (in a very inelegant way. How do people make it look easy? It's like when blokes leap over fences, and you try it and end up faceplanted in a cowpat). 'Oh, Maddie, I'm sorry.'

She touches up her lipstick with a slightly shaky hand, then slowly puts her bag down.

'You know about Jack?' The heavy sigh makes me frown. Jack was her first love and high-school sweetheart. It must hurt like hell.

I nod. 'Rachel told me.'

'I'm being stupid, it's not like we were still together, we split ages and ages before ...' Her voice is flat, and she's kneading her bag like a desperate kitten. 'When he went to uni, it was so hard, and his friends were all so clever like he is, and I felt stupid and out of it whenever I went to visit him. I just felt in the way all the time. And ... well, it seemed sensible to end it, but,' she looks at me with tear-filled Bambi-wide eyes, 'in my silly head, I thought one day he'd come back, and we could have our dream house and our babies and ...'

'Oh.'

'I know I was being stupid and impractical, I even had this picture in my head of the hanging baskets, with Surfinias, and the cute little box hedge that I trimmed myself.' This last bit does sound a bit impractical, but each to their own.

She sniffs. 'And I did tell him that splitting up was for the best, but, but ...' Her lip is wobbling again, and when she turns and looks at me full on her face starts to crumble. It is so un-Maddie-like there's a pain in my chest. 'I didn't really mean it! I saw them in Tesco, sharing a trolley, they had steak and strawberries!'

Hmm not exactly what you want to see when you've stacked up on meals for one.

She gulps. 'I only went in for some milk! How could he marry Sally? She was my friend!'

I sink back against the wall and stare. 'I don't know, Maddie.' I don't know what to say. To be honest, this is even more of a shock than Rachel marrying Michael. I mean, even if Maddie and Jack had split, you don't do that to a friend, do you?

'How did they even meet?' I dig into the past and honestly don't remember any signs that Jack and Sal even liked each other, let alone were going to get married one day.

'At uni.' Maddie sniffs. 'He said they bumped into each other, and were just friends at first, then ...'

This is going to be the wedding from hell.

What was Rachel thinking? Normally, you have to be careful about who you seat where, about not putting Aunt Mabel next to Granny Bee because they've had a feud that dates back to the days before you were born, or the groom's dad next to his mum, because she took him to the cleaners when they got divorced and has now married a millionaire and he is broke and lives in the part of town that *nobody* wants to live in.

But that's family, not bridesmaids!

'Oh, Mads.' Maddie has never been a huggie person, she's fragile and always so immaculate I reckon people are scared of either breaking her or ruffling her up. But I can't help myself. I grab her. She's slim to the verge of thin and feels as frail as a tiny bird but after a moment's hesitation she hugs me back, and her hold is surprisingly firm. Firmer than mine, because I feel shaky as hell.

'I'm going to sort this, they can't—'

'No!' She's clutching my upper arms, her gaze imploring. 'Please don't, please don't say anything. Don't make a fuss. Promise?'

'But—'

'This is Rachel's day, it's her wedding, I don't want to spoil it. And I'll look such a stupid idiot. Please!' Well, however frail she looks, there is nothing wrong with her grip. My arm is beginning to feel like a pin cushion. The pain must show on my face, because she suddenly let's go and smoothes my skin down with cool hands. 'Sorry. It was just a shock, I've not seen Sal since ... I knew, Jack told me, but I've not seen either of them, and ... Oh, Jane!' She's fighting a losing battle with the tears. 'It was just all the wedding talk, and imagining them ... I'm sure they're a much better match than we were, she's so much cleverer than me and can talk to him and his friends about important stuff, and she probably just fell madly in love with him, he's so nice.' There's a fresh outburst of tears.

'He is, he was.' He was. The Jack I remember was earnest and quiet, and, I thought, totally devoted to Maddie.

'It's my fault I split with him, it's not her fault, he must have ...'

I'm not so sure myself that none of this is Sal's fault. It does take two to tango. I mean, Jack might have been stupid enough (and hurt enough) to think Maddie really meant for them to break up. But Sal? Surely Sal should have known to steer clear? I've never trusted Sally, she is just like a girl I knew in primary school who stood on the back of my heel so that I lost my plimsoll and the three-legged race in year five ended in disaster. That woman is competitive with a capital C.

'I'll be fine.' Maddie dampens a paper towel under the cold tap and starts to pat her hot face and blotchy neck. 'I've moved on.' That is the most obviously untrue thing I have ever heard. 'We better get back, they'll be wondering where we are.' She flashes a brave smile and hooks her hand through my arm. 'Do I look okay?'

'Fab!' It's another little white lie, but like I said, sometimes needs must.

Rachel and Sally start guiltily when we return and jump apart. Rachel tops up the glasses with bubbly, and Sal looks everywhere but at Maddie with a false smile plastered to her face. If anybody looks our way now they'll think they've stumbled into the film set *of Stepford Wives* or an episode of *Humans*. Relaxed and natural we are not.

I really want to drag Rachel off to the loos again and have this out (and to take a photo, that washroom is amazing with a capital A), but that would mean leaving Maddie and Sal together. Which I don't want to do. Looks like I'm supposed to sit in the middle and stop fights breaking out. Keeping the peace has never been my forte.

Maybe it's Sally I should be dragging off to the loo's, and giving a good talking to. But then what am I planning on doing? Insisting her and Jack divorce? Splitting up a relationship. And for what? For all I know, they might be head over heels in love, he might be her 'one', she might be his 'one', and Maddie and him could just have been puppy love.

Oh, bugger. I can't do that. I just have to be calm. Rational. Supportive but not interfering.

But I still want to yell at her.

'What about you then, Jane?' I suddenly realise that Sally is talking to me. 'What have you been up to since we all left school, quite the little jet setter, aren't you?' She says it lightly, with a laugh at the end, but I know it's a challenge. 'Didn't make it as a nuclear physicist then? Rach tells me you're still taking your little photos.' How can somebody manage to smile nicely and sneer at the same time? 'Up the duff? Rich hubby? Oops, no ring, no time to get married?' I know that is a dig, she just *has* to know about me and Andy. I hate her.

'Didn't you know? She lives with Freddie!' Squeals Rachel, totally missing the heavy sarcasm.

'Who?' Maddie looks blank. Jack was the only boy she ever noticed.

'You know, Freddie!' Rachel says it with the conviction that if she repeats his name enough, everybody will remember. 'There was only one Freddie.' This is not said in a tone that says he was unique and memorable for his crazy antics, just that nobody else had the same name.

'Oh, they won't remember Freddie, it was a massive school, there were lots of—'

'Oh my God! I know!' It's Sal's turn to squeal now. 'Oh, fuck, not Freddie!' Bugger. She does remember. She is wide-eyed. 'You live with Freddie!' That is the look of somebody who will dine out on this for weeks. It will be all over Facebook,

Twitter, Instagram, Snapchat. Every inch of cyberspace basically. I can see her fingers twitching to get to her mobile. My subterfuge in Brighton is fucked.

'I don't *live* with him!'

'That's why we decided to make it a Brighton weekend, Jane is here with Freddie for a mini-break!' This is not what I wanted to hear Rachel say.

'Hang on a minute! It's not that kind of—'

Sally gives a low whistle. 'Wow, must be serious, weekend break in Brighton.' I'm not sure if she's being sarcastic or not now.

'It's not serious, we're friends and I needed a break, and he was coming here anyway, and—'

'Do I know Freddie?' Maddie frowns, interrupting my denial.

'Yeah, course you do. You know, that tall guy who was friends with Matt! They were in the year above us,' says Rachel.

They all sigh. Everybody knew Matt, he was the hunky one in a leather jacket. When you are sixteen, a seventeen-year-old poser in a leather jacket is swoon-worthy. Even if he will probably turn out to be a total dick.

Freddie was more the dreamy one in a jumper. Less swoon, more worthy. Not something most teenage girls notice.

Sal cackles. She is really enjoying this. 'You must remember him, Maddie. The geek! Freddie Flintstone!' He was called that because of his tatty old car, which belched its way into the school car park every day. 'Oh my God, I can't believe it! You can't seriously mean you hooked up with Freddie? He was such a geek.' Sally is laughing, and not in a nice way. That girl just has to be so competitive about everything.

'You should see him now, Sal,' Rachel chips in, 'he's grown into himself. He is hot, seriously.'

'Really?' Sal doesn't sound convinced. 'Well, why don't we ...?'

'What?' I don't like the sound of that.

'See him! Call him, get him over here.' She's smirking. 'Or we can all go to wherever you're staying!'

'No! He's busy, he's doing stuff, boy stuff.'

'So, he's still a geek? Don't tell me ...' she pauses for effect, ready to deliver the punchline, 'he works with computers or something?'

This is dangerously close to the mark. 'So what? He just happens to be smart. And he's lovely, and kind, and funny.' I don't want to overdo this, as I don't want them getting ideas about our relationship (or lack of it), but I do need to defend him. Freddie is nice. Seriously nice. 'He's grown up.' Unlike some people, I could add. Instead, I settle for an evil glare.

'Aww, that's so lovely, he was so sweet.' Maddie has got a dreamy look in her eye. 'I remember him now. He stopped to give me a lift one day when it was raining, he was so kind.'

See, some people remember the good bits about other people.

'He is lovely.' I give Maddie a smile. 'But hang on, you lot, I live with him, I don't "*live*" with him. We're flatmates.'

'You really should see him, though! He has changed,' Rach is on a roll, ignoring my protestations about '*living* with him'. I wish we could get back to talking about weddings, and maybe murdering each other. Much easier. 'It's not just that clever sexy vibe, you know, the Jude Law peering over his glasses in *The Holiday* vibe?'

'The what?' I blink at her, momentarily perplexed at where this is going.

'Ooh, I love a man peering over his glasses looking all professor-ish!' Rachel fans herself. I can't imagine Michael ever looking like a professor, but maybe this is her go-to fantasy when she's at the 'Help, I'm not quite turned on enough to come quick' stage. 'Doesn't everybody?' I look round, we're all shaking our heads. 'Whatever, anyway it's not just that, he is seriously hot.' She's doing that hand gesture, that can mean I've burned my fingertips, or can be rude.

'No, he's not!' I don't know why I said that. He is hot. And so am I. I'm hot. Red hot, my neck and face are burning. They're all staring at me. 'Well, he's okay, fine … like Mads said, he's lovely. But there's nothing going on. We just live together. Flatmates. We are friends.' I say it in every permutation to make it clear. 'He has girlfriends, lots of girlfriends, and I have …' I'm stuck now. 'I go out with people, men, other men. Me and Tinder, we're like that.' I do the cross-fingers thing.

'Well, if you're not going to introduce us today, then you've got to bring him to the wedding!' Sal is intrigued, I know she is. If she thinks he's hot she'll be all over him (married or not) like a black widow spider, and if she thinks he's not she'll be staring smugly at me and mentally awarding herself a win.

'I can't. One he's not invited—'

'Well, I …'

I interrupt Rachel. 'And two we don't do stuff together.' Often.

'So, you're not dating,' Sal has to point score, 'anybody? At all?'

'I'm not. I work all the time, totally unsociable hours. I like being single, it's, it's …' I'm struggling here. 'Freeing!' Yes, that's it. 'I am free! I can be who I want, do what I want, when I want. I don't have to watch stuff I don't want to, I don't have to put up with burps, farts. I don't have to shave my legs.' They're all staring again. 'Though, I do, of course.' Then I remember why we're here. 'Not that relationships aren't great of course, if you've got the right man, and you're happy, and …' Sally is looking smug. *Garhhh!* I direct my smile at Rachel. 'And you've found the one you want to spend the rest of your life with. I'm so happy for you Rach, really.'

'So am I!' Maddie squeezes our hands, so Sal has to jump in and slam hers on top.

'I'll drink to that! Marriage is the best!'

Oh, God, here we go again.

Luckily, Maddie is made of sterner stuff than she looks, she downs her glass in one and tops us all up though before speaking.

'So, where are you holding the wedding? It must be so exciting, planning it all! And your dress, have you picked a dress?' Maddie necks the second glass – okay, maybe not sterner stuff, but she's certainly resolved to not let her crap situation mar the evening. I flash her an encouraging smile, surely if Mads can push her personal feelings about this event aside, then so can I.

'And our dresses! I can't wait to see ours.'

'Oh my God, Rach, you have so got to tell us what you've already planned. My wedding planner was ace, everything was totally how I wanted it. It was magical.' Sal is back in the swing of it.

'Any unicorns?' I can't resist.

'White horses.' She ignores my snide comment, which is fair enough. 'We had two ... oh but we're not here to talk about me, are we?'

'Certainly not! Rach, dresses, tell us!'

'Well, it's all been so up in the air, but Michael has been so involved. He's amazing! Mum wanted me to wear this family heirloom, you know Jane, that dress she showed you photos of,' she rolls her eyes, 'lots of times?'

We laugh.

'But, don't tell me, you've gone with one of those slinky destination dresses like you've always wanted? Oh, Rachel, you will look so gorg.'

'Well, I was tempted, but then Michael's mum showed me this place she's been to, a really posh designer boutique.' She names the street and Sally fans herself dramatically.

'Oh my God! Yes, you *have* to get a dress from there.' Honestly, talk about gushing.

This wasn't what I was expecting, though. Rachel's family are loaded, but she's never gone for flashy stuff.

'I mean, at first I was all, no, no, but then Michael saw the website as well, and his whole family were kind of saying I should treat myself. You only get married once, don't you, it's only one day so Mikey said I deserved the best and I should go for something a bit more special. Me, but still out of this world, if you know what I mean?'

We do. We look at the photos on her phone and go all swoony and squealy, but I'm still a bit surprised. This wasn't the wedding we talked about when we were teens, but I suppose everybody grows up. Changes.

'He was dead sweet, he even offered to foot the bill if I wanted him to!'

She laughs, and we all join in. We know Rach's dad would never let anybody foot the bill. 'And you should see the brides-maids dresses they've got! We'll all go there next month and pick,' she claps her hands, 'I've booked a slot. You get bubbly and the place is all white, and posh, and the girl who owns it is lovely. What do you say?'

We all say 'Yes' loudly, and drink lots (and I mean lots) of bubbly and laugh. By the end of the evening I feel I might be warming to Michael, but am now totally confused about Jack. He just used to be so *nice*. And I know I'm going to have a humdinger of a bad head tomorrow.

'Oh, Gawd, how can it be last orders already? This evening has gone by so quick, it's been so fab.' Rach reaches out, and we all have a group hug over the tableful of empties, and the barman snatches them from beneath our boobs. 'Aww, I'm so lucky to have you lot.'

'We're all so lucky, this is so exciting!' Sal stands up. 'Let's have a room party! Come on, all back to mine, I've got a bottle of sambuca, it'll be just like old times.'

The old times with sambuca that I remember made me very ill, I am no longer friends with sambuca.

'Really sorry, but I'm going to call it a night, I can't keep up with you lot!' Maddie smiles, even through my alcohol fug I can see she's tired. She never was a heavy drink, she liked to have a laugh, but was never the 'let it all hang out' type.

'And I'm going to have to get back or I'll get locked out.' I link my arm through hers in a gesture of solidarity. Though it's quite a wobbly kind on my side.

'Ooooh, Freddie's waiting for her!' Sal cackles.

I settle for a wink. 'Who knows?' I'm going to regret saying that, but it does shut her up. Point for me.

'Well, at least meet us for breakfast, babe?' Rachel wraps me in a hug.

'Defo, you're on!'

'And you will all come to my engagement party next week, won't you? You will be home? We need to plan my hen party!'

It's her parting shot as I say goodbye to the three of them at the door of the bar. They all weave off up the road in one direction, and I head back to Freddie. My cool geek.

And I think I've just realised when I first started to fall for him. When I created fantasy Freddie. The day he came home clutching champagne, pizza and a copy of the game he'd been working on. The game that had gone viral, the game we played until 3 a.m. The game with a red-haired kick-ass heroine called Jane.

Chapter 11

Brighton was bliss. Partly because I had a bit of a Facebook fast (apart from posting the photos – which was a bit of a hit and run job). First, because I didn't want to read Coral's New York posts and I wouldn't have been able to resist, and second (and more importantly) for the first few days I was scared stiff I'd forget to disable my location and everybody (Coral and Crystal) would know I wasn't in Ibiza. And anyway, Freddie wouldn't let me spend more than thirty seconds a day doing it. He said it was bad for my mental health, and I needed a break.

I did realise though, after meeting up with the girls, that I was on dangerous ground. This particular secret was one that was now bound to come out. I'd kind of forgotten that the rest of the world, not just Coral, would see. And, before you ask, I *fully* intend on 'fessing up to everybody. Even before Rachel and my parents started to 'like' my pictures. So, I decided it was daft lying to Coral, she'd find out at some point. It was easier to just show her I was having a bloody good laugh in Brighton. And believe me Brighton is cool, just look on Insta. I got more likes within seconds of posting my first beach huts than my twenty-seven fake Ibiza photos had in total.

One massive bonus (always look on the bright side) of not being in New York though, is that I got a total break from Coral (I'm pretty sure her real name is actually Carol) and a bit of me time, which I haven't had for ages. Not that I got *that* much me time as Freddie seemed to think he was on some kind of suicide watch. Though when I broached it with him, he did say that suicide isn't all about walking into the sea, sometimes it's about burying yourself in carbs and slumping on the sofa all day, both of which can (according to Freddie) seriously shorten your life. He did however say this as we were crashed out on the sofa, stuffing our faces with ice cream, popcorn and beer, mid Netflix binge.

'And I want you to live a long and happy one, as long as you promise you're not going to keep trying to throw my old clothes away and pretend it's for my own good.'

'It is for your own good.' I pause *Killing Eve*, just as Villanelle strokes her finger along the blade of a knife. 'You'll never get the girl you deserve if you look like a tramp.'

'I don't want the girl I deserve, I want the ...' He pauses, mid-flow and his eyes narrow. 'You're doing that thing where you stop the convo about you by switching it to me.'

'No, I'm not.'

'Yes, you are. We were talking about your suicide, not my jeans.'

I give a deep sigh. 'Ha-ha all that was ages ago, I told you, I'm up for this wedding. I am so over Andy.' But I'm not, not deep down. I think it's the shame, the embarrassment, the loss that comes when you've invested everything into (as it turns out) nothing. I mean, what kind of girl gets dumped during her hen party? Although, as Rach said at the time, 'that says more about him than you'. This wedding is going to bring it all flooding back though, and I so want to be genuinely happy for Rach, not just faking it and pretending I'm somewhere else. As bad things go, missing Rach's wedding comes second only to missing my own.

'I was talking about Coral and New York, not him.' Freddie says softly.

'Whatever, I am not suicidal, I never have been. I'm not the type.'

He rolls his eyes. 'Anyhow, you're one to talk, you don't want a guy, so why should I want a girl?'

'That's different.' I stare at my ice cream, suddenly fascinated by the way the fudge bits manage to stay solid. Once upon a time, I did believe in forever guys, then I was shown the error of my ways.

'No, it's not.' His voice softens. 'Just because I haven't been publicly stood up ...'

'That's it, rub it in.' Having my heart broken was bad enough, but having it done in full view of the rest of the world really hurt. I might as well have held up a big sign with I'M A TOTAL FAILURE on it. See, I'm not completely over it. I might have fallen out of love with him, but not yet fallen out with the idea of being part of an 'us'.

Freddie ignores my interruption. '... doesn't mean I'm on a

hunt for commitment. Love isn't like that.' He shrugs. 'You can't always fall for the right people—'

'You're telling me.'

'—and if you don't want second best then.' He stirs his own tub of ice cream, then puts the spoon down. 'You have to stick with your old favourites, the ones you're comfy in.'

'We're talking jeans here?'

He ignores me, 'and don't try and stir things up.'

'I thought Andy was my first best though.'

'We're all allowed the odd mistake.'

'So how the hell are you supposed to realise when you have found the One, the best?'

'You know.' He's not looking at me now, he's miles away. 'Believe me, you know. Nobody else ever looks the same again.' He stands up abruptly and not for the first time I wonder what happened to lovely Freddie. Who did this to him? 'I better check the place is like Mum left it, we've got an early start tomorrow.'

I grab his hand to slow him down. 'Thanks, Freddie, really. You've been ace.'

He pulls free and ruffles my hair. 'De nada. Anyhow, I like being mates with you. It's cool.' He grins, then sighs and glances down at his mobile. 'Much better than all that complicated will they won't they, stuff ... and being scared of saying stuff that can be taken the wrong way.' He throws his phone down. 'Annie's not happy about me being here without her.' 'Nor with me,' I add in my head, though don't say it out loud. 'And,' his face squishes up, 'she's asking about moving in.' He threads his fingers through his hair, so that it sticks up in all directions.

My heart sinks. A ménage à trois would not be the same. 'Do you want her to?' I force myself to say.

'No, but I don't know how to tell her. She's nice, I like her.' He looks tortured.

'Just tell her the truth Freddie. She'll understand.'

'I don't think she will.' He shakes his head. 'I better get tidying. Bins out, stuff like that.'

'Freddie, what were you going to say before? You know, you didn't want the girl you deserve, you wanted, what? Who?'

He doesn't turn round, and his words are soft, but definite. 'I want the girl I fell for a long time ago. The one I always thought was "my One".'

'Who is she?'

He shakes his head. 'Not now, Jane.'

'Maybe you need to give up, move on, keep looking?'

'Maybe, or maybe not quite yet. I always was a silly, stubborn sod. You'd think I'd learn, wouldn't you?'

I smile. 'Not if she means that much to you.' There's a lump in my throat. I've never thought of Freddie as being madly in love with a girl. 'If she ever says yes, I'm totally buggered. Who am I going to talk to then?'

He laughs. 'Worry about that when it happens. Have you finished with that beer?'

'Sure, I can help you tidy up.'

'No, you just chill. Jane?'

'Yeah?'

'You know what I think you really need to do, to get over what happened?'

'Shag Bradley Cooper?'

'I'm being serious.'

I kneel up on the sofa, lean on the back and look at him. 'Go on.'

'You need to get your career sorted.'

'Career?'

'Your photos, you noddle!'

Nobody has ever called it a career before. Though I have been called a noddle.

'The pics you've taken here are brilliant. They're funny, clever. You need to get your finger out.'

'But I'm not—'

'You don't have to walk away from Coral, you just need to know in your head when you will. Get some credit, I don't know.' He shrugs, waves a hand. 'My name is on those games I write, I get some credit. You need to own it, Jane. Claim your life back, the one you want, not the one that jerk wanted you to have.' He has coloured up. It's quite a speech for Freddie and I'm left open-mouthed. He's never called Andy a jerk before either. 'I'm proud of you, you know.' It's a bit of a mumble, but I know he means it. Which brings a lump to my throat.

'Thanks.' It comes out all small and pathetic, but I don't think he hears anyway. He whizzes off as though he's overstepped the mark.

I slump back down on the sofa. He's right, I do need to own my life.

I also think I'm in trouble. Because just now, I wanted to grab Freddie and do things to him that have always belonged firmly in the fantasy box.

And he's just told me that he's never got over some other girl. That he's still waiting for her to come back.

Talk about rebound relationship, we'd be totally doomed.

So, while Freddie is tidying up, I distract myself with work. I un-post my last batch of Ibiza photos and, throwing caution to the wind, I re-post a load of silly seagull Brighton ones. Then dash down to the seafront and take some more.

It feels strangely liberating, as the wind buffets my face, and my hair lashes against my cheek.

It also makes me feel sad. I'll miss this place. And my time with Freddie. I mean I know we're together in the flat, but this has been different. As intimate as it gets with your clothes on, I guess.

I'm sad for Freddie, too. And when this wedding is over I'm going to help him find his old 'one' or persuade him to look for a new improved version. We can't both be miserable sods, hankering after relationships that were never meant to be, can we?

Freddie deserves to be happy. Being here, like this, has made me realise that whoever gets Freddie is a very lucky girl, loads luckier than I'd have been if I'd married Andy.

Andy never was one for eating cockles, laughing at seagulls or kissing turtles.

Andy would have thrown my camera into the sea and made me grow up.

He doesn't like sand in the bed.

Or *Killing Eve*.

I wish I could just stay here.

With Freddie.

Chapter 12

I've been at Mum and Dad's house for less than half an hour when my mobile rings. Luckily, it is not Darth Vader. Darth and I have only been on texting – and not speaking – terms since that horrible phone call. I'm hoping I've still got a job, but I'm not one hundred per cent positive. For all I know Coral could be packing Crystal into her mahoosive Louis Vuitton fake trunk and shipping her back as we speak. I hope she has to pay a premium for oversize luggage.

'Hey, I saw your posts on Insta! You went to Ibiza *and* New York? Jeez, you get around these days, girl.' Rachel laughs, to show she's kidding.

'Fuck, the Ibiza pics aren't still up, are they? I thought I'd deleted ...'

'Chill, they've gone. I was kidding. How was Brighton after we left? Any hot dates?'

That makes me pause. The image of Freddie and our shared sunset flickers into my head. Nope, better not go there. 'You were my only hot date!'

'Ha-ha, you're funny. That's why I rang, thought I better

check we were still on for tomorrow and you hadn't dashed off into the sunset with Freddie and dumped me.'

'Never! I wouldn't miss your engagement party for anything! Italian place on the High Street?'

'Bugger, didn't you get my email?'

'Email?' Hell, I've been so busy posting photos and having fun, I just haven't bothered checking. Which is so not me, I'm a 'refresh every 10 seconds' kind of person. Normally. Except now isn't normal.

'Oh, don't sweat it, it doesn't matter. But the whole thing kind of spiralled out of control a bit, and we've invited everybody! Mikey said why not, you only get engaged once!'

Mikey, it seems, only does everything once, apart from the obvious thing that he's done several times with several different women.

'So, Mum offered to do something at home. Much better, free booze and I only have to walk up the stairs when I'm drunk!'

'Fab!' Bugger.

When Rachel said the words 'engagement party' in Brighton, even though I was bladdered, a part of my brain went, 'Oh, Gawd, what do I wear?' Then at breakfast the next day she'd said it was at a restaurant we went to quite a bit, and I went *phew*, smart jeans, sparkly top, heels, sorted. Which is what I packed before heading to my parents. And a blingy necklace, which I had thought might be over the top, but I'd take it anyway.

The situation has now changed though. The necklace is

definitely not over the top, it is the only suitable part of my wardrobe, but obviously I can't wear just that.

Rachel's house is a whole different scenario. As is, 'We invited everybody.'

I did not arrive at my parents' house equipped for a flashy engagement party. I arrived with the type of small wheelie-case that makes it easy to make a quick getaway when you've heard one too many comments about eating toast in bed leaving crumbs, and the toothpaste needing to be squeezed from the bottom. I mean, I do love my mum, but loving somebody and living with them can be two different things altogether.

Now, Rachel might not be intending it to turn out that way, but it will definitely be *très pawsh*. This is because her folk are loaded. This isn't loaded as in you don't have to think twice about buying the book *and* the new lipstick. I'm talking seriously flush, though, surprisingly un-flash.

Their whole life went supersized the day her dad entered the *Dragon's Den* and came out with bucket loads of dosh and a whole load of TV exposure. When we were thirteen they upsized in a way that made my jaw hang loose. At that age you're not green eyed about stuff like big houses (just boyfriends, and new jeans and flash mobiles), you're just awe-struck.

Up until then, tea round at her house had involved being squashed round the Formica kitchen table and being able to see the TV in the lounge if you leaned back just a tiny (unno-ticeable) amount.

Now there was a TV the size of a car in the kitchen, reaching the lounge couldn't be done in high heels, and you could hold a party in her bedroom.

I know. We did. And now, my whole flat would fit in the third bathroom.

So however nice, normal and totally unflashy her folks were, the other party guests will be dressed to impress. I have to make an effort.

And who knows what 'everybody' means. It could even mean Andy, as we had made quite a foursome a few years ago and I know he is still good friends with Michael.

Normally I would log onto my bank account and check the balance then say to hell with it and go shopping. Now is not normal though. Now is post non-US trip, and like I said I am stony broke.

I check my coat pockets, and that little secret pocket in my handbag where I occasionally squirrel away a £10 note. I even rattle the piggy bank in my bedroom that Mum has kindly kept. It yields several old £1 coins, some hair grips and a trolley token.

I have reached such a desperate low that I am actually building up courage to ask Mum if I can borrow something of hers to wear.

Then I do a mental reccy of her wardrobe and all hope is lost. Let's just say, there are ways to do animal print that are on-trend and look wicked, and there are ways that say it is so over. I will be better dressed if I turn up in just my sparkly necklace.

I mean, I do love Mum, and she does have a certain style, but I'm not ready to turn into her yet. Or talk about hot flushes. Or keep my elbows off the table and my knees together.

There is only one way out of this, and it involves a man and next day delivery.

I need to talk to Freddie.

I glance down at my vibrating phone, and it's him.

It's like we have this weird connection. Like when you and your best friend suddenly realise your periods have totally tuned in. Like I say. Weird. He's a man.

'Freddie!'

'Jane, I have …'

We both speak at the same time. Both stop. Then start again.

'I am so screwed, I …'

'I've made a spur of the mom—'

We both stop talking again. But I did hear what he said. Spur of the moment? Freddie doesn't normally do spontaneous. Apart from the Brighton trip. And the day I told him how I'd been dumped by Andy, when he suggested we hold a wake for my (never to be used) wedding dress … Okay, he's spontaneous when he knows I'm having a crisis, which seems to have happened more times than it should have done lately.

'What do you mean?' That is said in synchronicity, so we both start laughing.

'You first.'

'No, you first.'

'Hang on a second.'

'What are you doing, there's an echo now.'

'I've gone into the bathroom.' I push the door shut and sit

on the loo. 'So Mum doesn't listen in.' I'd forgotten how nosy mothers can be. It's no wonder the teenage years are so tough, that you end up paranoid that you can't do anything right, and never get to do what you want. Big Mother is watching you (or reading your private stuff) and slyly making suggestions to try to get you back on the right track. I now realise Mum did not have any kind of ESP or worldly knowledge. She spied (or as she would say, kept a loving eye) on me.

'I've got my feet up, hang on, hang on, let me make a coffee.'

'Freddie! Are you suggesting this could take some time?'

'Yep.'

'Cheeky bugger.' I stop twiddling my hair and grinning like a teenager in love. 'Well, you're wrong! I just need you to do me a favour, if you've got time?'

'Always got time for you. Although ...' there's a pause in his voice, which makes my heart hammer. This isn't my 'Dear John' is it? When I discover he's got a new girlfriend who he really is into this time, and I'm going to lose my flatmate and my home. Is this why he rang?

'Although?' Be brave, Jane. Be brave. I cross my fingers and close my eyes. Please don't say you've fallen in love. Please, please.

'I'm going away for a few days to see a mate. I was just ringing to see if you want me to shut the curtains and set the light timer on? I wasn't sure when you'd be back.'

Phew. Or not phew.

'Going away, like today?' Shit, shit, shit. I'm going to have to borrow money off Mum. Or Dad. Dad is a better option, less explanation required, just more truth. A tricky one.

'Like tomorrow.' There's a smile in his voice, I can hear it. I can picture the lift at the corners of his mouth. The twinkle in his eyes.

Phew.

'Why, what's up?'

'I need a favour. I wouldn't normally ask, but I'm totally desperate. Say no if you want, I won't be upset.' Much.

Memo to self. When feeling in despair at being a singleton, or feeling overwhelming randy, or thinking similarly inappropriate thoughts when faced with a sexy man wandering half naked through your flat (or wandering barefoot on the Brighton sand). Remember, a friend is for life, not just for romance. Whereas a lover can be here one Christmas and gone the next.

So, value your wonderful friend, and do not allow yourself to lust after him in any way whatsoever. And definitely do not be tempted to paw him. Because that way will lead to disaster.

Freddie has saved the day. And my dignity. He has gone one better than Parcelforce and agreed to make a detour and bring me a dress. See, I'd be a fool to snog him and risk losing all this, wouldn't I?

Chapter 13

'It's too short, isn't it?' I like skirts just above the knee because if they're any longer they're at the top of my footballer-calves and make my legs look like tree trunks. Hem above the knee and I have shapely legs, hem below, I have chair legs.

Unfortunately, when I said little green dress, I forgot there were two. This is not the just above the knee one, this is the mid-thigh one.

I squealed when he handed the bag over, then felt like screaming when I peeped inside. But how could I even let on? He'd ventured into my room, rooted in my drawers and almost saved my bacon. And I loved him for it, even if my head was shouting, '*Sheeeet!*' in a very melodramatic way.

Maybe thick black tights would save the day. Or a long coat.

The coat idea is a no-go. Unless I wear a parka (bit heavy), or my Dad's black funeral coat (defo says funeral not wedding), which I don't think will work. For one, the sleeves are too long – I know because, in my desperation, I tried it on.

The tights do make my legs less noticeable, which is a definite bonus.

I am wondering about sewing the hem of the dress to them or putting my jeans back on when I hear Mum quizzing Freddie and decide I really do have to get a move on.

So I scurry downstairs, and accept his very insistent offer of a lift. Then discover that mid-thigh is fine, until I sit in a car. Or stand up. Or wiggle. Or move at all really. And that thick black tights just give this dress something to cling onto and climb up.

Hopefully this is a 'stand-still, clutch a canapé and chat' type of party.

'Can you just look the other way, please?' We've pulled up, so it is safe to ask. 'Ouch, bugger, oh, frigging hell, how am I supposed ...' Some girls can take their entire wardrobe off in a car and put a new one on. I can't. I don't think I was born bendy enough.

'What are you—'

'Trying to take these bloody tights off. Don't look, don't you dare turn round!'

'Oh.'

'Shit, I'm stuck, buggering, bugger. My foot is, can you ...'

'Am I allowed to look now then?'

'My foot is stuck.' Word of warning, don't ever put one foot on the dashboard when your thighs are bound together by a tight dress, and your knees are in the deadly grip of a gusset that believe me isn't giving extra stretch. 'I've got one foot on the dash, and the other is wedged under the glove compartment, and I'm getting cramp!'

'Oh, look, lots more guests arriving.'

'Shit, what, where?' I twist around and crick my neck. Seeing me spread-legged is so not what an engagement party is supposed to be about.

'Kidding. Here.' He hauls me upright on the seat, and my legs snap together like the jaws of a hungry crocodile.

'Thanks.' I take a deep breath and try to wriggle the hem of the dress down to a decent level. 'That was mean, saying that.'

'Sorry.' His grin doesn't say sorry, his grin says I'd be better off begging him to take me home.

'I should have asked you to bring my black dress.' The down to the knee, no cleavage showing, dress.

'Too late now.'

'I need to go back and change.'

'I thought you had nothing else to wear?' He wiggles his eyebrows suggestively and makes me laugh.

'True.'

He kisses me on the cheek. It's a fleeting touch of his lips against my skin, but it sends a tiny shiver all the way down to the base of my stomach. He's never kissed me before, he's blown kisses, hugged me. But never actually kissed me.

I look out of the window self-consciously and wonder what would have happened if he'd done that in Brighton. When we had our moment. On the seafront.

Oh, how ridiculous! I'm being daft, it was a friendly peck on the cheek for heaven's sake, not an invite to start fantasising. I've done it to him without thinking, it means nothing. He's just never done it back.

I dare glance back at him, knowing I've got pink cheeks, but he doesn't seem to notice.

Phew. That's good. If he ever guesses about the route my thoughts take me on sometimes, we're stuffed. He'd be out of here faster than a rocket out of a rocket launcher.

'Stop panicking, you look gorgeous. It will be great, honest.' He looks me in the eye. 'You'll be fine.'

He's right, well, at least on the dress front. I'm not sure about the physical contact kiss-front. It muddles my brain, or my body at least. Treading on dangerous ground.

'I'll be fine.' I've just got myself all worked up because this feel likes a big deal. It is the first step along the 'Rach is getting married and I'm going to her wedding' route. And that's why the kiss made me feel like that. Nerves. Panic. Nothing to do with lustful thoughts that are strictly out of bounds.

'You will. You just need to get this over with.'

'I do.' I'm still frozen to the spot.

'Go on then.' He nudges. 'Get your bum out of my car. The party will be over before you get there!'

I swing my legs out, knees glued together. I'm sure I read in Cosmo that this is the way ladies avoid knicker flashing. Although I think I might have already done that.

Which reminds me, I think I forgot to put my no VPL ones on. I really, really want to check. I think about pretending I've dropped my bag then I can have a sneak peek between my legs but that would look like I'm puking and would be weird with Freddie (well, anybody) sat next to me.

'Have fun.' He winks. 'You look amazing.'

'You wouldn't like to? No. No.' Inviting him in would start a million and one rumours.

As I wiggle my way towards the massive front door, keeping my knees together to avoid a riding-up incident, I realise I've got my fingers on my cheek. Where he kissed it. Bugger. I really am going to have to stop myself liking him quite so much.

It was a friendly gesture.

When he said I looked gorgeous and amazing he was just being nice, boosting my confidence.

Freddie is my flatmate. The perfect best male friend. And even if he wasn't, he doesn't do relationships. Apart from with the one from his past.

Like he said, mates are better.

'Aww, it's so lovely to see you again, Jane. How are you?' Rachel's mum wraps me in a Chanel-scented hug, then holds me at arm's length. 'You look wonderful!'

'All over that stupid bugger, are you?' Her dad nudges me in the ribs. 'Bet you've got a new man, eh? Is that him dropped you off? Where's he gone, parking up?' He winks. He's always been the 'bigger than life, dad-dancing, chasing you round the house, tickle you to death' type. Though I'm not sure that's appropriate with thirty year olds, even if it was when we were eleven. In fact, was it then?

'He's, er, a friend.'

'She lives with him!' Rachel bounces up and grabs me in a hug. 'Come on, come on.' She's pulling me across the hallway, and I manage a limp wave at her parents before she corners me and whispers in my ear. 'Don't worry, Andy isn't here.'

I resist the urge to do a fist pump. 'Thank God for that!'

'But Jack is.'

'Oh, no, you're kidding?'

'We had to invite him, I mean he is the husband of my bridesmaid.'

'I don't think you had to spell that one out.'

'Sorry.' She pulls an apologetic face. 'And he's the, er, best man.'

'Great, him and Maddie can walk down the aisle side by side. Bugger.'

'And Andy's an usher. I'm sorry, I'm so, so sorry, but he's been Michael's mate for so long just like you've been mine, but at least he's not here today.'

This is getting to be Ex's Reunited, without the united bit. There'll be a fistfight between the pews if we're not careful.

'You couldn't keep an eye on Mads, could you? I swear she's already had three glasses of bubbly, and you know she's never been a big drinker.'

'Sure. Of course.'

'Come on, let's get you a drink, then we'll find her. Oh, and Beth's here, isn't that brill!'

That one piques my interest. Beth used to be a real laugh, I'm not quite sure if she's completely reinvented herself, or whether the old Beth lies dormant beneath her motherly boobs, but I'm dying to find out.

'With the baby?' It could be hard to see beyond the bosom if she has a newborn clasped to it.

'She got a babysitter.'

'I certainly did.' The girl herself has popped out from the kitchen, clutching what looks to be a massive mojito. 'I wasn't going to miss this for anything. God, it's weird, I feel like I've forgotten a bit of myself, but it's so bloody brilliant being off duty! Bloody hell, Jane, it's good to see you, how long has it been? You've not changed, well, you have a bit, but the scaffolding is still the same!'

The old Beth is still there, and it's such a relief I start to cackle hysterically, then stop and bury my nose in the glass of bubbly that Beth has pushed into my hand.

She's got less black kohl round her eyes than last time I saw her, and her short spiky hair has lost some of its, well, spikiness, but there's a stud in her nose, a piercing at the tip of one eyebrow, and she still swears like a trooper.

Our parents didn't like her, but we all loved her.

'Mouth like a sewer,' more than one mother had been heard to say, when they all thought we weren't listening. Which made us even keener to draw her into our clique, we needed her in our gang.

'Oh, Beth, Beth, Beth, it's really you!' Maddie has crept up behind me and is now jumping about like a lunatic. I glance at Rachel, who mouths 'Prosecco' and grins.

'Mads, Mads, Mads, it really is!' Beth mimics Maddie, then grabs her in a bear hug. 'Now *you* have changed, what happened to mousy Mads?'

'Mousy? You didn't call me that, did you? Who called me that?'

'Everybody was mousy compared to Beth.' Sally's judgmental tone cuts into the conversation. We all spin round.

'Fuck me, it's the scarlet woman!' Beth laughs so loudly I can't help but smile. 'Just like old times, eh?'

They look at each other. Just like old times. Sal was never that keen on Beth, I think because she couldn't compete with her. They were too different, and Beth wasn't into one-upmanship, she did her own thing and to hell with what people thought. 'Corrupted poor innocent Jack, I hear, and,' her eyes are twinkling, 'squashed him under your well-maintained thumb.' Sal straightens her spine, her eyes narrow. Trust Beth to say what we've all been dying to, but not had the balls. Or been too polite. 'Wouldn't have thought you were his type to be honest, and,' she tips her head on one side (as I tip my Prosecco down my throat), 'wouldn't have thought he was yours. Don't you fancy a man who's a bit of a challenge, who can man handle you, in a purely figurative way of course. Although,' she laughs, a tinkly, pretty laugh that's always been at odds with the feisty girl we love, 'look where that got me! Maybe you should just stick with it, Sal. Sorry Mads.' She gives Maddie a quick hug. Beth all over. She always was as quick to kiss and make up as she was to shit stir and say what she thought.

Why the hell was I worried about my dress? Nobody is even going to notice what I am wearing with sparks like this in the air.

'Well, now, lovely ladies, bit of bad news, I'm afraid!' Luckily, Rachel's Uncle Peter lurches into the middle of our little group before it all ignites. 'Jack has had an urgent work call.' He's a vet. 'Apparently, a greedy snake has over done it on the fat mouse front and is choking! What's the chances, eh? Never a dull moment!'

What are the chances indeed? But this is good, and even better that the man in question hasn't dared to set foot within a hundred yards of our little group.

'Oh, Jane, I'm so, so pleased you said you'd be my bridesmaid.' I've never been good at juggling a glass of wine and a plate of nibbles, so Rach and I have found a spot on the stairs for a drunken catch up. 'Are you sure you're okay with it though?'

She's frowning with concern, and I can feel myself welling up. I can't lie, thinking about this wedding has been keeping me awake at night and making my stomach churn in the day. That's partly why I knew I had to feel good about myself this evening, being dressed to my best was bound to make me feel more positive, right? Well, that didn't start well. Although maybe having my legs bound together with a gusset is a sign.

'Of course, I'm sure. No way would I miss your wedding!' I hug her and take a moment to compose myself, and hope the tears go back in and not spill over my face – the one bit of me that didn't prove too much of a problem. I might not have brought an appropriate frock, but I did bring my entire make-up arsenal.

'Oh, Jane, I mean, I know this must be difficult, and you must hate weddings.'

See? Everybody is going to assume that if I say anything

negative, it's sour grapes, because I hate weddings. 'I don't hate weddings, just ones with Andy. And I'm not planning on one of my own any time soon.' Not that anybody is asking.

'I do love him, you know.' Rachel suddenly puts her plate down and grasps my hands in hers. 'I know you worry, but he's not the silly idiot he used to be at school you know. This is right, this is what I really want.'

'I know.' I smile. 'And that's all that matters.'

'The whole Sara thing was a silly mistake you know.'

I frown, I can't help myself. This has come out of the blue. Who is Sara? I don't remember a Sara from school. 'Sara? I thought it was Emily?' Oops, done it again, engaged mouth before brain. But, in the bright (too bright if you ask me) light of day, it is time to be honest. Somebody has to be. I owe it to Rachel to make sure she's not just going to have the best *day* of her life, she's going to have the best life.

'Emily?' She frowns, then suddenly laughs. Which rather takes me by surprise. 'Oh, God, Jane, I'd forgotten about her! That was so funny!'

'Ha-ha, yeah, how could you forget Emily?' The Emily incident was a long time ago, in fact a very long time ago. We were studying for our A levels, and it cemented our friendship as solidly as, well, cement.

Michael had been caught cuddling up with cute little Em in the school bogs by Ed, who had posted the photo on Twitter and it had gone *viral*. Well, fairly viral, viral within the school, which was pretty impressive back then. These days it would be seen more as a case of hiccups than a virus.

'That was so funny!' It wasn't at the time, but I can see

now that Rach might think it is. 'Emily was nothing, I mean that was *ages* ago, and I mean we weren't exclusive or anything.' She grins. 'Exclusive would have been so uncool. She was pretty uncool, anyway, wasn't she?'

I nod. She had been. Pretty, quiet, and a bit aloof.

'She was upset because her hamster had died. Do you remember?' I nod. That had been the story at the time. 'She was like, really upset and hiding in the cloakroom because she couldn't stop crying, and all Michael did was hold her hand. Typical of Ed to barge in and post a frigging photo on Twitter. He was so jealous of Michael you know, and he was so into Em. Anyway, Emily sent me this text saying how kind Michael was, and how lucky we were to have each other. She said it was hard to understand if you haven't had a hamster.'

I nod. It's hard to understand if you *have* had a hamster. 'So, erm, Sara?'

'Oh, no, she wasn't from school. She was the one in the photo at his works Christmas party, the one who rang me and said I was living in a dream world if I thought he was ever going to marry me.'

'Oh my God, right! That was when you ditched him?'

'Too right.'

I remembered this well, I'd just not known her name. Rachel had only ever referred to her as silly bitch and stupid cow. Never Sara. Sara was the reason she'd ditched him, and why I'd decided I didn't need to tell her about Lexie.

They'd split, it was over. My secret was safe.

Until they got back together again.

I'd been so proud of her when she'd bawled him out, even better she'd given his best jacket to the tramp he passes every day by the bus stop and locked him out of the house.

'He admitted everything to me before he proposed. It was so sweet, he was so honest and open about it and said that snogging her was the biggest mistake of his life, and he'd do anything to prove I could trust him. He'd been drunk but knew that wasn't an excuse. He's grown up, Jane.'

'That's brilliant, Rachel.' I cross my fingers out of sight under my knees. I really do hope she's right, for her sake. And for his, because if I find out that that he's still a serial shagger then he's going to be as dead as Emily's hamster.

But is now the time to tell her about Lexie? While we're clearing out the Michael closet?

'I've been going on and on about my wedding, what about you? You've still not told me about Brighton,' she winks, 'and Freddie.' The sudden change in conversation makes my mind up for me. Now is not the time to rock the boat. Michael is a reformed character. He's admitted his mistakes and they have clearly worked through it. Everything is going to be fine.

'Stop leering, you look creepy! There's nothing to tell. You know that! We're friends.'

'You do fancy him a little bit though, don't you?' She has her head tipped on one side.

'You're not going to get like all these other brides-to-be and try and get their friends hitched are you Mrs Matchmaker?'

'You didn't answer the question!' She laughs.

'I'm too busy to date, nobody would have me!'

'Freddie would.'

'Will you drop it? Friends works for us, it's,' Freddie's word jumps into my mouth, 'less complicated.'

'Hmm.'

'You know what it's like at the mo, I'm busy working for Coral. Once I've got established it'll be different.' I look her straight in the eye. 'I don't want a repeat of Andy.'

'I know.' She squeezes my hand. 'They're not all like Andy though, if you find a man who loves you because of your passion, your work, not in spite of it then you'll realise that.'

Freddie's back in my head. The one man who's always encouraged me, even helped me. The man who *likes* me for my passion, my work.

I feel the inward sigh and fight to keep it hidden, the man who really is out of bounds. Maybe I need to settle for kisses on cheeks and friendship and discount the prospect of ever finding a happy ever after and getting married. I push the thought down and put my best smile on my face.

'That's pretty deep after a bottle of Prosecco.'

She giggles. 'I've been saving it, I've got it written down.' We both drink our bubbly, slightly self-consciously. 'Coral's New York photos are pretty crap, nowhere near as good as your pics.'

I grin back. I love her solidarity. 'I'm going to really have to sparkle on the next shoot though, or I'll be dead meat.'

'Might be the best thing?' Her voice lifts at the end in a question.

'Have you been talking to Freddie?'

'No, why?' She looks at me suspiciously.

'Nothing.'

'He agrees with me, doesn't he? I knew it!'

'We talked a bit.' I shrug, trying to play it down. 'I know you both think I'm mad working for her, I think I'm mad sometimes.' I study my feet for a moment, trying to work out how to explain. 'But I'm not ready to break out solo yet.'

'Ahh, yeah, forgot you're Miss Perfection.'

'It's not just that, I need the contacts, I need to build my rep. You know I can't afford to take time out and do a course.'

'You don't need a course, your photos are fab!'

'Some people just look for stuff like that, where you studied, who you know.' I shrug and look her in the eye again. 'I didn't study so I've got to work on the who I know bit.'

'Sometimes you just gotta go for it, girl, even if you're not one hundred per cent ready. Work, new job …' There's a long pause. 'Man!'

I flick brownie crumbs at her. 'I knew you were going to say that!'

'Seriously, though, Coral is shit. She's bad news.' She's right of course, but everything is going great for Rach at the moment, her glass is definitely more than half full.

Mine is more on the empty side. Everything I touch turns crap. I need to get this right, when I jump ship I need to know it's the right time to let go of the security of a steady income, and I need to know I can prove to bloody Andy that this isn't a stupid little hobby. I'm not rubbish at everything. I have made some right choices in life.

I also need to prove it to myself.

'You don't need to tell me! I'm being a wimp, but I'm not ready to do it yet.' I daren't. What if it turns out that my

133

judgement about my abilities is as crap as my judgement on blokes?

'What does Freddie say?'

'Just that I need a plan, that I need her to credit my stuff.'

'He's not wrong, you know.'

'I know.'

Rachel knows about the sacrifices I've made because of this job though. I've had to cancel girlie night's out at the last minute before now, and she knows that it gets worse than that. After the dust had died down over my not-to-be-wedding, I'd realised that it was having to race off one Friday evening to attend to Coral that had probably been the final straw for Andy. He'd invited a gym-buddy and his girlfriend round for a meal. I'd forgotten and burst through the front door at 9 o'clock with a Chinese takeaway for two, a job lot of prawn crackers, and a lot of swearing.

To say it hadn't gone down well is an understatement. Particularly when the gym-buddy's girlfriend discovered she had a mild seafood allergy and her face swelled up like a blowfish and the rest of the evening we couldn't understand her as she sounded like she'd just had her mouth anaesthetised or swallowed a bag of marbles.

Coral has a lot to answer for.

I mean, I do know that if my relationship with Andy had been the genuine article then it wouldn't have mattered. He would have been happy to accept me as I am, a bit of a workaholic. That's just the way it is in jobs like mine.

'You know I'll help you any way I can, don't you?'

'I know you will, Rach. And I have got a plan. Freddie

helped me put it together.' She raises an eyebrow, which I ignore and instead just talk firmly in what I like to think is my professional voice. 'I don't intend working for Coral forever.' I also know that it's all about taking baby steps. Rachel's wedding is a biggie for me. I'm not so daft that I'm going to pretend it isn't. But once it's over, and I've proved to myself that I can survive trying on a bridesmaid's dress, a hen party, walking up the aisle, and seeing Andy all dressed up for somebody else's wedding, then I know I'll be ready to start putting my spreadsheet into action. Freddie loves spreadsheets, he'd run his entire life via spreadsheet if he could. And he helped me put one together. It's not exactly a five-year plan, more of an escape plan.

'Good! You're too good to put up with her crap, Jane.'

'You're telling me!' And I do know. 'Like I mean, all this blew up cos of Daniel's bloody pooch in a pouch.'

Rachel snorts Prosecco bubbles up her nose and splutters. 'He's not has he? I mean he does look well packed in those photos, but you never know what kind of padding is in there, do you?'

I bury my head in my hands, then peep at her through my fingers because she's giggling. She's happy, she looks so well, even tipsy. In fact, you know that phrase 'positively blooming'? That's Rachel.

Sugar! She's not, is she? I can't ask her outright, though, because she'll think, 1. I'm saying she's fat, or 2. I'm saying it's a shotgun wedding.

'Oh, goodness me, Rachel.' I'm rescued from the conundrum by Rachel's mother.

Who has just stepped onto Rachel's abandoned plate and has a skewered prawn on the heel of her shoe. 'What on earth? Oh, no, I knew this food was a mistake. Everything okay, girls? Dress fitting tomorrow, isn't that exciting?'

It's late by the time people start to drift off, and I'm the last to leave. Stopping for a last hug with Rachel and feeling so pleasantly tipsy I actually congratulate Michael in person. I hope the look I give him is piercing, and not squiffy.

They look so happy, hands entwined as we say goodbye that I feel bad that I've ever even thought about telling Rachel the dirty secret I know about her fiancé. Telling her about Lexie now could ruin everything and even a cynic like me can see that they're madly in love. How could I even think about hurting my best friend in the way Andy hurt me?

How could I ever risk her having doubts, having the whole thing ruined?

I let him kiss my cheek, then I weave my way down the driveway happy in the knowledge that I'm doing the best thing for everybody. Keeping my mouth shut.

Now all I have to do is sneak into the house without Mum hearing, or I'll get the kind of inquisition that no self-respecting woman over twenty-one should ever have to endure.

Chapter 14

'Hey, Jane! Looks like you've had a good night.'

Freddie is sprawled on the sofa, looking completely at home, a can of beer in his hand. He grins at me lazily, brushing his floppy fringe back with long fingers.

Bugger. I am so drunk I've somehow found my way back to my flat, or even Brighton, rather than my parent's house. How much have I spent on the taxi fare? I'll be bankrupted!

I stare at him, aghast.

Then notice the silver photo frames on the polished wood sideboard.

Phew. This *is* my family home. It is not Brighton, or our flat. The 'polished' bit is the give-away – no dust bunnies here, and the fresh smell, and the absence of socks on the radiator, and empty pizza boxes on the table.

And the fact that you can take more than one step without knocking your knees or elbows on a piece of furniture.

'Had to persuade your mum not to lock you out, I promised I'd wait up for you and call out a search party if you weren't back at a reasonable time.' He tilts his head on one side, and I copy, which makes me feel a bit dizzy. 'You're really pissed, aren't you?' I nod and he goes a bit blurry, so I blink to bring him back into focus.

'What are you doing here?'

His grin broadens. He's got a nice grin, and a nice mouth. A very nice mouth, I'd not really noticed it before, but now I realise I am fixated. He looks quite kissable. I watch his lips move, not really hearing the words. 'Don't you remember? You asked me? I'm going to Rob's tomorrow, and you said it was easier if I wanted to stay here? I brought your dress?'

He ends on a question. I shake my head to try to get rid of the kissing idea. I must be totally plastered, really drunk to even think stuff like that. That's what vodka shots, champagne, a very weird reunion and wedding news does for you. Well, for me.

'It is okay, isn't it? I can go.' He looks worried, and I want to hug him and pat his head and tell him everything will be okay. I must not. He is not my boyfriend, and he is not a dog, and those are the only two instances where that type of behaviour is acceptable.

'Of course, it's okay, Freddie dear. I thought I heard voices! Have you had a nice evening, darling? You look a bit flushed.' Definitely my parents' house, unless my mother has taken to wandering around random properties in her nightwear. Unlikely.

I nod. It's always wiser to say as little as possible when I'm drunk, and my mother is not. She shifts a china robin on the mantelpiece three inches to the right, as though to justify her presence.

'Freddie has been telling us all about his friend and this

tiny island he lives on. Fascinating, he's such a nice boy,' she says this as though he's not in the room, 'just the type you should be sticking with, dear. I always said that Andrew was a bit too big for his boots.'

'Did you?' This is news to me.

'Well, not to your face of course dear, it's up to you to make your own decisions,' she shifts the bird back, 'and mistakes.'

'Thanks, Mum.'

'But he was so assessing, I think he had his eye on our bungalow you know!'

'I didn't. I can't for one second imagine Andy, or any man, coveting your bungalow.' There is a funny noise, I think Freddie is sniggering. Quietly. I risk a glance his way, and there is a definite smirk.

'Are you drunk?' Her eyes have narrowed.

'Tipsy.'

'Hmm, well, don't eat all the cheese, and don't break anything.' She edges the china birds closer to the wall with her elbow.

'Cheese?' Freddie is grinning, enjoying the entertainment.

'Oh, you've never seen anybody eat like our Jane after she's been out drinking.' He has. 'Give her a wedge of stilton and she's worse than a mouse.'

'Mice are tiny. They nibble.'

'Whatever you say dear. A herd of mice. But anyway, you're much better off with this one than that horrible Andrew.'

She gives me a hug. *This one* looks startled.

'Oh, don't start, Mum, we just live together!'

Her eyebrows go up a notch.

'In different rooms! We're friends.'

'Well, that's nice. Respectful, though not entirely practical, I mean isn't it better to try a slice of pie before you buy the whole one?'

'Mum!' I want to scream, but I'm too drunk, and tired, to summon the energy.

'Anyway, Freddie's friend sounds lovely, as well. Maybe you should go to the outer Outer Hebrides and meet him if you don't want sex with this one.'

'There's only one "outer".'

'Sorry?'

'It's the Outer Hebrides.'

'Oh, well, it sounds very remote, a very long way north. A man like that could be just what you need, all rough and rugged, and you'll get a breath of fresh air as well. London isn't good for you, you know. Too many fumes and no sea.'

'We haven't got sea here, either!' I'm not so drunk that I make the mistake of saying I've just been by the seaside, with Freddie. That would make this far too complicated.

I remember now though. Freddie's friend Rob lives on an island, bird watching and seal herding and stuff like that, with his dog. He's a ranger. I've already got a mental picture of him; all rough, rugged and craggy (him, not the scenery) in a thick jumper and sturdy boots striding across the island. He's a little bit Poldark, but with a beanie instead of the funny black hat, and he obviously wouldn't strip to the waist to go scything as it is bloody cold 'oop North'. He'd build a fire, and drink whisky.

When Freddie called (during the dress crisis), it was to tell me he was off to see his mate Rob, but that he was more than happy to make a minor detour. It wasn't minor, but it was in the whole scale of driving to the Outer Hebrides, I suppose. Anyway, he did mention how far it was, and the fact he'd be kipping in his car as he couldn't really afford to stop over anywhere guaranteed not to have bedbugs and drug dealers. So, I said, why not stop over on our sofa. My parents wouldn't mind. It might even stop Dad going on at me about getting back in the saddle, and Mum scowling at him and saying it was a shame nobody went dancing these days, it was the perfect way to meet a nice young man.

I think I must have a 'use by' date stamped on my forehead.

'Have I missed something?'

Oh, Gawd, now Dad has joined the party. And he's in his Christmas flannel pyjamas.

'No, Dad.'

He kisses me on the forehead. 'Lovely to meet your young man, sweetie. He's charming.' Even though he whispers this in my ear, everybody hears.

'That's what I was just saying.' Mum gives me a pointed look. 'Don't be shy about it, darling. At your age you really do need to get out there dating while there are still some spare men of your own age.'

'Well, actually, given the high divorce rate there will always be spare men.'

Mum frowns. 'Sorry dear?'

'Well, they don't just disappear into the ether, do they? We're all very environmentally conscious these days you know, we recycle everything including the guys.' I hope Andy was considered not fit for recycling and dumped in a landfill site with all the crap nobody cares about.

'Well, you don't want second hand, do you dear?' She's back in full flow.

'Run-in could be an advantage, well, it is with cars.' Dad's contribution is accompanied with a wink. 'Upcycling,' he adds with a grin.

'Right now, I don't want to upcycle, recycle, down cycle or do anything on a cycle. Or with a man!' I think I've made myself clear. All three of them fall silent. 'I invited Freddie because I owe him.' Oops, they all look interested again. 'For bringing my dress, and for Brighton.' Why did I say that? I so wasn't going to.

'But you've never been to Brighton! Old people go there don't they?'

Dad shakes his head at Mum. 'No dear, that Jamie Oliver went there, don't you remember? We watched him on the TV with his friend. Cooking.'

'That was Southend-on-Sea. On the pier.'

'Well, it's similar. They had lots of young people eating with them.'

'I think they were film crew. Television people do that you know, they're not the real people who actually live there you know. They're drafted in! I mean, look at all those people Nigella invites round for lunch!'

I want to scream.

Mother turns her attention back to me and frowns. 'But why would you go there? Your little photographs aren't that famous, are they dear?'

'Look, you couldn't go to bed, could you?'

'Well, it is rather late. You won't be long, will you? Shall I turn your sheets down?'

'Mum!'

'Cocoa?'

I growl.

They go. Dad is chuckling. Which is sweet, though he winks at Freddie again. Not so sweet.

Things are getting a bit desperate when even your parents are trying to force you into bed with a man, aren't they?

The silence resettles.

'What happened at the party then? How did it go?'

'It was totally weird.' I stare at Freddie, swaying on the spot. Me, not him. He's got thick eyelashes, I've not noticed them before, and I'm suddenly dying to get in close and study them better. 'I mean, the whole bridesmaids thing is a bit of a 'mare, what with Mads and Sal, and Jack, who was there. But Andy wasn't.' He nods. 'But she'd also invited this girl I've not seen for yonks.'

'Come on.' Freddie pats the space on the sofa next to him. He is totally chilled and at home, even though he's never been here before. 'Come and tell Uncle Fred all about it.'

I want to make some clever comment, but I can't. Instead I crash down, and Freddie drapes a heavy arm round my shoulders. It feels comforting and nice. Safe.

'Come on, spill.'

'What do you mean, spill?'

'Well, you getting this bladdered isn't normal.'

'I'm just tired.'

'Aww, Jane.' Freddie laughs softly and hugs me a bit tighter. 'You look nearly as cut up as you did when your boss did the dirty, what's happened now?'

I spill. I find that several drinks remove my ability to hold back. 'God this wedding is going to be such a disaster. I'm worried about her getting married.' It bursts out abruptly.

Freddie grins. 'Oh. I get it now, you're jealous?'

'No!' I pummel him with a cushion, then realise it's one of Mum's best ones and she'll kill me, so I plump it back up.

'Oh, hell, shit, sorry. It's the whole wedding thing, isn't it? Still hate them, do you?' Freddie pulls an apologetic face.

He knows all about my cancelled wedding. He helped Rachel pick up the pieces after the hen party that will not be mentioned. That's how he got to know her. They bonded over my broken heart.

'Jane?' Freddie's soft voice brings me back to the present.

'It's not that.' I know everybody will think it is. 'I don't hate weddings, just my own, I do actually like weddings,' I nod vigorously as though that will make it true, 'other people's weddings, but I don't like Michael. How can she do it?'

'This is just about Michael?'

'It is.' Even though I walked out of the party resolving to leave well alone, I'm finding it tricky now they're not in front of me looking all loved-up. I am also feeling guilt.

Freddie shrugs, and hands me a beer and despite (or maybe because) of the fact that I've already drunk far too much, I take a swig. 'But it's not you who's marrying him is it? It's Rachel, so if she thinks he's okay, if she loves him and he ...'

'But he's not okay, she just can't see it.' I slump down a bit

144

further in my seat. It's hard to put into words, but I've always thought she could do better, and that she'd realise that and move on. Not marry him.

'You don't think maybe Michael is okay, but the whole Andy thing has made you, you know a bit ...' His words are tentative, I can see he's struggling for the appropriate word, so I help out.

'Paranoid?'

'No, I wasn't going to say that, I was thinking wary.'

'You just think I'm over thinking this don't you?' I have to admit, that deep down there is a niggling doubt that maybe Michael is fine, and it's just me making a big deal out of some silly incident that happened over a year ago. That he's forgotten all about it, brushed it under the carpet, realised just how much Rach means to him. And he'd never do it again. Maybe all this has blown up in my head because I feel so guilty about not telling her at the time. But it doesn't help that I just don't like him.

'I'm just wondering if maybe you're just not quite as trusting as you might have been?'

'Trusting's the word. I wouldn't trust him as far as I can throw him, which believe me isn't far at all. In fact, I'd have to push him.'

Freddie grins, and I giggle back, then get serious again.

'I'm really worried he'll let her down, that she's making a massive mistake. I don't like him.' It's on the tip of my tongue to tell Freddie all about Michael and Lexie, but I shouldn't. It's my secret. The less people who know about it the better. That's the whole point of a secret, isn't it?

'Aww, Janey.' Freddie hugs me, he's good on the hugs front. 'You don't have to like him. Not all guys are like Andy you know, we're not all stupid twats who don't know a good thing when we see it.'

'He was terrible at school, he was always messing her about.' That's where it all started, my distrust of Michael. It's hard to forgive and forget a guy who's made your best friend sob her heart out.

'Maybe he did it to make her jealous? It could have just been all front, showing off?'

'Or maybe he's just a randy sod.'

'We were just kids.' His voice is soft.

I nod. He's right, what Michael did as a teenager at school really shouldn't count against him now. They were just kids, playing around, playing at love. I could have drawn a line under all that, laughed it off I guess. If it hadn't been for Lexie. The girl who'd made me wonder if he'd ever grow up. The one I can't tell Freddie about.

I let my head fall onto Freddie's shoulder, and fight to keep my eyes open.

'I'm sure he's grown up.'

I'm sure Freddie has to be right, it will all be fine. Michael will have grown up and be a different man.

'I just don't get ...'

'You're not supposed to get other people's love, Jane. Are you? You're just supposed to be happy for them.' He shrugs.

'But I don't think he's her one.' Would Freddie see this differently if I told him the whole truth? That it wasn't just silly childhood kisses that are bothering me?

'Who knows? Maybe they both want comfort, companionship.'

'We're not still in the eighteenth century!'

He ignores me. 'Maybe having the chance to watch the movies with her fave man, share his life just for a bit is better than not at all ... all different reasons.'

'You make it sound like he's got some illness and is about to die. I do not wish he'll die, honest, I just wish he'd walk away if he doesn't mean it. That this isn't some one-upmanship – marrying her just to stop her going off with somebody else.'

'Maybe he does mean it, or maybe she loves him enough not to care.'

That bit makes me blink. 'Can you love someone enough not to care?'

Freddie just shrugs.

'But what if he doesn't love her, enough?'

'That's a chance we sometimes have to take, isn't it, Jane?' His voice is soft. 'Sometimes we just have to trust that our instincts are right. I know you did, and it didn't work out. But shit happens. Maybe it won't for Rach.'

'But what if it does?'

'It's her choice, her chance, isn't it? If she loves him, and she doesn't go through with it, then she'll be like your mate Maddie, won't she?'

I think of poor Mads. And the one she let get away, the one she accidentally pushed away, and my heart actually physically contracts painfully.

Or I've got bad indigestion from the beer.

Freddie has a point though.

Michael can't be the one Rachel let get away. Even if I'm right. But, dear God, I hope I'm wrong. I love her too much to see her in the state I was.

'It might never happen Jane. It probably won't. Nobody saw a problem for you, did they? And ...' he pauses, 'maybe he just is a bit of a jerk, but he's got it out of his system now. I bet his parents are a fine example of married life.' He grins, then squeezes my hand. I hadn't realised our fingers had somehow got entangled. 'You can't live her life.'

'I know.' I say sadly. I look up at him. 'I've got enough trouble sorting my own life out, so I'm obviously crap at knowing what love is, it's just ...' I'm about to tell him about Michael, about what I saw. About the moment when I'd suddenly been so sure that he was a louse. But I stop myself. Some secrets are better not shared.

'Your life is fine, you're fine.' He edges up the sofa, disentangles himself.

I sigh, feeling the coldness of the gap between us. 'It's not just Michael, though, it's Mads and Sal, I mean, Jack's going to be there. And then there's Beth, the one I hadn't seen for yonks, who just loves winding Sal up.' I bury my face in my hands. 'When we've all had a drink I just know it's going to blow up.'

'And you promised Rachel you'd be her barrier?' He smiles, a softer gentler smile than his normal cheeky grin.

'I feel like I'm one sandbag against a tsunami.'

'Oh, I wouldn't call you a sandbag.'

'I feel like a sandbag.' I feel all comfortable and heavy, and like I never want to move again.

'Come on.' He prods me in the ribs. 'I guess I need some shut eye before I set off for the back of beyond.'

'Shit sorry, it's so late.'

I don't want him to go though. I'm selfish. I talk just to keep him here. 'Is it nice? The outer Outer Hebrides?'

'Beautiful. The most wonderful place you can imagine. You can be yourself there.' He ruffles my hair as he walks round the back of the couch.

My 'take me with you' reaches him as he hits the stairs. He turns, winks, 'one day maybe. That would be nice.'

'I've got to make this the best day ever for Rachel, haven't I?'

This is my moving on, wiping out Andy and my horrible nearly-wedding forever.

'That's what friends are for. Night Jane.'

'Night Freddie.'

I lie down on my bed and look up at the ceiling. It's painted midnight blue, with twinkly stars and every time I look at it, I'm taken back to my childhood and simpler times. It's the perfect ceiling for meditation and pondering life, the universe and everything.

I wonder what Freddie means about being himself in the Hebrides, I thought he always was himself. My eyes are gritty; I close them and the room doesn't spin, it whooshes. As though I'm in a boat, on the water, and I'm rowing all the way to the Outer Hebrides to see a man and a dog and a beautiful sunset.

Chapter 15

'How do you feel?' Rachel is sitting at what has always been our favourite table in the transport café at the edge of town. We used to come here when we wanted to get away from everybody. We could plot in private, and not be found.

Meeting here is like a reunion, a chance to catch up before we face the fray. Sorry, enter the bridal shop. Last night, it had seemed like a good idea, and we'd laughed about having our greasy spoon hangover cure. This morning a long lie-in seemed like a better idea.

A bit queasy is the understatement of the year. I don't think staying up until 4 a.m. drinking beer with Freddie was a very good idea.

'I feel like I did after your 21st birthday party.'

We'd raided her parents' drinks cabinet and regretted it for days afterwards. I think it was the mix that did it, and the fact that we were both on some weird grapefruit and kiwi diet. Who knew you could puke long after all the multi-coloured contents of your stomach had been emptied down the toilet?

'Me, too. That's why I thought we should come here! I've ordered.' She grins.

I grin back. Not sure whether our hangover cure of a greasy breakfast will still work these days. Or whether it would send me running to the bogs, which you honestly don't want to run to. They always used to be a toilet paper free zone where you had to hold your nose to stop yourself gagging.

This is going to be kill or cure. At least it's taking my mind off the idea of going to a bridal shop and looking at dresses, which made me feel all trembly when I got out of bed this morning.

At least if I end up puking or coming over all faint, I can blame the breakfast now and not the fact that the very thought of wedding shopping has brought me out in a cold sweat.

'Here you go, my lovely.'

Two plates of food appear, and they look quite different to how I remember. No grease in sight. I sniff cautiously. My stomach only lurches a little bit, and the smell of bacon makes my mouth water. In a good way I hasten to add.

We eat in silence. Slowly at first, then speed up when we both realise that what is going down is staying down.

'Crumbs, I needed that.' I wipe the back of my hand over my mouth and take a good gulp of coffee. I still feel pretty ropey, but human ropey rather than zombie ropey.

'Heard from Queen Coral?'

'Nope.' I shake my head. 'I've decided I'm going to forget her and enjoy my break! Now come on, tell me about your bloody wedding plans. I can't believe we didn't get chance to talk about them last night!'

'It's all so totally amazing.' She's hugging her mug of coffee and has that dreamy look in her eye. 'And,' she really is glowing now, 'we're getting our dream house! His parents and mine clubbed together to give us money towards the down payment on this new house on the Laidlaw estate. Oh, gosh, Jane, you should see the plans, it's going to be amazing!'

The Laidlaw estate is one of those posh, gated-community places. The type with security cameras and gardeners. 'Wow! That's fabulous.' If it had been anybody else I'd have worried that their motivations for marrying Michael were suspect, but Rachel is doing it for love. I know she is. And, actually, her parents are better off than his anyway.

'It's got four bedrooms!'

I am speechless. Four bedrooms means it's a family house, she must be expecting twins or triplets or something. 'Impressive, you'll be well set up for a family.' How do I say this? 'If you're, er, planning on starting one, like soon?'

Her face falls slightly, which makes me wish I'd never asked. 'I'd love to, but Michael says it's for the future, he doesn't want to rush things. He says we're too young and he's not ready for the huge responsibility, he wants it to be just the two of us for a while. Isn't that nice?'

'Ace.' I have to stop thinking negative thoughts, but there are two rocketing round in my head. First, Michael doesn't want responsibility and secondly at least if there's no baby and it all goes wrong ... which it won't. Of course, it won't.

'I'll bring the plans next time we meet up, if you'd like to see them that is? I get to pick my own kitchen, and everything.'

'Of course, I want to see your house! So what kind of kitchen?'

Picking out electric appliances isn't really on any wish list of mine but each to their own.

'It's so difficult to choose, but Michael is great. He's got this image in his head already. I wasn't sure about the whole minimalist thing, but he's persuaded me. It's timeless, you know.'

Sexploits aside, this is just one of the things that's always made me wary about Michael. He persuades Rachel to do stuff and he's gradually taken away her ability to decide what she really wants. I know relationships are all about compromise, but it always seems to be her that is always giving way. A bit like the toxic relationship I have with Coral, but that's called boss and employee. It's acceptable, even if it's not very nice. And it's a stepping stone, I'll be moving on when the time is right. But the time to move on from your marriage is never supposed to be right, is it? Gaining two years of experience before quitting for a new challenge isn't exactly de rigueur, it's not the done thing at all.

'You don't fancy something with character, you know, a bit different?'

'Well, I did see some nice stuff, but he's right, we've got to go with the house, what will work.'

'Great, can't wait to see it!'

'He's been ace over the wedding plans as well, I don't know how we'd have done it without his ideas, and he's so busy at work as well.'

'Fab!' The niggle in the pit of my stomach grows. Why does

this all feel like it's all about Michael and what he wants? 'What have you decided on, where are you getting married?' I just know she's either going to name the poshest restaurant in town, or the small estate with the Jacobean hall on the outskirts. She's lusted after both places since she was sixteen. Our dream wedding locations. Well, apart from a Caribbean island, but I'm not sure that's Michael's bag. He's the type that broils in the sun.

'Well, we were going to have a big marquee at my parents' house. They've got a massive lawn so we could invite all our really good friends. But then when we started to make a proper list we ended up with a hundred and fifty!'

'Wow!' This could become my new, most overused word. Rachel has always dreamt of a small and cosy wedding, saying her vows surrounded by just her nearest and dearest. But one hundred and fifty people and a manicured lawn on the outskirts of Windsor? That is some leap.

'So then,' there is a dramatic pause, 'Michael said he wants to show me off, and we can't not invite everybody, isn't he sweet? So, guess what?'

'What?' I daren't guess, it might get me in trouble.

'We booked Startford Castle!'

I'm confused. '*The* Startford Castle? But that's, like, where, it's like where celebs go.' This was so not what we'd always talked about. This was the totally over the top type of wedding venue we'd taken the piss about.

I stare at Rachel. It's like she's morphing before my eyes into the type of girl we used to laugh about.

'Well, it is my wedding.' I detect a trace of huffiness in

Rachel's tone. 'And like Michael said, I'm only going to do it once, and as Sal said, everybody will be watching and tweeting about it.'

I'm about to say, 'they will?' But I bite it back.

'Stuff Sal for a minute, stuff everybody else. This is your wedding, Rach. It's your day, the one *you* will remember. No offence, but nobody else who sees it on social media will give a damn a few weeks later.'

'Tell it like it is!'

She is so not happy with me. I reach out, touch her hand and hope that the contact will show her that I mean well, that I want it to be right for her. That I'm saying this for all the right reasons. 'I will! Sorry, but it's what *you* want that's important, Rach.'

'This is what I want, Jane. I thought you'd be happy for me!' She is frowning. 'I know you hate weddings.'

'Oh, for God's sake, I don't—'

'But I thought as my best friend you'd be able to put that to one side rather than just picking fault with everything.'

'I'm not picking fault.'

'You are! Look, I'm really sorry about what happened, you know I am. I thought you'd want to be involved. But if you can't handle it and you don't want to be here then just say the word.'

I can feel hot tears prickling in my eyes. 'Rach, I do want to help you plan your wedding, honest, I'm so happy for you.' I look her in the eye, hers are glistening, and I know mine are, too. 'Maybe I'm not completely over things.' I gulp, and blink to clear my vision. 'And it is bringing it all back, but

I'm so happy for you, really. I'm not anti-marriage, I'm not. Not for you.' Her fingers tighten around mine. 'I'm sorry, I didn't mean to criticise. Honest, say you believe me?'

She nods. 'I am sorry about what happened to you.'

'I know you are, you saved my life after. You're my best friend.' No way can I spill my Michael-doubts now. There is no way she'd believe me, she'd just think I was trying to cause trouble between them. I try to steer us back onto safe ground. 'It's just it's so different from what I thought you'd do, it's so,' I struggle for a word, 'big?'

Rachel grins, her normal good humour restored. 'I know, it's amazing isn't it?'

'Totes.' What else can I say? If that's what she really wants, then it is amazing. I could have said lots of other words though, I'm not usually a 'totes' kind of person, but my brain has frozen. 'But you are sure this is what you want and how you want to do it, Rach?' I try and ignore the way her smile has slipped slightly again. 'I mean, you always said you wanted to get married at a quiet little spot with just a few people ...' See, I'm my own worst enemy, the second we get back onto solid ground, I shake the tree again. Luckily, Rachel isn't taking me too seriously.

'Oh, God, that was when we were kids, Jane. This is now, this is real! Anyway, his mum talked to mine, then they insisted we should go the whole hog! Oh, Jane, you should see what the wedding planner came up, you've never seen anything like it, it's going to be amazing.' All I can think of is His and Her Beckham-style thrones, a million white doves and my bestie standing in the middle of it in the biggest meringue dress you've ever seen. With a tiara. I feel queasy again. 'I'm so lucky!'

'He's the lucky one, getting a girl like you!'

'Aww, thank you.'

We have a hug.

'To be honest, we've not actually arranged that much yet, so I wanted to ask a massive favour ...'

She pauses. I wait. The silence lengthens. It's getting awkward.

Then I realise she's waiting to be cued in.

'Ask away!' I am going to have to make up for my bad thoughts about the groom to be, I am going to throw myself wholeheartedly into helping my best friend arrange her wedding. I am, I am, I am!

'Will you sort my hen party with Beth?'

Oh, shit. The hen party. The scene of my humiliation, the event I made a complete spectacle of myself at. If I never had to go to another hen party in my life I'd be happy.

Except I do have to. I'm Rachel's best friend. I have vowed to throw myself into this in every way possible.

She's waiting, so I nod and smile in what I hope isn't a sickly way. 'Of course.' It comes out croaky, so I try again. 'With Beth?'

'Yes, Beth! I mean you know me so well, but I didn't want to force the whole thing on you, 'cos I know how busy you are, and she pointed out she's got lots of free time and she's ace at organising stuff.'

This is code for what we both know – I am not a planner by nature. I wing it.

'Beth?' I get the 'somebody else doing it', but not the Beth bit. As in, the Beth with the baby so she can't be a bridesmaid bit.

'Well, she really, really wanted to. She said like, as she couldn't be a bridesmaid she wanted to do something, you know, be involved. So she asked if she could do this. That is okay is it? I mean I know you're my bridesmaid and ...'

At least with Beth involved this will be nothing like my hen party, it will be totally alternative if I know her. This is good.

'It's more than okay. Beth's cool, she will do a way more awesome job than I would.' I pause. 'But what about the baby? I thought that's why she couldn't ...'

'Well, like she said, she can do this at home, or online, it's her kind of wedding present to us she said. Isn't that sweet?'

'Er, yes.' Beth could never be described as sweet. But she has, as they say, got her shit together. Even if she doesn't look like she has. Although, God knows how the baby happened. The shit without the together.

'She's going to come to the fitting, just to like ...'

'Tell us how pretty we look in pink?'

'Sod off.' Rach flicks the froth off her cappuccino in my direction. This place never did cappuccino last time I came, wow how it's changed. 'Beth's our guest of honour.'

It is beginning to dawn on me though why Beth passed on the bridesmaid role. She is *so* not pink, flouncy, or slinky in satin. She's more black leather and Doc Martens.

She is a laugh though, and if Rach tries to swaddle us in

anything 'icky, then if anyone can save us it will be Beth. With her potty mouth. And truth.

I sometimes wish I was more like Beth. Willing to say what I think, and to hell with the consequences, 'cos, you know it will work out for the best.

The clock on the wall suddenly catches my eye. Bloody hell, talking about swaddling. 'Look at the time!' That's the thing with wedding planning, all of a sudden your whole life is controlled by the clock, driven by dates on the calendar. You're caught on this treadmill of 'stuff that has to be done'. That might explain why when mine stopped I felt like life had lost all purpose.

That, and the fact I was no longer going to be a wife, potential mother, and house owner. I'd been about to take that giant leap into a new future and fallen flat on my face. My feet had been taken from under me and I'd floundered.

After I'd unpicked all the planning that had been in place.

'Sugar,' Rach downs the rest of her coffee. 'We're going to be late. Come on, come on. Oh, God, Debs will kill me!'

Debs, it turns out, owns the bridal shop. I know this because above the window it says 'Deb's Divine Dresses'. I expected something slightly different from a posh designer frock shop. I don't know quite what, maybe Esmeralda's Emporium, or Beatrice's Bridal Gowns. Know what I mean? Anyway, Debs is at the door, and she is as lovely as Rachel said.

'Come in, come in my lovely. The other girls are here, I let them try on one of those dresses you've been looking at while they were waiting. Hope you don't mind? And I've opened the bubbly, we're all set for some fun!'

I'm not sure I'm up to 'fun', but when the bubbles hit my nostrils I don't feel nauseous, which is a definite improvement on how I felt two hours ago.

Then I try the dress on.

Chapter 16

We are the walking dead. 'We look like a flock of Miss Havisham's on a bad day, though I think every day was bad for her.' I am definitely the winner in the looks-closest-to-a-zombie stakes.

There is nothing wrong with the dresses. The dresses are gorgeous. Beautiful figure-hugging satin sheaths that any bridesmaid would be thrilled to wear. But, right now, we are the problem. What was definitely a wonderful shade of ivory on the clothes hanger, is beige when it is draped over three pasty faced bridesmaids to be. On a good day, in the sun, we might look okay. Today, not so.

We need colour.

We are staring at our image in the vast wall to ceiling mirrors. You can't not stare at yourself, there is no escape, they are everywhere. As are the bright lights.

Want to see how big your bum looks? Sorted! Want to see if you really look as green round the gills as your mother said in a slightly pointed tone as she tried to force cornflakes down your throat and you tried to refuse without needing to rush off and be sick? No probs.

'I think we're more Addams Family actually.' Maddie catches my eye and giggles. If we'd not all had the hangovers from hell we'd be laughing our heads off. Though, saying that, if we hadn't got hangovers we'd look a hell of a sight better.

'*Shh!*' Rachel, who is looking remarkably perky after her fry up compared to the rest of us, giggles.

'You lot are going to have a whale of a time at the wedding!' Debs is grinning at us, as she passes out glasses of bubbly. 'Now, come on, gorgeous Rachel, let's show this lot what a bride really looks like!'

Rach is ushered away, and we go back to studying our reflection.

Pale, wan and interesting does not say 'wedding', does it? Even if we are dressed in the 'pastel soft tones to create the perfect dreamy backdrop'.

We don't need ombre hues, we need a solid skin tone that will reflect in our faces and make us look human again.

The bridal shop is dazzlingly bright and white. We are all stood like rabbits in the headlights, eyeing up the complimentary chocolates as though we're expecting them to attack.

'How about these wonderful forest shades? They're so natural.' Debs has reappeared and is stroking a floaty dress that should say nymphs and woodland glen but is currently shouting out Appletini. Which is something I don't want to think about right now.

It is making me feel queasy. Well, queasier.

'Not green. Please not green, not today.' Normally, green looks good on me. Today, it will merge in with my skin tone.

'Who's Miss Havisham?' Maddie is frowning.

'Some old sad spinster that Charles Dickens invented,' says Sal, and Maddie raises an eyebrow. 'English lit, remember?' I don't think she does, she wasn't hot on lesson attendance. Well, she attended, but she didn't really concentrate. She wrote love letters to Jack and practised her married-name signature. Which at the time seemed a way better use of her time, maybe in hindsight not so much.

'Oh, God, I remember!' That surprises me. 'It was so romantic, and so sad. She was jilted and wore her wedding dress every day after that. And left the wedding breakfast and cake on the table.'

'Stupid idea. It would have gone mouldy.' Snarky Sal is back. 'Cake doesn't keep that long, does it?'

'Maybe that's what I should have done with mine.'

They all stare at me, shocked.

We don't generally talk about 'the wedding that never was'.

Even I stare at my reflection and am happy to see it is smiling back. The smile gets bigger as I look. I feel shit, but I feel strangely good about myself as well. In a mental, not physical way.

This isn't as bad as I thought it would be. I am standing in a bridal shop, trying on dresses and I feel okay. Not about to burst into messy tears or feel the need to stick my head down the toilet. This is a good sign, I am going to be able to cope with the whole wedding thing, even if I'm still not so sure she's picked the right groom. Minor point.

'It was a real ball ache trying to work out what to do with three tiers of fruit cake.'

'I thought it was four?' Rachel shouts from the part of the room that's been curtained off.

'I smeared one all over his windscreen, remember? But I hadn't got the energy to do another. It's bloody hard work crushing fruit cake, all gritty and fruity and blobby. Sponge would have been a damned sight easier.'

'Or cupcakes?' Maddie is grinning mischievously. She's got a sense of humour that I've never detected before. 'Think of all that buttercream you could have shoved in his wiper blades and down every hole!'

'I like that, I like it very much!'

'What did you do with the dress?' Sally is pressing a peach creation (which rather unfortunately reminds me of a cocktail I had last night) against her body.

'The shop sold it for me.' I shrug. 'I suppose I could have shortened it and done a Miss H.'

'She went the full monty, wore hers in all its glory.' Says Maddie.

'It must have smelled, nobody mentions washing it, do they? They don't wash well, do they? Designed to be a one-off wear, no wash label included.'

'*Eugh*. She didn't wash it, was she mad?' Sally is juggling her boobs about in her dress and tweaking it at the sides to see what it would look like if holding her breath was a normal state of play. Maybe it is for her, maybe she has the type of self-control that will sort stuff like that. Me? I'd rather rely on a corset, and the brute force required to lace it up tightly enough.

'Yep, totally doo-lally. Spurned, heartbroken, bitter and revengeful. Bit like me.'

They all laugh.

'You had a lucky escape, Andy was a twat.' We all stare at Sal.

'He turned her down.' Whispers Maddie in my ear.

'Ahh, makes sense. A woman scorned and all that.' I whisper back.

'At least he had impeccable taste, even if he was a bit of an idiot.' She hugs me, and Sal eyes us up suspiciously.

'I was not scorned!' She gives Maddie the evil eye. 'You're just being spiteful. A woman scorned, ha, it's you that—'

'Don't, please.' Oh, Lordie, I'm not expected to be barrier like today, am I? You must be kidding, hungover and tired. I'd sink down on my knees and beg Sal not to be nasty, but I don't think Debs would like it. Even though the carpet is pristine.

'Well, bugger me, if it's not the three wise monkeys!'

'What?' We all spin round, and nearly tumble – slinky satin dresses were not designed to spiral.

'See no evil, hear no evil, speak no evil!' Beth cackles.

'Beth!' I find my voice.

'Beth! Beth, you've got the baby!' Maddie is second to recover.

Sal just shoots daggers.

Beth is grey around the edges, with dark shadows under her eyes that are two shades worse than mine. And a face white enough to match the towel slung over her shoulder.

'Beth, Beth! Hiya! Isn't it exciting!' Rachel has stuck her head round the curtain and is waving madly. Then stops. 'You've brought the baby!'

'Oh, what a darling!' Debs manages to shimmy past and drape a cover over the chaise longue diplomatically and is back with Rachel without missing a beat. 'What's he called?'

'Joe.' Beth smiles. 'Sorry, guys, had to bring him. The sitter ran away 'cos he keeps puking.' Beth slumps down on the plush chaise longue and grabs a glass of fizz, baby attached to her in a sling thing. 'Which is what I'd like to do, if I had the bloody time. I'm telling you girls, God made you knackered after birth for a reason. It was so you didn't have the time or the energy to go out and get shit-faced. I need a caffeine drip.' She waves a hand randomly, blowing air kisses. 'Loving the frocks, ladies!'

I am wobbly, hungover, and was sucking up caffeine like it is was a life-support system not long ago, but Beth makes me look like I've stepped off a catwalk.

'Oh my God, enough about me,' she stops her air-kissing and studies me, 'you still really rock the casual look though, Janey babe!' She gives me the thumbs up. 'I could never pull off that just out of bed look, though you've got the perfect hair for it! Hasn't she Rach? The bed-head hair babe.' She laughs again, so much that the baby whimpers, so she stops abruptly.

I want to thump her – and hug her at the same time. It's always been like that with Beth. She doesn't always give people the best first impression, but underneath it she's lovely.

'I can't believe it's so long since we all got together, and you two are still like this.' She points at me and Rachel and crosses her fingers. 'I was dead jealous when we were at school.'

'You weren't?' I really can't believe that at all, Beth is not the jealous type.

'Oh, yeah, sure I was. I never had a bestie like you two.'

'Oh, I don't know.' Sally is sounding spiky. 'We were one big group, weren't we? And,' she stares at me, 'some of us have drifted apart now, haven't you?'

'Not really.' I stare back. 'You don't have to be in each other pockets,' or weddings I could add, 'to stay friends.'

'You were part of the gang, Beth.' Rachel adds.

'You were more a part of the gang than me.' I say.

Beth shrugs. 'I know, but it wasn't quite the same. All those adventures you two used to have in the old days.' She grins at me, but it looks strained. 'The way you led her astray!'

'I did not. You were the one who led us all astray!'

'Mebbe.' She rubs her baby, who is making mewling noises, on the back. 'God, look at us now though. Well, look at me!'

We are all looking.

'Oh, God, the secrets I could tell!' She laughs, then it dies as quickly as it appears, and is replaced by a look that's a mixture of angry and sad. 'Kidding. No secrets, just me being stupid enough to believe some stupid jerk would stick around for more than one poke.'

'One?' I stare at her, slightly shocked.

'By the time I'd pulled up my knickers, he was talking about his ex.'

'Oh, shit.' I put my hand over my mouth.

Beth shrugs, and squeezes her baby a bit more tightly. 'It's fine, and I got Joe, the best thing that ever happened to me.' Our gazes lock for a second over the downy baby-head. In those few seconds, I can see she loves him to bits, but she's hurt, angry as well. And who can blame her?

'Oh, Beth.' Maddie rushes round the back of the seat, so she can lean over and hug her. 'Men can be such bastards, can't they?' Then she goes beetroot red as she remembers where we are. And why. 'Sugar, I didn't mean … well, I mean, some men,' she's flapping her hands and spinning round. 'I mean some men are fantastic, they're—'

'Shit, fuck, buggering …' We don't get to find out what the fantastic men are, as the darling baby has just projectile vomited right in Beth's eye, over her shoulder and all over the carpet at Maddie's feet.

Maddie squeaks and shoots backwards, topples over an unfortunately placed pouffe that is acting as a coffee table displaying bridal magazines, and lands on her back.

There's the tiniest of sounds, that might have been ripping, of the gossamer, ethereal creation that she's currently wearing.

'Wow, that is bloody impressive. Who knew such a small creature could control such a stream of regurgitated milk? Respect.' I high-five Beth, Joe splutters. 'Oh my God, I've got vom in my eye!' I flap my hands, smear the stuff further into my eye. 'Shit, I'm going blind.' I mop my eyes, realise I'm doing it with the hem of a satin dress, shriek, close my eyes, stumble back, and trip over Mads' ankles.

'Well, I'm sure he didn't do it on purpose, little cutie pie!' Trust Sal to side with the baby. She's gliding across, all coo-ey and concerned. Impossible to ignore.

'Hell, sorry, Mads, sorry Jane.' Beth leaps to her feet, and baby Joe, with a new target in sight treats us to a spectacular finale. At least I hope it's a finale.

We all stare at Sal. He's managed to hit her right between the boobs. We watch as it trickles down, pools in her cleavage.

There is a deathly hush. Broken by, '*Ta-dah!*'

Rachel leaps out from behind the curtain, a vision in white satin and lace. 'What do you th—'

She freezes.

Joe dribbles, then smiles. The widest most genuine smile in the world and I can't help it. I giggle. Maddie looks at me and starts. Beth puts her hand over her mouth, but then starts to snigger, and snort. Sal is still staring down her front, aghast.

Which makes it even funnier. Nothing like getting your just desserts. Or in this case, Joe's.

'Oops! I guess I shouldn't have jumped up like that and jolted him.'

'I guess not.' The venom drips off Sal's words in a pretty blood-curdling way.

'Oh my God, let me hold him!' Rachel, oblivious to the vom-soaked Sally has her arms outstretched.

'No!' An alarmed Beth, clutches Joe tighter to her chest and he starts up a wail that could compete with a pack of baying wolves. 'The sick! Your dress, you don't want, you can't ...' She's backing away as she speaks, the chaise longue gets the back of her knees and her and Joe collapse in a heap.

'But I just—'

Rach is interrupted by Darth Vader. Which from the look on Beth's face is a good job. I've never seen her panic like that before.

I scrabble to my knees, and slither across the cream carpet towards the very cute and very expensive looking chair.

'Don't touch my French Louis XV chair!!'

The screech reaches me, just as I put a slightly sticky hand out. It misses the chair, makes contact with my handbag – which I pull down.

Lovely Debs groans with relief and sinks onto the carpet.

'I need Bristol!' Coral's words echo into the silence, as I've accidentally put her on speakerphone.

'Bristol?'

'It's so fucking authentic. Get me a shot of that seagull with those limited edition Doc Martens I gave you.'

'Oh, you mean Brighton.'

'Bristol, Brighton, whatever. How the fuck am I supposed to know? New York is so overdone, it's like pissing in a hail-storm getting noticed here.'

'But—'

'What is it with you and your fucking buts? Just get off yours and earn your keep.'

'I'm on holi—'

'Just do it. Gotta go.'

I flop back on the rather comfortable carpet and stare at the fake regency ceiling.

'I thought you said she was thinking of staying out there?'

I tilt my head, so I can see Rach. 'Sounds like the love affair is over.' I smile. 'Cool dress, you look ace by the way.'

'I do?'

'You do!' We say it together, all four of us. Three bridesmaids and one puke-covered guest of honour. Finally, all singing from the same hymn sheet.

'Really, Rach.' I soften my tone and stare at her. 'You're the most gorgeous bride I've ever seen. Michael will be blown away.' There's a lump in my throat. This had been me, not so long ago. I had the most gorgeous dress in the world, a dress that pulled me in in the right places and showed off a figure I didn't know I had. A dress that was supposed to blow Andy away, at the wedding that never happened. My bridesmaids had all been excited for me, and we'd celebrated with bubbly as I twirled and spun my way round the shop in impossibly beautiful shoes, with my hair piled up on top of my head.

I can't ruin Rachel's wedding, and I can't let anybody else. I have to make this the best day of her life. Michael's secret is safe with me.

'You look amazing.' She does, and this is all about her from now on, not me.

I can feel the tears well up in my eyes, but I daren't wipe them away due to the risk of baby vom. So, I have to let them brim over.

Joe belches, and the moment is spoiled. It was nice while it lasted though.

Chapter 17

'Freddie? Freddie! You've not seen my red Converse, have you?' As normal, I'm late. This is because I had another 'urgent' call from Coral. Her calls are always urgent, and I have been known to put my foot down when they're really not, but this was something that I could handle.

She's just received a new handbag from an on-trend designer who is destined for BIG things. This is a scoop, and her photo *has* to be up before anybody else's.

It just has to.

The hashtag will go viral, and she'll be back to queening it over Daniel and his dog.

I'll also be queening it. I've been thinking about what Freddie said when we were in Brighton, and realised he was right. I might not yet be ready to cut the shackles, but I am ready to start chipping away at them. So, I'd folded my arms the other day and faced up to her. I wanted my tag on the photos.

I've been building a portfolio up while I've been working with her, but have no followers of my own, and after the New York fiasco (when she had to bin a whole load of Crystal's snaps, ha) I felt it was now or never.

I might not be ready to break free from her yet, but I am going to have a plan. I'm going to start digging the tunnel, metaphorically of course. Along with chipping at the chain.

As Freddie said, she actually needs me more than I need her right now, and if I'm going to put up with the shit, then I might as well put some of it on my roses. I think he got a bit confused, but he means well. So, anyhow, we agreed that just as Rach's wedding is all about her, and nothing to do with my disaster, my photographic career is all about me and nothing to do with Andy thinking of it as a hobby.

Freddie has told me that no way should I waste any opportunity to make my dream come true. That I need to have a game plan (he likes a game plan – after all, he does write computer games and he knows exactly how they're supposed to turn out) and be the kick-ass version of myself that I used to be.

He's right. Andy dissing my work, then dissing me, did kind of leave me wondering if it was all a pipe dream, but Freddie believes in me. He also pointed out that all my friends do, too, that it's not just Rach, but also Maddie and Beth, and (begrudgingly) Sally who like my pics. And if Coral says yes to my demands then that proves something, too.

She said, yes.

Woohoo!

So, I got my tag. Tiny but hey, the grand masters only had a mini signature in the bottom of their masterpieces, didn't they?

There is no answer from Freddie, so I start to grab T-shirts and jeans. Then it happens. My T-shirt moves. Without my assistance.

Oh. My. God. We've either got a poltergeist or a rat.

More likely a rat. In our beautiful bijoux apartment.

It moves again. Sugar.

The important thing is not to panic. Or scream. Stay calm. Get a long stick and poke it out.

I scream and jump on a stool.

'What the hell, Jane, are you okay?' Freddie is standing slightly breathless in the doorway. I give him a sideways glance but keep most of my attention on the drawer.

What if it gets out? Makes a run for it? It could end up anywhere.

'Shut the drawer, shut the drawer!'

'What?'

'Quickly! And get a stick!'

'A stick, why?' He hasn't moved.

'To poke it with! Get the broom or something. There's a rat or something, look, look,' I point so wildly I nearly lose my balance. 'There's something, there's something, something moved! It's alive, in my drawer.' I'm waving like a loony, my heart is pounding so hard I need to sit down.

Freddie edges towards the drawers. Sideways. Brave, but not full on.

'No forget the stick, just shut the flaming drawer. Poking it might make it angry, it might leap at me. Rats can leap, can't they?'

'Guess so.'

'But grab that blue top first, that one, with the stripes. There!'

He looks. Then grins. Then chuckles.

'Don't laugh, do something!'

Then, he belly-laughs, which makes me kind of want to laugh, except it's not funny.

'Freddie!'

'You silly bugger!' He fishes in the drawer then holds something up triumphantly. It's not very rat-like, but it is furry. Ginger and furry. 'It's a kitten! I wondered where he'd gone.'

'What the frig is a kitten doing in my undies?'

'He's a surprise.'

'A surprise.' I step down off the chair, and peer into the drawer, to double check there isn't a rat in there as well. 'I could have killed him!' I shout, and the little thing flinches. 'What if I'd battered him? Oh my God!'

'He was in my room.' Freddie looks downcast. 'I thought the door was shut, I was sure ...' His voice tails off.

I gaze up at the very interesting ceiling. 'Oh, er, I might have,' cough, 'opened it, popped in to borrow your mirror.' Freddie has the only full-length mirror in the flat, and he doesn't normally mind if I pop in and use it. Though, I do normally ask. Because of course that's his private room, and we don't wander in and out of each other's bedrooms. That would be weird. 'Sorry.'

'I should have left him in the basket.'

'No, no, it is your room. I shouldn't ...'

'I thought you needed cheering up. If you don't want him, I will. Or we can share.'

'He is cute.' I stroke his tiny head and he opens his mouth in a silent mewl.

'What shall we call him?' Freddie is grinning, he knows he's got me.

'You're being serious here?'

'I am. Totally.'

I think for a moment, remember what this little kitten was like when I was trying to take a photo of him and his gang. The way he danced across the floor, flung himself up the blinds.

'I've got it!' I grin triumphantly. 'Louie!'

'Louis?' Freddie looks at me warily. 'Like St Louis?'

'No.' I punch his arm lightly and lean in closer so I can touch the tiny paws. 'Like Louie Spence.'

''Cos of his dance moves?'

'You got it!' Little Louie stares at me, all wide-eyed and innocent. His little tongue is sticking out, I think he forgot to put it in.

'He's so adorable, I could eat ...' I glance up at Freddie and suddenly realise we're practically in a clinch.

He's staring at me, not the kitten. And it's just like that moment in Brighton when our gazes met, then we both decided the sand was more interesting.

Except this time there is no sand. And he doesn't look away. Nor do I.

We both stare. And I can feel the heat bubbling up inside of me.

He kisses me.

For a moment I'm stunned. But his mouth is so warm, his lips so gentle against mine it makes me want more. I want to taste him. Touch him.

The kitten is nestled between us, but his other hand is on my arm, and the warmth sends a shiver down my spine.

He blinks. 'He's not the only adorable one.' His voice is hoarse. Then he takes a tiny step back and holds Louie up between us. 'Sorry. Sorry, really sorry. I shouldn't have ...'

'We shouldn't, we can't ...' I take the kitten, I can't not. I swallow hard. We shouldn't. We really shouldn't. Freddie is my friend.

'No.' His voice is low, flat. 'Sorry.'

'Freddie, I didn't mean, it's not that I don't want ...' But Freddie is gone, striding off to his own room, leaving his name lingering in the air behind him. I know I said it quietly, so quietly maybe I didn't want him to hear. I'm not sure.

The gentle click of his door closing echoes around the flat.

For a moment I stare at the kitten. Then I carefully put him down and carry on dressing, in a daze.

I touch my lips. The spot he kissed still feels the same, still normal. But inside my heart is hammering and everything feels out of kilter.

He kissed me. Properly. Like full on lips and a hint of tongue.

Oh, hell, we snogged! That wasn't supposed to happen, ever.

Have we cocked everything up?

Or, and this is a massive 'or', because inside I'm feeling all the fuzz and tingles that I can't remember ever feeling with Andy. Is it true that my fiancé never was the one? That I had a lucky escape. That *this* is what it feels like to find 'the one'.

Except, he's just run away, and he's sorry he ever did it. And I'm sorry. And, shit, I told him we shouldn't.

Is everything going to go wrong now?

I sit on the edge of the bed, and help Louie clamber up the cover until he reaches the summit. My knee.

His spiky tail is ramrod straight, and his eyes the bluest imaginable.

'Miaow.'

'Is this how Rach feels when she kisses Michael? Is this why,' I pick him up, tickle his velvet-soft tummy, 'people do the daftest things?'

Louie doesn't answer. He just purrs. Incredibly loudly, so that it shudders through his whole body.

'Oh, God, Louie, what am I doing? What if this changes everything? No, no I'm being stupid. It was one little kiss. It will change nothing.' I need to keep my fingers crossed on that one. More like I need to keep my legs crossed, because if he kisses me again I might just make the biggest mistake of my entire life.

Who in their right mind would risk losing their best friend, their home, the person who believes in them, their sounding board? The man who is bloody perfect in every way. Except for not wanting to commit to a relationship because they've already met and lost their true love.

I smack my forehead.

Right now, I'd be tempted.

I'm confused.

Chapter 18

'It looks, a bit, er, green.' I gulp as I frantically rub away at Rachel's scalp working up enough lather to wash a whale.

I rinse it off. It looks worse. My beautiful blonde bombshell of a girlfriend is now more Hulk than princess.

'Ouch.'

'Sorry.' I'm getting a bit frantic now, scrubbing away like my life depends on it. And it might. 'Conditioner, we need conditioner.'

God knows why I think conditioner would make any difference at all. Her hair is still green, but it's now green slime. Ever seen a seaweed-covered slipway? Well, you're getting there.

I'd thought this was a good idea. Me, her, a bottle or three of bubbly and some girlie pampering the week before the hen party.

We could bond, I could make up for all the nasty thoughts I'd had about Michael, and all the negative things I'd said about the venue. I could make sure everything was going to be perfect.

I might have been mistaken.

Especially on the perfect front.

'I'm sure it can't be that bad.'

'Worse. Do NOT look.' Bugger. I wrap it in a towel and wonder if my hairdresser takes emergency calls at this time on a Thursday evening, or if she'll be up to her eyebrows in vodka shots.

'How is mine looking?' I've got my head down, and water in my ears and eyes, and I reckon from the way Rach is kneading my scalp with her fingernails that we're going to be even-stevens on this one. Ish.

'You know you were after coppery highlights? A hint of spice?' Rachel is going at it so hard I think she's dislocated my neck.

'You might need to think more orange.'

'Orange?'

'Turmeric rather than paprika.'

I'm no culinary expert, but I get the gist.

'Brass rather than copper.'

'Brassy?'

'Definitely brassy. Where the hell did you get this stuff from?'

I'm not sure brassy is the bridesmaid look she's after. Though I'm not sure sprout is the bridal look either.

'Shit.'

'Exactly.' Rachel is surprisingly calm given we are now alarmingly close to D, or rather W-day. Although this could be shock. I reckon seeing her reflection will shake her out of it.

I thrash about, desperate to see, and she resists. Then eventually gives in.

She sheds her towel. We stare into the bathroom mirror, side by side.

Honeyed highlights, and hot paprika we are not. More you've been slimed and I've been tangoed.

'Fuck, Michael will kill me.'

'Well, it will be a day to remember.' I say in all seriousness.

'After all you only do it once.' She adds.

I glance sideways at her, and her face is straight. For some reason, this is too funny not to laugh at. My mouth twitches. Her nostrils flare, which means she's trying hard not to laugh.

Two glasses of bubbly and hysterical tears later, I manage to stop laughing for long enough to ring Lucy, my hairdresser.

'Give me fifteen minutes!' This surprises me. Lucy has always seemed to be the 'drink until you drop' type.

'What the hell?' Lucy picks up the face mask. The next task on my list. If it hadn't been for the highlighting disaster we'd be all charcoaled up by now. 'You weren't going to use these?'

'Weren't? Of course we are, saying goodbye to blackheads and massive pores forever.' Word perfect on the blurb on the packet. Me and Rach high-five each other. We've got through rather a lot of Prosecco while we've been waiting. Stress drinking.

'No way, ladies. If you think your hair is bad, you wait and see what this can do to your faces!'

We blink at her, owl style.

'Sit.' She points at the stool and I push Rachel forward first. Her need is greater than mine.

We never do get our hands on the face masks. There is a

lot of tutting and eye-rolling, but Lucy's expert hands have soon reverted Rachel from ocean floor mermaid back to siren, and I'm still a bit orange, but more flame and less satsuma.

She's also plastered us in a home-made face mask, after whizzing home to get a cucumber. Like you do. Got one handy? She'd asked ... as though I should have. Doesn't every girl, said Rach, with a wink.

'Both of you pop in the salon on Monday and I'll finish the job. Providing yours hasn't all snapped off.' She pats my head, which I suppose is to lighten the blow.

'I so need this.' Rachel takes a long swig of bubbly, then leans back against the pillows with a sigh. 'Thanks Jane, this was such a nice idea.'

'Even if turned out to be a disaster?'

'Well, at least we didn't put the face masks on.'

I wrinkle my nose and feel my face crack. 'This one's bad enough. I think I've set.'

She giggles and squeezes my hand. 'It is so nice to get away from everything, you can't believe the amount of stuff we've had to sort. Good job Freddie's not here to see us like this!'

'True.'

'Where is he by the way?'

I screw up my face and try to look nonchalant. 'No idea, out with mates?' The thing is, I really do have no idea. Yeah, we are free agents, but we tend to shout out where we're going and when we'll be back. But since kiss-gate there's been an air of embarrassment. An awkwardness. I want to kill it, but I don't know how.

It's making me feel all queasy in the base of my stomach.

At this rate I'll be losing both my best friends before the month is out.

I don't think hanging on to his trouser leg as he drags me to the door and begging him not to leave me is going to work though.

'You normally know where he is.' She's giving me a funny look.

'Not any more.' I sigh. Well, if I want to make sure we're as close again as we ever were, sharing is caring. 'He kissed me. We kissed.'

'Shit! Really?' Her hand flies over her mouth. 'Kissed, like proper kiss? Snog?' I nod. 'Tongues?' I cringe. 'And it was shit?'

I shake my head. 'It was awesome.' Then I burst into noisy tears. It's the drink speaking, that and the fact we're getting all emo about the big day approaching. Honest.

'Wow.' She wraps her arms round me, and the hug makes the tears fall faster.

'But,' I hiccup through my tears, 'he's my friend, I don't want to mess that up.'

'You can still be friends, Jane, but better. Michael's my best friend, the best one in the world, apart from you of course.'

'But I'm not the right girl!'

'But you don't know ...'

'No girl matches the one Freddie fell for ages ago. That's why he doesn't date seriously. Nobody else is good enough.'

'He told you that?'

I nod. Then wipe snotty tears from my face. 'In Brighton. If I fall for Freddie I'll lose everything.'

'Oh, don't be sil—'

'I won't have anywhere to live again, and I won't have him as a friend, and I'll never ever get married.'

'Oh, Jane.' Rach hugs me closer and kisses the top of my head. I feel mothered. 'Things will work out the way they're meant to. Honest, look at me and Michael. We've had our ups and downs, and he's been a git and a complete dick, but we're meant to be.' She pulls away a bit and looks at me. 'Freddie would never hurt you. He'd never kiss and run.'

I sniff. I want to believe her, I really do. But hasn't he just done exactly that?

ACT TWO

The Hen Party

Chapter 19

'This is a really weird way to start a hen party.' Sal's voice carries across the moor as she stalks down the path on her six-inch heels, dragging her very noisy wheelie-case behind her. Reaching us, she glances from me to Beth, then back again, before parking the suitcase, adjusting her shades, and folding her arms. 'You pair have really lost touch with Rach, haven't you? I mean if you'd asked me—'

'We didn't, because she didn't.'

'Didn't what?'

'Ask you,' says Beth, reasonably. 'She asked us.' She flashes a finger between the two of us. 'Because we're her ...' she pauses, leans in, and I don't know which is more wicked, her grin or the look in her eye, 'besties.'

I grin back, I can't help myself. I'm feeling good, and not even Sal can puncture my mood. Freddie texted me! We've been ships passing in the night for a few days and I've been torn. On the one hand, I wanted to barricade the door so he couldn't escape, hold the coffee hostage so he had to come looking for it, grab him, pin him down (for explanation, not carnal, reasons) and insist that nothing has changed.

I'm fine about the kiss, and now we can move on. Exactly as we were.

On the other hand, I've been terrified that if we do talk he'll say things have changed between us, that he's now checking every day that I've not moved his stuff in the kitchen cupboards, that none of my clothes have sneaked into his side of the flat – which is tricky, as we don't really have sides – and that quite honestly maybe I need to move out before things escalate. Or, and this would be a low blow that would send me back into the post-hen-night spiral, he'll say the kiss was crap and he doesn't know why he did it.

So, it would be better to carry on skirting round each other, and the issue.

Anyway, crisis averted! We're cool.

'*Soz I've been avoiding u, am a prat*' – I love that he is so honest – '*but not sorry about the kiss. Adorable people need to be snogged, and it was my turn. Feel free to snog me if you ever think I deserve it. Well, any time really. Movie date night on the sofa tonight? Hands free – I promise. Let's not mention this again though, for the sake of my fragile ego?*'

'Movie night if I can pick.'

'You're pushing it now! I only said I was a prat.'

'Ha! I'm still going to pick. And as the other prat, Chris Pratt, would say – I like to do Garfield Mondays.'

'Eh?'

'Can we do Monday instead of tonight, I'm at Rach's hen party this weekend.'

'So, I'm just a hangover cure?'

'Something like that.'

'*You're using and abusing me.*'

There's a long break in texts, while we both ponder the sensible answer to that. Well, at least, I do.

'*How about I pick you up from wherever it is, then you don't have to worry about a taxi the morning after?! Call it me making up.*'

'*You're a star. Here's where it's at!*' I send him the address. '*Will text a time as soon as I know, if that's okay?*'

Like I say, we're cool. Though a bit of me is disappointed that he didn't declare undying love, the need to strip me naked on the kitchen worktop, and a realisation that his previous love was now a thing of the past.

Hands free isn't great. Though he did say I could snog him if I wanted.

And hey, we're friends. That beats everything.

'*Pfffft!*' Sal is still spouting off. 'The girl is getting married in a castle, she likes nice things these days, she's ... she doesn't want her last big single-girl blow out to be a party in the park!' Sal is scowling. I reckon she's more bothered about herself than Rachel, at least I hope so. And we haven't completely cocked this up. Most of it was Beth's idea, but I threw myself behind it totally.

'Don't worry ...' Beth pauses, 'it gets worse. Promise.' She's enjoying this. 'That's why you need spare clothes. Who knows, maybe we're sleeping under the stars!'

Sal's look is replaced with one of horror. 'I am *not* sleeping in a tent. Not for anybody!'

'Not even for your best friend, who's getting married soon?'

'Sod off. This isn't what she'd expect me to do! And I've brought nice clothes, not, not ...'

'Camping clothes?'

'And don't you have a baby that needs looking after?'

'Ooh, the bitch is back. Well, for your information, Joe's not a milk-sucking leech!'

'Sorry?' Sal frowns. I hold my breath. I'd thought it was Sal and Maddie that I had to be barrier like with. Turns out it's a Sal sandwich.

'He's not stuck to my boob 24/7 you daft bint, I just ping him off now and then like this.' Beth flicks her finger off her thumb, and I cringe. 'And I did bring him, we're going to all take turns getting up in the night.'

Sal is turning a funny shade of pink. 'But he pukes!'

'Not all the time.'

Maybe I should step in, calm things down. But then again, maybe not. Sal has always been a bit cold and calculated, which is why I don't get why Jack married her. But hey, maybe it's all down to fizzy kisses that make you go all disorientated and fuzzy inside. So, I shouldn't judge on that one. But neither am I inclined to step in. Yet. Obviously if they start to roll on the grass ripping each other's hair out I might.

'Oh, my goodness, sorry, sorry. Traffic. Have I missed anything?' Maddie is standing before us, perfect matching pink trolley bag and hairband, with a nervous smile on her face.

'You have got to be kidding? You've not brought him?' Sal and Beth still have horns locked.

'Of course, I haven't! I expressed, you know ...' She makes a milking-the-cow gesture. 'Gold top all the way.'

'You've not missed anything important!' I hug Maddie, then whisper in her ear. 'Just some Beth baiting!' She giggles and relaxes a bit. When we were at school, Beth always used to say that harmony was boring, then would proceed to wind people up to the extent that somebody was bound to blow and cause a scene. In Sal, she had the perfect candidate, as she'd had a bit of a humour bypass and was so competitive she never realised that she was being teased. 'Anyway,' I go back to normal volume, 'you're not late, Rachel's not here yet, and she's bringing Michael's sister Daisy, and a mate from work called Claire.'

'Oh, good.' Maddie smiles properly for the first time. 'I like Daisy.'

'I do, too.' I do, she's sweet, nothing at all like Michael. It's hard to imagine they share the same genes.

'Hi, er, are you Rachel's friends?' I nod. 'I'm Claire, from her office.' Claire stops short of our group, nervously shifting from foot to foot, clutching her bag. I can't blame her, Beth and Sal are still squaring up, and Mads and I are huddled together watching from a safe distance.

'Oh, wow, yes! Hi!' I leap on her enthusiastically hoping her arrival might defuse things. 'I'm Jane, and this is Maddie, and that's Sal and Beth.' I point them out in turn. 'Dump your bag with the rest and give us a hand to get the rugs out if you like. Rach and Daisy should be here soon.'

I can't actually blame Sal for being a bit tetchy, when she's turned up all ready for a night in some glam location and discovers it's a rug and Domino pizza in the park night. Even Rach is a bit confused when the Deliveroo guy turns up two minutes after she does, and starts dishing out the 'Mega Night In with added extras' deal. She's side-eyeing Sal, and Beth and I are trying to keep straight faces.

'Party in the park!' I grin at Rachel. 'We thought we'd go all nostalgic.' Beth and I high-five, pleased with ourselves. 'Remember when we used to do this when we were in the sixth form?'

She nods tentatively, and it's obvious she's not entirely convinced that this is the best hen party ever.

'It was girls only, we used to pelt the lads with pizza, if they came near!' Beth adds.

'You're not telling me you've planned a pizza fight?' Sally sounds horrified, and Rach has what can only be described as a fixed smile on her face.

'Fab!' Rachel bravely tries to sound excited.

'Oh my God, I nearly forgot!' Yells Beth and reaches for her bag. 'The coup de foudre!'

'The what?' Mad frowns.

'I don't think you mean that!' For the first time, Sal shows the glimmer of a smile. 'Unless you've got some hottie hidden in that tiny bag.'

'Wha?' Beth stops furtling.

'A coup de foudre is a bolt of thunder, love at first sight, just like me and –'

'Oh, for fuck's sake, if you mention his name!'

'I was going to say me and my pug, Charles!'

'You've got a pug?' Maddie leans forward. 'Oh I love pugs, they're just so squishy and …'

'Called Charles?' I interrupt. This bit is funnier to me. 'You've called your dog Charles?'

'He's very regal and talks to plants.' Sal's expression softens. Forget Jack, I think we've just discovered who her true love really is. Apart from herself of course.

'I think you mean pees on them.' Beth interjects. 'Anyhow, stop interrupting. This is more important!' And she whips out a bottle of Prosecco.

Claire, who has been pretty quiet, shifts uncomfortably on her corner of the rug, Maddie cheers and Sal rolls her eyes.

'Well, thank heavens, you at least had the sense to bring some alcohol.' She does however follow up with a smile and I heave an inward sigh of relief. Looks like hostilities have been suspended for a bit.

'Come on.' I chivvy them along. 'Eat up, you need to line your stomachs for what's coming next!'

'You mean there's more?'

'Do I detect a hint of sarcasm, Sally.' Beth raises an eyebrow, but they do seem to have a truce.

'When I had my hen party I ... shit, what the f—'

Beth manages to dump her whole glass of Prosecco in Sal's lap. Oops, okay they can't be nice to each other for more than two minutes. 'Sorry. Chill, it'll soon dry, alcohol evaporates doesn't it? More anybody?'

This has not got off to a good start, but I know it will get better. I just know it.

Fifteen minutes later, with pizza and Prosecco done and dusted, there is a noisy hoot of a horn.

'Quick, quick, you're going to love this!' Beth is cramming

the small litter bins with cardboard, she's told Maddie to dispose of the bottles and plastic cups in another, and I'm rolling the rugs up as fast as I can. There may be pizza in them, but who cares?

Beth and I stand at the door of the bus and wait nervously as the others hand their cases to the driver to be stashed.

'Oh my God!' Sally is so close behind Rachel as they go up the step she practically falls in, but she finally looks happy. Sitting on the grass put her so far out of her comfort zone that she was pricklier than a hedgehog. Here, I'm sure, she can forgive Beth every jibe. Which is handy.

'This is amazing.' Rachel does a twirl before landing on a seat. 'Where on earth did you find this?'

I grin. 'You likey?'

'Oh, me likey. Definitely.' She pats the seat.

'Welcome to the boogie bus! A booze cruise has got nothing on this.'

There's a bit of a stunned silence as everybody gazes round in awe, and me and Beth give each other the thumbs up.

Then we get the party started.

The disco lights are on, the champagne bar is open, and we're ready to party.

I haven't got a clue where we've parked up, but I don't really care. It's to be hoped it's in the middle of nowhere as this bus has some sound system as we dance our way through the '70s and '80s and have a blast with the karaoke.

Maddie and Sal seem to have buried the hatchet (but, luckily, not in each other), Beth has completely let her hair

194

down and forgotten to try to needle anybody. 'I'm not leaking milk am I?' She peers down her front.

I grin and shake my head.

'I've not had my boobs bouncing like this for years!'

The only person I'm worried about is Claire. She's had one dance, but seems to be trying to down the entire contents of the bar on her own. Well, with Maddie's help actually.

'This is ace.' Rachel spins me round and distracts me. Wrapping me in a three-way hug with Daisy and we 'Party Like It's 1999', trying to avoid Sal's flailing arms and the chance of a black eye.

The music slowly fades and the lighting changes, and Rachel screams. 'A pole! A pole! Pole dancing, how did you know?'

I reckon this, not the Prosecco, is the pinnacle of our achievement tonight. Who'd have thought that having a pole between her legs was all that Rach had ever wanted?

She's wrapped round there in an instant. It's not elegant, it's not good, but it's bloody funny. And awesome when Sally actually mounts the bloody thing as though she's been taking lessons from Pink!.

Beth and I sit back, and wallow in our awesomeness and we watch them make complete dicks of themselves in a good way.

The boogie bus is a triumph.

I chat to Daisy about the photography course she's doing at college.

And Beth huddles with Maddie in a corner whispering about who knows what.

And Claire gets very, very pissed and voms out of the window, because even though I've tried my very, very best to include her, it's hard when you're quiet and just not part of the gang.

And then the driver starts up the bus and we're off again.

'All out, cases are here, ladies.' Our driver is obviously used to dealing with inebriated hens. He herds us off in the same way you would if we were the actual feathered, clucky variety. It works well.

Daisy and Claire opted out of phase two, so they yell goodbyes and stay put, and Beth swears a lot after discovering an emergency text (and lots of missed calls) from her mum insisting that her baby son is on hunger strike and needs the real deal. So after some major foot stamping she climbs back on board and shouts out that she'll be back in the morning after performing her mothering duties. And, to Sal's horror, displays her boobs to illustrate the point.

Which leaves three bridesmaids and a bride to be.

We all stand in the darkness, slightly stunned as the bus drives away. Then Sally points.

'We're staying here?'

'We certainly are.' I smile as I look at the entrance to the very posh spa hotel, and then glance over at Rachel, who gives me the thumbs up.

'This place is supposed to be awesome!'

'No tent?' Says Sal, as though she can't quite believe it.

'No tent.'

She smiles, her face transformed. She has found the perfect

place to park her suitcase. 'Come on, girls.' She's so keen she's leading the way to Reception, dragging Rachel behind her.

'Be with you in a sec, you check in!' I call after them, hanging back to breathe in some fresh air.

This is phase two. Sleep and pamper. I need sleep, I really need sleep. My feet are killing, and I feel more than a little bit tipsy. So tipsy in fact, I could swear I just saw ... No. It can't be.

'Jane, any chance we can, erm, talk?'

I have been accosted just outside the entrance hall. By Jack.

Sobering up normally takes about eight hours. I reckon this takes eight seconds.

'Oh my God, what the hell are you doing here? You can't be here! Shush, out, out.' I'm bundling him down the steps as we speak, and glance nervously back to check that nobody has seen him. Nobody meaning Maddie. 'Stay!' I waggle a warning finger.

He nods meekly as I storm back over and make sure everybody has checked in and is heading for bed. 'You go up, I've got to check a couple of things for tomorrow!' They go, too tipsy and knackered to complain.

'What the ...' I bundle the unfortunate Jack into what I think is a bin store. It's dark and smelly anyway. 'Why are you here?'

'It's Michael's stag do.'

'Here?' This I cannot believe. 'Here?!' I say it again. 'But it's a spa hotel! Why the hell did you come to a spa hotel, and you knew we were coming!'

'No, we didn't! Michael hadn't got a clue where you lot

were going, and Sally told me you and Beth were behaving like children and wouldn't tell anybody.'

Okay, I'll do a U-turn on that one. I glare though, because of the behaving like children remark. 'It was a surprise! And it's still a country house and spa!'

'I know.' He looks miserable. 'It was a complete cock-up. We left it too late to book anything else.' I don't ask him who 'we' is, because I've a horrible suspicion it involves the man I do not wish to speak of. 'Andy looked around' – ha-ha, I was right – 'and said it was this or nothing, we had to settle for a whisky and wildlife weekend, except it wasn't a weekend, it was Thursday to Saturday.'

He looks so down I start to laugh.

'We've been up to our knees in bogs and deer shit stalking the master of the moors.'

'Master of the moors?' This is beginning to sound like a kinky kind of murder mystery weekend. My laugh is starting to sound slightly hysterical.

'A stag.'

'Oh, then what, did you shoot it?'

'God, no! I'm not into that bloodlust thing. It was amazing, so majestic.' He perks up a bit. 'I got some brilliant photos.'

'I bet!' I feel a sudden pang of jealousy but haven't got time to dwell on that. 'Are you sure when you booked a stag party there wasn't some kind of misunderstanding?'

Jack laughs. 'Maybe. Then we came back here for a lesson is whisky. We're off in the morning though for some bird action.'

I raise an eyebrow.

'The feathered type! We're flying birds of prey.' He looks so downcast it's hard not to laugh. 'We have to get up early.'

'Very early?' I try to ignore the giggles and give him my stern look. Stern, but drunk. He does look worried, so it might be more stern than drunk.

'Well, not early, we've got breakfast included and we can't ...'

'Fine.'

This *is* actually fine, we've organised breakfast in the suite we booked for Rachel. A proper girlie start to the day before the pampering starts. I can keep the two tribes apart.

'Well, why do you want to talk to me?' I glare. We avoided each other at the engagement party. He quails. 'I used to like you, you know, before ...' I'm not normally quite this outspoken, particularly when it's none of my business. But we all like to think we're a good judge of character, don't we? And when you've known somebody for years ...

'Is Mads okay?' It comes out in a rush.

'Okay? Well, yeah, absolutely fantastic, deliriously happy. She is *so* looking forward to walking down the aisle with your *wife*, instead of you.'

He flinches and looks even paler than he did before. But that could be down to the security light that has just flashed on.

'I wouldn't go to the wedding at all, but I'm best man, and Sally would—'

'Never forgive you if you didn't?'

'Something like that. She's very friendly with Rach and Michael. She calls us,' he looks even more dejected, 'the fearsome foursome.' I can't help it, I snigger. Nobody would have ever called Jack fearsome. 'We do, er ...' there is a pink flush along his cheekbones and I actually start to feel a bit sorry for him, 'dinner parties.'

'Cosy.' I am surprised Rachel never let on just how close she was to Sal these days, but I suppose couples do things like dinner parties, and I'm not part of a couple. And she probably didn't want to upset me.

Jack sits down on the step that leads to the side entrance of the hotel. 'I do still care for her, you know.' He gives me a sideways look, beneath his floppy fringe. 'Mads. I've never stopped loving her, but she told me we needed to move on. That it wasn't working any more.'

I sigh. 'Did you try and get her to change her mind?'

'Not at the start, I mean I'd got carried away with uni, my new mates, the freedom.' He picks at the blades of grass that have grown between the paving. 'I've been a jerk, haven't I?'

'If you say so.'

'I did try and talk to her in the summer hols, but she was away with her parents in Italy most of the time, and I'd arranged a break in Barcelona with the boys, then I had to go back and find a flat, and, well, the summer was over.'

'And then?'

'And then I bumped into Sally, and she was dead understanding. She really listened, you know? We talked and she made me see why Maddie had broken things off. She told me if I ever needed somebody to talk to, a mate from home, and, well, one thing led to another, then she thought she was pregnant, and ...'

He doesn't need to say any more.

I'd always thought Jack was decent. And maybe he was.

'Sal said Mads was cool with it.'

'I bet she did.'

'I didn't realise she wasn't until we'd bought a house back here and bumped into her in the supermarket ...' He pauses. 'God, she looked so upset.' He looks upset himself now. 'She just dropped her sprouts and ran. They went everywhere.'

For a moment I ponder the scattered sprouts, then realise he's still talking.

'I never meant to hurt Mads, we were over, we'd been over for ages. Years.'

'Not in her head you hadn't.' I say it quietly.

'I didn't know that. She was so definite when she told me, then I was away and didn't see her, and ...' He stops messing with his watch and looks at me. 'Sal isn't all bad, you know.'

'I guess she isn't, or she wouldn't be our friend, or your wife.'

'I think she got carried away with the idea of being together, we both did. I am really fond of her though.'

'Fond?'

He laughs. 'Fond, though I think we both talk to that dog of hers more than each other. She's been good to me, and we've had a laugh, done all kinds of stuff together ...' He pauses. 'I can't leave her.' He's talking as though he's persuading himself. 'Marriage is for life, I promised. I promised, Jane. Oh, hell, I've made so many bloody mistakes, I've been so stupid.'

I stand up. 'You are a complete twat Jack.'

'I know.'

Then, without stopping to think about why, I hug him. Because he looks just like the old Jack I used to know at school. Cute and huggable. Which is a mistake, because he's so shocked he takes a step back, and falls over the small wall, and throws his arm out to stop himself.

'Aarghh, shit, fuck.'

'Jack?' I've never heard him swear before, well, not properly, loudly, like that.

'Hell fire, it fucking hu—'

He sticks his arm out and we both stare. There is a sharp sticky out bit where there shouldn't be. Then he keels over, and my stomach does a very unhealthy flip.

'Jack, Jack!' Shaking him isn't doing any good. He's out cold. I risk a look at his wrist again. There are bones on the outside that should be on the inside. My stomach lurches alarmingly so I look the other way and do a panting thing to try to stop myself from heaving or passing out. I think I've picked it up from maternity scenes on *Holby*, but it's working for me even if I'm not having contractions. 'Hang on, hang on.' I don't know why I'm saying hang on. He's not going anywhere.

It takes bloody ages for the ambulance to arrive, and even longer for the receptionist to raise one of the stag party. Andy.

We stare at each other. He's totally pissed. So pissed he thinks he's been summoned to shag me. 'This is a fucking good dream. Come here, darling. Oh, God, I've missed you.' He lunges, I dodge. He nearly ends up in a pot plant.

'Don't you dare trip up and break something.' If he does, I'll murder him.

'I'm not breaking anything, just your sweet little—' He staggers round in a circle and prepares for a second charge.

'You've been watching too many crap films.'

'I do love you.' It's like watching a bull go after a red cape, a drunken bull. 'I miss you.'

'No, you don't Andy, you dumped me! In the middle of my hen party!' I side step and he staggers past.

'Oh, yeah, but I still love you. I dream about you.' He shakes his head. 'I feel dizzy.' He blinks. 'I knew you'd forgive me in the end.'

'No, I haven't bloody forgiven you. You never even asked me to forgive you! Not that I would!'

'You called me. You said you needed me.'

'I need you to help Jack, not needed you in that way you dipstick!'

'Let's go to your room, I'm sharing mine with Jack.'

'We're not going to anyone's room. It's Jack, Jack!'

He frowns. Andy never was at his best when he was smashed.

'You need to go to hospital with Jack! He's got a bone sticking through his skin!' I am hoping shock tactics might help concentrate his mind. Oops, mistake.

'Bollocks.' He sinks down, sliding with his back against a pillar and passes out. I'd forgotten he was so squeamish.

I end up packing Jack into the ambulance myself and leaving Andy snoring in the lobby.

'You don't need to come with me, Jane.'

'Are you sure, but ...'

'It's fine, it's only a broken wrist.' He winces. He's very pale, green at the edges. 'I am sorry about Mads you know. But I can't dump Sal, she's a nice person.'

'What you and Sal do is your business, but don't hurt Maddie any more, stay away, eh?'

I don't hang about to hear his answer. He's the same Jack he always was. The one I used to like. Maybe he didn't do the dirty, maybe he really didn't realise he'd hurt Mads. And maybe Sal didn't either. She just saw a nice, single guy and went for it.

Only problem now is, he's just more or less told me he still loves Maddie.

I've never liked secrets. The Michael one is already giving me a crisis of conscience. And now I'm supposed to keep this secret as well?

I have a headache. I need to sleep.

Chapter 20

'Whoever decided chocolate and massage are a good combo should be given a medal.'

Rachel's words are slightly muffled as she's got her face stuck in one of those holes that posh massage tables have, she's also having her back pummelled, so it comes out a bit staccato, but I get the gist.

When Beth insisted on going with the 'indulgent' package, I'd thought the chocolate and rub down came separately. My first thought had been that maybe that's why the massage tables *do* have a hole, my second thought had been that nibbling on a Flake while you have the knots beaten out from around your shoulder blades could be a bit of a choking hazard, and pretty messy. Turns out its messier than that.

'Oh, God, that smells good.' I groan as melted chocolate is slapped on like a liberal dose of massage oil.

'Orgasmic.' Sighs Beth.

Maddie giggles. 'Really?'

'When you've been starved of sex for as long as I have, being smothered in chocolate is my dream fantasy. Oh, Lordie, just there, yeah, oh, yeah. Harder.' She moans. 'This beats the Mars bar we reverted to last time.'

Even her masseur starts to splutter. 'Mars bar?'

'Don't ever use anything that's got a layer of toffee. It gets a bit icky, didn't think I'd ever get out of my hair.'

'Hair?' Says Maddie, raising herself on her elbows. 'What was it doing in your hair?'

Sal laughs. This is good, I think we're bonding over chocolate.

'Think Brazilian rainforest rather than Brazilian.' Sighs Beth.

'Oh.' Maddie buries her red cheeks back in the hole in the table.

'You lot couldn't all lie still and enjoy your pure indulgence experience, could you?' the masseuse asks.

'Ah, knew it was Galaxy.' Rachel sighed. 'I'm going to have to tell Michael about this. Do you do couples?'

I wonder if you came as a couple, you'd be invited to lick it off each other at the end?

Freddie would like it. He's one of the few men I know that will fight me for the last Rolo and insists on buying Quality Street all year round. He's all green triangles and soft centres, and I get the toffees, fudge and nuts. We just fit together so well, and it's weird but when he's not with me I feel like a part of me is missing. Not knowing if we'd fallen out for good had been horrible, it had scared me. It had made me realises just how big a part of my life he is, and how much I miss him when he's not there. Which is a bit scary. But I'm not sure if I could have enjoyed this weekend if I hadn't known we were cool again.

'Normally, but I'm not sure with you lot!' The girl who has been doing my massage laughs. 'Right, ladies. I will leave you to relax in the warmth for a few minutes, then you can make your own way to the shower room, and no licking, this doesn't taste half as nice as it smells!'

'I hope we don't set.' I stare down at the polished wood floor.

'If you're as hot as I am, there's no chance of that.' Rachel starts to giggle. She sits up and looks at me. 'Race you to the showers, I want to try and make a Rach body imprint on the glass!'

Ten minutes later and Beth and Sal have been whisked off for manicures, Mads is having a facial and Rach and I are heating our blood up to boiling point. At least that's what it feels like. I'm melting, or about to erupt like a mini volcano. I haven't decided which yet. I feel too weak for logical thinking.

'I don't think I was designed to lose this much sweat.'

'Oh, Jane.' Rachel giggles and puts out a hand, and I cower.

'No! Don't touch me, I'm like a teabag, it will all spurt out. I'll be a pile of shrivelled bony bits on the floor.'

I'm dying to tell Rach about Jack. To tell her that I'm sure the silly idiot still loves Maddie as much as he ever did. But I can't. If I do then she'll feel she has to tell Sal. They're the fearsome four after all.

Much as Sal winds me up, she's also a mate, and like I said to Jack – I do like her. Some of the time. And even if I didn't, I wouldn't want to be instrumental in wrecking her marriage.

207

And I want to tell Mads that it's all okay. That maybe one day. But that wouldn't be fair on her either.

All these thoughts disappear from my head in an instant when I notice the look on Rachel's face. She's not giggling any more.

'Am I doing the right thing, Jane?'

'What?' I know she's not talking about the ladle of water she's just chucked over the already hot rocks.

'Getting married.' She stares blankly at me.

'Of course you are, you love him!' I can hear a note of panic in my voice. 'Don't you?'

'Oh, yeah, I love him.' She nods. 'But it's all the other stuff. What if we end up disagreeing about money, kids,' she screws up her face, 'we had a big row over how much he wanted to spend on new kitchen appliances.' She laughs weakly. 'Oh, God, that sounds pathetic, it's nothing, I'm making a thing about nothing.'

'Rach, it's not nothing if it's bothering you.' I don't know what to say. Cancel the wedding is the obvious one (okay, I still don't like Michael as much as I should), but that feels like dangerous ground.

'Oh, it's not really bothering me. I'm being,' she takes a big breath as though trying to clear the thoughts out of her head, then starts coughing wildly as the hot air hits her lungs. 'Shit.' The tears are streaming down her face, and she doubles over. 'Bloody hell, I can't … I'm going to die.' We both dive headlong out of the sauna and she stands doubled over gasping for breath. After an age, and much rub-backing and concerned noises from me, she stands up and fans herself with her hand.

'I'm fine, I'm fine. Really.' Then she smiles wryly. 'Forget what I said, it was all crap, I'm going crazy. It's all this wedding stress, it's driving me loopy. I can't think straight, and I keep getting in a panic about everything going wrong! I reckon all brides must get like this.'

'You sure?' I frown at her.

'Oh, yeah, it is definitely sending me crazy!'

I didn't really mean that, but she gives me such a firm hug, and such a big grin I decide I need to let sleeping dogs lie.

'What's next then, boss?'

'Shower!'

'Wow, this Brides Bombshell is the best cocktail ever!' Rachel closes her eyes. 'It's bliss, I am so going to have to have one of these after the wedding. You two are geniuses, or is that genii?'

I laugh. 'Just call me a genie!'

Booking the cocktail masterclass was our masterstroke. A gin cocktail each to make on arrival, followed by the big surprise. A drink tailored to each of our favourite spirits and mixers. The bartender had come up with the names and is currently flipping his cocktail shaker. He stops, and with a flourish pours my drink.

'Your One Hot Chick, madam!' He winks.

'Wow.' I stare at it, salivating. My first instinct isn't to drink it though, it's to preserve it forever. 'I'm sorry, but I need to break the number one rule of Hen Club.'

There were many reasons Beth and I came up with the rules of Hen Club, but the number one reason was to avoid embarrassment the morning after the night before. This particular hen and her chicks have enough scandals and secrets attached without adding to the list, so number one rule had to be – no mobile phones. Because, you know as well as I do, that if you have your mobile at hand, and you're drunk, and you're having an hilarious time, and you are with all your besties, then you'll just have to post a photo on social media. Won't you? Yeah. Exactly.

Number two rule was no holding back. Number three rule was no heels under three inches, number four rule was no getting off with anybody, or even talking to anybody of the opposite sex and number five rule was no talking about work, secrets, scandals or anything other than the here and now. This was one Beth and I firmly agreed on. She obviously didn't want to talk about 'the father of the baby', and I didn't want to accidentally talk about 'Michael's indiscretion', 'Jack's damaged heart' or 'Maddie's big mistake'. There's a time and place for everything.

Anyhow. I need my phone. I need to take a photo. This isn't want, it's need. 'I won't take pics of anybody, just the cocktails, please.' I look round at the other girls, clasp my hands together and beg. 'Pretty please, they are just so awesome and it's my job. Please?'

'Let's vote on it girls!' Shouts Beth, raising her cocktail to her lips.

Luckily, it is unanimous. And the bartender reluctantly hands over the box so that I can retrieve mine. He has taken his duties very seriously, and we did make him swear that on no account would he let us persuade him to give us them back. But he has seen the vote. And he has been given full authority to snatch it back if I start shooting right, left and centre.

Unfortunately, my impromptu photoshoot has an immediate negative effect. Okay, it was totes my fault for uploading one to Instagram. But it was just an automatic reaction. Shoot, edit, upload.

Despite the fact that we'd agreed this was a day off, Darth Vader couldn't resist. Coral is calling. I'm very tempted to ignore her, but instead I accidentally put her on speakerphone.

'Product placement, product placement! Get one with the fucking bottle!'

The others are totally confused by the lack of introduction, but I know Coral.

'Photoshop it in, anything, then tag it! My God, you silly cow, how could you not tag it with the gin! And why is it not on my IG?' The last question is said in a slightly plaintive tone. Coral doesn't really do plaintive, just hurt, or confused, if she thinks it will get her attention.

'It's not on your IG 'cos it's my photo.' I say reasonably. 'On my Instagram. I do have my own, you know.'

'Your fucking photo?' She is confused now, I can tell.

'My day off, my life, my photo.'

There is a long silence.

'Well, get it on mine, I *need* to be associated with that gin. They love me!'

'My tag?'

'Whatever, just do it. Bill me.'

Because I am drunk, I push my luck. 'Photoshopping isn't very authentic though.' I say, thinking back to Brighton-gate.

'Fuck authentic, I need that cocktail.' She doesn't say please, she just assumes I will comply.

I will.

I need the money. And it is a bloody good photo, even if I say so myself.

'Phone away, now!' Orders Rachel, and the others start up a chant. I giggle and grin back at Rachel, who is looking happier than I've ever seen her. Her outburst in the sauna just had to be last-minute nerves, no way would she be as bubbly as this if she didn't love Michael to bits, and looking forward to her big day.

'Sorry, Coral, gotta go. Orders!' I toss my phone at the bartender, who expertly catches it and deposits it back in the box.

But not before I've noticed a text from Freddie saying he'll see me tomorrow, which makes me un-proportionally happy. We're back to normal texting! After 'the kiss' I thought we'd ruined everything, now I know we're going to be okay. Though I'm not quite sure what okay means. Losing Freddie as a friend would be so bad I'm happy to swear off lip contact with him forever, if it means we're going to stick together.

I suddenly realise my fingers are on my lips.

Kissing Freddie was nice. More than nice.

Maybe there's a way of making this work *with* kisses?

'Oh my God, Oh my God, Oh my God!'

Maddie and I are weaving our happy way back to our

shared room at 2 a.m. and she is extremely drunk. I've never seen her like this, normally she's a couple of drinks girl.

Even though I've had a fair few cocktails though, I do remember she's been in a huddle with Beth. Which kind of explains things.

'I don't know what to do Jane!'

We have tumbled into our shared room, and all I want to do is crawl into bed – fully clothed, without taking my make-up off.

'What about?' I don't really want to ask, I just feel duty bound.

She sits down on the bed next to me, and leans in, so she can whisper conspiratorially in my ear. Even though there's nobody else here.

'I've been talking to Beth, you will never believe what she told me. I shouldn't tell you, but I've got to!'

I stop thinking about crashing back on the bed. 'Tell!'

'It's Michael, he's ...' her tone drops down to an even more hushed level, 'slept with—'

'I know!' I put my finger on her lips. I don't wait to hear any more, I don't *want* to hear her say the rest, to say that woman's name, but I am so bloody relieved that there's finally somebody I can talk to. Somebody else who knows about Lexie!

'*You know?*' She blinks at me.

'I know! I found out a while ago, but I didn't know what to do ... whether I should tell Rach now, or later, or never.'

'Oh, wow!' Mads is shocked. 'Beth didn't think anybody else knew!'

'It is all over though, I mean it was ages ago.'

'Oh, yes, definitely.' She nods her head violently. 'Definitely. Beth said it was.'

'So, I kind of thought maybe it's better just forgotten?'

'Oh, I don't think that's the right thing.' She's now shaking her head. 'I was so shocked when she told me. I mean, Michael!'

'Frig!' This reminds me that Beth knows as well, everybody knows except the one person that really should Rach. 'Does Sal know as well?'

Maddie shakes her head. 'I don't think so.'

'I don't think we should tell her.'

'Me neither.' Maddie shakes her head violently. 'She'll just shit stir, she'll go straight to Rachel, I know she will.'

'Maybe I should talk to Beth, see what she thinks?'

'No, no,' says Mads, 'she told me in confidence, I mean I don't want her to think she can't trust me, and I've blabbed to everybody. I mean I only told you because I'm drunk, and didn't know what to do, and seeing as you knew anyway then ...'

'I did. Don't worry. Okay.' I take her hands in mine. 'It's our secret, for now. Yes?'

She nods. 'And Beth's.'

'And Beth's. But she won't say anything, will she?'

'Not yet, but ...' She looks doubtful.

'I'll work out what to do, when we should tell Rach. There'll be a good time.' Except I'm not sure there will be. Maybe the good time has passed.

We hug, then Maddie climbs under the sheets and I head for the bathroom.

'Night, Mads, sleep well.'

'Night, Jane, you, too.' She sounds sleepy, and drunk. 'Maybe Beth should talk to Michael first?'

'No, no.' I frown. But it does sow a teeny seed of an idea in my befuddled brain. Maybe it's me that should corner Michael, tell him that if he doesn't come clean then somebody else might do it for him. Maybe that is the only way to sort the mess out.

I stare at my reflection in the mirror.

I've got no choice now. Rachel's got to know.

There's a hard lump blocking my throat. What if this means history will repeat itself? Her wedding will be cancelled just like mine was, she'll go through all the pain and agony I did. Doing this to her will be the worst thing I have ever done. It will destroy her, just like it nearly destroyed me.

The memories I've been stamping down flood my head. My beautiful dress, the church, the cake, the flat we were saving up to buy together, the bright, amazing future we'd got planned. Together.

I can't do it. I can't do that to her.

I have to do it.

Michael has to do it. He has to tell her. If he tells her, and he loves her as much as she thinks then it will all be okay. It has to be. They'll be able to move on from it. They love each other.

I take a deep breath to steady my nerves, and chase away all the horrible thoughts. First, I will sleep on it and see if some kind of magic solution comes to me in my dreams and I don't have to worry about it ever again.

Chapter 21

Oh, bugger. My lift has arrived. Or rather, it seems, two of them have.

This could be embarrassing.

There are two open car doors, two men looking at me expectantly. Freddie has his head slightly on one side.

After his text saying he'd realised that he'd been a prat avoiding me and was glad we were going to be friends still, I'd messaged him back this morning with a brief: *Is 11 a.m. okay? Thanks! x.* I'd been desperate to add: *Can't wait for movie night … not so sure about it being hands free though …* However, I refrained, as he might have withdrawn the lift offer, and the friends offer.

Or he might have agreed with me, then taken me out on four dates, made me madly happy, before panicking, started to check for signs that I was looking for my happy ever after, changed the locks, broken my heart, and changed my life for ever. In a bad way.

And gone back to searching for the girl who stole his heart.

Andy is leaping up the stone steps, as competitive as ever. 'You are looking great.' He leans in and kisses my cheek, his hands on my upper arms immobilising me so there is no chance to dodge. Just to throw my head back and invite a kiss on the neck – creepy, as that was always his go-to never-fails erogenous target – or a Dracula-style love bite. So, I keep my chin pinned to my chest whilst trying to look cool. Freddie's eyebrow has cocked, so that obviously didn't come off. He folds his arm, leans against his car and looks amused.

Andy smells familiar, which he would. Sadly, he's still not turned into a horse-headed toad like I'd wished he would. Word of advice, those 'cast your own spell' websites are shit. He never rang begging forgiveness, or complaining of stomach cramps, or turned into a toad. Horse-headed or otherwise. Like I say, crap. Spend your money on wine or vodka and then you'll be able to believe all the evils have happened even if it's a one night only thing.

'Er, thanks. What are you doing?'

'Sorry.' He takes a step back. Runs a hand through his hair and shuffles his feet awkwardly. Very un-Andy-like. 'Thought you might need a lift back to town? I wanted to make it up to you, for the other night?' He seems to have adopted that habit of making every statement sound like it ends with a question.

'I was way out of order, totally drunk and when you rang our room I just jumped to a stupid conclusion. Can't believe I did that, sorry.' He does look sorry.

'Fine. No problem.'

'It's not fine, Jane. Nothing is fine, I need to explain.'

'Nothing to explain. Nothing, absolutely nothing.'

'But Jane, I need to.' He gives me the plaintive, sincere look that used to drag my heart from my chest and leave me all pounding and breathless. 'I was a complete dickhead the other night, I was just so drunk. And I think I was wrong about the wedding, I've made ...'

I don't stop to hear what he's made. 'Sorry, got to rush, Freddie's waiting.' I kind of slither out of his grasp and go hurtling down the steps, catching my heel on the last one and practically diving headlong into Freddie's car. Luckily, the door is still open, or the ambulance service would think we'd got them on speed dial.

'New bloke? Thought it was a hen party?' Freddie asks.

'That's Andy.'

'Ahh, thought he looked familiar.'

'It's really good of you to come.'

'I wanted to, though if you'd rather ...' He leaves it hanging. 'I didn't realise you'd arranged ...'

'Oh my God. No! I didn't arrange for.' I wave towards Andy. I still don't want to say his name. 'No, no, never. No, I didn't ask him, there was a cock-up, the stag was at the same place, but nobody knew. Well, not until Jack cornered me, then I had to call Andy to come down because of the ambulance, and he was so pissed he was useless and fainted, so Jack went on his own and I left Andy in the lobby and went to bed, and now he's trying to apologise. Well, I think that's what he's apologising for.'

'Ambulance?'

'Jack broke his wrist, he tripped over this wall when we were talking, and it wasn't my fault.'

'Oh. Right.'

'And Andy said he still loved me, but he was pissed, he probably doesn't even remember saying it, and he didn't mean it.'

'It's none of my business.'

'Oh, it is, it is, I want you to know. That was all just him being weird!' I put my hand on his arm, realise what I'm doing and move it quick. Which isn't cool at all, I mean before the kiss I used to touch him, and we're supposed to have forgotten it. We are supposed to be in the this-is-not-awkward zone now. So I put it back. 'I didn't see Andy again until just, and I don't know why he thought I'd want a lift.'

'Who knows?' Freddie shrugs, closes my door then bangs the boot shut. He gets in.

I glance back. Andy is watching. He waves, grins. So, I do a half-hearted wave back, a regal but slightly limp-wristed flourish, just to show that I don't care.

Then it hits me. I really don't. Care, that is.

I can feel the smile twitching at the side of my mouth, or I've got a bad nervous tick.

He means nothing to me. I can wave now, I no longer have the urge to strangle him or stick two fingers up. Or batter him over the head with the nearest thing to hand. I stick my hand out of the window and wave again. Just to double check.

'If you'd rather go with …' Freddie slows the car down.

'No, no, just drive, please.' I need to get away, before Andy decides the wave is another summons and comes hurtling after us. 'But I just realised I don't.'

'Don't what?'

'Love him, even if he does love me, which he doesn't.'

Zara Stoneley

'Oh.'

'I don't care at all. I don't even care if he's sorry. Can we go faster, please?'

Freddie drives. In thoughtful (well, I hope that's what it is) silence.

'You know what? That's the first time I didn't feel the need to throttle him.'

'You've made up?'

'The opposite. I've finally realised that he means absolutely nothing to me.'

'Really?'

'Absolutely.'

'Did you have a good time?'

'Great. But it's so nice to be heading home,' I pause, 'with you.' I snuggle down under my coat and close my eyes, but not before I've sneaked a sideways look at my best mate. The man who seems to have burrowed his way into my heart. He's smiling.

Chapter 22

'What are you up to now?' Freddie takes the bottle of beer I'm waving in front of his face and does his waggling eyebrow thing. I've never known anybody with such an expressive face.

'What makes you think I'm up to something?'

'Ha-ha, promise me you'll never play poker. Come on, what's up?'

'It's Jack.' I sigh. I've got to talk to somebody, and when I tried Louie he headed for his litter tray. Since getting back from the hotel I've not been able to get Jack out of my head.

'Guilt trip about breaking his ankle?'

'It was his wrist, and I didn't break it, he fell.' I pick up the remote and flick through the channels, with the TV on silent. I don't have to tell anybody. I should keep this to myself. Let them work it out themselves. Let sleeping dogs lie as they say.

I turn the TV off again, half turn to look at Freddie and sigh. 'He still loves Maddie.'

'So?'

'But he's married to Sal, who he likes a lot and doesn't want to hurt.'

'Ah. You sure about this?'

'He told me.'

'Was he drunk?'

'He didn't seem it, he seemed pretty sober for somebody who was on a stag weekend.'

'Tricky then.'

'Are you going to tell me to mind my own business?'

'No, never.' He gives me a mate's hug, then pulls back in a way that could be reluctant, or that could just be wishful thinking on my side. 'It's cute how you care so much.' His beautiful dark eyes make me feel all warm and squishy inside.

I swallow, clear my throat. 'Cute?'

'Just carry on, forget the cute. Tell me about Jack.'

I can't forget the 'cute', but I probably should. 'He says marriage is for life, so he can't leave Sally.'

'Honourable.' He says it like he means it, but he's still gazing at me as though he's got other things on his mind. It's unsettling. Distracting.

'He is.' I crash on but can't stop staring back at him. 'I always liked Jack.'

'Until you slagged him off for marrying Sal.'

'Yeah, but I think he's just too *nice* for his own good. I mean, it's just so sad. Maddie loves Jack, Jack still loves Maddie, they should be able to be with the one that's made for them.'

'Bit of a mess, isn't it?'

I'm not sure if he's really talking about Jack here, or something else. Like us. Either way, he doesn't know the half of it.

'So you don't think I should tell her?'

'You and your girlfriends have got complicated lives. But

222

the timing isn't always right, is it? And,' his tone is so even and reasonable I wonder what's going to come next, 'Andy still loves you, but you're not getting back together,' he shrugs, and leaves a longer than normal pause, 'are you?'

'Never! He's not my One, I know he's not, and,' I pause, I've never told a soul this bit, not even Rachel, 'in the last text he sent me, he called me matchstick!'

'What?'

I tap my head and wait for the penny to drop.

'He didn't?' He grins, his mood suddenly lighter.

'He did. I mean, there's no going back from that, is there?'

'Jane?'

'Yeah?'

'That kiss.'

I look at him warily. We'd not mentioned our kiss. The awkwardness between us had kind of been side-stepped because of the way I'd dived headfirst into his car after the Andy incident. No strained 'How are you?'s had been required after that.

'Horrible?'

'Not horrible. I was lying when I said we should just forget it. I can't.'

'You can't?' I gulp. To say the air is tingling between us would be to disrespect a good thunder storm, we're super-charged. Even Louie makes a run for it, his little tail stuck up with so much static he can't try to get away from it fast enough.

'And I'm not sorry. I can't be sorry for doing something that was that good.'

'Good?' I've gone monosyllabic.

He frowns at me. 'It wasn't good for you?'

'Oh, yeah, yeah, yeah, it was good for me. Definitely good for me. *Wow!* Ace. I should shut up now, shouldn't I?'

'Carry on for a bit. It's good for my ego.' We do that silent stare thing. 'How good?'

'Don't push it, it was only one teeny tiny kiss.'

'Would you risk another one? A bigger one. Just so you can rate it?'

'It scares me.'

'I'm scary?' His gentle smile is anything but scary. And the way he's looking at me, all earnest and intent is unsettling, in a goose-bump kind of way, but is making me want to move closer, not further away.

'No. Kissing is.' I lick my damp lips, and swallow hard. 'Like you said, it's complicated. And like you said, the timing isn't always right.' Why do I feel all bubbly and expectant?

'Sometimes it's perfect.'

'I don't want to ruin what we've got, Freddie. What if we try it, and like it too much, and we get carried away, and ...' I know if I was drunk I wouldn't be saying all these things, I'd be climbing on top of him. But I'm sober. 'The last few days without you have been weird. Horrible. I don't want to not be friends, to risk a lifetime without you.' I suddenly realise I'm edging closer, even though what I'm saying and thinking should be sending me the opposite way.

'I would, if it meant a moment of pure magic.'

I stare into his dark eyes, then something snaps inside of me. 'Oh, to hell with it, I could get run over by a bus tomorrow.' I put my hands on his face. Rest my finger on his perfect lips.

He pulls back a tiny bit, a very tiny bit. 'You're only doing this because you might get run over?'

'You know I didn't mean actually run over, it's a figure of speech. I meant maybe I need to seize the chance, live for the moment.'

'That'll do me.' He closes the gap between us, his lips are only centimetres from mine. His fingers are in my hair, and my scalp is tingling. His mouth is covering mine so lightly I wouldn't know we were touching if it wasn't for the way my whole body is reacting and I'm desperate to get closer. Oh, Gawd, I think I might be clutching at him. But wait, it's okay, he's clutching back, and his hand is on my bum, and we're wrapped so tightly together, I can feel every (and I *mean* every) centimetre of his body.

'Bugger.' His mouth breaks away from mine, as there's a loud clatter and the biscuit barrel tumbles to the floor. He spins me round, the hard work surface digging into my back, but who cares? I tease at his bottom lip with my teeth, as he curses and pushes me back.

'Ouch!' Banging your head on a kitchen cupboard door-knob is so unsexy.

'Sorry.' He's paused, short of breath. 'You okay?'

'Knob, nothing, don't stop now!' I grab a handful of T-shirt, pull him in tighter, and he lifts me, plonks me on the work surface in a way I'd normally think was unhygienic, but it's not. It is so not, it is fantastic, it is—

'Sugar.' There's a crash, hell I've just swept a whole bag of

Tate and Lyle's best granulated onto the floor. 'Forget it, forget it.'

Freddie manfully spins round in the small space, taking me with him, hanging on like a monkey with my legs wrapped round his waist.

'Bugger.' My elbow hits the fridge freezer.

'Flaming heck.' He cracks his toe on the wine rack and there's a good chance that the one bottle of wine it houses has just crashed to the floor and right now might be spraying the kitchen with a layer of supermarket best Merlot. But who cares? We stagger into the living room lips melded together, apart from the odd escaping swear word.

We're out of the tiny kitchen, oops forgot to navigate the sofa, over the back and nearly breaking our necks as we land, then bounce and tumble off to get wedged on the rug with our heads between the bookshelf unit and a stack of DVDs.

'Okay?'

'Okay.'

We're ripping clothes off each other, which isn't working and is frankly a health and safety issue. Scrambling back on to the couch as we go.

'Let's do our own.' I pant out. Which is nearly as dangerous, when he's half on me and half off. 'Shit.' A little ginger face has just appeared over his shoulder and blue eyes are staring at me. 'Get him off my back, don't want to hurt ...'

I whisk poor little Louie off Freddie's back – 'No, little buddy, not now.' – and deposit him on the chair.

'I hope you're not talking to me?'

I glance back up, and he's all I can see. Freddie. Staring

down at me with dark, dark eyes that are definitely intent on more than friendship.

I've seen his bare chest before, but this time it's different. I can *really* see it, every arousing inch, every contour. The red marks that my nails have left as I clutched at him, the unfashionable wisps of hair that are suddenly the most on-trend thing ever in my eyes. The dark shadow that snakes down between our bodies, to where his belt meets the waistband of my jeans.

'No way.' I tug at the buckle, and he chuckles, easing himself higher so that his hip bones meet mine. There's something sexy, something demanding about the clash and I grab more desperately at the buckle.

Then we're going, on the move, rolling off the stupid, too-small sofa again.

'Stay here.' His words are strangling, because he's taken over the belt duties, whilst coming in hard for a teeth-jarring kiss that is making my lips throb and my body desperate to get in the action.

Hot flesh hits hot flesh and for a second I freeze. This is it. We are totally naked. My best male friend has his very male parts snuggled between my thighs and we're on the brink of changing everything.

'Oh my God, do it!'

He does, and I can't help the little scream, followed by the near-hysterical cackle, which must be the un-sexiest thing ever. But Freddie just grins and goes for it, and we roll, and hit furniture and get carpet burn and fluff where it shouldn't be, and we laugh and groan and shout and then … it's over.

'Wow.' Freddie props himself on his elbows and blinks down at me. There's a pause, this could get sticky. Well, it is sticky, but awkward, you know what I mean. 'Talk about Mission Impossible!' He wipes the sweat off his brow.

I can't help but grin back. Then smile. Then laugh. 'My stomach hurts, get off, get off!'

'Loony!' He tries to roll but there's not enough room so he kind of back off onto his knees, then clambers to his feet, and offers me a hand.

He hauls me up. And we're back in the position we were in before. Skin to skin, but on our feet this time.

'Okay?'

He looks worried. I reach out, stroke my hand down his cheek. 'More than okay.'

And he kisses me, then backs off, pulling me with him.

'Yours or mine?'

'Yours.' I blow him a kiss. 'You're tidier than me, and anyway,' I can't stop grinning, 'I don't want a damp patch.'

'Ha. Who said you'll get the chance to make one?'

I do. I get more than one chance. Then afterwards, I flake out with my head on his slightly hairy chest until I'm woken by a rude banging.

On the door. Not the other, ruder, type.

Chapter 23

'Oh, sorry.' Andy doesn't look sorry. 'Not interrupting anything, was I?' He also doesn't look like he thinks he is.

I don't normally scramble to the front door with a sheet wrapped round me, bed hair and the aura of somebody who has spent too few hours asleep and too many hours with their hands on a fellow human being, but I thought it was a delivery. I have ordered the most amazing play den thing for Louie, one with scratch post and tunnel and dangly things, and a feather on a wand and ... well, I thought it was amazing, and I am sure he will. And you know what delivery guys can be like, don't you? Knock-and-run round here, and a card stuck through the door inviting you to drive 30 miles up the motorway to your 'nearest' depot to collect. Which you do, then discover that after a two hour wait they can't locate it.

So I'd grabbed the closest thing to hand, a sheet, and stumbled to the door yelling out 'hang on' and 'don't go' as loudly as I could.

From the smug look on my ex's face he thought I knew it was him. As if. 'Not going anywhere honey!'

'I thought you were a cat activity centre with added extras!'

'Oh, yeah?' He grins. 'I'm all about the extras.' Talk about cocky.

'Fancy fresh orange?' Freddie strides up behind me, then stops short. 'Oh, Andy. Hi.'

Andy's grin fades, and his eyes narrow as he takes in Freddie in PJ bottoms and nothing else and me wrapped in a sheet. Us discussing breakfast choices.

It's classic. I should be punching the air. Instead, I find myself turning a colour that will outdo my auburn hair any day of the week.

'I never say no to something sweet and juicy in the morning, do I, Janey?' He recovers and winks. I want to gag.

Full marks for recovery, into the negative for cringe-worthy. How did I ever think I wanted to spend the rest of my life with this man? I was deluded, crazy.

'Sorry?'

'Bugger, sorry, didn't mean to …' He suddenly looks awkward, embarrassed. 'I just, it wasn't easy to come round, I've worked myself up into—'

Freddie gives him a look, then squeezes my shoulder, and wanders off to squeeze the oranges.

I don't know quite what to say.

'Why are you here?' My brain isn't up to niceties and working out what I should and shouldn't say. It is still sleep-fogged.

'Sorry. You, erm, well, look busy?' He rolls his eyes in the direction of the kitchen.

I fold my arms and decide not to comment.

'Look, I'm, erm, sorry.' He shifts about from foot to foot, and forgets the script, and just like that bravado-man is replaced with the man I fell for. The man I was going to marry. 'For everything. We ended on a bad note.'

'A bad note? A bad note?' My tone shoots up an octave. 'You dumped me on my hen night!'

'Maybe the timing wasn't great, but I was drunk and things just came to a head and if I hadn't said something I'd have exploded.' He flares up, trying to justify what he did.

'You'd have exploded?' I'm spluttering. I can't believe the man. 'You texted me!'

'We needed space.' He looks at me, dejected and slightly pathetic.

'We?'

'Okay, I did. But I want to make it up to you,' he doesn't say 'apologise' like any real man would. 'I miss you, Janey. We can at least call a truce, can't we? Be friends? Like you and geek man here.'

I glare.

'Sorry, sorry, that came out wrong again didn't it? It's just so frigging hard.' He runs his hand through his hair, and it's like a light-bulb moment in my head. I get it.

I stare at him.

One of the things I'd fallen for with Andy was his total self-confidence and self-belief, the way he'd make decisions with total certainty, the way he liked to take care of me. Now I realise that he never was sorry, he never knew when he made mistakes, he was often selfish. Apologising and seeing things through other people's eyes was something he never did.

Things that come as naturally as breathing to lovely Freddie.

I'd not really analysed it before. Never realised how little compromise there had been, until I'd moved on.

I *had* loved Andy once, but he'd never been the right guy for the grown-up me. Maybe for the teenager, who'd been wowed by such a masterful man, but I'd outgrown him. And he'd realised that.

And he'd been scared.

He just hadn't stopped to think about how I'd feel when he'd announced his findings when he did.

'I know it's hard, Andy. You never were very good at apologies, were you?'

He looks confused, then is distracted by Freddie coming back bearing orange juice in one hand, and Louie in the other.

'I know I said look after her mate, but this is going a bit far.' Andy guffaws. He sounds like a donkey. Bravado-man is back, and I want to slap him

Freddie looks at me, 'he didn't …'

But I barely hear him. 'Look after me? Look after me?' I seem to have got into this thing where I have to repeat everything twice, but it's the only way I can believe he's actually coming out with this crap. 'How dare you! And as if you give a rat's arse. You didn't even know I'd moved in with Freddie!'

'I do give a rat's arse! It was for you babe, for us, that's why I did it. I just thought we'd got our whole lives ahead, so why rush, why risk fucking it all up?'

I want to give him a good shake. But instead, I sigh and

try to let the anger out. I'm not going to let him wind me up any more. He's not worth it.

'Yeah, you're right Andy. I've got my whole life to do what I want.' I poke him in the chest, I can't help it. 'I don't need looking after. I've got friends,', poke, 'a job,' Andy splutters, I ignore it, 'a cat, well, maybe not a whole cat, a kitten, half a—'

'You don't like cats!' He moves forward as though he's going to grab my poking finger, and the rest of me, and I leap back and cannon into Freddie.

'I never said I don't like cats.' I address this to Freddie, then repeat it for Louie. 'Honest, I just said I hadn't got time for cats.'

'Aww, come on, Jane. I only want to talk, a coffee, maybe?'

'No, go away, Andy, it's too little too late. Sod off out of my life.'

'Not friends?'

'No!'

'We can talk things over, clear the air?'

'No!'

'Not even for Rachel's sake? She wouldn't want us falling out at her wedding ...'

'*Arghh.*' I think what I make is a kind of strangled cat noise, because Louie's normal plaintive squeak turns into a yowl of panic and he scrambles free from Freddie, practically walks up the wall, lands on Andy's head and does a head over heels down his back before heading for the outside world.

'Crumbs. Bloody hell! You better not have left the outside

door open.' I shove him out of the way and fly down the steps after the cat.

'Oh my God! Louie, Louie! Louie!!' I spin round on the doorstep desperate to see a flash of ginger fur. 'Here, kitty, kitty. Oh, shit.'

Don't ever dash out in only a bedsheet. Just saying. And if you do, don't do a twirl. The embarrassment of being wrapped ever tighter and falling over would have been fab compared to this.

I have unravelled.

'Shit, shit.' I gather up the sheet as fast as I can and try to cover my boobs and bottom at the same time, with the same tiny piece, which isn't working as somebody has just hooted their horn. 'Morning, morning!' Act cool, as though this is normal. Oh, Gawd, now it's got snagged on a bush.

But it hasn't. It has got snagged on the claws of a tiny kitten. 'Oh, thank God for that. Thank you, thank you!' I offer up thanks as I reel in the cotton with him attached to the end, then gather him to my chest, realising as I do that only one breast is covered. But I don't care. Well, I do, when white van man thanks me with a rude hand gesture.

'Bloody hell, are you okay?'

Freddie is staring down at me, holding out a hand. I grab it and am halfway to my feet, when he's shoved aside. I plop back down on my bum.

'Jane! What on earth, it's only a cat you know.'

I hold Louie up for Freddie, then scramble back to my feet via my knees, and rearrange my sheet as though it is normal street attire.

'You,' I poke Andy in the chest as I push my way past him, 'are an arse.'

He laughs heartily. But it's his false laugh, I know it is, and I feel a little sorry for him. That he feels he has to do this. 'I always did love you when you were in a feisty mood, you've no idea what it did to me.'

'Normally, it made you yell, because you didn't like me standing up to you!' This was true. Our biggest blow ups were when I stood up to him. 'And you have no idea what I'm already doing for Rachel's sake! And,' I turn back, 'Louie is not *only* a cat, he's my cat! Well, our cat. Mine and Freddie's cat.'

Andy raises an eyebrow, and I can just tell he's about to say something I don't want to hear.

So, I link my arm through Freddie's and pick my way gingerly over the gravel, leaving Andy outside.

A long shower, getting dressed and feeding Louie calms me down.

'Gone a bit cold.' Freddie pushes the toast towards me and we look at each other.

'Sorry about ...' It's not quite how I imagined the day would start.

'Cool. It's not a problem, unless ...'

'Unless?'

He puts down the knife that he's been scraping burned bits of toast off with. 'Unless you wanted him to come round? I mean, that makes me look a bit of a plonker, doesn't it?'

'Oh, God, Freddie, no! You're not a plonker, no way ... that,' I wave my hand towards the bedroom, 'was, you know ...'

He raises an eyebrow and I feel myself burning up under his scrutiny.

'Amazing.' It comes out very small. Except amazing is a big word, maybe I've overdone that. 'Great. Nice.'

'You've gone from amazing to nice there.'

'I know.' I twiddle with the toggle of my sweatshirt self-consciously, then when there's no response I glance up.

'If it helps,' his voice was soft, 'I'd go with amazing.'

'It does.' I swallow. 'I didn't want to sound you know, pushy, like OTT when we've only just ...'

He laughs, then leans forward and kisses me. 'Jane, we've known each other for ages. This isn't a meet-cute that's gone from bus stop to bed without stopping for refreshments.'

'I know, it's just we've known each other for ages as friends, and this is a bit ...'

'Unexpected?'

I shake my head. I want to be honest with him, and although it was slightly unexpected in that it actually happened in *real life*, I'd been living it over in my head for quite some time now. I think I'd been willing it to happen.

'Out there?'

'Yeah, it is a bit out there. It's just I was trying to stop it happening Freddie.'

'Stop it?'

'Because we've been such good mates.'

'And you didn't want to spoil it?'

'You got it.' I really didn't want to spoil it. Sex changes things, doesn't it? 'Freddie? Did Andy really ask you to look after me?' Is that why he was on suicide watch when we first moved in together? Why he's taken me to Brighton, taken me to bed? I swallow hard. I don't want to believe Freddie would do that, I want to believe he looked after me because we're mates. That what happened last night was because we'd both tumbled down the slippery slope of lust.

I want to believe in him, even if there isn't an us.

But, right now, I'm feeling fragile. Great but maybe-wrong sex, followed by a run-in with the man you nearly married can mess with your head. Especially when you've not even had a cup of coffee.

'Did he bugger! I hardly know him.' Freddie looks hurt.

'No, of course you don't! Sorry.' But I had to ask, just in case.

'We weren't exactly best buddies at school, were we? You heard him – I was geek boy, he was … Well, to be honest I thought he was a bit of a twat.'

'You did?'

'I did. And did he really care enough to ask anybody to look out for you after …'

'Ouch.' Point taken though.

'When you ran out after Louie though, he did pat me on the back so hard I nearly fell down the stairs, then said,' he puts on quite a good Andy voice now, 'maybe you guys should cool it, give Jane some space to work things out.' I try not to laugh when he does an Andy *ha-ha mate* at the end. 'He said you were on the rebound, I wasn't your type.'

'The sod! Give me space! Why do I need space?'

'That's what I thought, but I reckoned I should mention it. In case you do want to take some time?'

The toast lies untouched between us. The melted butter starting to solidify in a not-nice way.

'Freddie. I think I've had enough time, don't you?'

He nods.

'Andy's a total knob.'

Freddie stirs his coffee. I just wrap my hands round my mug. Feeling awkward. Watching him but pretending not to.

I like him, I like him so much it hurts. And Andy isn't right, but maybe I was. Maybe we should have just stayed friends.

'Have we fucked everything up?' He speaks abruptly.

'I don't think so ...' I keep my voice low, sneak my hand across the table closer to his. Him saying out loud the words I've been thinking makes up my mind, I don't want this to mean we've messed up. 'Do you?'

He wraps his firm, warm fingers round mine. 'No.' He leans forward, kisses the tip of my nose. 'Definitely not.' Then he kisses my lips, a firm smacker. 'No way. How can anything that good be called 'fucking up'?'

'Shall I put new toast on? Start the day again?' Louie brushes against my leg, then starts to clamber up, and looks very pleased when he reaches table level.

'I'd love to, but—'

'But?' Here we go.

'Rob rang while you were in the shower.'

'Outer Hebrides Rob?'

'The one and only. He's broken his arm and asked if I could go up for a few days, help out a bit.'

'Oh. You're going to the Outer Hebrides?'

'I am, if it's okay?'

That's weird, Freddie asking me if something is okay. That definitely shows we are now on a different, post shag, footing.

'Well, yeah, yeah, sure, whatever. When?' My heart does a bit of a wobble, along with my bottom lip. I never felt this, kind of, turned inside-out all of a quiver after a night with Andy. Just goes to show, doesn't it, how wrong you can be when you think you've got it right?

'I better get packing. I've got some code I need to debug, and I can do it from up there, and, well, I thought with the wedding you'd be busy, and I'd be in the way.'

'You'll never be in the way! Well, not unless you hog the bathroom like you did last week when I was dying for the loo and late for work.'

'You'll be okay?'

I nod. 'I'll miss you.' I wanted him to be here, with me, at the wedding. I know now that I'm not going to need him to be there to catch me, that I'm not going to fall, but I just wanted him to *be there*. But I can't say that. Not yet.

He kisses my nose. 'I'll miss you, too.'

'Theoretical question?'

'Fire away.'

'If you knew a secret about your best friend,' he nods to show he's listening, 'and decided not to tell them because it could upset them, and you thought it wasn't really important any longer.'

'Mm.'

'And then you found out that some other people knew the

secret, too, and you were scared that they might tell your best friend. Would you tell her first?'

Freddie smiles. Then drops a kiss on my lips. 'Jane, whatever it is you think you need to tell Rach, you'll know when the time is right. When you love somebody, you know.' He shrugs.

'What if I'm scared she'll hate me?'

'You're not scared. You'll do what's right for her, not you.'

'How will I cope with this crazy wedding without you?' I'm on the verge of begging him to stay, but that could just send him running in the opposite direction. Crazy wedding, crazy woman.

'You can always call me, text. And I'll be back soon. It can't get any crazier though!'

'Thanks, Freddie.'

'Welcome.' He smiles. 'You couldn't give me a lift to the station, could you? In like, an hour?'

'Sure, shit is that the time? Bugger, I forgot! I'm supposed to be going up for the final dress fitting. Oh, bugger, bugger, bugger.' I dump the cups in the sink. 'I need to go soon, now.' I grab my car keys, check my purse is in my handbag and make a dash for my bedroom and make-up case. 'Come on, come on, I can still drop you off.'

'Stop.' Freddie is in my way, hands on my shoulders. I have no option but to stop. He kisses me, a quick peck on the lips. 'I'll get a taxi, you get going.'

'Are you sure, I mean I can drop you?'

'I'm sure. What about Louie?'

'I'll be back later, he'll be fine, won't you?' Louie stalks off, tail in the air. 'Then Lora said she'd look after him any time, so it'll be fine for the rehearsal and wedding when I have to stay over.'

'You sure you don't want to stay over at Rachel's tonight?'

'Positive.'

'Good.' I'm wriggling, but he's holding firm, then he kisses me. This time it's a proper, toe-curling kiss that makes me reach up for more. 'Go on, go!' He lets go abruptly.

'Tease!'

'Tease yourself, if you don't go now I won't be held responsible for my actions!'

I grab my handbag, slip my shoes on and leap into my car. Freddie is waving from the window as I drive off, little Louie in his arms.

I don't stop smiling even when I get stuck in the mother of all hold-ups on the motorway.

Not until I turn into the car park near to the bridal shop.

Why has Freddie taken off so quickly? Did his mate really ring, like exactly then?

Of course, he did. I'm being totally stupid. Freddie wouldn't lie to me, I trust him. And it's not like we're in a big relationship, we've had one shag.

Maybe he thought I meant it when I yelled at Andy that I didn't need looking after. But I do. Just by the right person. I'll ring him, just a very quick call.

There's no answer.

I try again. And again. Just to be on the safe side.

So, I leave a cheery message hoping he has a good trip (Gawd, I'm beginning to sound like my mother. What kind of person wishes the guy they've just had incredibly hot sex with a 'good trip'?). I need to delete it, but in my panic I don't hit 1 for more options, I hit end call. Bugger. I hate voicemail. Who listens to them anyway? Hang on, that's a valid point. He won't ever listen to it. I will send a text, a cool text.

'Too much, too much.' I am so not cool. I stab at my screen, deleting some of the kisses but make one jab too many and off it goes. Bugger.

That was so over the top.

Now he'll think I'm completely crazy, and he'll be dying to escape (when he comes back), except he'll be too nice to say so, and he won't actually be able to escape unless he moves out. So not only have we ruined our friendship and will have to spend the rest of our lives, or at least the rest of the notice on the apartment, hating each other, I have completely ruined the chance of touching his lush body ever again.

Freddie is allergic to deep relationships. I know that. I have seen how he picks the wrong girls, just so that he can keep things light and have a reason not to get involved.

My mobile slips out of my fingers. Am I another 'wrong girl'?

No. I refuse to believe that. What we had just as friends was far deeper and more meaningful than any of his flings that I've seen. And Freddie is not a user. Freddie looked after me when I was desperate, took me to Brighton to cheer me up. Gave a kitten a home.

It will all be fine, I'm just over reacting because of the Andy thing.

I take a deep breath.

I am fine. It is my new mantra. I can be cool and relaxed about this.

I try to call him again, just to make sure. He might want to talk to me.

There is still no answer. Fine.

Shit, not fine. I've seen the time, and now I'm not just a fashionable 'nearly on time', I'm a 'this could have the bride-to-be in a panic' ten minutes late.

Chapter 24

I slide to a stop outside the bridal shop, surreptitiously check armpits to make sure the lovely Debs is not going to refuse permission for me to try on my dress (though it is mine, so there must be some leeway), then throw the door open casually.

'... and flame-throwers!' Shouts Rachel.

I stop dead, and double check I'm in the right place, and also not hallucinating. I am, and I'm not. 'Flame-throwers? Bloody hell, I'm only ten minutes late and you're about to torch something!'

Rachel laughs. 'You're never going to believe this, Jane!' She wraps me in a hug, then steps back. 'Mikey has booked flame-throwers and thousands of white doves!' She is jumping up and down on the spot and waving her hands about like a cheerleader.

I cackle. I can't help it. It's a bit like my hysterical reaction when she announced she was getting married. I couldn't control the sound that just came out.

That comment has thrown me straight back to the moment when she told me where the wedding was going to be held. When the vision of the whole doves, thrones and Posh and

Becks type thing had leapt into my head. 'Sorry, God, I hope the two don't get too close together?'

'What?' She looks puzzled, but Sally is laughing.

'Ha-ha. Oh my God, flaming doves! It'll be like having a flock of Phoenixes.'

'They rise from the ashes, not get turned into them,' says Maddie.

'We're ready for you!' Debs is clapping for attention, and ushers Sally away towards the changing room.

I grab my phone. 'You were wrong.' I text Freddie. 'This wedding has just got crazier!' I add lots of doves and flame emoticons. Or at least I think they are, I'm always terrified of mistaking one for something else and sending a totally inappropriate one that will upset somebody. I might just have declared my love of barbecued duck.

'Oh, bugger, sorry, I forgot my shoes!' The beautiful satin shoes arrived a few days after we chose the dresses and are sitting in a box in my wardrobe. Miles away.

'Borrow these!' Debs smiles. 'Size 5, isn't it?'

'I promise I won't forget them on the day! It was just all a bit hectic, Andy came round and ...'

'Andy came round?' Shrieks Rachel, Debs stops mid zipping-up, Maddie nearly falls over, as she's in the middle of putting a shoe on, and Sal stares. Her mouth open. 'Shit, you're kidding?' Rach leaps towards me, towing Debs with her, tripping up over Maddie's other shoe and nearly landing on top of me. 'To your place?'

'Yep.'

'When the hell were you going to tell me this!'

'I am now.' I steady her by the elbows. 'It only just happened this morning.'

'And?'

'And.' I shrug. 'I realised what a knob he is.' I really wish I could tell her about the look on his face when he saw Freddie, but I can't. I can't just blurt out what happened last night, can I? 'He let Louie out!'

She giggles. 'Oh, God, you must be so totally over him if you're more bothered about the bloody cat.' She high-fives me, laughing.

I try to look annoyed, but it's hard. 'He's not a bloody cat, he's my kitten. I love him, I'll have you know.'

'I know you do.' She grins, I grin back.

'I don't want to rush you, girls, but dresses?' Debs has shoes in one hand, my dress in the other and is looking flustered. She's probably trying to rush us out before Beth and the projectile vomiting baby arrive.

This time when we line up in front of the mirror, it is different to the last time when we were hung-over, pale and pasty. This time we are not the cast from *Shaun of the Dead*, we look amazing. Even if I say so myself.

'Wow.' Maddie smiles back at me in the mirror. 'We look pretty damned good, don't we?' She piles her hair on top of her head with one hand and does a twirl.

'Fab.' Rach slips into the gap between me and Sally, and links arms with us both. 'You okay?' She whispers in my ear as she squeezes my arm.

'Yep.' I am. I hadn't realised until now just how much I'd been dreading this moment. This reminder of the last time Rach and I were dressed in our bridal wear for the final fitting – but last time she'd been the bridesmaid and I'd been the bride. 'Really fine.' There's no empty, sick feeling at the pit of my stomach and it's because my heart and head have finally come together and agreed that this is all about Rach, and not me. 'Seeing Andy again made me realise what a bloody escape I had!' Okay, I might never forgive his shit timing, but he did make the right move. For both our sakes.

'Oh my God, this makes it feel so real! I'm so excited.' She giggles nervously, clutching my arm, and I hug her close. And I hope with every bit of my heart that she's going to be okay, that the secret I've been keeping from her for so long isn't going to destroy everything. Rachel deserves the perfect day, she deserves to be happy, she deserves the perfect life.

'Oh, Rach, me, too.' I say the words softly, into her ear. 'It's going to be amazing.' Because maybe if I say it, then the words will come true.

Our dresses fit perfectly, beautiful soft satin sheaches that slink their way down to our ankles. The high, wide neckline makes even my neck look elegant and long, and the cinched in waist somehow makes each one of us look like we have a perfect hourglass figure – even though we are all different shapes and sizes! They're so classically simple and gorgeous, they bring a glamour that I could never have imagined.

'We look so ladylike!' Maddie giggles.

'And sexy!' Sally laughs as she spins round, to display the thin straps and plunging V. 'Clever, eh?'

Debs has indeed been clever. Very clever. She's given me an elegance I didn't think possible, and carefully picked out different pastel colours that suit each of us perfectly. The soft green of mine brings out the colour of my eyes, lifts the colour of my hair. It's so perfect it brings a lump to my throat, and as I look at the other girls I can see that despite the joking, they feel the same way I do.

'Right, girls, out, out before you start to blub! We don't want any nasty stains before the big day, do we?' Debs is doing her best to herd us away from the mirrors and back towards the changing area, and we let ourselves be rounded up.

I'm dying to call Freddie and update him, but instead I send him another funny text. I am a tiny bit miffed that he still hasn't replied, but I suppose he must be on the train, or a boat, or something. I'll call him later. When I get home. Reassure him that Louie and I are coping.

The flat is eerily quiet when I get back. It never seemed quiet before, but now it does. I miss Freddie even though that's ridiculous. I only saw him a few hours ago! And nothing has really changed, has it?

Freddie has never responded to my texts straight away, but I didn't notice before because it wasn't as important. We were just friends. That's it! See!

Except as I scroll back through our exchanges I realise he did. Reply quickly. Almost instantly. And yet, now, after our friends-to-lovers shagathon, there is nothing. Zilch.

This is worse than after the first kiss, when it all got awkward. This is radio silence and it's making me feel sick.

Maybe he's lying ill somewhere? See this is the problem when you fall for somebody, suddenly every little tiny absence is magnified into a possible disaster.

'Oh, Louie, I'm going to have to be a batty cat lady and talk to you! Louie? Louie?' I rattle the cat biscuits and wait for him to come tumbling in.

Except he doesn't.

Which is why it seemed so quiet when I came in.

The windows are shut, the door was firmly shut when I got back.

I open every cupboard, root in every drawer and even look behind the radiators.

He's not there. Then I realise, neither is his bowl, or his food, or his favourite toy.

It's then I notice the note, left on my pillow.

Taken Louie with me. Thought it would be easier for you! X

I scrunch the note up, hold it tight in my fist. Is this a sign that at the end of the day, all males leave me eventually, even my flaming cat?

Chapter 25

'Oh, my goodness.'

Maddie is crying. Not just her normal discreet sniffle, but full-blown fat blobs of tears cascading down her cheeks. She hiccups, then blows her nose loudly.

'Mads, what's up?'

'It's so lovely, so romantic, everything I thought I'd ...' Her voice tails off. 'So beautiful.'

We are in the chapel where Rachel is going to get married, all together for the rehearsal and acting like a group of nervous virgins on a first date. Which we definitely are not. Virgins. Though we are nervous.

Well, I am. I am very nervous. My stomach feels like its got bats, not butterflies in it.

This should have been me, the next wedding I attended should have been mine. But somebody pressed the fast forward button on my life and we skipped that and we're here, at Rachel's.

I close my eyes for a second, fighting for control, scared that I'm about to make an idiot of myself. In my head I can see myself, in my beautiful wedding dress and my throat feels all blocked, and dampness starts to flood my eyes. I shut them tighter, dig my nails into the palms of my hand. But I can still see the image.

I stop, glance up at my groom, waiting where he should be waiting.

Then he turns to look at me, and he smiles.

And it's Freddie.

I open my eyes with relief, blink away the dampness in my eyes, and breath. Properly. It's like I'm breathing properly for the first time in ages. I said to Freddie that I didn't care about Andy any more, and I did mean it, but now I can actually *feel* it. I'm free!

'It's only the rehearsal you daft bint.' Beth nudges Maddie in the ribs, and she makes a funny mouse noise, totally oblivious to my moment of release. Which is probably a good thing. 'You're worse than my baby.' But she puts an arm round Maddie's waist and squeezes. 'It is kind of moving though.' She sighs. 'Almost like watching lemmings jump off a cliff.'

'Lemmings?' I frown at her.

'Shush.' Hisses Sally, but the three of us just huddle closer and carry on.

'Suicide mission, boom, straight off the cliff.' Beth does a soaring up motion with one hand, followed by a splat on the palm of the other.

'Beth!' I think I may have broken the whisper barrier. I mean, I know I was slightly anti-Michael at the start. But we're at the practically up the aisle stage now, all done and dusted, and now is not the time and place to declare that marriage is like a suicide mission. 'They love each other, it's not like that at all!'

Beth widens her eyes and opens her hands. 'Just sayin'.' She's got her innocent look on, but I know she knows about Michael – and I know she doesn't know I know, but I feel myself burning up anyway.

Maddie giggles, and Sally glares.

I frown. I'm with Sally, the last thing I want is Beth spilling about the Lexie fling, because nothing, absolutely nothing and no-one is going to be allowed to ruin Rach's day.

Everybody else turns round and stares.

Michael winks, oblivious to what we're actually discussing, and his mother pokes him between his shoulder blades. 'Concentrate young man, you only do this ...'

'Once,' we all chorus, at a whisper, of course. We are in a place of worship, after all, and we shouldn't be taking the mick out of the groom-to-be.

But it is funny. Too funny. Probably because I feel on a knife edge, and this is tipping me into hysteria.

I've never been thrown out of church before, but this could be my time.

'They are all full of hope.' Beth's tone of voice is dreamy, and for a moment I think she's had a rethink on the love and marriage thing. 'All on their way to something heavenly, only to discover it's actual heaven, or—' she pauses dramatically, then lowers her tone several octaves and makes the duh-duh-duh noise of doom. 'Hell!' Oops, she is still with the lemmings.

'Stop it, Beth.' I punch her arm.

'Joke!' She grins at me good-naturedly and I can't help but

grin back. It doesn't sound like she's about to drop a bomb into the proceedings, and she is taking my mind off Freddie and the fact he might be stranded out at sea or something.

It is also taking my mind off Andy who has become a bit stalkerish. There have been many texts since the morning at the flat and they are annoying. I'm ignoring them in the hope he'll get bored.

Up until now, ignoring Andy has not been a problem. But today, he is stood next to Michael and Jack, and I keep catching him staring at me, which is unnerving. I wish Freddie was here, and not lost in the back of beyond. Then we could stare back at Andy in solidarity. Freddie is good at solidarity, and listening to me chuntering on about this wedding, and Coral, and he's actually quite a good sounding board when it comes to my photos.

I blink. I hadn't really thought about it before, but he has, as they say, a good eye for colour and form. He's so much more than a kind-hearted geek who can write computer code, he's got a sensitive, artistic side, I sigh, and feel all mushy inside as my head is flooded with thoughts of his sensitive fingers and creative moves in bed. Oh, bugger, I can't be thinking that in church! I will be struck down!

'Phew, thank goodness that's over, it was so weird.'

'Weird?' I raise an eyebrow and take the glass of bubbly that Rachel is offering, and we sit down in the window seat together. It was our seat when we were younger, slightly hidden away, a good place to share secrets and spy on the grown-ups.

I'd been worried about dodging Andy when we were sorting

out lifts back to Rachel's house after the rehearsal, but Beth had solved the problem by jumping between Michael and Rachel and announcing that all the girls were going back together.

'I kind of felt a bit panicky in the chapel.' Rachel looks at me. 'Is that odd? It's kind of made it feel real. Up until now, I've just been running round planning stuff, but it's just felt like wedding stuff, not *my* wedding stuff.'

'I know what you mean.' I hug her and try to blink away the memories. My wedding had felt real, which is why it hurt so much when that one text exploded the dream into smithereens. And it's why Rachel's day has to be perfect. I won't let Michael's past, Beth's gossiping or Rachel's nerves come between her and her happy ever after.

'I am doing the right thing, aren't I?'

'What do you mean?' I look straight into her eyes, which are as damp as mine. 'It's a great place to get married!'

'I didn't mean the place, I mean getting married. It's so big, so important. How do I know it's right?'

'You know, Rach.' I keep my arms wrapped around her. 'You love him, don't you?' I try not to let my own feelings seep into my voice.

'Of course I do.' Her laugh is strained, wobbly. Then she nods her head vigorously. 'Of course I do! I'm being silly. Everybody gets last minute nerves, don't they?'

I hadn't had last minute nerves. I had been rock solid certain I was doing the right thing, right up until the point of finding out I wasn't. But I suppose I'd never got this close. This last-minute.

'It'll be fine, the real wedding will be fantastic, I know it will.' I squeeze her.

'I know, but then everything will be different. I'll be Michael's wife. I'll be a Mrs!' She rolls her eyes at me, then we grin together.

She suddenly sobers. 'It won't change us, will it?'

'Definitely not.' I squeeze her into another even tighter hug, blinking away the tears. 'Never.' I wonder if it will change 'us' though, I mean it can't not, can it? I'll be back in the apartment with Freddie and Rachel will have her new home. Different things to do. Couple-things with people like Sally and Jack. Making baby-things.

Adulting-things.

Oh, God, this isn't why I finally broke my only-friends rule with Freddie, is it? It wasn't a subliminal message from my brain, saying that I was about to lose my best friend Rach and I had to get back on the 'date, marry, procreate, die' wheel, as well, was it?

'You are going to tell Coral to go screw herself, and sort your career out properly?' Rachel prods me.

'Soon.' I nod.

'Honest?'

'Honest.' More nodding, I'm like that dog in the Churchill adverts. 'Me and Freddie had a big talk about it, then I made a plan. I know I've stuck with her longer than maybe I should, I realise that now, but I needed her, just like I needed you and Freddie.'

Rachel nods, squeezes my hand.

'It's been safe, my security blanket as well as a good stepping stone.'

'But you're ready to let go?'

'Nearly. I'm going to prove to everybody, but most of all to myself that I can do this.'

'That's my girl.' Rach hugs me, tears brimming in her eyes. She wipes them away. 'And ...' she pauses, 'what about Freddie?'

'What about Freddie?' I'm trying to sound casual, but I'm pretty sure the blush is heavy duty.

'Oh, come on, Jane! Have you even bloody snogged him again, yet? I bet you have, admit it!'

'Okay.' I sigh. Take a deep breath. It's only fair, if we're having an honest and open discussion. 'I slept with him.'

Rachel screams.

'Shhh.' This is not something everybody should know about.

'Oh my God!' She clutches her left boob, then starts pounding on it like Tarzan having a heart attack. 'He should be here now! I'm going to text him, ask him.' She's grabbing her phone as she speaks and lifts it out of range when I try to grab it.

'Rach stop!' She stops. 'There might be a problem.'

'Problem? Rubbish, don't you see Jane, you two were meant to be! It was fate, meeting him again just when you did, when you needed him, and—'

'I think it might have been a massive mistake, the biggest mistake in my life,' although surely that was Andy and not what happened with lovely Freddie? 'I've not heard from him for days and he's in the outer Outer Hebrides.'

She frowns. 'What do you mean, not heard from him?'

'I've texted and texted, and called and left messages, and nothing.'

'Nothing?'

'Not since he left. His phone goes straight to voicemail.'

'Oh, frig. Oh, Jane, that's horrible. Maybe he's had an accident and is lying in a ditch somewhere, or,' she adds quickly, 'a hospital, or been arrested, or lost his phone.'

I sniff. 'I'll go with the last one.'

'Sugar.' She puts her hand over her mouth. 'I didn't mean to say anything really horrible had happened. He'll be fine, fine, not dead or anything. Just not able to text. I mean it's not like him to not text you is it?'

'Well, it wasn't before, but that's when we were just mates.'

'But I can't imagine that Freddie—' She suddenly grabs my arm. Hard. 'Oh my God, look!'

'Where? What?'

'There.' She nudges me hard in the ribs and inclines her head in the way you think is inconspicuous when you're drunk but is actually like waving a giant placard in the air. 'Have you seen who Jack is talking to?'

I look.

He's standing in the slight alcove of the doors that open onto the terrace, partly hidden by the floor length heavy drapes. A spot even more secret than ours.

'I still can't quite believe you broke his arm,' whispers Rachel in my ear. 'I bet not many people have wedding photos where the best man is in plaster, do they?'

'I didn't break his arm. He fell over.' I give her a playful nudge in the ribs.

'Yeah, yeah, yeah. I'm beginning to wonder about you!'

'Who's he talking to? Your dad?' I lean forward a bit, I can't quite see the other person.

'No, not Dad! Keep your voice down, look, look!' She points wildly.

We both lean forward and nearly fall out of our window seat.

'Bloody hell.' This snaps me out of my wallowing about the future.

Jack has shifted to one side slightly, and there's no mistaking who he is talking to. Beth. Their heads are close together, as though they're sharing a secret. 'How weird is that?'

'Very, he's so not her type.' Rachel tuts. 'She better not be trying to bloody wind Sally up.'

This has just crossed my mind as well. Beth loves to needle Sal, who, luckily, isn't anywhere to be seen at the moment. But what worries me more is that she might be telling him about Michael and Lexie. I feel sick.

'Oh my God. They're hugging! She never hugs anybody!' Why would they be hugging if she was gossiping? She can't be making a play for him, can she?

'Ouch.' Rachel yelps and I suddenly realise I'm clutching her hand.

'Sorry. But this is wrong. Jack is married to Sal, Jack still lo—' I stop myself a second too late. I never intended saying this to Rach. Rach is Sal's friend. They are the fearsome foursome.

'Jack what?' Rach is staring at me.

'Nothing.'

'You were going to say loves! Jack still loves ...'

'No, I wasn't! Well, I was, he loves Sal, he's married to Sally.'

'You said still loves. Oh, no.' She puts her hands over her mouth. 'Jack still loves Maddie?' It's a whisper, the kind of whisper that is really quiet, you know when something falls out of your mouth because your brain has just added everything up?

'I could be wrong, I just, he ...'

'He, what?'

'At your hen do, when I bumped into him ... He was saying he missed her, and never meant to hurt her, and didn't realise that she didn't mean it when they split up.'

'She didn't mean it? What do you mean she didn't mean it?'

I study my hands, then finally decide to look her in the eye and come clean. 'I promised to keep it secret, because Mads really doesn't want to upset things, or Sal, or anybody, but she told me when we were in Brighton. You know when she was dead upset?' Rachel nods. 'She told me she'd done what she thought was best at the time for both of them. She didn't think she fitted in with his new uni friends, and would mess things up for them, but,' I take a deep breath, 'she thought he'd come back one day and they'd live happily ever after.'

Rachel sighs, then grabs my hand. 'Wow, really? She really thought that?'

It's my turn to nod.

'Wow, poor Mads. It's no wonder she was upset when she bumped into them. And you think he ...?'

'I dunno, really, but I know he misses her, but he'd never hurt Sal. He said so, he said he could never leave her.'

'What a mess.' Rachel shakes her head. 'Poor Sal.'

'Don't say anything, will you?'

We sit in silence for a minute. Then Rach gives a little gasp.

'They're hugging properly now! He's hugging her!'

I'd forgotten we were spying on him, well, not actually forgotten, just a bit distracted.

'If he's still in love with Maddie, what the fuck is he doing groping Beth?'

'I wouldn't say groping!' His hands aren't anywhere they shouldn't be. But it does look pretty intense. Like any second now it could turn into groping.

'They're staring into each other's eyes, he's touched her cheek, it's one step away from orgasm!'

'Rach!'

'Do something! If Sal sees them she'll scratch Beth's eyes out and have his balls on a platter!'

This would actually solve quite a few problems.

But I don't say that. I just think it.

Luckily, they've pulled apart a bit, so I don't have to leap into action. Even at this distance I can see Jack looks upset rather than amorous. And Beth looks like she might be on the verge of tears, which is totally un-Beth-like. And he's still got his hands on her shoulders and is pulling her in for another hug.

'Beth doesn't do hugs.' Rachel is frowning. She has a point, this was just what I'd been thinking. I, at least, have never seen Beth in a clinch with a man.

'True. Though she must have done at least some hugs, to make Joe.'

'Shit! Joe!' We both have the thought at the same time. Stare at each other in open-mouthed shock, then stare back at Beth and Jack.

'Bloody hell, Jane. You don't really think?'

I don't want to think, but I am. Gawd, the baby isn't his, is it? Really?

Why else would she have cornered him though? Why else would they be in a huddle and both look so upset?

'It can't be.' I say this, but only half mean it. 'No. No. It just can't be. What about Maddie? Oh my God.' I put my hands over my mouth. 'I nearly told her that he still loved her!'

'Well, it's a bloody good job you didn't. Poor Maddie, and what about Sal? Flipping heck, I didn't think Jack was like that!'

'Oh, hell, I've just realised, that's what he meant!'

'What do you mean?' Rachel stares at me, puzzled.

'When I was talking to him at your hen party. He said he'd made so many mistakes! I thought he just meant marrying Sally, but he didn't, did he? That would just have been one mistake! I thought he was the perfect match for Maddie, I didn't know he dished it out right, left and centre.'

'He's never come on to me.' Rachel sounds a bit affronted.

'He's never come on to me either!' I fold my arms and feel slightly miffed. Not only have I misjudged the man, twice, he's worked his way through most of Mads friends. And, I have to admit the uncharitable thought: what's wrong with me? Not that I'd ever want one of my friend's boyfriends to come on to me of course, that would be totally wrong and screwed up. But nobody wants to be the one girl that a guy passes on do they? It's like being the last one to get picked for a school team. And that kind of thing lives with you, believe me. 'Bloody hell, do you think Sal knows?'

We both take our gaze off Beth and Jack for a moment and let this sink in.

'I always thought he was the quiet one.' Says Rach.

'Me, too. Though my mum always said to watch out for the quiet ones, but I think she meant girls.'

'No wonder she's been so bitchy with Sal.'

'She's always been bitchy with Sal.' I say, for the sake of fairness. 'Sal baiting was her hobby at school.'

'This is going a bit far though, isn't it?'

'Do you think Beth has only just told him? I mean, she did say she hadn't told the father, and he does look pretty upset.'

'But huggy? Very huggy for a guy who's just discovered he's a dad. Would he be huggy?'

'God knows!' Then she smiles, a wistful, dreamy, very scary smile. 'I always thought he'd make a nice dad.'

I shoot her a look. 'Why've you been thinking about Jack being a dad? That's well weird.'

She shrugs. 'Sal isn't keen on having kids, but he is, and, you know, well, Michael's been putting it off as well and, well, it gets you thinking about guys you know doesn't it? Who'd want to be a dad, who'd be a hands-on type. Who'd run a mile.'

It doesn't get me thinking like that at all. Right now I'm

happy weighing up whether a guy, one guy in particular, would be good with kittens. Mine was. Just not with me it would seem. How can he still not have replied to my texts?

It's not crazy-possessive to expect a reply is it? It has been days. Lots of days since our night of passion and his hasty exit.

Unless he's trying to work out how to tell me it was a mistake.

Freddie hates confrontation, he goes out of his way to finish relationships in the nicest way possible.

I shake my head, I think I need to get back on track here and concentrate. 'But what about Sal? And Mads?'

When I'd pondered whether I should tell Maddie that all hope wasn't lost, I hadn't thought life would throw a curve ball like this. Thank goodness I didn't tell her, that would have been one mistake it would have been hard to recover from.

'Oh my God!' Hisses Rachel, clutching at my arm. 'It's Maddie!' She's shaking me. 'She's heading straight towards them. Do something, shout her, distract her! We need to head her off.'

The room is too big and too busy for that to work though. We watch, hearts pounding, unable to look away. Unable to move. We'd make crap action-movie heroines.

It's like that moment in a thriller when you just know it's about to kick off unless somebody does something quick. Which they never do. Where would be the fun in that?

'*Sheeeet!* Sal's over there as well.'

'*Owwww!*' I'm mesmerised, but Rachel's nails are digging so hard into my arm she's about to draw blood.

Maddie rounds the corner. Will she burst into tears, will she thump Jack?

'What the—' The breath I've been holding shoots out of me.

She's smiling at Jack. Okay, it's a bit shy and awkward, but it's a smile. She slips her arm through Beth's, kisses her on the cheek.

Rachel and I stare at each other.

They're laughing. Maddie is hugging Beth, who then takes a step away.

'Oh, no! She didn't see them all over each other! She thinks Beth is her friend.'

'She does?' Rachel frowns. 'At school they were ne—'

'No, but they are now. They got chatting at your hen party, and Beth confided in her and …'

'Confided in her? What about?'

Shit. I still haven't even worked out if I should tell Rachel about Michael's 'indiscretion', let alone the fact that everybody else seems to know.

I had been sure that *not* telling her was the best way forward, in the interests of making this the best, most memorable (for all the right reasons) day of her life. With none of the upsets I'd had. But knowing that the others all know has changed that.

Really, the only way forward is to come clean, before somebody else does it for me.

It has to be top of my list. I must do it soon. Very soon. And work out how to tell Maddie that Jack still loves her, not Sal, but he's actually just found out he's a dad so maybe he loves Joe more. 'Well, not confided, just, er, chatted and stuff.' Luckily, Rach is distracted.

'Beth's on the move. She's going, she's going, we need to follow her, ask her. Don't let her get away!' Rach grabs my arm and shakes it. Which catches me unawares.

'Shit.' We both lean forward. One lean too many. We start to lose balance and grasp onto each other tighter. Mistake. We both tumble out of our hiding hole, and land in a bit of a heap. In front of some jeans with torn hems that I vaguely recognise.

Freddie?

I look up.

It isn't. The disappointment is physical as it slams into me.

I want to cry.

It's bloody Andy.

Could this get any worse?

Chapter 26

Andy has changed out of his normal dress-down gear he was wearing for the rehearsal, and the chinos and open-necked shirt have been replaced with distressed jeans that are practically begging out for mercy, and a heavy metal T-shirt that should have been buried in the decade it was designed for.

Freddie's clothes have been over-loved, Andy's have been neglected and donated to a moth farm. I notice the light overhang of belly and realise this clobber probably dates back to when Andy was a student.

'How's it going, ladies?'

'Kill me now.'

'Sorry?' He laughs. I hadn't meant to say it out loud, but what the heck.

We both stare at him.

I want to shove him out of way so that I can watch Mads and Jack, so that I can see where Beth is going. I peer through his legs but they've all gone, so I crawl back a bit.

'Your hair looks funny.' The moment I saw him something had niggled me, there was something strange about his appearance. Now I realise what it is, he has had highlights!

'Variety is the spice of life, eh?' He winks.

I swap a glance with Rach, who is on all fours next to me, and looks like a cat trying to cough up a fur ball. She's not, she's trying to keep the giggles in.

'Bugger, you'll have to excuse me, I'm, I'm,' she leans in closer, and takes up the position of a sprinter on the blocks, 'I need a pee!' Then she's off.

'Is she okay?' Andy looks worried, and also looks like he's about to hunker down on the floor beside me. So I shoot to my feet.

'So, having a good time?'

'Great, great.'

'You're looking good.'

'Thanks.' I would say it back, but you know how I feel about lying, and the mess it can get you in.

'I know I got the timing wrong the other day, but I really would like to make up.'

I shrug. 'Look I'm sorry, Andy, but ...' I start to edge away.

'Stop. Please.' He puts his hand on my arm, and I freeze. 'I know it's not just the other day I cocked up. I want to apologise.'

He's looking me square in the eye.

'I really owe you that, Janey. I wasn't ready, but I should have said something earlier, tried to work things out rather than bashing on. But for ages I just kept telling myself it would be fine.'

I stop properly then and look at him. The man I'd loved.

He's still there, inside and I've just seen a glimpse of the guy I thought I'd known, the one I said I'd marry. Another human being, who'd known getting hitched wasn't the right thing to do. He'd just messed up how and when he told me.

'I reckon that message wasn't perfect timing, was it?'

I sigh. Heavily. 'Andy, anything would have been bad timing to be honest.'

'Maybe.' Now he's gone shifty. 'But I was running out of time, I didn't think. There was only a week left! Look Jane, what I'm trying so say here, is I made a mistake. I panicked. I wasn't ready!'

'And now you are?'

'I've realised I was being daft, nobody ever feels ready, do they? I mean, look at Michael and Rach, who'd have thought?'

Who indeed.

'But he's got his shit together. Calmed down.'

'And you've got your shit together? You're ready to commit?'

He smiles, his confidence returning. 'We could give it a whirl.'

'I don't want to Andy. I don't want to whirl with you, I'm done with whirling! We were never going to work out, not then, not now.'

'Aww, come on, I know you like Freddie, but we were the real deal, weren't we? You can't have just forgotten what we had. Remember,' his eyes twinkle, 'that beach in Mykonos?'

I do remember Mykonos. That Greek beach is a memory of our good times, our best times, but I can't go back there.

'Nothing's changed though Andy. We're still not meant to be. I've moved on, you need to as well.'

'But ...'

'I need to go. Sorry.' I start to edge past him.

'Is this about Freddie? Do you two guys really have a thing going on?'

My cheeks start to warm up, as in full on about to erupt volcano kind of warm.

'No, this is about you and me, Andy.'

'You hardly know him, it could be over in days, whereas you and me ...'

'I do know him!' And as the words burst from my mouth, all my doubts about whether snogging Freddie has been a disastrous mistake suddenly burst from me in some kind of hallelujah moment. I laugh. Andy frowns. Not very diplomatic of me I suppose, but it's like I've been shot straight in the jugular with something that's sent me sky high. Or dead. Not sure shooting stuff into your jugular is a good idea. Or legal.

But I know. What I did with Freddie might have been rash, stupid, lustful, mad, but it was inevitable.

We've been so bloody happy together, so in tune with what the other is thinking, so close it's as if our emotions have been meshed like flaming Velcro. So we let our bodies do the same. It would have been a travesty not to at least try it. Well, that's my excuse, and I'm sticking to it.

And if it doesn't work out, then obviously I'll have to spend the rest of my life with earplugs at the ready, just in case he brings a girl back.

And I will cry, I know I will. And stuff myself with carbs, and weep myself to sleep. But I'll be able to get through life, just as I'll be able to get through this wedding.

If the other bridesmaids don't kill each other first.

'I hope so, Janey. I do want you to be happy you know.'

'I will be.'

'Freddie's a good bloke. Cool dude.' He does a thumbs-up.

I think I have narrowed my eyes and am about to strike out. Andy has never called Freddie good, a bloke, or cool before. 'But is he really your type?'

'I'm dating him, it's not like we're not about to get married.'

I feel a bit sick. Seasick sick. Well, my stomach does, it's swishing about as though the waves have just started to swell. I mean, it's all well and good saying (or thinking) that it won't kill me if it's a five shags and out scenario, but really? Am I destined to only go for guys who won't ever make it down the aisle?

'But isn't that what you want? To get married?' Andy is frowning and looks genuinely confused. 'That's why I asked you!'

I already know Freddie has sworn off commitment because he's already found and lost 'the one'. Is this why I'm cool with it, because I really am as wedding-phobic as everybody thinks?

My God, Andy has a lot to answer for.

'Times change. People change.' I haven't heard a peep from Freddie since he left. But I need to. I need to hear him, see him, get hold of him. Tell him he doesn't need to be scared.

Andy grabs hold of my upper arms. 'Oh, Jane, are you sure?'

I wriggle, but he's got a pretty firm grip. 'Will you let go?'

I hiss through closed teeth, trying at the same time to smile at all the other passing guests.

'Are you sure you've not just confused being mates with, you know ... something more.'

I freeze. 'No!' Have I really? No, no, no! That kiss, that night in bed, falling off, almost tucking my leg behind my ear (didn't think I could still do that at my age). They way he nibbled my lip and sucked ... I shiver at the thought. Who knew that having your face sucked could make other parts of your body react like that? Who knew I'd be thirty before anybody was clever enough to show me!

That wasn't confusion. It definitely wasn't. I am puzzled and distracted, and slightly flushed, mainly because I'm thinking about Freddie, and haven't got a clue what Andy on about. Then I realise.

Too late.

Andy seems to have taken my rigid stance as an invitation. He must think I'm mulling things over, or deliriously happy (and speechless) that he's offering me a second chance. He lunges, his mouth half open, and all I can see are blubbery fat lips as he closes in on me.

I dodge and get an earful of tongue. Could be much worse, all things considered.

'What the hell are you playing at, Andy?' I kick him in the shin, hard. I think I might have shouted, and I reckon I'll be leaving him with a handful of my hair, but I don't care. He's welcome to the memento.

I duck down and do a kind of limbo dance as I shimmy out of range, waving to Rachel's Dad, who is watching from the side-lines and give me a thumbs up. He probably thinks we're inventing a new party game.

Then I spin round, and bump straight into a tall dark, handsome stranger. Warm hands rest on my forearms to steady me, and I look up, straight into a pair of familiar eyes.

Chapter 27

'Jane! You've grown.' He chuckles.

It's not a stranger, it's Rachel's brother, the one I had a crush on years ago. And it's fair to say he's grown a fair bit as well. He's maybe not quite as noticeably hot, but his eyes still twinkle, and he's got the most gorgeous dimples.

'Sam!'

'And you're looking totally gorgeous! Why did Rachel never tell me?' He grins, and his dimples deepen. Then he leans forward and kisses me on both cheeks, Spanish-style, and I get a waft of something that smells so delectable it has to be expensive. I take a deep breath and nearly swoon. I think it's a heady mix of aftershave, body warmth and shock from Andy's assault. 'You look amazing!'

'You are kidding? Have you seen her hair mate? It's bright red!'

This time I spin round so fast that I'm surprised I don't corkscrew into the ground. For a moment I stare, open-mouthed. Then I think I must squeal (rather loudly), because Sam covers his ears.

'Freddie!' I don't know whether to swipe at him, laugh or

cry. So instead I leap at him (well, on him, if I'm honest), and it's like coming home as he wraps his arms round me, as his warm lips meet mine and I taste the familiar wonderful smell.

Sam grins good-naturedly, but to be honest I hardly notice. All I can do is stare, and drink in Freddie.

I've never seen him all suited and booted before, and he still looks eye-poppingly good even though I've dribbled down his shirt and wrapped myself round him like a boa constrictor. He must have a crease-proof coating.

'You're here!'

'I'm here! Not interrupting anything am I?' He raises an eyebrow.

'Sam, Rachel's brother.' Sam sticks his hand out. 'I'll leave you guys to it, shall I?' Then he winks at me. 'Holler if you need anything!'

I am turning beetroot-red, which is so not fair.

'That's Sam?' Freddie's eyebrow goes up another notch. 'The one you ...?'

'Stop it! I was a kid, it was a crush! Gawd, I wish I hadn't told you!'

This is one downside of your friend becoming your boyfriend, he knows all of my secrets.

'Anything else you haven't told me?'

'Nothing. Well, nothing like that.'

Whatever Freddie and I have done wrong, we've never slipped up on the being honest and talking things out front. He knows nearly everything there is to know about me.

'Well, Andy did try to kiss me, but I dodged, and ended up bumping into Sam.'

'Try? Any contact? Should I march off and deck him?'

'No mouth to mouth contact. How did you get here?'

'Car.'

'No, but, you're with Rob, and you've not answered my calls, and ...'

'I was on my way back, thought I'd surprise you. That is okay?' He looks worried.

'Definitely. More than okay. My God, you look sexy!'

'Sexy?' He grins, ear to ear and he looks so happy I make a promise to myself to tell him more often.

'Definitely!' I stand back a bit so I can take another gander at him. 'You didn't answer my texts!'

He looks bashful. 'I forgot to take my phone charger, picked one up at the services on my way back and my phone practically self-combusted when I switched it back on!'

'Services?' I frown.

'Motorway? Petrol?'

'You went on the train!'

'Well, I didn't actually. After you'd gone and I decided to take Louie, and it seemed easier to drive. Have you ever tried to take a cat on a train?' He grins, then it turns into a sheepish smile. 'I missed you. I needed to see you, even if it is only for one night.'

'You drove all this way, just to see me, then you're going all the way back?' Wow! 'For one night?'

He nods. 'Must be crazy.' Then he strokes one finger gently down my cheek and a tiny shiver runs down my spine. 'Though I did leave Louie up there.'

'Totally crazy.' I gulp, forgiving him for leaving Louie. 'Nobody has ever driven miles just because they miss me.'

'Then they must be crazy, too.' He drops the smallest of lingering kisses on my lips, and I want to grab him and kiss him like I'm never going to stop. Instead I just let the warm fuzzy feeling spread through my body and I smile. Like a bashful teen. He smiles back.

How could I ever have thought I'd mess things up, that he wasn't coming back? 'Good job Rachel text, or I wouldn't have known where to find you. I'd have gone all the way back home and you wouldn't have been there!'

Home. I like the sounds of that. Our home.

'I'll be back for the wedding though, now I've got an invite. If you want me to?'

'Of course, I do!' I can't stop myself from grinning, and it does actually feel like it's from ear to ear.

'Wouldn't miss it for the world! Something tells me it's going to be memorable!'

He holds out his hand. 'Shall we grab a drink?'

It's a bit surreal, like an old-fashioned movie, when the guy says, 'shall we dance?', and the girl swoons into his arms and they do, to a full orchestra, with the moonlight shining through the open French doors, and everybody else magically evaporates.

Except it's real life, and I'm still feeling a bit giddy from all the weirdness of the rehearsal, and being cornered by Andy, and the shock of seeing Freddie again.

So instead of melting into his arms, I take a deep breath and slip my hand into his. 'Yes please, and I need help! This wedding will be memorable for all the wrong reasons if I don't work out what the hell is going on with the bridesmaids!'

The only safe place, I reckon, is the bathroom. I need somewhere we can't be overheard, somewhere to sit down and think. Well, lie down I think might be a better idea. And, no, not like that. I need the cool tiles, with a wet flannel on my brow.

My head is spinning.

So I drag poor Freddie off to the bathroom, lock the door, then lean against it for extra safety.

We need to come up with an action plan. I said at the start of this, that there were reasons for us girls drifting apart and now I know they were bigger than I ever imagined.

'Jack is Joe's father!'

'What?' Freddie looks at me blankly.

'Jack, the one who is married to Sally, but still has a thing for Maddie!'

'Busy boy!'

'That's not helpful.'

'Sorry.'

'He's just so nice, I can't believe he's a serial shagger. I mean Michael, yeah, but Jack?' I bury my head in my hands. Honestly, he's just so nice, and normal. Average build, average looks, twinkly smile, kind. A safe bet you'd reckon.

Well, it looks like everybody reckoned, not just Maddie.

'How could Beth do it? How could she sleep with him? And how could she be stupid enough to let his sperm do a happy dance with her egg?' Freddie has the hint of a smile on his face, which disappears when I glare at him.

'Happy dance?'

I ignore him. 'I never had her down as a sneaky bitch, I mean, she's snarky, but it's funny not hurtful. How could she have slept with Jack, and then be pretending to be friends with Maddie?' That's the bit that really stings. Her buddying up with lovely, heartbroken Maddie. 'They were in a huddle at the hen party, and she told her!'

Freddie frowns. 'That's good then, isn't it?'

'Good?'

'That Maddie knows about, erm, Jack.'

'Oh, God, no! She didn't tell her *that*, she told her about Michael and Lexie!'

'Lexie?' Freddie has a slightly startled expression on his face. 'Michael and Lexie?' He drags the words out slowly as though he's tasting them, and I realise I've still not told him my secret. My real reason for having gnawing doubts about the whole wedding.

'It's this woman I saw him at it with in an alleyway not long before me and Andy were getting ... Well, it was just before my hen party, and I was going to tell Rach and then things all went wrong, and I missed my chance, then they split and I didn't think it mattered. And I thought,' I run out of my breath and draw another one, 'I was the only one that knew, but now Maddie does, and Beth does.'

I look at him to check he's following, but he looks a bit dumbstruck.

'So anyway, the point is, what kind of a cow is Beth if she's having a go at Michael for being unfaithful when she's done something just as bad? She betrayed Maddie! At least Michael only shagged Lexie once!' I can't believe I'm saying something slightly in Michael's favour, or that I'm totally trusting his word on that one. 'At least that was a one off and all forgotten, but a baby lasts for ever, doesn't it?' Well, not forever, but the probability is that Joe will outlive us all.

Freddie frowns, but doesn't say anything.

'I blamed Sal for stealing Jack from Maddie! I mean I've never particularly liked her, but I got it totally wrong.'

'Maybe not totally.' Freddie says reasonably. 'I mean she did, didn't she?'

'I bet it was him made the running and she just took the opportunity, like he did with Beth!'

'Hang on, don't you think you're being a bit unfair here, jumping to conclusions. You said Jack still had a thing for Maddie, but he was doing the honourable thing and sticking with his wife, that doesn't fit with him being a total dick does it? That's good, isn't it?'

I frown. Stopped in full flow. He has a point. 'Okay, but it doesn't change the fact he's Joe's dad! This is terrible!' This is far, far worse than telling Sal that Jack might still be holding a candle for Maddie, this is a whole firework display. 'Should I tell her?'

Freddie shrugs. 'Do you need to, right now?'

'Oh, God, what is it with men?'

He raises both eyebrows.

'Sorry, not you, not all men. I just …' I sigh and sink down onto the lovely cold floor. Freddie joins me.

'Look, you don't need to do anything, do you? If Beth has told Jack he's the daddy then it's up to Jack to tell Sally, not you.'

'But Maddie will be heartbroken.' I bite my lip. 'And Sal will be fuming, and they'll all ruin Rachel's big day!'

'Maybe they won't, maybe they'll stay quiet until after. They've only got to wait a few more days!'

'What if Beth gets drunk at the wedding and tells everybody?'

I stare at him glumly, and he hugs me. I knew having Freddie here would make me feel better.

'Forget them Jane, concentrate on Rachel.'

'That's the other problem though. Beth knows all about Michael and Lexie and she told Maddie, what if she says something about that?' I never thought it would be Beth who'd be the loose cannon on the big day. 'I need to talk to Michael, don't I?'

'Maybe you do.' He has a slightly doubtful look on his face, which I decide to ignore. My mind is made up!

'I'm going to. Right now.' I scramble up off the floor, just as there's a very loud knock which means I stumble and land on top of Freddie. Which he seems to think is a very good excuse for kissing me. Can't say I have an issue with that.

'Hey, are you okay?' Somebody yells.

'Fine, erm, hang on.' I detach myself from Freddie.

'Getting desperate here!' The knocking gets a bit more frantic.

'Sugar.' I look at him, then hiss in a loud stage whisper that can probably be heard through the door. 'Erm, this could be embarrassing, you wouldn't, erm, mind going out of the window would you? I am chief bridesmaid, I have a rep to keep up here you know!'

I am only half joking, but Freddie eyes up the large sash window and before I can say another word, he's opened it. He winks. 'Always wanted to do this! See you in a bit!'

I flush the toilet so that the person out there knocking on the door is in doubt about what I've been doing, give my smeared lipstick a bit of a rub, sort my hair and try to stop myself giggling smugly. Then I open the bathroom door in as casual way as I can.

And I can't help myself. I groan.

Chapter 28

'Jane!' What do they say 'talk of the devil and the devil appears'? Oh, Gawd, I just want to go home. Back with Freddie to our little cramped flat.

'Sally!' Not the person I wanted to bump into. She peers round me, as though suspecting I might have somebody else in the bathroom with me.

As if!

'You are doing the rounds aren't you? Making up with Andy now.'

'I was not! And he's not in there if that's what you're thinking. Anyway, I thought you said you were desperate.'

'I can last a bit longer.'

'Well, I'm all done.' I try to dodge past her, but Sally is not to be deterred.

'He's still got the hots for you, hasn't he, Andy? Strange the way he dump—' She pauses as I glare at her. 'Did that. Guess some guys get jealous when you spend too much time at work, don't they? They like attention. But he's so mad about you still, and as for Freddie.' She fans herself, in a drunken fashion. 'Wish I had a guy like that!'

'Freddie's not my guy, he's a friend.' This isn't strictly true now, but I'm not sure quite where we stand so it will do for now.

'Call him what you like, same difference.' She shrugs. 'You are *so* lucky, *so* popular.'

I'm not sure if she's being sarcastic or means it.

'Did you need a wee?'

She ignores my question and tilts her head on one side. 'So why Jack?'

'Jack? What are you talking about?'

'At the hen night, you were talking to him ...' She pauses. 'For *ages*.'

'Ages?' I laugh nervously. 'Oh, I wouldn't say ages!' Flaming heck, I didn't realise Sally or anybody else had missed me, I thought they'd checked in and gone straight up to their room.

'Well, I would! Checking in was a 'mare and you were still not back when they finally gave us our room keys!'

'I was getting some air!' We're not exactly shouting, but it's getting a bit hot and confrontational. 'I needed to clear my head.'

'Whatever.' Sal waves a dismissive hand. She's good at that. 'But it must have been quite the heart to heart. Is there something going on between you two?'

'No!'

'So, what were you talking about?' She is peering down at me.

'Erm.' This is a tricky one. Luckily, she moves on before I spill the beans about Jack's feelings for Maddie, or his relationship with Beth.

'Were you talking about me?' She's looking a bit agitated, as well as very drunk, which isn't the Sally we all know, and at times love to hate. Our Sally is uber-confident, and never doubts herself or any part of her perfect life. Does this mean she knows there are cracks appearing?

'Erm, not really, why?' I don't want to add to the lies, but I don't think she's really listening.

'I need to talk to you, Jane. You're alright you know, and you can keep a secret, I know I can trust you.'

Oh, no, not more secrets. I might have to scream and make a run for it. This is the longest, most traumatic party in the history of man. I leave the bathroom and make my way back into the party room, but Sally follows hot on me heels, still determined to get something off her chest.

'People love you, you know.'

She must be very drunk. 'Er, thanks again.'

'I mean Rach loves you. And Freddie obviously loves you, too, it's the way he looks at you. I know that look, I want that—'

'Everything okay, Matchstick?'

This is what you call a rude interruption. Very rude. Where the hell is Freddie when I need him?

'What did you just call me?' I glare at Michael, hardly believing my own ears. But I am quite glad of the interruption. We have business to sort.

'Matchstick.' He shrugs. 'Me and Andy always called you that.'

'*Always?*' I can't believe he used that name. When Andy carelessly dropped it into his 'we are over' text to me, I hadn't realised that my stupid school nickname was still in common use. 'We aren't at school now, you know!'

He shrugs but seems on edge.

'Matchstick!' Sally giggles. This is what being drunk does for you, you forget why you were angry and start laughing at the drop of a hat. 'Ha-ha, matchstick!' And she's off, weaving in a zigzag towards the bar. I've never seen her this drunk before, which makes me think maybe I'm being mean, maybe she really does need somebody to talk to.

I'm tempted to go and catch her, which wouldn't be difficult, but Michael senses it and neatly moves to block my way.

'What do you want, Michael?' Michael and I avoid each other wherever politely possible. This is out of character. It's also me that's supposed to be looking for him, so this is all very odd.

'Have you told her?'

'Told her what?' I'm confused now. Does he know about Jack's secret, am I supposed to have passed the message on?

'About Lexie. Have you told Rach?'

'Oh. That! No.' I falter feeling myself blush and look round guiltily. Just talking about the girl I caught him tonsil-sucking down an alleyway next to Tesco's while I'm in the same room as Rach is making me all hot and bothered.

The image is as fresh in my mind as if it happened yesterday, not over a year ago. Oh, why the hell didn't I tell her on my hen night like I'd planned to? If Andy hadn't spectacularly dumped me I would have. I know I would have. None of this would be happening now. 'Why?' Bugger, Beth hasn't said something, has she? Or Mads? Does he know it's practically common knowledge now, and I'm the least of his worries?

'She's been acting a bit strange. She was just muttering on about men who shagged around, and,' his eyes narrowed, 'she was really upset. We're about to get married!' He is eyeing me up as if he'd like to have me struck off the guest list. See? We don't get on, and at times of heightened emotions (like on the countdown to your wedding) the slightest remark could lead to something nasty. I know. Believe me.

The twinge in my gut relaxes a bit though. I think this is about Rach spotting Jack and Beth, not about her being suspicious of Michael. Call me mean, but I'm not about to tell him that and let him off the hook.

I fold my arms, slightly defensively. 'Rach is my best friend, I want her to be happy.' It's a bit of a stand-off.

'So do I. Can't you see that?'

I glare back. My head on one side and study him. I have been trying to see that he loves her, that he's a reformed man. His shoulders slump slightly, and for a minute I feel sorry for him. The poor man does love her, and he's been stricken by guilt in the same way I have. Burdened by the fear that I could spill the beans any day.

'It's probably just last-minute nerves.'

I don't want to explain about Beth and Jack, about baby Joe. He'll shoot his big mouth off and tell everybody, and I could end up being the only bridesmaid left. 'But.' I take a deep breath. This could be my last chance to sort this out. It's now or never. This is my opportunity to do what I told Maddie I'd do. Get this out in the open. 'I don't like keeping secrets from her, I hate myself for not saying something, I should have told her about you and Lexie. She's my best friend, Michael.'

'I get that.' He seems to relax a bit. 'But we're for keeps, Jane.' He shrugs. 'I'll tell her myself if it means that much to you.'

Phew. I can feel the weight roll off my shoulders. 'Really? You will?' This is a turn up for the books. Has he had a nasty knock on the head that has turned him into a different person? I haven't even had to confront him, to insist on anything!

'It was just a slip up.'

Or rather a slip in. But that would sound bitchy. He is trying.

'Sure. I just want you guys to start with a clean slate, you know, no secrets.' I nod vigorously to drive the point home.

'So do I.'

'So you will tell her. Everything? Honest?'

'Honest.' He smiles then, a charming warm smile and I know why Rachel fell for him, and why she's prepared to forgive him.

'When?' I can't help myself, I'm still slightly suspicious.

He laughs. 'I've always thought you were a bit barmy you know, but you're a good mate, aren't you? Don't worry.' He pokes me on the nose, which is a bit annoying, but right now I can put up with that 'I'll tell her before the wedding.'

I'm shocked and impressed. So impressed I almost hug him, or that could be because I'm pissed not impressed.

He high-fives me, job done, then walks off in Rachel's direction.

'Everything okay?'

I glance up at Freddie, he looks slightly dishevelled after his escape through the bathroom window, so I brush him down. 'Erm, I think so.'

'So that's Michael?'

'That's Michael!'

'Hmm.'

'What?'

'Nothing.' He's staring after Michael in a not-nothing way. 'Just checking. He's changed a bit since school.' He snaps out of it then and grins, his gorgeous toe-curling grin. 'You did it then? You had words?' He raises an eyebrow, it makes me laugh.

'I did. He's going to tell her.' I'm on a high. Delirious.

'Definitely?'

I frown at him 'Definitely! It was just a one-off, and it was ages ago. You know what? I think it's all going to be okay, I think he does really love her!'

'Fantastic.' He kisses my cheek, 'so, it's all systems go?' and gives me a double thumbs-up.

'All systems go!' I'm shattered, but I have done my duty. 'You wouldn't mind if we called it a day and went home? If you don't mind that is?'

He smiles, slips his arm round me, rests his warm hand on my waist. 'I don't mind at all.' The way he squeezes my waist tells a story all of its own.

'Oh, er, I'm staying at Mum and Dad's, driving home in the morning. No, erm, nookie tonight.'

He laughs, a lovely rumbling laugh that fills me with gorgeous anticipation. 'I was thinking of skipping that, driving back to ours?'

'Mmm, I like the sound of that!' I'm grinning ear to ear, I know I am. 'I'll just say 'bye to everybody, won't be a minute!'

I'm just about to head off and look for Rachel, so I can say goodbye, when Maddie appears. She looks happy. I can't bear to pop her bubble and tell her that Beth isn't the new bestie she's pretending to be. 'Great party, isn't it? I can't wait for the wedding! Are you off?'

'I need an early night, I've, got a ton of work to do tomorrow. It's been fun though.'

'Great fun, and,' she shrugs her shoulders in excitement, 'I've finally broken the ice with Jack!'

Hasn't everybody? Well, not exactly ice.

'Oh great! Fab!'

'We had a good chat, he told me about you breaking his arm!' She giggles. I wonder what else he has and hasn't said. Then she hugs me unexpectedly hard. 'Thanks for talking to him Jane, you're brilliant. You should say bye to him before you go, I think he's chatting to Beth.'

'Beth?' I try to look neutral.

'They're probably talking about baby Joe again.' She smiles, totally at ease and benevolent. She must be totally pissed.

Yeah, yeah, I bet they are. I hug her back. 'Oh, right. What a mess.' Mess is not a big enough word.

Maddie sighs, then brushes my hair off my face. 'I know, but things work out how they're supposed to in the end don't

289

they?' A philosophical drunk. 'I'm glad Beth finally decided to come clean and managed to talk to somebody about it. It must have been so hard.'

'I. Suppose. So.' My words are coming out in slow-mo. I think I have woken up in another dimension. This is all too odd, and too much to cope with at this time of night after so much to drink.

'She didn't want to upset anyone, but she couldn't stay away. She needed to see him. It's so hard keeping a massive secret like that, isn't it?'

I nod. It certainly is. Then, I realise I can't help myself. I have to say something, it can't do any harm now. She knows about baby Joe, and she's obviously moved on now.

Just like Jack did when he thought she'd really dumped him. Though I need to be sober and have a calendar in front of me before I can be sure if Beth came before or during Sally. Definitely after Maddie though. I squeeze Maddie's hands. 'He did still love you, you know. He's still very fond of you.' I know fond is a bit of a crap word, but I don't feel I can push it any further.

'Really?' She smiles, then kisses me on the cheek.

'Really. He told me.' I grin. 'Just before I broke his arm.'

Maddie grins back, then pulls away and grins at Freddie. 'I can't wait to meet you properly at the wedding, you look so good together and I'm so happy for you both, you deserve one of the good guys, Jane! Ooh, I'm so excited! Night!'

'Night, Mads.' She doesn't hear, she's already gone.

'So, I'm a good guy, am I?'

'Yes, Freddie, you are an excellent one.' I am totally

exhausted after everything that's happened tonight. Talk about drama. But as I link my arm through his and smile up at him somehow I know everything will be okay. With Freddie by my side, how can it not be? 'Take me home, please?'

Chapter 29

We didn't make it home, but we didn't get to my parents either. We are currently shacked up in a Premier Inn and I have just got round to removing my bra properly, after an athletic workout that involved the shower, wardrobe, loo and bed. I mean you do have to use the facilities you are paying for, don't you? I make it a rule to either use or take with me every single complimentary packet of everything. Even the shoe-polishing kit and shower cap, they're quite useful as Christmas-cracker fillers, and go down better than the free trolley tokens the supermarket sometimes hand out.

Anyway, I've never used the facilities quite so thoroughly before, or left an impression of my bottom on a TV. Why don't they mount them higher, out of harm's way?

'I've got a confession.'

I am sprawled across Freddie's chest, twirling a hair and wondering whether it would be too obvious and prudish to pull the sheet over myself, as I don't think I can hold my stomach in much longer. He is running his fingers through my hair in a way that is making my scalp tingle. Other bits are starting to tingle as well, but I'm not convinced I have enough energy to do anything else just yet. Maybe I should suggest watching TV (after I've wiped it down) and a nice cup of tea – we've not used the kettle yet. 'You hate Mission Impossible, you only watched it for me?'

'Not quite.' The corner of Freddie's mouth is quirked up, but it's not its usual grin. He looks a bit like a Labrador that's been caught stealing the Sunday roast.

'What?' I frown, stop twiddling and stop thinking about how long the biscuits might have been on the tray.

'I knew about Lexie and Michael.'

'*What?*' My heart does a hiccup. I stop lolling on his chest and sit bolt upright, and stare at him with what could be a confused look on my face, or it could be more *I'm going to kill you*. Who the hell *doesn't* know about Lexie? Just Rachel? 'What do you mean, you knew?'

'I'm her friend on Facebook.'

'How can you be her friend?' How can the man I share everything with be Lexie's friend?

'I, erm, might have been out for a drink with her.'

'What?' Facebook friend is bad enough, but this is real, in-person, full-3D friend.

'In a group of course.' He adds hastily. 'She's friends with this girl I knew, we all went to a *Star Wars* convention!'

Lexie is the least '*Star Wars* convention' person I can think of.

'Ages ago,' he adds, as though that makes a difference. 'She talks about Michael all the time.'

'What? Talked or talks?' I eye him up suspiciously and

wonder who exactly this man I've just had rampant sex with really is.

'Talks.'

'Why the fuck didn't you tell me?' It comes out on a gasp, and then I stare at him and do a goldfish impression. I don't know what is most shocking, the fact he knows, or the fact that Lexie still talks about Michael – as though something might still be going on! And I don't know who I'm most angry with, Michael for so obviously lying to me or Freddie for not actually owning up to this earlier.

'I don't really know Michael, and I've not seen him for years, so I wasn't totally positive it was him from the photo she posted, until I just saw him tonight. He looked vaguely familiar, but I didn't realise he was Rachel's Michael.' He looks a bit miffed, which is most unlike Freddie, but I'm too wound up to take much notice.

'Not totally positive? But why didn't you say? If you thought it was him, why didn't you show me flaming photos!'

'Well, I didn't know that he'd ever had a fling with Lexie, until you mentioned it earlier, did I?' There's a defensive note in his voice. 'Then I realised it had to be him. There aren't many Lexie's about, are there?'

Well, that explains why he looked so startled and, well, uneasy. I'd just thought he'd been confused.

'It didn't seem to matter, and it doesn't, does it?'

'It does!' I can't put into words exactly why it is so important, but it is. This means that it might not be over. This means that Michael has been lying to me as well as to Rachel, and that he probably hasn't got any intention of telling her the whole story. The lying, deceitful toad! If I'd known this earlier I could have made him tell me exactly what was going on.

I scowl. I thought Freddie and I shared *everything*, I thought it was a two-way thing.

'Oh, God, Freddie!' I am so angry I can hardly speak. 'She's still talking about him! I should have known, I should have told Rach!'

'Well, it's sorted now, isn't it? Michael's going to tell her.'

'But they're this close,' I put thumb and finger together, 'to getting married and now you're saying that this thing between them happened more than just that once!' My heart is thumping so hard in my chest it feels like it's going to burst out. I feel sick, dizzy. This changes everything.

'Shit. I should have told her earlier, I knew I should.' I start to pace, then go faster, and charge round the room, grabbing clothes, and just, well, charging. I'm all pent up and feel all hollow inside.

I was so totally selfish leaving this until now, not telling Rachel at the time. And I am so angry at Freddie for not warning me.

'I can't believe you did this. You should have told me!'

'It'll be fine.' His words have an edge to them, and I know I've upset him, but I can't help it. 'Just calm—'

'Don't you dare tell me to calm down!' I know I'm over-reacting, but I can't believe he's done this. I can't believe that all along, when I've been telling him about my worries, my guilt, he's known the bloody girl at the centre of it.

Maybe it's guilt, maybe it's because these last few weeks

Zara Stoneley

have been a total emotional whirlwind for me, or maybe it's because in my heart I'm still worried that Freddie and I should have stayed just good friends, but all of a sudden I want to rewind time. Undo all of this. Not be here having this conversation.

'I didn't think it mattered, Jane.'

I know I've cocked up not telling Rach. I know Andy cocked up not telling me how he felt earlier, and I know that right now all I want to do is curl up in my own bed.

'You're as bad as they are! What is wrong with men? You're all as bad as each other!' The words burst out before I can stop them.

'That's not fair, and you know it!'

I know it's not, the moment the words come out of my mouth I know I'm not being reasonable.

'I don't know anything any more.' I know if this conversation goes on any longer, I might say something I'll regret.

'I think we better go, don't you?' Freddie's voice is tight, I just nod and don't say a word. We pay the bill, get back in the car, and head for the motorway.

We've been travelling for an hour or so when the silence starts to get at me. I hate long drawn out silence, it generally means something bad is about to happen, or already has.

We'll soon be home and I don't want us to be like this when we get there.

'Sorry, it's just I need to trust you, I thought you told me everything.' It comes out a bit stilted. 'I was a bit wound up and it just kind of tipped me ...'

'You *can* trust me! It's just ...' there's a long pause.

'What?' A feeling of dread wraps its way round my heart. I just know he's about to say something terrible, that there's another reason for him being so defensive about this. Apart from me being a totally unreasonable, shouty, cow.

'I'm pretty sure Lexie has seen Michael more than once. And quite recently.'

'*What?*'

'I promised I wouldn't say anything to anybody. I wanted to say something,' he gives me a sideways look, 'but she'd said they were sorting it, and I thought if I told you it might screw things up between us.'

I glare, I am speechless. Well, not quite.

'And I still wasn't totally positive that her Michael was Rachel's.'

'He's not *her* bloody Michael! How could you not tell me?'

He shrugs. 'It is up to them to sort it though, not us, isn't it?'

'Fuck.' I can't think of anything else to say.

He sighs, flicks the windscreen wipers on, and I watch them swish from side to side, and try not to explode.

'Look, Jane, I know all this has been difficult, so,' there's another long pause, 'I was going to suggest that after the wedding we do something different, make a fresh start.'

'What?' All I can do is stare at him. I'm still seething, and worrying about Rachel, and this conversation has just taken a very strange turn.

'Away from here, away from London, all the bad memories, people ...'

'They're not just *people*, they're my friends!'

'Well, you can visit your friends, like you do now. I've, erm, been offered a job in Scotland.'

'Scotland?' I frown.

'I thought maybe if you came as well?'

'But why would I want to go to Scotland?' I realise that could be taken the wrong way, as a bit of an insult. 'I can't, Freddie! I like it where we are. I need to be near London.'

'You don't though, do you? You can work from anywhere.'

'No, I can't.' It's my turn to sigh. 'All my contacts are here, the right places, people. You know that! And my friends are here.' If I have any left after all this. 'Rach, my parents.'

'You did fine with your Brighton photos.' There's a stiffness in his voice that I've never heard before. 'Take more like that. Strike out on your own.'

'I don't want to take more like that, *this* is my career.' I can hear the wobble in my voice. I'm not yet ready to start out on my own. Of all people, Freddie is the one that I thought knew that. That understood. He knows that! He's trying to force me to move before I can. I'm not good enough as I am, doing what I do at my own pace. 'I like what I do.'

'No, you don't.' He sighs again. 'You have to take the leap some time, Jane. Maybe now is the time. And it's a good job offer.'

I can't move, not yet. The life I'm living, working for Coral is what I need right now. The photos I'm taking for her are a part of me, they *are* me. I have to be good enough just the way I am, doing what I do. In my own time.

'It's my fault for barging in and rushing things, if you can't trust me then you obviously do need some space, time. Decide what you want to do. This isn't about me and you, is it? It's just about you, and your friends and doing things your way. And I can't compete with that.' His voice is scarily soft, and there's a note of finality that sends a shiver down my spine. This is it. He's going to walk away. I don't know how we've got to this, how it's all blown up.

'I do know what I want to do! And it is about me and you, but I need time!' I notice out of the corner of my eye that we've pulled into our road. 'But,' I have to say this, the thing that really bothers me about 'us', the thing that would always make me hesitate to take the giant step and follow him to wherever he wants us to go, 'I obviously can't compete with your perfect woman either, can I? The one you can't get out of your head!'

'There isn't *another* perfect woman.' His voice is dangerously soft. 'Just the one.'

I barely hear him. The moment he's pulled the handbrake on I'm out of the car and heading up to our flat.

I go into my room and close the door, then collapse with my back against it. There's the sound of him coming in, his steps hesitate by my door, then I hear his quietly close.

Reasons why you shouldn't shag your best friend: 1. He won't be your best friend any more, whatever happens; 2. You know he's a commitment phobe; 3. A tiny bit of you refuses to stop believing in love, which means the only way it can end is badly.

Chapter 30

Bugger. I've overslept again, and I've got so much to do. I practically fall out of bed as the alarm goes off and hit my head on the bedside cabinet. I really must move the bed against the wall. Safer all round.

I've overslept a few times recently. Since Freddie and Louie went – the first time. Then again after Freddie went – the second time. I woke up the morning after the rehearsal party to find he'd gone.

I'd known he was planning on going back to Rob's, but doing it like this, without us saying another word to each other makes it feel kind of final. Even if he did leave a note, with a kiss.

There is a physical pain in my chest, my neck is all knotted up and my stomach feels hollow, but I am not going to let it kill me.

I have a job to do, a duty, I have to make sure that Rachel knows all about Michael and Lexie, that she is totally, positively sure that the affair is over, and that Michael loves her, before she says, 'I do.'

Freddie *might* be wrong about Michael and Lexie, and

fingers crossed he is. It *might* just have been a one-off like I've thought all along, and Lexie's obsession with Michael *might* be one-sided. And he *might* have been telling the truth, and Rach's big day *might* still go without a hitch. But I have to be sure. She has to be sure. There are too many 'mights'.

And then I have to do something for myself. I have to kick Coral's ass and prove to myself (and anybody who will listen) that, 1. I can make a go of this, I don't need propping up by Coral any more, I am ready to be just me, and, 2. I can manage without Freddie, I don't need a man to define me, or to help me pay the rent. Well, it would be helpful as far as the rent goes, but I will work that one out, or find a box-room next to the railway, runway or motorway that is big enough for me and my camera. I can survive on baked beans and charity shop bargains, after all who needs cocktails and nice hand-bags?

Anyway, my current problem is I can't get to sleep. So I read. And scroll through Twitter, Facebook and Instagram to torture myself with the perfect lives everybody else is living.

Then I crash out at 4 a.m. and my body forgets to wake up again.

I clamber back on the bed and fling out an arm to turn the alarm off.

Then spot the time.

And realise it's not my alarm it's my front door.

My stomach flips. It's Freddie!

Common-sense kicks in before I'm even out of my bedroom. He's got a key. The flip becomes a churn. I hesitate, wondering if it would be much safer all round to dive back under the duvet. But then cave and answer the door instead.

Because I miss him. I miss his easy company, the laughs we used to have, the way he'd listen. I miss having somebody to turn to in the middle of a bad film and raise an eyebrow at. I'll edit photos and turn round to see what he thinks, and there's nobody there.

And I hate the empty space where Louie's bowls used to be. And I hate the sight of Freddie's toothbrush in the mug – but I can't throw it out. As long as it is there then it means he might come back. We might somehow be able to find our way back to how we used to be.

Silly, I know.

I've not heard from him since he went, and I don't know where he is or if he'll be back. It might only have been few days, but right now it feels like forever.

'Morning! Americano?' Sally waves the coffee cup in my face and neatly steps into the flat before I can refuse entry. 'Sorry.' She looks slightly taken-aback, no doubt by the look of disappointment that I can't help but feel. 'Were you expecting somebody else?'

'No. Nobody.' The flatness in my tone shocks even me. I need to lighten up. Call the police, or a private detective (though according to all the movies I'll get 'he's not been gone long enough' or 'we don't get involved in domestics'), or not worry until he's missed paying his half of the rent.

I'll be really screwed if that happens.

'How cute.' Sally is hovering just inside the door, and gazing round. She's never been here before.

At least she said cute, not tiny, or cluttered, or 'My God, I never knew you were this hard-up.'

'Don't worry, I won't stay long.'

She's misread my look of horror. I'm frantically trying to remember if there are knickers drying on the radiator, or the remnants of a two-day-old pizza on the table. I've been busy. What can I say?

'It's fine, fine. Come in.'

She takes the armchair, and I sit on the sofa, our knees clash and we both flinch. We look at each other awkwardly. Hands wrapped around coffee cups. Normally when we meet we have escorts. A one-on-one for me and Sal isn't natural.

'It's a bit embarrassing.'

You got it.

She takes a deep breath. 'It's Jack.'

'Oh, God, he told—' I mentally zip my mouth. One day, I'll learn that I have to listen, not talk.

'Told you what?' She frowns. 'What are you on about now?'

'Told me, told me you were angry about his arm!' Ha, think I covered that one well. 'Sorry, sorry, but it wasn't me, I didn't ...'

'Oh, whatever.' She waves a dismissive hand. 'Of course I don't blame you for that, it's nothing. Why would he think I was cross about that?' Her frown is even deeper this time. She'll need emergency Botox before the wedding if she carries on. 'You see that's the problem.'

'It is?'

'He hasn't a clue what bothers me. I mean, that's insignificant, isn't it?'

'It is? Oh, shit, yes, it is.' I nod frantically.

She knows. She's going to tell me the news and I'm going to have to prepare my 'I hadn't got a clue, what a shock' face. If I can be bothered. To be honest, right now, Freddie and Rach are top of my priority list.

'You see, this is the biggie ...' She pauses, and I'm going to burst if I have to hold this expression of shock back much longer. She leans forward. 'I was going to talk to you at the party, because I know you'll be sensible, and you can keep a secret, but then that stupid jerk interrupted.'

'Andy?'

'Jane, I've got to talk about this with somebody. You don't mind, do you? I mean I know we're not *that* close, but you can be objective, and you've not got loyalties. Rachel will just try and smooth things over, tell me it will be fine, and I can't exactly talk to Maddie or Beth, can I?' She rolls her eyes.

I swallow. My throat is suddenly very dry. Sandpaper. 'No. Good heavens, no, definitely not.'

She gives me a funny look. 'I've known for ages I guess ... well, had my suspicions.'

'You did?' It comes out all squeaky. I can't say more, though, because I don't know if it's something she spotted in little Joe's face that made her twig, or if Jack's said something.

I still can't quite believe that Beth would do such a thing, however much she dislikes Sally. However jealous she is.

This goes way beyond normal point scoring. Or feeling you weren't part of the gang at school.

Knowing Jack is the father, knowing they must have had a 'thing' has completely shocked me.

Beth has always been sharp and snarkey, but the person I would have least expected to shaft her friend. And, as for Jack, well, Jack honestly convinced me that he still had feelings for Maddie, that it had all been a complete cock-up, that he'd do anything to turn back the clock. But because he couldn't he wanted to be loyal, kind, to Sally. The woman he married.

I should have broken his bloody legs, not just his arm.

'I mean you just know, don't you?'

'Hmm.' I nod, encouragingly. I don't feel like I know anything any more. I didn't know Freddie was keeping things from me. I didn't know he was planning on moving. I didn't know he'd try to force my hand into starting up on my own when I wasn't ready.

'You can tell if things aren't right, but you just ignore them.' Sally is still droning on, but then she suddenly slumps, which catches my attention. Sally's bright smile drops. It is not Botoxed into place like I suspected. 'You just won't believe this, but Jack and I have not had sex for nearly six months!'

Whatever I thought she was going to say, it wasn't that. I nearly say I managed for much, much, longer, and despite popular opinion my body parts did not self-seal (they seemed to work better than ever after a break), but I don't think she wants to hear that. She does have a husband after all, my starvation period was self-imposed.

Luckily, Freddie had re-ignited the flame. All in perfect running order here, thank you. For now.

I try to concentrate on what she's saying.

'He used to go on and on about how he wanted kids, and I mean I know I wasn't that keen at first, I've got my career to think about, and my boobs and stomach, and I mean down there. Everything will flop, droop, expand, won't it?' I keep my mouth tightly shut. 'Not that it makes any difference if it's not getting attention. I mean how the frig does he think we'll make a baby if he refuses to ever try? And,' she really looks like she might cry now, 'I like sex!'

'Well, erm, maybe it's just a phase? Maybe he's busy at work? Got a lot on his mind?'

She shakes her head violently. 'I guess,' she gazes at me with sad eyes, 'I always knew things weren't right between us, I just kidded myself.' A tear plops onto her perfect cheek and she wipes it away, but then more follow in quick succession. 'I know he's only staying with me because he feels he has to.'

This is so shockingly close to the truth that I grab a box of tissues and start yanking them out and throwing them in her direction, hoping she doesn't guess I already know.

'Oh, Sal.' We've never been big on hugs, just the air-kissing type of hug. 'I'm sure that's not—'

'I bet everybody knows.'

She could be right.

'Oh, no, no, not at all, you're the Fearsome Four!' I laugh, weakly. Is this the point where I tell her that his joy stick has been over worked, that it's not her, it's him? That he has dipped his wick in one place too many and already has offspring.

Or do I keep my mouth shut. To avoid Rach's wedding turning into a bloodbath?

'He's just not interested, Jane. I wanted my life to be perfect, so I just made it that way.' She sniffs. 'Jack's never loved me the way he loved her.'

'He hasn't?' I'm confused now. How could Beth and Jack have had this thing going on, and nobody knew?

'She was his first true love, you never forget your first love, do you?'

Now I am definitely confused. No way was Beth his first love. I'm just about to check who we're talking about here when she rescues me.

'Maddie's the one he loves, Jane. Not me, and, I think getting married was a big mistake. Oh, Jane.' She crumples completely then, onto my shoulder. 'It's a sham. He won't leave me because he's too nice, but I know he's not happy. Neither of us are happy.'

'Oh, Sal, but you must have been happy at the start.'

She sniffs and lifts her head. Determined to regain her composure. 'We were, we loved each other. Honestly, we did, it wasn't like we were pretending. But however much I try to kid myself, we're so different.' She puts her head in her hands. 'I've seen the way Jack looks at Maddie when he thinks nobody is watching.' She gives a heavy sigh. 'He's never looked at me that way, and he doesn't even try these days.' And the penny suddenly drops. Her drunken outpourings at the rehearsal dinner, when she was talking about the way Freddie looked at me, were about her trying to tell me something altogether different. About herself and Jack. 'Nobody has ever looked at me like that.'

'I'm sure he loves you.'

'But there's love and there's love, isn't there? It's not right Jane, for either of us, is it?' I can't tell her that Jack feels just the same, or at least he did, until Beth popped up. All I can do is hug her. I mean, how the hell does Jack feel about anything?

'Do you know why I went out with him in the first place?'

I shake my head.

'I hooked up with him because of Maddie,' now I'm confused, 'because Maddie always said how nice he was, how brilliant, how kind, how amazing.'

'Ah.'

'And you know what I'm like.' Safer not to comment. 'I went for it, 'cos that's how I am. Maddie had given him the thumbs up, and he was open to suggestions.' What kind of man wouldn't be, when the full Sally siren mode was switched on and aimed at them? Like I've said, she's competitive, and she works bloody hard to get what she wants. Jack had been a project. 'If somebody has something great, then I want it as well. I need it. I needed Jack, do you get that? And he was amazing, she was bloody right, he's lovely, but he's gone right off the boil.' She shrugs, then wipes the fresh tears away with her forearm. 'I've been an idiot, love isn't a competition, is it?'

'It's not.' Flipping heck, she's going to say she's leaving him!

'I need you to do something for me. I know it's a massive ask, but you're the one person I know can do this right.' She blows her nose loudly, then lifts her chin and looks me in the eye. She's got guts this girl, and I have a sudden admiration for her, even if we'll never be best buddies. 'He likes you, so you've got to help me.'

'I have?'

'I love Maddie, and I love Jack, and I know that in a perfect world they would have stayed together. But it's not a perfect world.' You're telling me. 'So ...' She pauses, a very long pause, then grabs my hands.

For a moment, I think she's going to tell me that she wants to own up that she made a mistake, that she's going to give them a second chance. And if she'd told me this two weeks ago I'd be doing a happy dance. But now?

I needn't have worried, though.

'I need you to talk to them. I want you to check nothing is going on. And if Jack is going to carry on being such a misery, pining like some lovesick donkey, then I need to know. The no sex thing is bad enough.' She rolls her eyes. 'But it's not fair on me if he's going to be chatting and laughing with her all the time, is it? I can't just play second best, can I? I'll look a right idiot!'

I've gone from wanting to hug Sal, to wanting to shake her. It was always like this, she just can't help but be competitive, she needs to win. At everything. Instead I just groan.

'Will you talk to him? He'll listen to you.'

This could be tricky.

'Please, Jane? I mean, my marriage might end anyway, but I'm not going to be made a fool of. I need to give this one last chance, throw everything at it. But if we're doomed then I need to know so that I can make the decisions.'

'Don't you think it's better if you talk to Jack yourself? Or you could go to marriage guidance or write to an agony aunt, or something?'

'Marriage guidance is for people who can't sort their own problems out.' She huffs a bit. 'I can, I just want you to help, if that's not too much to ask? All I want is a decent sex life and him to listen to me when I'm talking to him and stop leaving the bloody towels on the bedroom floor, oh, and the toilet lid up, and squashing the toothpaste in the middle is annoying.'

I think she's got a pretty challenging list there – I reckon sex is the least of her problems.

If Freddie comes back though I'm not sure I can go back to living with him and not having sex. Or a cuddle on the sofa, or a snatched kiss as I head into the bathroom and he comes out.

Oh, God, what have we done?

'Just ask him if he's prepared to try, can't you?'

I nod, because what other choice do I have? And she picks up her coffee and waltzes out of my life as though a huge burden has been lifted.

So, what the fuck do I do now?

Chapter 31

Tomorrow is the first day of the rest of Rach's life, and I'm feeling good. Well, as good as can be expected. This is partly because I've just had a text from her:

Beth doesn't think she can make it to the wedding. ☐ Joe's got chickenpox. R x

I squeal and punch the air. Yes!

Okay, I'm not happy that the poor little thing feels like biting ants have crept under his skin, and it is a shame for Rachel that one of her besties won't be there. And Beth is entertaining. But, I mean, she is a bit of an attention seeker, and I wouldn't put it past her to go public after a couple of drinks, especially if there was a lull in proceedings.

Sal would probably castrate Jack on the spot, because although she's realised their marriage isn't perfect she is not the type to forgive and forget. And once she'd done that then she definitely wouldn't end up with a better sex life.

Rachel would be devastated, as they're the fearsome four-some, and any hope of a Maddie and Jack reconciliation would be out of the window.

No. Beth not being at the wedding is perfect.

I type a response:

Oh, no, what a shame. Hope he's not too poorly J x

Me, too. See you later R x

Then I grab my camera bag, mobile and a few other bits and bobs, and head for the door.

I've got a ton load of work to do before I head up to Rachel's tonight.

I've made it quite clear to Coral that I'm not prepared to be her dogsbody any more and told her all about my new IG account. I just know she'll have been on there and seen the comments, including the ones from Daniel, who absolutely adored the photo of Louie posing in his diamanté collar. It was a freebie, my first solo freebie! In fact, Louie had been approached by a supermarket, and agent and several pet product suppliers as a result – just before Freddie whisked him away.

I'm never going to be an influencer, I don't want that. I'm a photographer, but I want to be a respected one. And to make a reasonable living.

It makes me feel sad. Louie has gone. I really need to talk to somebody, find out how I can fight to at least get shared custody.

I blink away the upset, double check I've got my keys, then slam the door behind me. I haven't got time to blubber, I'm on a countdown. I have photos to take, a load that need editing and scheduling, and packing to do.

Outside, it's the most perfect Friday morning. The sun is shining, the blossom adorns the branches like the perfect bouquet and even the birds are excited.

This must be a good omen, tomorrow is going to be just perfect. I know it is.

Michael will have talked to Rachel, and hopefully told her *everything*, leaving me with a clear conscience, phew. After Freddie's revelation that Lexie had been more than a one-off slip-up, I'd confronted Michael. I had tried to meet him in person, but he'd dodged that one quite neatly, and he had been ignoring my phone calls until I'd texted him saying I had it on firm authority that his minor transgression had been major, and if he didn't talk to me within the hour then I'd be telling Rachel.

He called me three minutes later and swore that 1. It was over, and 2. He'd tell Rach everything.

You've no idea how much better I feel, knowing that the truth is now out there and whatever happens in their marriage is based entirely on their own decisions. I know she'll forgive him, and I'm sure it will make their love stronger. I just hope I've not cocked up, and she's going to feel she can never trust me again.

Now all I have to do is talk to Jack, for Sally, and try to find out if their marriage has a chance. I need to help my friends be honest and open. And it looks like Sal, Maddie and Jack have been anything but with each other.

Who knows what will happen, but as Maddie said things do have a habit of working out how they're supposed to.

I just hope Jack isn't now such a jerk that he moves from Sally to Beth, because it's the honourable thing to do. I might have to kidnap him and lock him away until he comes to his senses.

313

I've not checked my tea leaves, I don't drink tea it gives me a headache, and I've not got a feeling in my waters, but I do feel light and positive. Though that could just be because I've already had two black coffees and am on a caffeine high.

The day whizzes by, and I kick off my shoes with relief, dump my bags, make a drink then head through to my bedroom.

After a hectic day working, the flat seems even emptier than it did before, if that's possible, so I'm glad that I'm going to have to get a move on and rush straight out again.

Another evening here on my own would be depressing. I mean, for heaven's sake, I've now got to face up to the fact that I'm probably never going to be leading the charge up the aisle, I'm destined to forever be the bridesmaid. Which is something I don't want to brood about. Normally I would talk to Freddie, but Freddie is now part of the problem and not the solution. So, having proved myself right on the shouldn't-do-it front, I am now going to devote my life to my career. My way.

I grab my wheelie-case and start to throw stuff in. My bridesmaids dress is already at Rachel's, there was no point in me bringing it back here. But I need overnight stuff, make-up, posh frock to change into in the evening (we all agreed that would be a good idea) and fresh clothes for the following morning. Scared stiff I'd forget something crucial I made a list, so it's easy.

I have a minor panic, when I realise I don't know where my pretty satin bridesmaid shoes are, then suddenly remember.

I grab the box, shove it next to the suitcase on the bed and throw in a few final toiletries. Hair, and a splash of make-up and I'm ready to roll.

I'm actually quite pleased with myself, talk about organised and positive!

Everything gets tossed in my car, and I'm off – ready for my best friend's big day, and whatever lies ahead …

Chapter 32

'What's the matter, Jane?'
'Nothing. Absolutely nothing at all. I can't wait for tomorrow!'

We are spending Rachel's last night as a single woman at her parents' house. They have gone out for dinner with her Great Aunt Mabel, who they only ever see at weddings and funerals (she doesn't bother with christenings). Her mum has left us a massive lasagne, with a much smaller salad (too late to think about diets now, girls!), garlic bread, lots of soft drinks and one bottle of Prosecco (you need to be fresh-faced tomorrow – think of all the photos!).

I love Rachel's mum. I love my own as well, but if I ever got to pick a second one it would be Rachel's.

Rachel spoons a massive dollop of lasagne onto each of our plates, then adds a few lettuce leaves. 'I am so sick of salad, it's all I've eaten the past month.'

'Apart from the pizza.'

'And ice cream. Yeah, yeah.' We eat in silence for a few minutes.

'Well?' I should have known she wouldn't let it drop. 'Oh, come on, you can't kid me!'

'Really, it's nothing important, and this is all about you. Look, I've even brought you a cake!' I crack open the Tupperware box with a flourish.

I'd done a photoshoot the day before with this baker who made the most amazing cakes. He'd insisted I take one. 'They've been under the lights for ages, they'll be fine, but I can't sell them. Elf and safety and all that. And if I eat any more cake I'll get a saggy bottom.' We'd both laughed. He had the least saggy bottom I had ever seen. Talk about rock buns, his were just calling out for an experimental grope. And he was flirty. Believe me, if I'd been in the market for a quick fling, he'd have been the cherry on the top of my cupcake list.

But I'm not, so I just took the cake, muttered about colour saturation and shot off to edit the photos. They were good, definitely good enough to eat, and his Insta account sprung into life the moment he loaded one up.

'Wow, we should have got him to do the wedding cake. That is amazing!'

We both stare at the luscious icing, which is practically glistening.

'It looks too good to eat.'

'Bollocks.' I laugh, grab a knife from the block and cut into the cake. 'Believe me, these are as good as they look. They're all fluffy and melt in your mouth, and really zingy.'

I'd tried my hardest to make them look totally edible, because they were. It wasn't a case of not judging a cake by the cover, these were total bliss.

We both close our eyes as we eat and make the type of noises you'd never want to hear on a playback.

'Oh my God. This is orgasmic. He could make a fortune marketing these to girl's who've just split up, they are the best sex substitute ever.'

'I've totally cocked up, sleeping with Freddie.' It bursts out of me before I can stop it. I think it's Rach talking about sex that's done it – and the realisation that the best sex I've ever had in my life is probably over.

'I love my work, I don't want to move and start again, and he didn't tell me he knew ...' I can't tell her what he knew, '... stuff. Important stuff.'

Rachel drops her fork. 'What stuff, what do you mean, move?'

'We've had a row and I think he's dumped me.' Then something else bursts out of me, a big, fat horrible tear. I was going to be all casual and matter of fact about this. Not working out.

'But you slept together, you had amazing sex!'

This makes it worse. 'I know!'

'He drove all the way home so he could see you.'

'I know.' I think I've got my glum face on, it feels that way.

'You have got to be kidding me. I don't believe it!'

'I believe it. I mean I did know he's a total commitment phobe, didn't I? And I did know that I am a total dead loss when it comes to picking men.'

'But this is Freddie!'

'This is Freddie.' I wipe the dampness off my face and sigh, deeply. 'I thought he was different, I thought he understood about my work.'

'He does.'

I shake my head, feeling very sad, and very tired all of a sudden. 'He's been offered a job in Scotland and wants me to go and start again.'

'He wanted you to move with him? That's something isn't it? That's not dumping!'

'But I can't go yet! I mean, he's not as bad as Andy, he didn't say I should stop taking photos and learn how to touch type and photocopy and work a paperclip, but he did think I could just forget everything I've been doing and start again.' I pause. 'Well, he didn't actually say that.' He didn't, and it's unfair to accuse him of being anything like Andy when he's been totally supportive. Even as I'm explaining to Rachel it's all becoming much clearer about what our row was really about. Fear. I'm petrified about what I'd be risking if I went with him. 'Oh, Rach, I'm not ready, I'm too scared to take a massive step like that and risk losing everything, my friends, the money Coral pays me. I need to be here, Rach, near to London to do what I really want. And,' I try a smile. It's a bit weak, but I'm trying, 'I want to be near to you.'

'Oh, Jane, you're never going to lose me, wherever you are. And you'd have Freddie, if you went with him.'

But would I? I'd always thought I could never match up to his 'perfect woman', now I don't know whether she even ever existed.

'I might have overreacted a bit, but it was a shock.' And so was the fact that he knew about Lexie and had never told me.

'Oh, come on, you must be wrong …' She pauses. 'You said 'think'. How can you think you've been dumped? You live together!'

319

'Exactly. Except he's gone.' I make a pile of the cake crumbs on my plate.

'What do you mean gone?'

'Gone, gone. He was gone when I got up in the morning, I don't think he's coming back. I was horrible to him. I said he was as bad as all the other men I know!'

'Oops.' She flinches, then places her hand over mine. 'But you two were great together, you were closer than anybody else I know.' She peers at me. 'He even watched soppy films with you!'

'Yeah, we were great as friends. He's even taken my flipping kitten.'

'Yours? I thought it was his?'

'Well, technically, he's his, but he's ours.' Oh, heck, we have custody issues and we've never even been a proper couple.

'Oh, no, Jane. He was *so* cute!'

I'm not sure if she's talking about Freddie or Louie now.

'So funny, and the way he danced in front of the mirror, and when he didn't realise his tongue was sticking out.'

'You are talking about the cat now?' I hope she is.

'Oh, hell, sorry, but I can't believe Freddie's gone. I mean, he's got to come back, he lives with you.'

'The flat seems so bare without Louie.' And without Freddie, but I can't say that bit out loud yet. Nor can I imagine life without Freddie.

'What makes you think he's actually gone, gone? I mean, didn't he say he was going back to his mates for a few days?'

'Well, yeah, but it was a massive bust up.' I shake my head and do a wide-mouth frog smile. And try not to cry.

Rachel squeezes my hand. 'Maybe,' she takes a deep breath, as though she's about to say something she knows I'm not going to like. 'Maybe you've not got over what Andy did, that you're not, well, trusting him like you need to? Did anything happen that ...'

I shake my head vehemently. I can't tell her why I no longer feel like I trust him one hundred per cent. 'Oh, God, I've ruined everything by sleeping with him. He was my mate. I love him.' I do a funny hiccup at the end.

'Love like in like a lot, or as in,' Rachel clutches at her heart area dramatically.

'Stop! I don't know! But it doesn't matter now!' I don't know why I am being so over the top emotional. I guess it's all the heightened feelings because of the wedding, and the fact that I need to tell Rachel that I've been the worst friend ever and kept secrets from her. Well, one major secret.

She's going to hate me.

I'm set to lose both my best buddies in the space of a few days. And all because of sex. Sex is evil, it should be banned.

Cake is the way forward.

'Aww, Jane. Are you alright? You look really bad, like you looked after the vodka chase competition.'

I shake my head. I do feel a bit nauseous. That's what keeping secrets does for you. But I have to pull myself together, for her sake.

'I'm fine, fine, I'm being daft.'

She puts her hands over mine. 'He'll come back, I know he will.'

'I know, I'm overreacting.' But the question is, when he

comes back, what then? Can we go back to being just good friends, or will it be too awkward, too different?

'Just chill, I know it'll be fine. I bet he turns up for the wedding! How long is he supposed to be away?'

'I don't know.' I shake my head. 'He just said a few days more. But why did he even need to go back? Why had he planned that?' I frown. Had he engineered that row? Had he done it on purpose, because he's so rubbish at finishing with people?

'Maybe something happened, I mean if his mate's broken an arm or whatever maybe it hasn't set, or something.' She pulls a face, we both know she's clutching at straws. 'He'll be back, Jane.'

'Yeah, sure. I'm being silly.'

'Not silly, just letting what happened with Andy get to you again. Don't. It'll be fine, he'll be back. He'll forgive you, whatever you said!'

'You're probably right.' I doubt it.

I look at her. It's now or never. I feel sick, but I know I've got to check she knows about Lexie. Be sure she knows about the woman that nearly came between her and Michael, the woman who also seems to have come between me and Freddie.

One step at a time.

'There is something else as well. There's something I need to ask you, Rach.' I've got to. I don't know if Michael has stuck to his side of the bargain or not, but it doesn't matter any more. He told me he'd come clean before they walked down the aisle, he promised. If he has, then I'd hate it to come out that I knew and hadn't told her, and if he hasn't, well, he can't blame me for messing everything up, can he?

Well, he can. But it's Rachel I'm bothered about, not him.

There is no way can I let my best friend say 'I do' in front of all her friends and family – and be the only one in the dark. If somebody said something to her on the day, and it all blew up, I'd never, ever forgive myself.

'That sounds serious!' Rachel dishes out more Prosecco. Will one bottle be enough? I can't do this over a glass of water.

'Rach, I need to ask you something. I know it'll sound strange but, it's something I talked to Michael about and he said ... Oh, hell, Rach, has he talked to you?'

'You're being a bit weird, Jane. What's up?'

'Has he told you about, well, that he,' how do I put this? 'Did he tell you he had a fling?' I spit it out and cower, waiting for the fallout.

'A fling?' There's an edge to Rachel's voice.

'A woman he—'

'I know what a fling is.' She gets up, picks up the plates and carries them to the dishwasher. Speaks with her back to me. 'You know about Lexie, don't you?'

Phew, he told her.

'Well, yes, but ...'

'How long have you known?'

'A while. I would have said—'

She turns and fixes me to the spot with her gaze. It feels like I'm on Mastermind, in the spotlight, but if I get this wrong I will lose the one person that matters most to me. 'Why didn't you tell me?' Her voice is soft.

'It was all such a cock up. I was going to tell you at my hen party.' Wow, I just said that without feeling the slightest bit sick. 'Then things went tits up, and I forgot all about it, then there never seemed the right time. I never thought ... and then you guys split up and it didn't seem important.' I swallow hard, hoping she'll understand. 'Then you got back together, and you were so happy. Rach, you'd sorted out all the problems, all the misunderstandings.'

'But why didn't you say something when you knew we were getting married?'

'I wanted to, but then I thought it wasn't fair. You'd made up, he'd explained everything, he loved you, you loved him, Rachel.' I hesitate. 'And I didn't want you to hate me for being the one to tell you, or to think I was jealous or something. You know, sour grapes, anti-wedding Jane! I didn't want to stir things up, there was no point.'

'Stir things? That's a funny way of saying it.'

'You said he'd changed, that he'd moved on, realised what a jerk he'd been. He'd apologised for everything, explained. That you were getting married.'

I wish Freddie was here now. He'd know exactly what to say, he wouldn't be making a cock-up like I am. I can feel the panic start to flutter in my chest.

'I didn't want to upset you for no reason, Rach. I didn't want ...' I have to say it: 'I didn't want you to think I was trying to cause trouble, to split you up.'

'Oh, Jane, I'd never think that.' She sits back down at the

table. Wraps her fingers round the stem of the glass. 'I was mad at him when he told me.' She peers up at me. 'Did you make him tell me? Is that what you were talking about at the dinner?'

I nod mutely. My mouth dry. 'You saw us?'

'I saw you. I thought it was a bit odd, then I thought,' she smiles weakly, 'you guys were trying to make up, get to know each other a bit better. Why tell me now?'

'You're getting married, I wanted you to know before you did, no more secrets.' And everybody else in the congregation knows.

She sighs. 'Shame he couldn't make that decision on his own.'

'But he did.' I nod rapidly. 'He did the right thing, I mean I didn't, oh, God, you didn't think I'd blackmailed him or anything? I mean, I just suggested, and he agreed.'

I am so relieved that Michael has done the right thing. 'I doubted him, I was wrong. He loves you to bits Rach, he's your one.'

'I know.' She smiles then, her grip on the glass loosens.

'Do you still want me to be your bridesmaid?'

She reaches out then, puts her hand over mine. 'Of course I do.' Then she raises her glass. 'Thank you.'

We get off to bed early. Rachel's parents and her Great Aunt Mabel make sure of that.

There's a bit of a strained atmosphere between the two of us, but they don't seem to notice. I think they're too excited.

Her mum insists I see her hat. Her dad shows us his top

hat and tails and does his Fred Astaire impression. Then they start reminiscing and break out the photos of us from school and we both decide it's time for bed.

I'm tired, but when I climb between the sheets I can't sleep. Oh, God, I wish Freddie was around to talk to, to tell me I've done the right thing. Or at least responding to texts. I take a deep breath, if I was prepared to risk everything with Rachel, then why aren't I prepared to do it for myself? Why can't I have the guts to actually confront him? Except I'll have to track him down first.

I'm going to have to. The moment this wedding is over I am going to hit the road.

Okay, he's ignoring my texts and voicemails, but I have to give it one last try.

I pick my mobile up, and it's a good job speed dial exists because my fingers are trembling so much it's hard to do anything.

I'm holding my breath as I wait but, luckily, it's not for long. It clicks straight through to voicemail. Again. And my whole body sags with disappointment.

I text him and tell him if he doesn't get back to me soon then I'm going to call out a search party. He'll be on wanted posters, on milk bottles, or *Crimewatch*.

Then I Google his friend Rob, and finally hit gold. He *is* on Facebook. From the description and photo, it has to be him. How many rangers called Rob with a broken arm can there be in the Outer Hebrides?

I send him a message, asking him if Freddie is there.

Check it's been delivered then stare at the screen until I fall asleep.

It's as though Freddie has disappeared off the end of the earth, into outer space, not just gone to the Outer Hebrides.

When I wake up next morning, ranger Rob has replied. 'He's been a brilliant help, not here now though. Have you tried his phone?'

I throw mine at the wall.

Of course, I have.

And more to the point, where has he gone? When did he leave?

'Jane? Breakfast is ready. Hurry up!'

I hurry up. I'll message him again later. Find out exactly what Freddie said to him, and if he told him where he was heading.

And if he's still got my cat.

I have made a decision, so now I have to shake him out of my head and concentrate on Rachel and the biggest day of her life.

'Coming!'

ACT THREE

The Big Day

Chapter 33

This has to be a nightmare. Any second now I'll wake up and laugh hysterically. I have arrived at the hotel all bright-eyed, bushy-tailed and bubbling with nervous excitement and flipped open the boot of my car with a flourish so that the bellboy can carry my cases.

I do it with a flourish because I am excited about there being an actual bellboy. This is the first time I've stayed in a hotel that is posh enough to actually have a bellboy.

Mistake.

I wave him away as the most awful smell ever hits me. 'Back, back.' I splutter. One hand over my face, I try not to gag as I lift my suitcase out, then resort to holding my nose as I reach for the box with my shoes in.

Oh, my, it just got worse. It's not just a little *eugh* smell, this is a total stink that catches at the back of my throat and makes me want to heave.

And it is strangely familiar.

And it is the box that smells, not my car boot.

I drop it, the lid pings off and a shoe rolls out onto the gravel.

'Oh, shit.'

Luckily, Rachel is not with me. Rachel's dad has already dropped off her and her mum, and I've followed in my car. So, it's there for me in the morning. It's mid-morning and we are all assembling at Startford Castle to get ready. We have a make-up lady, hairdresser and who knows what else lined up to pamper us.

Unluckily, my mother has appeared out of the blue to 'help'. And I have stinky shoes.

'Language, darling. You'll never keep a nice man if you—'

How could I not have noticed until now? I put those shoes in my car, they travelled all the way up the motorway with me.

They stayed in the confined space overnight, so that I wouldn't forget them, and the smell built up.

I have to admit it. This day has not got off to a brilliant start.

'No mum. I'm not swearing – look!' I kneel down, tentatively lift up the shoe by the tip of the heel and hold it at arm's length to double check. I have no idea why I think I need to double check. I drop it like it's on fire. There is no mistake, it is definitely liberally coated in ...

'Cat poo!' Declares the bellboy loudly, then drops his voice. 'Sorry, but it is, isn't it? My gran used to have six cats and, cor, they could stink. If they weren't peeing, they were spraying, and if they weren't doing either of those, it was that.'

Well, at least Louie did leave something behind for me to remember him by. He has poo'd on my satin shoes! Bugger!

Bugger, bugger, bugger. I toss it back in the box, trying to use my fingernails and not my fingers, and slam the lid down.

My shoes. The shoes I am supposed to be wearing for the wedding!

What the hell do I do now?

I'm supposed to be colour co-ordinated.

'Oh, Jane, how could you?'

'I cannot believe you just said that, Mother! It's not my fault!'

'Could Housekeeping help?' I glance up, I'd completely forgotten the bellboy. He's trying to keep a straight face. They must train them well at this place.

'Unlikely.'

He pulls a funny face, but gamely takes a step nearer. 'We can try though, Madam.'

It takes industrial strength cleaner to get rid of the smell, I know it does. 'I've only got ten minutes, they'll all be waiting for me!'

'You could leave them with me?'

'No way.' Smelly shoes have to be better than no shoes. Maybe.

'I'll tell the girls, dear.' Mum is flapping her hand in front of her nose and keeping as far away as she can. 'You go with this man, and I'll distract Rachel!'

'Don't you dare tell her what's happened, make something up!'

'I'll say it's woman problems, shall I? Had to pop home for emergency knickers?'

'Mum!'

'Well, come on then, hurry up.' He stops being a formal

bellboy and turns into a normal bloke. A bloke who bravely grabs the foul-smelling footwear in one hand, and me in the other and whisks us both over to Housekeeping.

We gather quite a crowd of helpful staff, and many bottles of detergent, bleach, furniture polish, carpet spray and 'I'm not quite sure what it is but it worked on that nasty stain on the carpet in Room 403'.

The head of Housekeeping dabs carefully at the shoe.

'Sorry, sorry. We need to be quicker.' I can't wait any longer, I grab it from her.

'But the colour might ...'

Too late, I've sprayed bottle number 3 on it, switched the tap full on and started to scrub.

The jet of water is slightly stronger than I expected, it hits the heel and sprays straight back at me. 'Yikes.' I'm dripping.

'Here love, give me that T-shirt and we'll dry it in a jiffy.' One of the girls has a towel in one hand and is practically stripping my top off with the other. We have a bit of a tousle, which she wins. Leaving me semi-naked in a room of strangers. But there's no time to worry about nudity. I look back at my shoe.

Silence falls as the water turns the colour of the shoe.

'Bugger.'

'It might not be colour fast.' Finishes the housekeeper.

'Yes. Fine.' The damp patch spreads, the whole shoe is changing colour before our eyes. And it still stinks. And even more dye comes out as I frantically pat it with a kitchen towel.

'See,' says one of the staff, pointing to a tiny label she found in the shoe box. 'Protect from damp it says here.'

Crying is not an option. I need an option though, anything. Running round in my bra clutching a stinky shoe is not helping.

Stop. Think. I pat my hair dry with the towel.

'I know!'

'You know?' They all chorus.

'My car.' It's the only option. I reclaim my T-shirt, grab my soggy shoes and dive out of Housekeeping, back out of the hotel and slide to a gravel stop next to my car. Which, luckily, hasn't been parked somewhere else yet.

I fling open the boot.

'Thank God for that!' They are still there.

The limited-edition Doc Martens that Coral had sent over, and had expected me to Photoshop into an 'authentic' Brighton photo long after I'd returned home. Pah, she really needs to look up the meaning of 'authentic'.

Weirdly they are almost the same colour as the shoes I've just trashed, give or take a shade or two. Well, they are limited edition, they do happen to be in my size, ultra-comfy, and nobody will seem them under the dress.

Phew, it is such a good job that Rachel ignored Sal's suggestion of what she thought were the sexier short dresses. Give me a good cover-it-all length any day of the week,

Sally just wanted to show off her endless pins, we all knew that.

What the hell, I've no real choice.

Nobody will notice if I slip them on quietly, they'll all be busy getting ready.

'Everything okay?'

'It will be.' I shove the shoes into a carrier bag, nod at the bellboy, throw my shoulders back and paste on a smile.

And check my phone. Still no message from Freddie, still no update from Rob – who is probably chasing seals or untangling seagulls or something.

I gulp as I look up the big stone steps towards the very posh entrance hall. I am hot and sweaty, have dripping hair and a soggy top. I truly hope no other guests are going to spot me as I head up to the room.

'You're fine.' Bellboy winks at me. 'It's quiet at this time. Come on.'

Chapter 34

I didn't really notice my surroundings when I dived down to Housekeeping with my smelly shoes, but this time I do.

Startford Castle is the place dreams are made of. The word amazing was invented for places like this.

I can't help gazing round open-mouthed as I check in at Reception. It's not just a castle by name, it's like an actual castle.

There's a hushed silence that's all to do with splendour rather than spookiness, and with its wood-panelled walls and exposed stone I can see why it would be perfect for the medieval banquets they hold here.

The old oak floorboards feel soft beneath my feet, the dark brown leather chairs and sofas make me feel like I've stepped back in time and I turn round slowly trying to take it all in.

If Rachel wanted a fairy tale wedding, she's certainly picked the right place.

I peer past Reception and spot a large lounge, with an absolutely massive carved wooden fireplace, and windows to the ceiling with enough material in just one drape for curtains in my flat several times over.

It's all plush reds, golds and greens that work in harmony with the natural wood, leather and stone. And there are books. Bookcases that reach from floor to ceiling, stacked high with old books that I'd really like to rush in and touch.

The staff are obviously used to this reaction. They wait patiently as my hair drips on their rug, which is probably hand woven and cost more than my home and all its contents.

'The ladies are all in Room 264, if you'd like us to leave your belongings in your room and take you straight there?'

'Oh, heck, yes, please, I'm late!'

'Jane, you're here!' Rachel jumps up. 'Your mum said you'd gone off with a man! Where've you been? I thought you were right behind us.' She doesn't pause long enough for the shoe story. 'Sit down, here, here, here.' I'm forced onto a stool. 'You need your make-up doing first. Sarah's done us, you're next.'

'Where's Mum gone?' I look round suspiciously, half expecting her to jump out of a wardrobe.

'Don't worry.' Rachel giggles. 'We sent her off to supervise the table laying.'

'Does it need supervising?'

'Nope, but I'm sure she'll find something to tweak.' Rachel knows my mum well. I'm sure we both have the same vision of her in our heads right now. She'll be checking cutlery and glasses for smears.

The next hour whizzes by as I'm powdered, painted, primped and generally prodded about. Eyes shut, open, mouth like this, look up, head up, keep still, left hand please, don't you dare move.

I could never, ever be a model. All this sitting in one spot while being manhandled and perfected is hard work. My fingers are totally twitching for my camera, but I'm not allowed to shift from my stool until the bridal conveyor belt has been processed.

As my last ringlet is dropped into place I glance to my left, and Maddie and Sal, then to my right where Rach is sitting and cannot believe we've actually got to this point. It's been exhausting. I am totally, absolutely, one hundred per cent knackered.

I am never, ever going to be my best friend's chief bridesmaid again. Well, by that I don't mean I'm expecting her to need a chief bridesmaid again, because obviously in a few hours' time she'll be waltzing down the aisle towards her one and only, and a lifetime of love and happiness.

But if I ever have *another* best friend, who decides to get married, I'm not going to be chief bridesmaid. Final.

We are actually the sweetest foursome though, I'm including myself in that because, whatever, I actually look quite good in this dress.

I take a deep, steadying breath in. My hair has been smoothed and waved and actually looks sleek and shiny for once, my nails all look the same length and are minus the splodgy bits I normally end up with when I varnish them myself, and my eyes kind of ping. That girl was a genius with her flicky eyeliner, both eyes look exactly the same! It's a miracle!

And I don't think anybody has spotted the shoes yet.

'Hey! Hey, everybody, quick, Beth's sent a video!' Rachel

has finally been given permission to move her hands, and the first thing she's done is grab her tablet. 'She tried to ring earlier but nobody answered, so she sent this. Look!'

She holds it up and hits the play button.

'Hi gang, Gawd, I bet you all look gorgeous. Send me photos!' Beth is clutching a happy little Joe, who giggles as she waves his hand. 'The little man is feeling better, but he's still a bit itchy, so I thought I better stay away from the wedding in case I've caught it! Miss you all.' Beth holds Joe's hand and blows a kiss off it, and he beams.

'Miss you, Beth!' Maddie waves and blows a kiss and my heart twinges. Her and Jack would have been so good together.

Who knows what will happen. One day, the daddy secret will be out, when Joe is old enough to understand probably – but for now they're both happy. We're all happy. Happy, happy, happy. Even Sally, when I glance her way, seems chilled.

'Anyway, wanted to wish you a fabulous day, Rach. Hope you all get rat-arsed and enjoy the dad-dancing, and I'll see you soon! Oops, I better go, nappy time.' Beth pulls a face.

'Better out than in, eh?' Sally winks at me, and I know she's going to be okay. I guess, like me, it was a huge relief, a burden lifted, when she owned up to herself, and me, about the state of her marriage. At least she has an action plan now, even if I suspect it is doomed.

'Defo.' I cross my fingers in my lap and send up a prayer that Beth won't think her secret is better out in the open until at least Sal and Jack have had a chance to talk.

'Have a drink for me!'

'Several.' We all yell, even though we know she can't hear us.

We'll miss Beth of course, the one that couldn't be a brides-maid 'cos of her baby, and that's probably good. If she was here then she'd be shattering the sweetness and light with her barbs and the bosom that we're all a tiny bit (secretly) jealous of. And I couldn't cope with the stress of knowing that any minute she could spill the beans about Jack.

Anyhow, we've got our shit together at last and are getting on.

I mean, okay there might still be secrets to share, but as far as I'm concerned, my biggie has been spilled.

Rach catches my eye and I mouth 'gorgeous' at her. She is. She looks the perfect bride. She smiles back at me, a nervous and slightly tentative smile. I'm not sure she's one hundred per cent forgiven me for not telling her about Michael's 'slip-up' earlier, but she's happy. I'm happy for her, and oh so bloody relieved that the secret is finally out. I couldn't bear to carry that in my heart as I watch her say 'I do'. I mean, I could have been responsible for her whole life being fucked up. Well, obviously, not responsible, that would have been Michael who carried that, but I would have felt like I'd let her walk into the lion's den without a spear, or anything. Not that Michael is a lion, but you know what I mean. She wouldn't have been armed with the facts, she would have been wandering inno-cently where innocents shouldn't wander.

I'm glad it came from him as well. Like it needed to.

I do still feel a bit like I'm walking on glass at the moment though, and one false step and I could end up in quick sand,

and I think she feels a bit the same, but I know we're going to be alright. I'll make it up to her, we'll soon be back how we were.

'Oh, no.' Rach suddenly frowns, then starts to root around on the dressing table. 'Where's my something blue?'

'What?' I snap out of my 'how to make it up to Rach' list and stare at her blankly.

'This is my something old,' she points to the beautiful antique sapphire and diamond ring on her right hand, 'this is my new,' her dress, 'borrowed,' she points at her head, and for a moment I'm confused, then I manage to lock onto the hair comb. 'So where the fuck is my blue. My blue Jane!' Her voice has gone up several octaves on its way to hysteria. I get it, this isn't normal Rachel, this is nervous, excited, I'm about to get married Rachel. And everything has got to be right. 'The blue is my garter, where's my frigging garter?' Her mum, who is helping us get ready, winces. She's not used to hearing Rach use the F word.

'Oh, hell, sorry, sorry!' I know it's my fault, I should have made sure she had everything before we started to get ready. It's my job. The one job I should be more than capable of doing.

Which I would, if I hadn't been late because of the shoe incident. 'Where is it? I'll go and get it.' I say, hoping it's not been so forgotten it's miles away.

Rachel, who's been frowning, suddenly smiles at her reflection. 'I remember! It's in my makeup case, it is, I can practically see it.' She gathers up her dress. 'Come on!'

'Come on where?'

'I got them to put all my stuff in the bridal suite. Quick, quick. Oh, bugger, where's the key card, the key?' She's throwing stuff left right and centre on the dressing table, then turns to the bed, and her pile of clothes. 'Here! What a relief, it could have been anywhere.'

And we're off!

She flies out of the room, with me hot on her heels. Her in her gorgeous wedding dress, and me in my beautiful slinky bridesmaid dress that really isn't designed for running. I'm doing a bit of a duck waddle if I'm honest, flipping my legs out from the knee down and hoping she doesn't spot my shoes.

'Rach, Rach ...' I grab her arm and pull us both to a halt. 'Slow down, or my dress will be split right up to my bum!'

'It's fine, it's fine, come on.'

'That's easy for you to say! I just heard a ripping noise, and you do realise I've got no knickers on?'

'Ooh! You've sorted things with Freddie! Expecting fun later?' She winks, wriggles free, then grabs my hand.

I don't have the heart to say no, because today has to be perfect, so I just summon a happy grin of my own and tell another little white lie. White lies don't count, they don't hurt.

'Counting on it!'

She giggles. 'Me, too! Come on, you have just *got* to see our room! It's amazing!'

We zoom down the corridor, the plush carpet sinking under our feet and I suddenly feel light. She forgives me! We're still best friends, it's like somebody had loosened a huge weight that's been dragging me down and I've been released.

'Wait for it!' She pauses, her hand on the door handle, then, '*Ta-dah!*'

She flings the door open and I step in first, prepared to have my breath stolen away.

'What the?' For a moment I think I'm hallucinating, there's a ghost in the room!

Then I realise body flesh that colour, moving in that way has to be real.

'There's been a mix up, somebody else ...' But as the words tumble out of my mouth I realise that there's not been a mix up with the rooms. Not unless the groom-to-be has booked two.

It's like a punch to my gut, it actually, physically makes me tremble with shock. And if it has that effect on me, then what's it going to do to Rach?

I fling my arms wide and back out, trying to take her with me, but it's too late. Rachel is right behind me, she's so close she can't help but look over my shoulder. And she's not going to let me push her anywhere.

'Michael!' We both scream the name out together.

I blink. This can't be happening.

Something blue has taken on a whole new meaning. This is blue movie. This is Michael's bottom and a pair of boobs bouncing in harmony.

'Mikey!' That one comes from Rachel and is like the roar of an injured animal.

'Oh. My. God!' That's me, much lower key than Rach. I feel sick. I put my hand over my mouth. 'Lexie!'

'Shite.' That's Lexie. She covers her boobs and stares at us.

The bouncing dwindles to a stop. It's like watching a yo-yo run out of steam.

Lexie flings long legs out high like she's doing cabaret and gracefully dismounts. I'd be impressed if I wasn't so bloody angry and to be honest this would actually be funny if it was happening to somebody else, somewhere else.

'Fuck, oh, shit, I am so screwed.' This is not the most appropriate thing for Michael to say at this point.

He scrambles backwards, and Lexie rolls off the bed and into hiding, obviously working out the best way to exit.

'*That* is Lexie?' Rachel looks at me, grief stricken, and I nod then reach out to hug her, but she pushes me away. '*That* is frigging Lexie?' She directs it at Michael this time, taking a step towards the bed.

He cowers and for a moment I think he's going to crawl under the covers.

'Oh, for fuck's sake, have you finally finished?' This rather surprisingly sounds like Beth. And when I spin round there is a reason for that. It is Beth. She is standing in the bathroom doorway, clutching Joe, and looking even angrier than Rachel. She is also staring at Michael.

'But you're at home, Joe's ill.' I frown. She isn't, though. She's very much here. They're both here. 'What are you doing in there?'

'I was checking it out for posh toiletries.'

'Wha?' I stare at her.

'Freebies? You do realise how hard it is as a single mum, don't you?' She fishes what looks like a Jo Malone candle out of her bra.

345

'Well, I … but … bathroom.' My words are struggling with each other and coming out in a random order.

'What do you mean finished? You've been listening?' Michael finally speaks again, and he's furious.

'Well, I didn't want to, did I? I told the staff I was planning a surprise and they let me in, then next thing the pair of you tumbled in and had your clothes off before I had chance to say anything! Have you any idea how traumatic it is to sit in a bathroom for that long, listening to all that wailing when you've got a baby? Jeez, I'd forgotten people made noises like that when they shagged!'

'Beth!' I shout this in an attempt to shut her up, and to stop Rachel keeling over.

'That's bang out of order.' Michael has regained some confidence.

Beth laughs, but she doesn't look or sound amused. 'It was the only way I could bloody corner you before you walk up the aisle, with your bloody trousers down! Christ, you are such a total wanker! I knew you were a shit, sorry,' she directs this to Rachel, 'but I didn't know you were quite such a loser.'

'What does she mean, corner you? Who the hell is that Mikey?' Lexie has jammed her boobs back into her bra and is glaring. 'What does she want?'

'To introduce him to his bloody son before he gets married!' Beth shouts. And the rest of us shut up.

Lexie is the first to recover, managing to smack Michael right in the chops. 'You've been having an affair?!'

'It wasn't an affair, it was one flaming night, a one-night stand when he was *single*,' Beth yells back, stressing the last

346

word, 'and look what I got!' She holds Joe up, who looks around wide-eyed, then launches into full scale howls. 'And who the fuck is this?' She adds pointing at Lexie.

'You know who she is!' I yell, finally getting a word in. 'This is Lexie!'

'How the fuck does she know about Lexie?' Michael stops trying to back off the bed, which he's been quietly doing for the last couple of minutes.

'Beth, you told Maddie you knew all about Lexie at the hen party!'

'Did I bollocks. What are you on about?' I get the benefit of Beth's glare now, it is scary.

'Oh, there you are Jane! What a beautiful baby.' My mother beams at Joe. 'He looks just like Michael, now fancy that! Now,' she bumbles on oblivious to the effect her words have had. 'shouldn't you girls be getting ready, it's not the right time for a room party I wouldn't have thought. And your father has lost his best cufflinks, the nice ones I got him, you know those with the rose, the Lancashire rose, do you know where they are, dear?'

'Out!' I yell, then soften it. 'Please, Mum.'

'Oh, I do hope I wasn't interrupting something! You do all look a bit tense, but there's no need to shout, dear. I was only asking ...' She pauses by the door. 'That man should have his clothes on shouldn't he?' Then she pops on her glasses and peers over the top. 'I thought it was you Michael! Chop, chop, don't want to keep the guests waiting. I'll be off now then, see you all soon! So exciting, so exciting, I've been waiting for a nice wedding ever since yours was cancelled.' And she wanders off down the corridor. I resist throwing my shoes at her head, which I think is quite restrained.

'I really don't know what you're on about, Jane.' Beth's words drag me back to the situation in hand.

'You said you knew, about Michael, about his ...' I pause; indiscretion has been the word until now – well, transgression is his word – but it's a bit late for niceties: 'shagging around.'

'Oh, God.' Beth clutches her head. 'I told Maddie about Michael and *me*,' she spits the words out as though they taste nasty, 'Not about that tart!'

'Oh.' That has stumped me. Somehow, I have completely got the wrong end of the stick. 'You mean when Mads said Michael had slept with somebody, she meant you?'

'You bastard.' Lexie, obviously not one to sneak out under the cover of a row, lamps Michael one again. 'You said I was the only one!'

'It's not my kid, honest!'

'You still slept with ...' Lexie pauses, and gives Beth the once over, 'her.'

'The kids name is Joe, and he bloody well is yours, you sneaky two-timing excuse for a man!'

'Oh, for fuck's sake, it didn't mean anything. I only shagged her once, to get back at Rachel,' he glares at her, as though it's partly her fault, 'for dumping me. I wanted to show her. I was pissed off!'

'You did it to get back at Rach?' Beth's voice is suddenly small, smaller than it's ever been, and she's quivering.

'You can't have done, you wouldn't ... Joe can't be ...' Rachel finally speaks again, the small wavering words effectively silencing everybody.

'He's not. He's not, you're right! He can't be.' Michael seizes on Rachel's words, and gives her a lapdog look, I'm expecting him to start panting and licking any second now.

'He is.' There's no sign of Beth's anger now. Her voice is flat, unemotional. 'He is.' She turns to Rach. 'I am so, so sorry Rach. It was one night, he said he was single, you weren't together. I know I should never, ever have done it, but to be honest Joe is the best thing that ever happened to me, but the worst thing I've ever done to a friend.'

'But what about Jack?' I stare in her direction, totally confused.

'Jack?' Beth turns to stare at me. 'What are you talking about now? Honestly Jane, keep up. Why would Jack be here?'

'Jack isn't Joe's dad?'

They all stare at me, then Rachel suddenly whimpers. 'Jack isn't Joe's daddy, Michael is. Beth's right. Just look at his ears.' We all look at baby Joe.

'What's wrong with his ears, there's nothing wrong with his ears!' Beth pulls him closer to her, possessively, covering his ear with her hand.

'Nothing is wrong.' Rachel's voice is level, more certain than I've ever heard it. 'Jane's mum was right. Just look at his face.' She suddenly grabs the baby from Beth and advances, cradling him gently. 'I was digging through your old baby photos with your mum, looking for some to put up on the big screen later. He's the spitting image of you, Michael.' She thrusts him

349

forward, and Michael flinches, then she very gently hands the baby back to Beth. 'He's yours alright.'

'Rach I'm—'

'How could you?' Rachel's voice is soft. 'How could you, Beth? You were supposed to be my friend. You were nearly my frigging bridesmaid. I am so glad you weren't, I am so, so …' Rach pauses, 'this is why you wouldn't do it, isn't it? You've been shagging him, you are so dead to me.'

Beth nods. 'I'm so ashamed, but it was just one night, honestly. However much you hate me – and I don't blame you if you do – you have to believe me. He said you'd split up, and I moved out of town as soon as I found out. I went to my cousin's but then I couldn't cope, it was such a shit hole and I didn't have any money, and it was so bad for Joe so I came back to stay with Mum.'

'That's why you disappeared for a year?'

She nods glumly. 'Then your mum bumped into mine, and I knew she'd tell you, and I knew I had to do something. I wanted to tell you, honest I did, and I wanted to tell him.' She nods her head towards Michael. 'But he kept dodging me, that's why I wanted to sort the hen party, so we could be at the same place and he'd have to talk to me.'

'But he didn't?'

Beth shakes her head. 'I never managed to catch him on his own. There were always people about, and then at the dress fitting, I really wanted to be there, but I was scared stiff you'd look closely at Joe, that you'd see …'

'Which is why you wouldn't let me hold him?'

Beth nods.

'Oh, for heaven's sake, will you lot shut up, you're giving me a headache. Are we done here, lover boy?' Lexie is languidly pulling a blouse over her head and messing about with her hair. If she's after the just-shagged look, she's got it cracked. 'Same time next week, or was that the grand finale?'

'You bitch! You total cow!' Rachel who has been in a stunned lull suddenly seems to find a second wind. She starts to hurl clothes at Lexie's head, she catches what has to be Michael's boxers in the face and flings them at him. Then neatly fields her own undies and wriggles about trying to get them on. Michael is edging backwards, gathering his stuff as he goes, and I don't know if I'm supposed to bar the exit, help with the clothes tossing, or hurl insults. 'I want to talk to you!'

Lexie, who is now partially dressed is heading for safety and manhandling me out of the way.

'How long have you been doing this? How long? Tell me!'

Lexie shrugs, and doesn't look half as guilty as she should. 'Only a few times.'

I feel really ill now. How could I not have told Rachel earlier? How could I not have trusted my instincts, known that he was as trustworthy as a sack of weasels? A *few* times?

Freddie must have been right when he told me Lexie talked about Michael. Shit, why the hell didn't he tell me earlier?

Lexie wriggles her way fully into her skin-tight jeans and zips them up. Right in front of us – the cheek, just to show us her sexy toned abs and thin thighs. 'Are we done here then?' She even has a thigh gap. Bitch.

'Stay right there!' Rach loses interest in Lexie as she spots her husband-to-be edging towards the door. All her focus is now on Michael, who is looking round wildly for an escape route and at the same time trying to hop into his undies.

'I can explain, darling.'

'In our bridal suite?!'

'Really, honey, I can …' He's given up on running and is crawling towards us. He's down on his knees, about to beg and I know I should go and leave them, but I'm weirdly fascinated, frozen to the spot. Trying to avoid looking at his dangly bits. He really should have bought some better knickers for his wedding day. Something snug.

'You said it was over! You said it happened once!'

'We've not done it for ages. It was before I asked you to marry me. It meant nothing. Honest!' His hands are clasped together.

'Honest? Honest? You've just done it again! You wouldn't know honest if it bit you on your pimply bum.' Rachel is so angry she can barely spit the words out.

'Nothing? What do you mean it meant nothing? You bastard!' I thought Lexie had found an escape route, but obviously not. 'You said you'd tell her!' She's pulling her boots on as she speaks, and glances over at Rachel. 'He said he'd tell you that it wasn't just once!'

'And that makes it okay, does it?' Rachel's voice is icy cold, but I can hear the quiver in it.

'Oh, grow up, Lexie, how've I had time to tell her?' Michael is so full of his own importance and so keen to justify himself, he seems to be missing the point here.

'You agreed, last night!' Lexie is positively growling.

'Told me what? That the wedding is off?'

'No, I—'

'What then? That you love her?' Rach points at Lexie with a shaky finger.

'Hell no!'

Lexie hurls her boot at him. Then turns on the scorn. 'You spineless idiot!'

'I couldn't tell her before, I wasn't going to risk screwing everything up. What would I do then?'

'Well, it's time you flaming well found out!' Rachel takes a step back. Then another. I make a move towards her, but she brushes me away and storms out.

I spin round, ready to follow her. 'Rach, Rach.'

I've got one foot in the corridor when Michael shoves me out of the way and rushes after her. 'Fuck. I didn't mean that, Rach ... come back, darling, Rachel! I love you! You're all I need.'

I get my balance back, and hesitate, not sure if it's my place to interfere.

'Oh, for fuck's sake, it's not like I want to marry him.' Lexie barrels past, nearly flooring me, then slings her bag over her shoulder and I have to duck to avoid a black eye. 'I just thought she should know.'

'And so did I.' Says Beth sadly, still clutching Joe to her chest. A tear plops its way down her cheek, and lands on the baby's head. The tears become a steady stream, and I want to hug her, even though she's been a complete idiot.

'Why didn't you do it earlier? Why now, Beth?'

'This was my last chance! He's been avoiding me and

blocking my texts and everything.' The stream turns to hiccups. She wipes her face with Joe's top. 'Oh, shit, it's all a mess, isn't it?'

It's then I notice the time. The others will be wondering where we've got to. They'll be finishing the champagne off. Her mum will be adjusting her hat. Oh, bugger, her mum.

Guests will be arriving!

'Fuck! Come on, Beth!'

I run down the corridor, glad I've got sensible shoes on, and am just about to put a hand out to open the door when it flies open and I nearly fall on top of Maddie and Sally, who are on their way out.

'We were just coming to find you. Where've you been? Rach needs to have her veil put on.'

'There might not be a wedding.' I slow down to draw my breath. All this running around is bad for me.

'What?'

'What's happening?' Maddie sticks her head further out of the doorway as we hear a loud male yelp.

'I think Michael might have caught up with Rach!' I cringe, but at the same time hope she's kicked him where it really hurts. 'Come on, come on.'

'What? Michael's here? Oh, no, he didn't see her in her dress, that is such bad luck!' Maddie shakes her head as I grab her hand and drag her out of the room.

'Worse!'

'What the f—' Sally is trotting behind us 'Where are we going, shouldn't we be getting ready?'

'Come on, quicker!' I try to hurry them along, scared of

what we might find when we catch up with Michael and Rachel. 'We've got to catch them up. Michael was with Lexie, bonking her brains out!' I might have just informed the whole hotel, but there is not time for niceties, or long explanations. I need to cut to the chase.

'What?' Sally has grabbed my arm so hard I'm spun round to face her. 'Bonking who?'

'This girl called Lexie.' I look at them glumly. They're going to find out sooner or later, how can they not. 'In the bridal suite.'

'Oh my God.' Sally puts her hand over her mouth.

Maddie clutches my arm. 'Oh my God, no. Not really? He was with a woman? Are you sure they weren't just chatting?'

'No-clothes chatting? Horizontal? Jiggling bits? And she knows about Beth, too ...' I glance back at the tearful Beth.

Maddie's eyes well up with tears. 'Oh, no. Why now?'

'What now? Tell me for heaven's sake!' Sally has a grip of both of us, and we are clearly not going anywhere until she's satisfied. 'What has she done? What have you done Beth?'

'Oh, no, Beth?' Maddie's voice is small, upset, and I grind to a halt.

'Yes.' Beth hiccups. 'Sorry, so sorry, it's all my f—'

'It's not your fault.' I shout, I think it's the sense of urgency making me do that. 'Well, not *all* your fault. Oh, for heaven's sake, we need to catch them!'

'*What?*' Screams Sally.

Beth has gone very pale, even worse than before, she looks like she's about to be sick. 'Michael is Joe's dad.' She sniffs and puts her hands over her eyes.

'Oh my God, you are kidding me?' Sally looks from Beth back to me wildly. 'Fuck me. Michael's? You fucked Michael?'

'Only once.' Confirms Maddie.

Sally laughs, slightly hysterical. But it gives me a chance to pull free and set off in pursuit of Rachel again.

'Oh, hell, are you okay, Beth?' Maddie hugs Beth. 'And Rach? How's Rach? Oh, hell, oh, hell.'

'Why did Jane think he was Jack's?' Puffs Beth, who is carrying the extra burden of a baby, but has jeans and sneakers on so is one up on us in the mobility stakes.

'Jack's?' Sally is horrified. 'My Jack's? Why on earth would you think that?' She pokes me in the back. 'You're not telling me she's shagged Jack as well!'

'I didn't think, well, I did, oh, forget it.'

'I can't forget that!'

'Jack has never been with Beth, I'm sure he'd never do that. Would he?' Maddie is staring at me as well now, her voice quavering.

'Can you all bloody shut up and run!' I flap my hand, but Sal is not to be flapped away.

'You thought Jack was Joe's dad and you never told me, you let me make a complete tit of myself talking about him and Maddie!'

'No, I didn't. You didn't, I—'

'Why were you talking about me and Jack?' Maddie is dabbing at her eyes again. 'I've never done anything with him, honest Sal, we'd never, I mean you're married, he's yours, you …' She is wringing her hands together in agitation, huge tears threatening to spill from her eyes.

'For fuck's sake, shut up!' They shut up. 'We'll do all this later! Right now, it's Rach and Michael that are important. Maddie, I just wish you'd told me that Michael was the father!' I shouldn't have said this, it all kicks off again.

'I did! You said you already knew!' Maddie pulls a face.

Sally stares at both of us in turn. 'Okay, let's calm down. How did you know Mads?'

'Beth told me when she was drunk, at the hen party.' Maddie looks at Beth, who nods.

'And I told you, Jane!' Maddie prods me, to get my attention back on her.

'You knew?' It's my turn for the inquisition from Sally.

'Well, no, well, I got confused.' I sigh.

Maddie is frowning at me. 'Confused? I told you after the cocktails, in our room! I told you Michael and Beth had, well, you know, and you said we'd work out how to tell Rach.'

I realise now why I got this all so wrong. When Maddie told me that Michael had slept with somebody else, I did my usual trick of jumping in before she had chance to finish her sentence. I didn't let her explain.

'You never exactly said Beth's name.'

'I said Beth had told me, confided in me.' I can tell Maddie is getting frustrated with me.

'I got my wires crossed, I just thought you meant she knew about Michael and Lexie!'

'Who the hell is this Lexie?' Sally and Maddie ask the question together.

'Long story. Later. Please? Come on, we've got to find them!'

Even though we've been walking and talking, we've not exactly been in a hurry. It's all been a bit stop and start.

We've lost ground. We all hurtle down the stairs, and there's no sign of Rachel, Michael, or Lexie.

'There, there!' Sally points. It's not hard to spot Rach in her white dress if you're looking in the right direction.

Michael obviously caught up with her, and the roles have been reversed. She's after him now.

They're heading for the marquee, and we scurry after them. Slowing down as we get closer. Not wanting to intrude, but really needing to be there for her if she needs us.

Michael drops down to his knees, clutching at her arm, then when she shakes him off, clutching his own hands together. Practically begging. Now he's got his hands out in a 'not my fault' manner. I'm sure his mum would clip him round the ear if she was here, I mean the grass stains are never going to come out of those trousers.

Rach is crying, throwing her hands up.

I take a step, I need to help. But Maddie puts a staying hand on my arm.

'They've got to sort this out themselves, Jane.'

He's on his feet, putting a conciliatory hand on her shoulder. Explaining earnestly.

All I can hear is the pounding in my ears, and us all panting as I strain to hear what they're saying. Is this it? Is this where she forgives him?

Rachel shrugs him off and takes a step back, until her back is against the table. She's yelling now, and he's yelling back. It's hard to hear what they're saying but the words 'bastard', 'two-timing piece of shit', 'fucking princess' and 'who do you think you are?' do carry surprisingly well.

She prods a finger in his chest.

His hands are on his hips.

We glance at each other. Uh oh. Defensive stance.

This is looking dodgy.

It is then that it happens.

The cake.

We'd all been concentrating so hard on her poking finger (and so had Michael) that nobody noticed her other hand. The one that is clutching the top layer of her beautiful wedding cake.

'This is the bit you save for the christening!' She yells so loud, we all hear every word. For a moment, the whole world seems to freeze, and then, in slo-mo, she does it. Launches it straight at his face. 'So you might as well have it now!' She grinds it in, then she spins round and is grabbing the next layer while he's still scraping chocolate out of his eyes. But he sees. 'No! No, Rach, be reasonable!'

'I'll give you reasonable! You're never going to get a first anniversary, so you might as well eat it now!'

I've never seen a man move so fast, he's pelting across the grass, and shouts 'just think about it' over his shoulder.

'I am frigging thinking, you two-timing, money-grabbing imbecile!' Rachel kicks her shoes off and is running like she used to do in the 100-metre sprint. She was fast then and she's pretty impressive now.

He doesn't get far, he's so busy checking if she's making up ground that he doesn't notice the flowerbed.

It's not a spectacular fall, more a messy tumble. And he does notice when she plants one foot on his chest, leans over and very deliberately mashes the second cake into his face.

I reckon she spots Lexie out of the corner of her eye a split second before the rest of us do. 'Stop right there, you cow!' Michael makes a grab for her ankle, and for a moment she's on her knees, then she has scrambled free, kicking him in the chops, and is after Lexie.

It's a pretty close call. The pair of them both look quite fit, but I reckon Rachel's fury is more empowering than Lexie's fear. She's gone from cocky to desperate in a moment.

Rach is gaining on her as they get to the ornamental lake, but Lexie doesn't stop. She hurdles the wall, gallops on into the shallows, gathering water lily's as she goes then flounders out the other side.

'Do you think somebody should go and tell Rach's mum?' Sally has her head on one side.

'I think she already knows, dear.'

We spin round, and Rachel's mum is there. She picks a piece of cake up, pops it in her mouth and chews thoughtfully. 'Rather nice.'

'Lovely.' Remarks my own mother, licking her fingers. 'Sponge is so much better than fruit cake, and so chocolatey! So on-trend! Have you tasted it girls?' We all shake our heads, wordless. 'You don't think somebody should be videoing this, do you? You could have a YouTube hit. We could go viral!'

I am gobsmacked, I don't know what to say. I'm really tempted to just dig into the amazing cake, but I resist.

'We never were that keen on him,' says Rachel's mum, 'but you can't tell your children what to do, can you?'

'Oh, no!' Says mine.

'Oh, look, she's coming back. I think I'll make myself scarce, she might want to talk to you first. I'll be having my make-up retouched if anybody needs me.' She pats my hand and straightens the flowers.

Mum links arms with her. 'If you need a hand, I know exactly how to cancel a wedding you know. I mean, Jane's didn't quite get to this stage, but ...' They wander off, their voices fading.

I cringe. I'm over my complete cock-up of a non-wedding, but I so didn't want this to happen to my best friend. I feel queasy. How can I ever forgive myself for the part I've played in this? This was supposed to be the best day of her life.

Chapter 35

'I'm going through with it.' Rachel flicks a piece of cake out of her fringe, then picks her shoes up from where she'd abandoned them.

'Oh my God Rach! You can't be serious!'

'But Rach!' Sally takes her hand. 'Don't do something you're going to regret, please don't, it makes life so complicated. Believe me.'

We're all talking at once.

Maddie takes her other hand. 'You've got to go with your heart, Rach. Follow your heart, not your head. You can't still love him ...' she pauses, looking scared, 'do you?'

'Of course, she doesn't!' Says Sal, ever competitive and tugs on her other hand.

We all hold our breath as we wait for the answer.

'Oh, girls, you're the best.' She hugs both of them, and Maddie pulls me in as well. We're all a bit shocked, now that the action is over, and it wouldn't take much to have us all in tears. Maddie looks the worst, I know she's blaming herself so I give her an extra hug.

Rachel sniffs. 'It's okay, honest.' Her voice is shaky, and so is her smile, but there's more than a hint of determination in it. 'I need to sit down though, my legs have gone all funny.' Maddie leads her into the marquee, and over to the raised platform which I guess was where the DJ was supposed to be entertaining us later.

She sinks down, her white dress pooling round her, and we all plop down.

I think Rach catches the look on Maddie's face, as she runs her finger along the bunting that is wrapped round each pole.

'It's awesome, isn't it?' Her voice is soft, the words catch, and it brings a lump to my throat.

Maddie jumps, as though she's been caught stealing sweets, and pulls her hand away. 'Totally.' She smiles at her sadly.

We all gaze round at the amazing marquee.

'Beautiful.' I nod.

'Too good to waste.' Says Rachel.

'Rach, please think about it. This is the rest of your life. You can't get married just because you've arranged the most perfect wedding ever.' There is also the question of the groom, who she's just smeared in cake and chased off the estate. Somebody is going to have to go and get him, and it's not going to be me. I'm all out of bridge-building attempts and forgiveness for Michael.

'Jane.'

'No, hang on, I've got to say this. You want me to be honest with you, Rach?'

'Yeah.'

'Well, I don't get it, after everything he's done, how can you still marry him? You know he's a lying twat. He's a dad, he's slept with your friend, and he's slept with Lexie again after he told you it was a one off! It's your big day,' I hate to use Michael's phrase, but I have to, 'you only do it once, or at least you're only supposed to. Oh, Rach.' I hug her harder. 'He's really not worth it. You don't have to do this. Are you positive this is what you want? I can send them all away?' I'm shitting myself at the thought of having to go round and explain to everybody. But I will if she needs me to. 'I could talk to your mum.'

'Aww, Jane, you'd do that for me?' She clears her throat, then grins. 'You should see the panic on your face! Look, who said anything about getting married?'

'You did!'

'No, I didn't, I said I wanted to go ahead with it. I said I couldn't waste it.'

Sal gives her *the stare*, I'm not surprised Jack hasn't found it easy to leave her. 'You aren't making any sense.'

'She's deranged with shock,' says Maddie, pulling her close.

'No, I'm bloody not! Are you lot not listening?'

We are all hanging on her every word, and it's not working for any of us from the expression we've all got on our faces.

'We're doing it without him!'

'We're what?'

'We're having a wedding without the groom! I'm not going to let him win, I'm not going to let him ruin everything.'

'That's a bit, well, alternative.' Sally is musing it over. 'But *good* alternative.'

'It's paid for, we're all dressed up. We've got to do it! Let's get this show on the road Jane. Girls? Help me? Please?' Her voice is low and quiet, it's a bit scary. But she sounds determined, and to be honest I don't think any of us know what to say.

'Everything okay? I can't find Mi—' A male voice stops mid word, and we all spin round.

It's Jack, all debonair and gorgeous in his suit. He looks so dashing, and different, just like a man about to go to a wedding. 'Michael.' He finishes as he takes in the remains of the smashed wedding cake, and the shoe-less bride. 'What the hell's happened? Has somebody broken in? I'll call the police.'

He's reaching into his pocket for his mobile as he speaks.

'Oh, don't be ridiculous.' Sally scowls at him.

'Sorry?' Jack's voice is low, and he stares back. An impasse. And suddenly even I can see what she meant. This pair are such a total mismatch, how she ever thought she could shoe-horn him into the love-shaped hole in her heart I don't know. He's a triangle when she's looking for a square. This has got nothing to do with Maddie, it's about her, her and Jack. A truth she's tried to ignore, then found out she couldn't any longer.

Trust Sally to bash on, though, unwilling to admit she'd got it wrong, that she couldn't make it work.

I'm not quite sure if Sally needs a doormat, or somebody to spar with, but either way Jack isn't the man for the job.

'Michael's gone.' Rachel smiles sadly at Jack, but he's still got his gaze locked with Sally's. 'But if he turns up at the chapel will you get rid of him, please? I don't want to see him ever again.' There's the slightest wobble in her voice, but she's fighting it, and something tells me that although this has all been a massive shock, some part of her isn't surprised.

'Gone?' Jack frowns.

'Gone!' Shouts Sally. 'Your friend happens to be a two-timing—'

'My friend?' Jack frowns. 'Hang on, this isn't my fault, I didn't know anything about this.' He looks at Rachel, a mix of confusion and disbelief on his face.

'I know you didn't.' Rachel says softly, 'I'm not blaming you Jack.'

'You must have had some idea.' Sally's voice is scornful, and the flash of anger that plays across Jack's face is such a surprise I can't think of a thing to say.

'Why? Why would I have had any idea? Did you?'

'You must have suspected he was sleeping with that girl, and you knew he'd slept with Beth!' Yells Sally. 'You know, the Beth you were all cosy with the other night?'

Jack folds his arms. 'So, because I listened to her, and said that, as a bloke I'd rather know if I was a dad, this is all on me, is it?' He shakes his head slowly. 'You always have to find somebody to blame, don't you, Sally?'

'I do not!'

'Yes, you do. And you always want to make sure that you run other people's lives for them.'

'I know what's best!'

'No, you don't.' His voice is dangerously soft. 'You don't Sal, you don't even know what's best for yourself, for us.'

'I do! And it's not you!' Sal is red in the face and all wound up, and I'm sure she didn't mean for those exact words to pop out of her mouth, she was just trying to win the argument. She was just trying to win.

'Exactly.' He shakes his head. 'We need to talk, don't we? God knows I've tried to make this work Sal, but it was never going to, was it?'

'Shut up! You don't know what you're saying.'

'I've shut up for too long, and I do know. I do, Sally. This is way overdue for both our sakes, but I can't do it any longer. I won't do it. I'm sorry, I really am, but it's over.'

'Oh, don't be ridiculous. What do you mean, over?'

'Over.' He signals a flat line with his hands, which looks pretty final, and non—negotiable. 'You can't force yourself to love somebody can you? And I know you know exactly what I mean. Neither of us is happy, we've been dancing around each other, me being a drip trying to do the right thing. We've forgotten who we really are, and I've just realised I can't carry on doing that. And you don't want to either, do you?' He looks her straight in the eye, and she wavers. Glances away, turns her wedding ring on her finger.

'Oh, for heaven's sake, why do you always have to be right?'

This is rich coming from Sally, who always needs to be right.

'I'll go and tell everybody what's happening myself!' She glares as she brushes past Jack and we all know that she just needs to get away. To process this and come up with a new plan. Then she looks back over her shoulder, and the spark is still there. 'And don't think for one moment that you're having my car!'

Jack turns to Rachel. 'Erm, sorry, I didn't mean to … Not today, on your day. It just kind of came out, and …'

Rachel opens and shuts her mouth for a moment, then comes to. 'Better out than in, Jack.' She smiles. 'She'll be fine, she's tough our Sally.'

'And you're right, in her heart she did know.' I add.

'I'm still sorry.' He glances again at the remnants of the cake. 'For everything. What do you need me to do?'

'I need to talk to Jane, but can you go and warn Mum and Dad? And can you make sure Sal is okay? Maddie?' I'd almost forgotten about Maddie, who'd been sitting quietly in the background watching the drama.

'Oh, hell, look!' I point down the driveway. There are cars, and even from here I can tell that they're wedding guests – the hats are a give-away.

'Oh, no!' Wails Rachel. 'Everybody's arriving. I don't want them going to the …' her voice wobbles for a moment. 'Chapel,' she manages. 'Can you and the ushers divert them? For drinks? Quickly, please?'

I squeeze her hand.

There's a chapel attached to Startford Castle, and the wedding service was going to be held there, before everybody headed over to the marquee.

'I'm on it!' Jack, relieved I think to have something useful to do, spins round. Then stops. 'Coming?' He holds a hand out, and just like that, Maddie slips hers into his like it's meant to be. There's a lump in my throat. Again. And a prickle of happy tears. I am seriously going to have to do something about these waterworks when this wedding is over and done with. I never used to cry. Ever.

'Tell Mum I'll be back soon?'

Maddie nods. We're all a bit shocked, now that the action is over, and our lives seem about to change for ever.

'And, erm,' she shouts after Jack, 'could you get somebody to break the news to Michael's parents? I don't think I can really face them.' For a moment her face crumples, and she grabs a napkin off one of the tables.

'Oh, Rach.'

'I'm fine, I'm fine.' But she isn't. She's been going on adrenaline up until now, fired up with anger and pain, and now it's gone all quiet. Just the two of us, and I can see it hurts.

'We can cancel everything.' I squeeze her shoulder and try a tiny smile. 'My mum knows exactly what to do!' She sniffs, then grins, a tiny grin back.

'Bloody mothers.'

'Where would we be without them?'

'Knock, knock?'

Our heads shoot up at the sound of Beth's voice. You've got to admit it, the girl has got guts. If that had been me I think I'd have been on a train to the Outer Hebrides after an announcement like that. Ouch, I don't want to think about the Outer Hebrides, I really don't, and I'd promised myself I wouldn't. Not today. My job is to sure Rachel's day is memorable – which I think has been achieved. But for all the wrong reasons.

'Can I say something?'

'Fire away, this day can't get any worse, can it?'

'Right.' She takes a deep breath, and I think she's been rehearsing this speech while she's been standing on the driveway watching Michael and Lexie being chased off the premises. 'Okay. Right.' Even with a rehearsal this has shaken Beth, I've never seen her stuck for words before. She's jiggling on the spot as well, which is partly for Joe's benefit, but more because she can't help it I suspect. 'I am sorry,' she looks down, then forces herself to look back up at Rachel, after a quick glance in my direction, 'I don't expect you to ever forgive me, but I wanted you to be happy. Honest, I would have never told him if I'd have thought it would have hurt you. He wasn't interested in me, I know that, I really do.' Her voice wobbles. 'I didn't know he only slept with me because I was your friend.' She sniffs, but battles on, and I really want to hug her. But I can't, this is Rachel's call. It's between them. 'No excuses but I was so drunk, I bumped into him in that pub we all used to go to? He kept buying us all drinks and when everybody left he persuaded me to stay, and I hardly knew what was happening. A quickie in the park behind a bush, how crap a way is that to conceive a baby? He was just making a point, Rach, getting back at you. I think he thought you'd find out, that I'd tell you.' There is a long silence. 'I just wanted you to know. I'll go now, shall I?'

'Oh, Beth.' Rachel shakes her head. 'I can't just forget this, I don't know if I can ever forgive you totally, but I believe you.' She nods her head. 'I know how bloody charming he can be. And he basically just said the same to me, that we'd split, and he was angry, and you were there. Sorry, I don't mean to sound cruel.'

'Don't be sorry, I deserve it, I deserve it all. I'll go. I just wanted to check you were okay, that we ... Oh, Rach, I don't know how to make this right.'

'You can't, can you?' She sighs. 'Nobody can make it right. You don't need to go though, stay, enjoy my non-wedding.' She smiles, a weak but I reckon forgiving smile. Rach is nice like that. We should all be more like Rach. 'Just stay out of my way for now, okay?'

We both watch as Beth backs away without a word, bouncing Joe in her arms.

I look at Rachel. I am mildly – okay, massively – shocked by her decision to party on, though not by her decision to forgive Beth.

I'm not sure I could do this, no scrub that, I know I couldn't do it. But it's her decision to make. So I swallow hard before carrying on. 'Are you sure you're okay?' Silly question.

'Great.' Her voice is flat, motionless. This does not sound great.

She blinks at me. Her eyes are red-rimmed, and she's pale, but there's a determined air about her.

'Did you know, Jane? About Beth?'

'Shit no! Honestly, I only knew about Lexie, and that was ages ago, and I thought you guys had split up for good after the other time.'

'Joe *is* his you know.' She throws her hands in the air. 'He never even wanted kids, he'll be a shit dad. They did it once! Once, and were shit-faced.' She rolls her eyes. 'So that's okay then.' She rests her head on my shoulder. 'And I guess Beth was trying to do the right thing, telling him.'

'I had no idea, Rach. I would have told you. I honestly thought it was Jack. You know I did, we both did when we saw him and Beth together! And before that, I'd just assumed it was some guy none of us knew.'

She sniffs and sits up straight. 'I'm not letting him beat me.' Her gaze drifts from mine, and she looks out over the tables. But I don't think she's seeing them. 'You were right you know.'

'About what?'

'Michael. I should have listened to you. I know you've never really liked him.'

'I wouldn't say I've not ...'

'It's okay. Honest. You never trusted him, did you?'

'I just wanted you to be happy, Rach.' I say, dodging the direct question.

'I know. It's not just Joe, or Lexie, I was trying to ignore all my doubts, but it's all suddenly started to add up.' She gives me a sideways look, and I understand now why she was having doubts, why she'd asked me before if she was doing the right thing. At her hen party, and the night we dyed our hair. 'That's why I'm not completely in bits. It's better this way. We had a row the other day, over money and I very nearly called the whole thing off.' She plucks at the napkin. 'I should have done.'

'Row?'

'Yeah. That's why I totally flipped when I saw them together. I mean cheating on me is bad enough, but the rest is even worse.'

'What do you mean, Rach?'

'I opened his bank statement by mistake, I thought it was our new joint one.'

'Oh?'

'He's broke. Aren't money, kids and commitment the biggies you need to agree on before you tie the knot?' She laughs, a harsh little laugh and doesn't wait for an answer. 'Well, we've not sorted out about children and he's lied about other people, so I guess the money thing is the final straw. He was just after my money, Jane. Not me.'

'No! I don't believe that. He did love you, Rach. You guys have been together for ages.' I could add on-and-off, but I don't.

'Maybe he did love me at first. But that wasn't why he wanted to make up, why he proposed. I've been kidding myself.' She dabs at her eyes with the hem of her dress. 'That's what all this is about.' With one gesture she includes everything, the hotel, the dress. 'He talked me into all this 'cos it was what he wanted, so he can show off. It's all front with Michael. He's broke Jane, I didn't realise but he's completely broke, and so are his parents.'

'Are you sure?' I think about the BMW he always drives, the smart suits. His mum's insistence on Rachel's designer dress. The doves and bloody flame-throwers.

'Oh, God, I've been so stupid, Jane. I got totally carried away with the whole romance, the wedding, everything I dreamed of. He just stoked my ego. He's clever, and I've been a total idiot.'

'No, you've not been stupid. You loved him, Rach.'

'Maybe I loved the idea of 'us' so much, I ignored the fact that we'd changed, grown apart. And,' she gives me a weak grin, 'the fact, he's a dick.'

'Well, yeah, maybe he is a bit of a dick.'

'A massive dick.' She rubs the back of her hand over her eyes then suddenly, and unexpectedly, smirks. 'Nice shoes by the way.'

'Ahh, you weren't supposed to notice!'

'Oh my God, how could I not! You've got DM's on, they are aren't they?'

'Limited edition!' I grin. 'Sorry, Louie shit on my wedding shoes.'

'You're kidding?'

'No joke. Then the entire Housekeeping department here tried to help me scrub them clean, they've kind of got a tie-dyed look now.'

She hugs me. 'What the hell. Those are far cooler. I'm well jel. Come on, I need make-up if I'm going to do this. The full trowelled on look.'

'You are sure about it, Rach? Nobody will mind if you don't.'

'Are you kidding? This is the biggest party of my life, I might never get the chance to do it again.'

She slips her shoes on and I take her hand and haul her to her feet. Her cheeks are blotchy, she's a bit snotty and her eyes are red-rimmed, but she's smiling.

'Then can we get bladdered?'

'You got it!'

We high-five, link arms then weave our way back across the lawn like a pair of drunken old fogies.

Until she stops, by the flowerbed that Michael landed in.

We both stare at the crushed flowers, the remnants of cake crumbs, and the single pink fondant rose that is surprisingly intact.

It is so sad it nearly starts me off again.

She looks me in the eye, then throws herself into my arms and a big hug. Her voice is small when she whispers into my ear, small and slightly broken, but her words are clear and determined. 'I would so love to pretend I forgive him, and pretend I'm going through with it, because I want to humiliate him in the same way he just humiliated me.' She sniffs. 'I'd love to get him to the ceremony, then tell the whole bloody world what he's done. But it's better this way. Without him. I think there have been enough secrets haven't there? It's time to be out, loud and proud.'

'You got it!' I gaze at my best friend, and I'm so proud of her it makes me well up. She is so much stronger than me. I'd always thought I was the one looking after her, but I know now that I never was. True, we've looked after each other's backs like good friends should, but Rach is the one with Girl Power. Rach is handling this so much better than I did when my own wedding fell to pieces. I'd never needed to worry about what the knowing would do to her. 'You're amazing you know.' I say softly.

'You might have to remind me of that later. Anyhow,' she smiles weakly, 'I couldn't catch him, he ran too fast, and in this dress.' She opens her arms wide and we both look at her dress.

We laugh then I hug her back. 'It is better this way and of course I'll help you. If it's confession time, can I tell you mine?'

'Spill.'

'I think I love Freddie.'

'I know.' Her voice softens. 'I *know* you love Freddie, you daft cow! So, what you gonna do about it?'

'I'm going to hunt him down!' We both laugh. 'Come on, before I do that we're going to have a bloody good party. The best damned wedding without a groom anybody has ever been to!'

Chapter 36

'Aren't you going to get changed, dear?'

Rachel's mum doesn't even raise an eyebrow when we stagger into the room and demand emergency make-overs. She just produces gin and tonics in the biggest glasses you have ever seen. You can always count on her in a crisis, she's totally no-nonsense and calm. The type of person who you can rely on to cater for extra dinner party guests at the last minute. Or to cancel a wedding as the guests are arriving. She must be upset, but she doesn't ask a single question, cast any reproving looks, or even say, 'I told you so.' Which my mum would have been very tempted to do.

She hugs her daughter, and it's then I see it. Just how similar, and close, mother and daughter are. They're both stunningly attractive, but both kind and capable underneath. They're picker-uppers, problem-solvers.

They're both very determined.

'I've paid for it, so I'm going to wear it. It's not like I can wear it another time, is it?' Replies Rachel, looking down at her dress.

Her mum, for once doesn't tell her that sarcasm is the lowest form of wit. 'Maybe, but it's a bit grubby along the bottom, though, dear.'

'And this bit that sticks out, it looks like somebody has blown their nose on it?' My mum adds, peering over the specs she's put on.

'Does it matter?'

'It might do to you later, when you look back.'

Rachel sighs. 'I'm not sure this is a party I'm going to be reminiscing about, Mum.'

'Oh, you should!' It's my mother again. My groan might have been a bit loud, but she ignores me. 'I mean you might not do it again!'

'Mum!'

'Well, there's no sign of you doing it, is there, Jane? Give me five minutes, Rachel. Five minutes. I know what to do!' We think that is the end of it, but she bustles off and ten minutes later is back with the head housekeeper, and a pair of shears.

'This lady does alterations!'

'Well, not, I'm sorry madam, but ...'

'Oh, come here.' Before anybody can object, Rachel's mum has grabbed the massive scissors. 'On the stool darling, then I can get it level. How short?'

Rachel giggles, and clambers on to the stool, hanging on to my shoulder for balance. 'Oh, Mum! She used to do this when we were at school, emergency alterations!'

'It's going to fray, but I'm sure that's trendy!' I've never seen Mum so excited about dress alterations, the two mothers are egging each other on like giggling schoolgirls, and I have to say it is a fantastic dose of light relief after all the drama.

'On-trend, they say now, Mum.'

'Do you want some slashes in it, like in those jeans we saw?' Her mum is gabbling on as she chops, and I'm a bit worried Rach is going to lose a leg, or we're going to have to rush off to A&E with a severed artery.

'Oh, yes! So on-trend!' Shouts my mum – I'm not sure what she's been drinking.

'No!' Rach yells, and, for a moment, I think she has been injured. 'No slashes!'

'Oops, you made me jump! Don't shout darling, I'm not deaf. Oh dear, I've gone a bit off-piste, must be the gin. Never mind, I'll improvise!'

Within minutes the fishtail has flapped to the floor, and the improvisation means there's a sexy slit that reaches nearly up to her hip bone. 'I'm not sure your father would approve of your knickers showing, but I'm sure I've got a safety pin somewhere!'

Rachel rolls her eyes, but all the distractions have turned her back to her normal pink colour.

'Oh, and your father has sent an email, sacking that man.' Adds Rachel's mum.

I raise an eyebrow. 'Sacking?'

'That was another thing,' Rachel says sadly, 'he begged for a job with dad, so he could be a proper part of the family. I didn't realise that he'd been practically sacked from the other place. His firm said they'd give him a good reference if he went quickly and quietly.'

'Oh.' Just how bad a person was Michael?

'Well, it's over and done with now, Rachel. Stand up straight, dear so I can check the hemline.' The dirty hem has been cut away, and the new edge sits on her toes. Not that I think anybody will be notice, they'll be looking at her lovely legs.

'Right girls.' Her mum claps her hands at me and Maddie, who has just arrived, slightly pink and breathless, and for a moment I think we're going to be attacked with the shears. 'Off you go, put your evening dresses on! Shoo, shoo.'

After all the commotion and tears, it's nice to be mothered, and easy to not think and just follow orders and do as you're told.

I glance out of the window to see that Jack and the ushers are assembled on the driveway and are already directing people to the main entrance of the castle.

'Oh my God, so many people are arriving!' Rachel has gone as pale as her dress. No doubt the reality of it all has just hit.

'Shall we send them home?' I'm worried it will all be too much. 'Last chance?'

'No.' She downs the rest of her G&T in one. 'We're going to do this.'

'I'm off to find your father, dear.' Her mum checks her reflection and pats her hair. 'So much more exciting than a normal wedding! Good for you, darling.' She kisses Rachel on the cheek and hugs her, then whispers conspiratorially in her ear. 'Now that horrible man has gone, your father has asked them to bring the good wine out instead of that cheap stuff! Right,' she brushes her hands together, 'they've put us in the grand hall for reception drinks, instead of that draughty tent.'

'Marquee, Mum.'

'It's a tent where I'm from dear.' See? That's what I mean about Rach's folk, they're very grounded and normal, as well as obscenely rich. 'But we'll eat and dance in it later! See you down there, don't rush, we'll get the party going. Another hour and they won't even remember they were expecting a wedding!'

'Oh, I think they might.' Says my mother. 'Why didn't you do this, Jane? We can start a trend!'

'Well, I hope you're not letting that man have any of these presents!' Great Aunt Mabel has parked herself in the entrance hall and appointed herself receiver of the gifts. Ignoring the fact that Rachel's mum seems to be trying to get people to take them away again.

I'm not sure what Mabel and Rachel's parents have said, but apart from a few extra tight and prolonged hugs, everybody seems determined not to mention 'that man' or why we're really all here.

The meal actually goes without a hitch – after Jack, at the very last minute, notices the display of Michael photos that Rachel has assembled and hides them under the table.

The remnants of cake have been swept away, along with everything that might allude to a bride and groom, and the staff have miraculously replaced the 'top table' with a normal one. And we've all decided to sit wherever we want, which means Sal and Beth have been dragged off by Aunt Mabel and hidden on a table behind Rachel, and Jack has positioned himself behind a marquee pole so that Sal can't send him the evil eyes. Unfortunately, my mum and Rachel's are sat next to each other – which could be asking for trouble, but at least it means our dad's can quietly consume the vintage wine without being told off.

'I think I'm a bit pissed.' The tables are being moved to one side, which means we've had to stand up.

'Me, too! Look.' I nudge Rachel, which is a mistake as we both stagger.

Maddie is standing next to the bar giggling girlishly and looking radiant, and no prizes for guessing who she is gazing at.

'They look cute together, don't they?' Says Rachel.

I nod. 'I'm glad Jack and Sal finally had the guts to face up to things, they both deserve better.'

'Like you and me, eh?' Rachel high-fives me. 'Back in a sec, just off to get another drink.'

I go back to leaning against a pole and staring at Jack and Maddie. If there is such a thing as a happy couple today, it has to be them. They do look cute. They look like they are two halves of a perfect whole and would never be quite the same without each other.

Maddie catches me watching her and waves, then says something to Jack before running over and wrapping me in a bear hug.

'Looking cosy there?' I hug her back.

It's funny, but she's so excited she doesn't do her normal looking bashful, or blushing. It all just comes spewing out.

'Jack insisted I help him tell everybody about the changes to the plan.'

I nod.

'We got talking.'

'And?'

'And he told me he was sorry for believing me when we split up. I mean, it's stupid, it was my fault, he was supposed to believe me.'

'You're funny, and obviously a good actress!' She does blush then, I'm happy for her.

She looks down at her feet, then under her eyelashes at me. 'Did you know him and Sal were having issues?'

'I had an idea they weren't one hundred per cent. But you know Sal.' I shrug. 'She hates to admit defeat. If anybody was going to make him stay and suffer, she would!'

'You cheeky cow!' The sound of Sally's voice makes me jump, and makes Maddie look guilty.

'Oh, Sally ... Oh, I'm so sorry, I—'

'Oh, shut up, Maddie.' She shrugs. 'I'm only going to say this once. Okay? So don't ever expect me to admit it again, but he looks at you in a way he's never looked at me. Once we moved back here and bumped into you it was so bloody obvious.'

'Oh, Sally.'

'Of course I am devastated, you idiot.' She says it affectionately though, none of the old Sally malice. 'But I'll get over it. Plenty more fish in the sea,' she raises an eyebrow, 'just not that particular sprat. Right I'm off to find another cocktail, and,' she winks, 'you can tell him I'm going to be keeping the handcuffs and vibrators!'

'What?' Maddie opens her mouth wide in shock. Sal sniggers and sashays off.

I hug her. 'Joke Mads. You know what she's like. And anyway, who wants second hand vibrators?'

We both shudder.

'Sally is going to be okay, isn't she?'

'She is.' I nod. 'I never thought I'd say this, but she is. Funny isn't it how you can get people wrong?'

'It is.' Maddie is talking, but I know she's not really tuned in to me, she's only got eyes for Jack, who is still waiting at the bar for her.

'Talk about eyes meeting across a crowded room. You better get back to him before you both make me feel a bit icky.'

'Do you think we should stay away from each other for a bit, you know, to be fair to Sally? I mean, I'm sure she's really upset and just putting on a brave front.'

'I'm sure she is upset.' I nod. She will be, I know what it feels like to split up with somebody, even though you know deep down it wasn't right. It still hurts. 'But I reckon her and Jack have known this was inevitable for a while. Don't miss your chance Maddie.'

'Sal came and told us that she's been offered another job you know, back where she used to work. If Jack hadn't done something now, she'd have persuaded him to move, then I'd have never seen him again.'

'It figures, she always did like to be organised.' It doesn't surprise me, once Sal makes a decision that's it. She goes for it. It wouldn't have mattered if Jack had kissed her feet and begged for them to give it another go, she wouldn't have. 'I'm glad I got it totally wrong about Jack.'

'Wrong?'

'You know! About the baby. Me and Rach must have been mad thinking it was Jack!'

'True.' She smiles.

'Can I ask something? At the party after the rehearsal you said Jack and Beth were talking about the baby, and he hugged her. That's why we thought ...'

'Ahh, well, she was upset, and he was being nice, trying to help.'

'Right.' I nod. I hold up my hands. 'It's all my fault.'

It's all coming back to me. Her words. The words I misunderstood. I can hear them in my head. Gawd, it's no wonder Maddie was chilled about it, she knew Joe wasn't Jack's, she knew he was Michael's! And there was I thinking she'd gone all Zen and was behaving like a bit of a drip. Along with Jack. Two drips.

'It's not your fault,' says Maddie, with her reasonable face on, 'Jack told her it was better to come clean, you know be honest about it?'

'That was what they were talking about? Why he was hugging her?'

Maddie nods. 'And I agreed, I mean it's better to be honest and open isn't it? And the father should know, and Joe deserves ...' Her voice tails off. 'I just didn't think she'd do it today!'

'Nope. Maybe not the best timing, but you know how impulsive Beth can be.'

'I certainly do. But I still like her.' She grins, and I grin back. 'Thanks for telling me Jack still cared.'

'Cared? Don't you mean fancies the pants off you?' I hug her. 'Now go on, go and ask him about those handcuffs!'

Maddie giggles. 'You okay?'

'Yeah, I'm off to find Rach.' I'm not that okay really though. Seeing Jack and Maddie together has made me realise how much I miss Freddie. Right now, I'm missing him more than I ever thought I could miss anybody. I tell him everything, he's the person I turn to when I need to talk stuff over, when I've had a shit day, when I've had a good one and want to celebrate.

And I miss holding his hand. We only had a few days hand-holding, but it was good. I flex my fingers, trying to remember how it felt and instead I remember the touch of his hand on my waist, my stomach, the way he touched every inch of my body before slowly making love to me.

My eyes water, my fingers go to my throat. Oh, no, I mustn't cry, not here. Not now! I've not cried yet, and I'm not going to.

He'd made my eyes water in an altogether different way an hour or so later, when we'd made rough, passionate love. We'd also broken the bed.

The smile tweaks the corner of my mouth. It could only happen to me and Freddie.

He'd grabbed hold of the headboard with one hand to stop it banging on the wall, and a few thrusts later it was on my head.

Weakened screws I reckon. But Freddie swore it was his pure macho strength.

I need to find him, ask him if he'll do it again – before he leaves for Scotland for good.

We need to end on a good note, because everything else between us up until now has been too wonderful to destroy. I want happy memories, even if I can't have a happy ever after with Freddie.

Sally is dancing with the bartender, who she's been making eyes at since he mixed her first drink. She looks happy, more girlish I guess as she flirts with him. I reckon now she's made the decision to walk away from her marriage she feels a whole lot better.

Okay, maybe Sal and I are never going to be bosom buddies, but I reckon she's not so bad, and she will find somebody she can truly love – or at least find a career she can.

Rach has kicked Michael out of her life for good, and Mads, sweet, patient Mads hasn't barged in and upset anybody else's marriage. She's waited.

I'm proud of my friends. They might be a little bit mad, a little bit reckless, but deep down in their hearts they've done things for the right reasons.

And Beth? I still like Beth, and I guess she did try to do her best to get herself out of the mess she'd created.

Maddie drags Jack on to the dance floor and I can't help but smile. He's terrible. He looks awkward and self-conscious, but he doesn't care. He's there because she wants him to be.

Chapter 37

'The things you do for love, eh?'

There's a fan of warm breath on my neck that makes me feel weak and dizzy. I must finally be going mad, all this emotion has finally sent me doolally. I've always said too much excitement isn't good for me. I close my eyes. But the feeling doesn't go away. Instead warm hands rest on my shoulders.

I freeze. Then glance to my right, then my left. I know those fingers. Oh, my goodness, do I know those fingers! Just like I know that voice, that smell.

But this can't be happening, they can't be real. So, I pinch the back of his hand.

'Ouch!' He laughs. 'Is that some kind of ancient greeting ritual I don't know about? Or does it mean piss off?'

I spin round on my chair, which clearly isn't meant for spinning.

'Oh, bugger.' I'm on the floor, and scrambling like mad, getting tangled up in the chair legs and then finally managing to grab his. Leg that is.

I drag myself up it in a very inelegant way. Tuck my hair

behind my ear, as I'm pretty sure I look a complete mess and heave myself upwards. Past non-designer rips in his jeans, past knees that feel familiar, circumventing a crotch that definitely looks familiar and finally reaching the top. 'Freddie!' I prod his face, just to be sure. 'You're here.'

'Ouch. Yes. Nice hair!' I think he's commenting on my orange stroke hint-of-spice highlights, which have been expertly toned down since he last saw them, but still have a bit of a way to go on the blending in front.

I ignore him and glare. 'You're not lying in a ditch dead!'

'Erm, no, not yet, though from the look on your face you'd quite like me to be?'

'Where the hell have you been! I've been calling, texting!' Now that the shock of knowing he's actually here has eased, I am flooded with anger. Practically hopping mad. I can't stand still. There are too many words trying to get out of me. If I wasn't gripping his arms I'd have taken off and joined the designer balloons that are bouncing about in the roof space. 'I spoke to Rob!'

'I'm so bloody sorry ...' He pauses. 'For everything.' It's then I realise that he's actually out of breath, and all hot and sweaty. Which can be a bit *eugh*, unless it's somebody that you like to be hot and sweaty with. 'I'd promised Rob I'd go back, but I got back here as quick as I could. I needed to talk to you, I needed to see you.'

'As quick as ...' I am speechless. 'You've been away for days!' Okay, not totally speechless. 'I thought you'd gone for good!'

Freddie takes a step away from me, and my heart takes a dive. I don't want him to go.

389

'For good?' He frowns. 'I wouldn't, I can't. I swear ...' he pauses, and crosses himself, '... on Louie's life, I would never just walk out on you.'

'Speaking of Louie, where is my bloody cat?' I look around, even though it's pretty unlikely he's come to the wedding.

'At home. I've brought him back, to stay? I know I said some stuff, but I was kind of hoping you hadn't gone off me? Us? Maybe, if you'll still have us both back?' he takes a deep breath, moves back closer, which is nice, and put his hands on my forearms.

'I've not gone off Louie! But you left without talking to me!'

'I left a note!'

'One bloody note, then ignored me.'

'I wasn't ignoring you! I wanted to speak to you, honest. I know I was stupid not telling you about Lexie, but I'd never lie to you, Jane. Never.'

'But you said you were leaving, for good. Going to Scotland!'

Freddie brushes his fringe back from his eyes and I'm transfixed by those beautiful eyelashes, those dark eyes that look slightly sad right now, those lips that I know are firm and warm.

'I was a jerk. It was stupid, spur of the moment, I was jealous!'

Freddie, jealous?

'That rehearsal party was hell! Michael had been watching you all night and Andy couldn't take his bloody eyes off you! I thought at one point he was about to drag you off.'

'I'm not easily dragged Freddie, I'm quite solid.' Freddie was jealous!

'And I just wanted us to get away from it all, give us a chance.'

'We've got a chance without moving Freddie.'

He carries on as though he hasn't heard me. 'I didn't stop to think about your friends, and your work, and needing to be here. I was being selfish, I was just scared that just as I thought we had something it was all going to disappear again.'

'You've never been selfish Freddie.' He hasn't, not ever.

'I wasn't trying to undermine you.'

'I know.' I sigh. Freddie has always been ultra-supportive, why should that have changed now? 'It's my fault, I was running scared and just jumped to conclusions. I kind of thought that you agreed that I was crap, that Andy was right it was all just a pipe dream, a silly game and a waste of time.'

'You've never been crap Jane.'

'I'm sorry, I just overreacted, thinking I was getting myself into the same kind of relationship all over again.'

'I'd never do that to you.'

I put my hand up to stop him. 'I know, listen I—'

'I'll stay here, I don't need to move, it's only a job.'

'It's not only a job, Freddie, it's your job and it's important. And so is mine. I was going to say that I know I don't need to be here forever. You can take your job, and I can do mine, we can work it out. But I do need to be here now, just for now until I've got going. I know I can do it – you made me see that.'

'So we've still got a chance?'

'We always had a chance Freddie, except I was scared, about you, and your bloody perfect woman.' Isn't the green-eyed monster a total pain in the arse? She only appears when things are serious, when it really matters. Sticking her oar in where it's not wanted. 'What if I can never live up to her?'

Freddie's voice is soft and his eyes meet mine, hold me there and I'd be happy for this moment to last for a long, long time. Just me and Freddie. 'There's only ever been one woman Jane. Just you.'

I stare at him, confused about what he's saying. 'Just me?' What does he mean exactly?

'I've had a crush on you since we were at school.'

'*School?*' To say I am gobsmacked would be an understatement.

There's a pink flush along his cheekbones which makes me want to kiss him. 'Why do you think I helped you make your photo exhibition the best? I couldn't believe it when we bumped into each other in the estate agents, I thought it was fate.' He looks rueful.

'So you weren't scarily stalking me?'

'Well, yeah, maybe.' He grins. 'Then you were heartbroken, devastated by what that shit had done to you, and I realised it was all wrong. I might have been waiting for you, but you still loved him.'

'But you stayed anyway, you rented that place with me!'

'I couldn't not, Jane. I wanted you to be okay, I couldn't help trying to look after you which I thought might freak you out a bit if you guessed, so I guess I might have dated more than I should have.'

Is he saying what I think he's saying. 'I'm your other woman?' This is confusing as hell.

'You're the only one. The bloody perfect woman! My God, Jane, I've tried to get you out of my head, believe me.'

'Oh, thanks!'

'I've gone out with other girls, had a good time, thought it was working, then, bam! I've realised it wasn't the real deal, it wasn't good enough. I needed you, or nobody. But I didn't think you'd needed me. I'm not daft, I never wanted anything one-sided.'

'I always need you Freddie. I like talking to you, you were the only person I was bothered about talking to.'

'And I like talking to you.'

'You're my best friend, and I thought we'd cocked it all up.'

'Never. Friends?'

'More than, I hope?' There's a question in my voice, reflecting the one in my heart.

'Lots more than.' He's smiling, leaning in and I am so looking forward to kissing him again that I close my eyes and hold my breath and clench various bits of my body with anticipation.

'Oh my God! Freddie!' Rachel launches herself at Freddie, knocking him out of kissing orbit. 'You're here! See!' She grins at me.

'I know.' I feel like telling her to sod off, and dragging him back into position, but that would be rude. And it is *her* not-wedding, and it's her I should be thinking about, not my own lustful longings.

'Sorry I'm a bit late.' Freddie smiles at Rachel, then hugs her. 'Looks like I missed all the fun. How did it go?'

Rachel laughs. 'It didn't. Haven't you told him?'

I shake my head. 'Not had time yet, we've just been ...'

She rolls her eyes, then does a puckering kissing thing with lots of *mwah*s. 'Catching up.'

'What do you mean, it didn't?' Freddie looks from me to Rach, and back again.

'Long story. No wedding.'

Freddie is opening and closing his mouth like a goldfish. I hold it closed for him.

'I should have realised after the rehearsal I suppose. That was ace, apart from my bridesmaids giggling on the back row like a load of kids.' She rolls her eyes, and I shrug with all the innocence I can muster.

'Haven't a clue what she's on about! Must be nerves, she was hearing things.'

'Lemmings.' The word is barely audible as Maddie glides past, but it sets me off again, and Maddie, and Rachel. Who is laughing, but looking confused.

'Lemons?'

This makes us laugh even more.

'What was that? What did she say?' Rachel narrows her eyes. 'And I always thought you were the nice one Maddie!'

'I am!'

Freddie raises an eyebrow. 'Don't ask!' I hug Rachel. Then look at Freddie again. 'Drink?'

'I'm so glad you're here!' Rachel grins and slips her arm through his. 'He's an honorary member of the gang now. Go on, go off and make up, I won't watch!'

Maddie slips her arm through Rachel's. 'Go on Jane, go. I've got to talk to Rach about the honeymoon!' She giggles. 'We're going to make it a girl fest! Go on, go, we'll fill you in later!'

I go.

Freddie orders a pint, and a nice glass of wine for me and we stand and watch the others.

'Sounds dangerous, a girl fest?'

'It does. God knows what they're planning now, but we can't let Rachel go on her honeymoon on her own, can we?'

'So, what happened?'

'Well …' Where do I start?

So I start at the very beginning, and keep going until I get to the end. 'So voila, a wedding without a groom. Who'd have thought Michael was completely broke. He's a total gold digger. That was one secret that was buried too deep for any of us to spot!'

'Always said he was all talk and no trousers.'

'No trousers most of the time by the sounds of it.' I sigh. 'I mean Beth, how could he? How could she?'

'And I missed out on all that, no wonder my phone was on fire when I got back to civilisation!'

'Is Louie okay?'

'He's fine. He's missed you though.' He rests his fingers under my chin and kisses me gently. 'We both did.'

'Missed you, too.'

'Fancy a boogie? I reckon I'm nearly as good as Jack!' I laugh, then stop abruptly as I spot Andy. 'Can you wait a mo? I need to do something.'

His gaze follows the line of mine. 'Ah, Andy! Shall we do this together?'

I nod and clutch his hand a little tighter. Together sounds good. He's got hold of my hand, and even leaning back and digging my heels in isn't helping. I'm just being towed, ski style.

'Hey guys!'

Andy is drunk. He's just done a double thumbs-up, then staggered sideways and put his arm round a tent pole. Even Andy doesn't date tent poles.

'Andy.' I have decided to do this formally, with my phone voice on. 'I wanted you to be the first to know, that I am sure, I am totally positive, and we're not just friends.'

He looks at me blankly. 'Eh?'

'Freddie and I!' I hold up our joined hands. 'Just so you know, that I'm sure. And I don't want you to text me or anything.'

'Or anything.' Repeats Freddie.

'So you love him now?'

I nod. He probably won't remember any of this in the morning, but at least I will know I've said it.

'You did love me though, once?'

I screw my mouth up into a maybe. I mean, now I come to think about it, I'm not sure I did. Not really. Maybe in the way I loved my hamster, or my dog, no, not my dog, my dog was special, but definitely my hamster. But I can't say that.

'Well, you loved me enough to say you'd marry me, didn't you? And you've not said you'll marry him, what does that say?'

'You're a dick.' Freddie doesn't flinch.

'I'm a dick, fine, but the dick she wanted!' Andy finds

himself very funny, he's going to fall over if he laughs any louder. He's also attracting attention.

'Enough, stop it, you're making me feel sick. I don't want a dick!' I shout this rather too loudly, in a bid to stop them bickering. The people who weren't staring before, are now. This is definitely a wedding nobody is ever going to forget.

'Don't you?' Sally frowns. 'Well, I do.' Her barman, who she has by the arm, tries not to look even more pleased with himself than he already was.

Rachel sighs heavily. 'Me, too, I'd give anything for a dick right now.'

Maddie has stuck her hand up. 'Me three!'

I want to scream, so I do. And point at Andy. 'But not that one!'

'Nope, not that one.' My three friends chant in unison as they stand behind us, arms linked.

I'd like to say that Freddie flattened Andy, or chucked him in the fountain at this point, or something heroic happened. But it didn't. Andy just laughed and started to smooch the tent pole and everybody lost interest.

'Well, that about sums him up.' Says Sally, then looks at Freddie, who has just draped his arm round my waist. 'Now, get a room lovebirds!' Sally laughs, a deep throaty and decidedly dirty laugh then turns her attention back to her man. 'Come on gorgeous, let me show you how to tango.' The poor barman is dragged off by his tie, and Maddie, Jack and Rach drift towards the bar.

'Shall we take her advice?' Freddie is gazing straight into my eyes, in that way that brings me out in goose-bumps. All earnest, but deep, dark and sexy. He has eyelashes to die for. And the rest.

'Loving the shoes by the way.'

I glance down at my Doc Martens.

'Shall we?' Freddie offers his elbow, so I slip my arm through his.

'That would do nicely kind sir.' Louie will just have to stay home alone for one night. Tonight, I am going to make full use of my gorgeous four-poster bed and Jacuzzi bath.

With Freddie.

'I know Scotland's off the agenda, but you are going to come to the Outer Hebrides with me, aren't you?'

'The outer Outer Hebrides?'

'That's the one! Rob's dying to meet you.'

'Can you wait a bit?' I nod over to Maddie, who's just given me the thumbs up. 'It's just, that girl fest thing. I'm due to go to Barbados on Rach's not-honeymoon with the girls, and we're off tomorrow!'

'When I've waited half my life, what's one more week?'

'Well, two, actually!'

He laughs. A gorgeous deep rumbling laugh that I thought I might never hear again, and my stomach does a little flip.

'Does this mean you'll buy new jeans now?'

'I never dump the things I love, even when they're old and tatty, 'cos to me they're never past their sell by date.'

'Tell me more about this girl you fell for.'

'Which girl?'

'You know, the one.'

'Shut up, you noddle.' He laughs.

'When exactly did you first realise you fancied her? When she was thirteen, fourteen?'

'When I spotted her dancing behind the bike shed with her best friend, yelling out some funny song lyrics.'

'That was Girl Power!'

'You're not kidding me!'

He winks, then leans in closer, and this time there are no interruptions. This time we kiss. This time he touches my lips, my waist, the small of my back, my neck, and I hate to sound all girly and drippy, but this time I swear he touches some secret little spot deep, down in my heart where nobody has ever been before.

I think I've found my *One*.

Acknowledgements

This book has not been the easiest to write. My wonderful dad passed away the day before it was finished, and the revisions that inevitably followed – which needed a light touch and laughter - were written as our family tried to come to terms with our loss. Dad was always known as Peter, but he was christened Frederick, and it seems fate that my gorgeous hero Freddie shares the same name. Dad was every bit as generous, supportive, loyal, loving, clever and bright as Freddie, and will always be my hero. I'll miss him every day, as will my mum. They had the type of happy ever after that many people can only read and dream about.

I've always known that as an author I write the first draft alone, but that it takes a team to produce the final, polished version and it has never been truer than with this book.

I can't thank enough the terrific, talented trio who always take care of me – my fabulous publisher/editor Charlotte Ledger, my agent Amanda Preston, and my editor Emily Ruston. Thank you for inspiring and encouraging me every step of the way, for being smart, funny and supportive, and for always being there when I need you.

Thanks also go to my lovely author friends who go above and beyond the call of duty at times. This book wouldn't have made it out into the big, wide world without Mandy and Jane, and the wise words and virtual hugs from the Savvy Authors.

I'd also like to thank all my mates, and my many friends on social media, for all your hugs, love and kind words – it really has made a difference.

Thank you as well to my wonderful supporters on Facebook, in particular Pauline Ricketts, Llainy Swanson and Debra Finney whose wonderful Hen Party ideas have found their way into the story.

And lastly a big thank you to you, for reading this story. I hope you've enjoyed *Bridesmaids*.

Zara x

HELP US SHARE THE LOVE!

If you love this wonderful book as much as we do then please share your reviews online.

Leaving reviews makes a huge difference and helps our books reach even more readers.

So get reviewing and sharing, we want to hear what you think!

Love, HarperImpulse x

Please leave your reviews online!

amazon.CO.Uk   **kobo**   goodreads   L♥ve**reading**   iBooks

And on social!

f/HarperImpulse   **𝕏**@harperimpulse
⊙@HarperImpulse

LOVE BOOKS?

So do we! And we love nothing more than chatting about our books with you lovely readers.

If you'd like to find out about our latest titles, as well as exclusive competitions, author interviews, offers and lots more, join us on our Facebook page! Why not leave a note on our wall to tell us what you thought of this book or what you'd like to see us publish more of?

/HarperImpulse

You can also tweet us @harperimpulse and see exclusively behind the scenes on our Instagram page www.instagram.com/harperimpulse

To be the first to know about upcoming books and events, sign up to our newsletter at: http://www.harperimpulseromance.com/